Showtime

ROADIES SERIES

ERIKA VANZIN

Want to get more FREE from Erika?

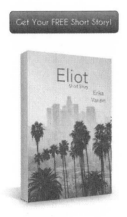

Sign up for the author's New Releases mailing list and get a free copy of the short story "Eliot." You will periodically receive free short stories and unique chapters.

Click here to get started:
https://www.erikavanzin.com/newsletter.html

To all who love to color outside the lines.

Simon

Ten years earlier

"What the hell are you doing here?" I look up at Michael, who has just sat next to me on the bus.

"Imagine my surprise when I woke up this morning and found half the bed empty and your clothes gone."

I take a breath and look out the window. The number of people in line to get on this bus is too long and slow. I pray for the doors to close and leave the station as fast as possible.

"It's more of a surprise that you got up at seven this morning. That's normally the time you go to sleep."

He doesn't respond, but I feel his gaze on me. He's not joking like he usually does, and his seriousness puts me in a bad mood. I got up early and dressed in absolute silence to avoid seeing this look—it makes me feel guilty.

"How did you find me?" I ask him.

"Joe can't keep his mouth shut. He acts like a bad guy with that baseball bat behind the counter, but when it comes to keeping an eye on strays he drags into his place, he's worse than a mother hen. All love, friendship, and doing the right thing."

I smile because Michael is repulsed by anything related to affection. Even Joe's. That man is the closest thing to a father the three out of four of us have ever had.

"How the hell did you get on the bus without a ticket?" I ask him when the vehicle closes the doors and moves from the station.

He shows me a piece of paper with a sly grin and a raised eyebrow. "I stole it out of the bag of someone in line. And you? You don't have the money for a ticket."

It's hard for me to hold back a smile. I shrug my shoulders and look again out the window at the road and Manhattan traffic, full of cars and pedestrians bustling at this time of the morning. "I stole it out of the pocket of someone in line."

Silence falls like a wall between our two seats. It's strange because there's usually never a second of peace with Michael, nor awkwardness. He plays down everything with a joke, so the fact that he's quiet makes the air between us heavy.

After half an hour of tortured silence stuck in the city's slow traffic, Michael gives in, wanting to know more. "So, are you leaving the band?"

"It's not like we're the Rolling Stones. You can change bass players and the fans won't freak out." The four drunkards who regularly frequent Joe's bar will be happy not to have to put up with us making noise while they get drunk all afternoon.

"Who cares if we're famous or not? Don't you care about us? We got out of that crap thanks to the band, doesn't that matter to you?"

"You decided to leave behind the life you had before going to juvie. I just looked for a way not to go crazy while I was there. I have someone to take care of, who I don't want to abandon."

None of us ever talk openly about our life before we ended up in prison. A little story, a phrase that suggests a bit of truth, but nothing honest and open, exposing our feelings. They know I grew up in a foster family, that there were other kids with me, but it ended there. They have no idea what I left behind in that place.

"So you think the solution is to go back to robbing banks?" There's disappointment in his voice, as though he expected something more from me.

"What should I do? Clean toilets at Joe's for a hot meal until I get old? It's not like we're rolling in the money playing music," I bark.

Michael decided to give up everything and everyone, erase his past. But I don't want to do that. Robbing banks allowed me to provide for the person I care about. I've already lost two years being locked in there. What does he expect me to do? Sit here waiting for something to change?

"We'll find something, but you're not stuck with being a professional criminal."

"Michael, don't you get that I don't have many choices? I've been in prison, I don't have a diploma, I don't know how to do any kind of work. I do what I know best, which allows me to take home enough money for me and someone else. Stop judging me for how I decide to provide for myself."

Michael tightens his jaw and frowns at me. He seems almost angry, and I'm a bit sorry. He's not to blame. We ended up together in that prison and helped each other to get out of it, but we don't have the same ambitions, the same vision for the future. At some point, you have to be realistic and understand you can't live on hopes and dreams.

"Is this person more important than us? Is that why you'd

trade the happiness of three friends? *We* have been close to you in the worst moments of your life. Where was this person when you were in juvie? Because I don't remember them ever coming looking for you. And now you'd give up the ones closest to you for someone who gave up on you."

The thickness that grips my stomach almost makes me vomit. Nicholas was only thirteen years old when they arrested me. Now he's fifteen; how could he visit me in prison? He's not old enough, but Michael can't know that. The guilt at not being there to protect him makes me hate myself and the stupidity that landed me behind bars.

"You don't know what you're talking about, Michael."

"Then explain it to me."

"I don't want to explain it to you! It's none of your business," I snap, and regret the words as soon as I see my friend's hurt look.

The rest of the two hours pass in absolute silence, even when we get off and walk together for forty minutes. I wish I had the courage to tell him what's happening to me, why I can't stay with him, Thomas, and Damian, but I am not capable of it. It's not just my story, and I don't want to betray Nicholas's trust.

We arrive in front of the house where I'd grown up since I was five years old. It's where all my memories are linked, beautiful ones and ugly ones. It's quiet. Not a living soul inside, and I'm a bit disoriented. There's always someone coming and going, windows open, doors slamming, shouting inside. I walk hesitantly up the sidewalk that leads to the porch, and it takes me a few seconds before knocking on the red door.

No one answers. Michael is holding his breath next to me.

I don't know what he expects to find here, but he looks as nervous as I am. I knock another time, but no one comes.

I walk to the window and spy through it, seeing the worn brown leather sofa, but there's not a living soul nearby, not even the TV is turned on, the usual background in this house, day and night.

I go around to the side gate that leads to the backyard and open it. The grass is up to my knees, the house seeming almost uninhabited. I try to open the patio door into the pastel yellow kitchen, but it's locked. Another oddity that shakes me.

"There's no one there anymore, if you're looking for the kids who lived with you." Mrs. Sanchez's hoarse voice draws my attention to the other side of the worn-out fence that divides the backyards of the two neighboring houses.

I approach the half-destroyed wooden planks, seeing a familiar round face with tubes connected to an oxygen cylinder welcoming me on the other side. "How is there no one left? There were seven kids, were they all adopted? Even Nicholas? Where did they take them?"

"After they put you in jail, one of the kids got hurt, and they came to pick him up in an ambulance. Social services came to check and took away the others from their custody as well."

My heart sinks into my stomach, cold as if it had stopped beating forever. "Do you know where they went? Have they been placed with another foster family?" My voice trembles, and I feel Michael's hand on my shoulder, supporting me.

"I don't know, but it's been two years since there were kids in there."

The words rumble between my chest and brain in an echo

that makes my head spin. He isn't here. Nicholas hasn't been here for two years, and I didn't have the faintest idea. Is that why he no longer answers my calls? But it still rings—why doesn't he answer? Doesn't he want to be found?

I can feel my breath getting shallow, the air struggling to enter my lungs. How do I find him? How do I take care of him? Not knowing if he's okay torments me. Michael's arms wrap around me and pull me tightly into his chest. Only now do I realize my eyes are closed and my hands clenched in fists at my sides.

"Will you come home with me now? We're your family, Simon. There's no one left here waiting for you." Michael's whisper hits my chest like a loud banging.

There is no one left to take care of.

I thought I was different from the rest of the Jailbirds. I thought I had a reason to go back to my old life, but it looks like that reason couldn't wait for me. The pain that creeps into my chest is so searing it takes my breath.

"Come home with me, please, Simon," Michael begs, holding me tight.

"I thought he would wait for me," I say barely in a whisper.

"Maybe he had no choice." Michael's tone is not patronizing, not an attempt to console me. He really believes it.

At thirteen, you can't decide who to live with. When you're inside the social services system, someone decides for you whether to stay or change families. But knowing this doesn't soothe the pain. I follow Michael without a look back when we leave the house and the hope I had of returning to the only love I've ever known in my life.

PRESS *Review*

Hi, Roadies!

How are you spending the holidays? Another year flew by, and we're here summing up twelve hectic months on this New Year's Eve. Looking back at what happened this year is undoubtedly essential at Jailbirds Records, especially in this challenging year where uncertainty ruled the roost—leaving a well-established record label for a whole new adventure.

However, all things considered, the choice turned out to be the right one. It reflects the values of honesty and transparency toward the fans the Jailbirds have always tried to maintain. And the fans' support has repaid the efforts of the enormous amount of work that a new record company entails. The success of the surprise concert tour was terrific and gave an injection of confidence worth much more than any contract with the big names in the industry.

Happy New Year, Roadies! This post is for you, who have always supported the Jailbirds since the beginning of their career. This is their way of wishing you a year full of happiness and dreams come true. The Jailbirds are looking forward to giving you some awesome surprises in the coming months.

Be Kind and Rock'n'Roll,

Iris

87,486 Likes 74,698 Tweets 58,672 Shares 9572 Comments

CHAPTER 1
Simon

"Ten! Nine! Eight!"

Thomas's house is as meticulously decorated as a furniture magazine or one of those Pinterest pages where even the drink coasters are decorated. The snowflakes in the candle centerpiece are so realistic I didn't touch them, for fear they'd melt.

In one of the band's now rare outings, Thomas told us that Iris has a new passion for resins, transforming a room in their house into an art studio where she does strange experiments with silicone molds and chemical agents worthy of a meth lab.

"Seven! Six! Five!"

I watch my friends, glued to the TV tuned to Times Square, watching the big ball come down to announce the arrival of the new year. I study Levi's curious eyes, and I realize that in just a year, so much has happened that fifty years could have passed. I would not be surprised if tomorrow morning I woke up and found myself, almost eighty years old, sitting on the porch enjoying my retirement.

I'm happy because we've finally freed ourselves from the weight of the lies we carried with us from our past. We've taken back the freedom they denied us. Still, I feel restless, looking for something I can't even identify.

"Four! Three!"

At twenty-eight, I have four houses, more money than I could spend in a lifetime, a career that, despite everything, is going well, and friends who show their affection for me constantly.

Yet I'm here, in this room, looking at the centerpiece and wondering how the hell Iris created such a complicated thing, instead of enjoying the excitement of an old year ending and a new one beginning. The anticipation for a new beginning isn't there, like in other years, with a pleasant squeeze in my stomach.

"Two! One!"

I shift my gaze from the smiling faces of my friends to the silver balloons covering the floor. The red confetti sticking under our shoes. The bread crumbs from the appetizers fallen on the floor from the huge table still covered with dishes of leftovers from our dinner.

The grapes, the lentils, the donut-shaped cake, the beans are all dishes traditionally meant to bring luck, money, prosperity for the new year. But I don't know where to start eating them because I already have all these things. What's the point of wanting more if it doesn't take away this restless feeling I've had for a while?

"Happy New Year!"

The cry draws my attention to my friends who exchange greetings with smiling faces and happiness in their eyes. Damian grabs Lilly by the ass and pulls her in for a kiss that looks like a prelude to a fiery night rather than a New Year's greeting. Evan hugs Levi, who makes a disgusted grimace when Michael takes Faith's face in his hands and delicately touches his lips to hers. Thomas kisses Iris before leaving her in Emily's clutches, looking at her with a lover's eyes.

Everyone has someone to turn to for the first thought of the year while I'm here, standing still, watching the happiness that swirls around me, never reaching me.

I grab the heavy sweater from the back of my chair and head down the hallway leading to the backyard. When I set foot outside, the icy air hits my face and I put my hands in my pockets to avoid freezing. Shivering with cold and cursing myself for not wearing a jacket, I look up at a dark cloudless sky and breathe. The air freezes my chest, and I close my eyes.

Beyond the wall surrounding the backyard, the city is in full swing. People shouting, music coming from some open window, someone else blowing those annoying trumpets that seem to materialize in massive amounts on the shop shelves during the holiday season. I suppose that's the price to pay when in Manhattan, where it's forbidden to have fireworks.

I don't smell gunpowder on national holidays anymore, and I miss it a bit because it reminds me of those few moments of my childhood when I was really happy, when we allowed ourselves to be children for one day.

"Everyone's wondering where you ended up."

I turn to Evan, who joined me out here. His lips form a smile, but his gray eyes scrutinize me, trying to read my thoughts.

"Really? Or did you come here to make sure I didn't run away?"

Evan shakes his head and looks away. He is freezing inside his elegant coat and scarf, and when he snorts, trying to hold back a little laugh, the white cloud of breath creates an almost ethereal halo on his face illuminated only by the streetlamps.

He shrugs his shoulders and glances at me before looking again at the grass beneath his feet. "They're still in that honeymoon phase, where they only have eyes for their lovers. You'll see, sooner or later, it will pass, and you'll go back to going out with them like before. They'll be your old friends again."

A disconsolate half-laugh slips out before I can hold it back. "Don't you feel like an idiot when they invite you out, and then show up with their woman and flirt all evening, or talk about how perfect life is as a couple? I don't know what excuse to use anymore to say no to their invitations."

Evan smiles and nods. "I usually say I have work to finish."

"Yes, I can't use that excuse. They *are* my job."

Evan chuckles.

"It's not that I can't stand their conversations. It's just that I feel like I have nothing in common anymore... We're not in harmony anymore, and I miss those moments a little. I miss arguing over the pigsty tour bus or teasing Michael about his one-night stands. I miss talking about music, concerts, what we do for a living. Am I ungrateful? They're my friends. I adore their women, I should be happy for them, and instead, I'm here complaining."

I study the wrinkles that form on his forehead when he furrows it in a serious expression. "You're not ungrateful. You're just the last of your friends to have a partner, and that sucks. I think it's almost an unwritten rule that, at a certain age, one at a time, your friends fall in love and you're still alone, looking like an idiot. But they'll come back to their senses and start to act normal again. You may not go around partying like you used to, but you'll come back to sharing the same interests."

I breathe in and hold my breath. I stopped looking for a woman. I don't know what's wrong with me, but every time I'm interested in someone, after a few dates, my enthusiasm diminishes.

Most of the women I meet want to know about the rock star lifestyle. All the conversations focus on my career, on the crazy experiences they expect me to have, but my life's not like that. I find myself telling my bandmates' stories instead because I'm not a rock star. I'm just a guy who likes to make music for a living. That's it. But they don't care, they don't want to get to know me better. They want to know about my celebrity lifestyle.

The thing I crave most is finding a woman I feel good with, who likes a simple life, away from the spotlight, drama, from complicated things that keep you up at night. But I stopped looking for her.

"You mean the 'curse of the last single?' They could make a movie about it."

Evan looks at me with a smile, then looks at his red, freezing hands. "Do you think going on tour would make you feel happier?"

A sound something like a roar comes out of my chest. "Yes, please! I need to go back to playing live, not just in the studio for the new album."

Evan smiles and nods but says nothing more. "Shall we go back in? It's freezing out here." He turns around and climbs the stairs without giving me time to answer.

"We were looking for you!" announces Michael when we return to the dining room where everyone has taken a seat at the table and is swallowing grapes.

I sit down, grab a lucky grape, and put it in my mouth.

"Can you tell us why you're so mysterious today?" Thomas asks Michael what we were all wondering this afternoon when we came here to help them set up for tonight.

My best friend looks at Faith, who lowers her head and blushes, unable to hold back a smile. That simple gesture makes my blood freeze in my veins because I know what's coming. I know what he has to announce. When they returned from their trip to Mexico, she had an engagement ring on her finger. We toasted, congratulated the woman who managed to convert Michael to marriage. The tender way he caresses Faith's hand now, Levi biting his lips to keep his mouth shut, can only mean one bit of news.

My stomach twists in a grip that hurts. The grape I just ate struggles to make it past the lump forming in my throat. I wish I had a remote control to press "pause" and compose myself before the news about to come out devastates my chest with an explosion. I should be happy, Michael's my best friend. I want him to be happy, and at the same time, I want to stop this moment before our friendship changes forever.

"Faith is pregnant."

Three simple words I can't stop. Fifteen letters, violent as a slap. The silence that follows seems to last for hours, then Lilly's ecstatic squeal starts the noise of chairs screeching on the floor, friends congratulating, hugging, patting each other on the back.

I do my part, getting up from my chair, putting a smile on my face I hope will appear sincere as I walk the six feet separating me from Michael with the slow pace of a funeral march.

He has teary eyes, the idiot grin of someone who's deliriously happy. He embraces me with so much enthusiasm I'm sure he couldn't wait to share this moment with us, his family.

I wish I was on another planet. I hug him back with almost no conviction, and when it takes him a while to let me go, I'm so uncomfortable I want to push him away. Almost. I stay there with a fake smile on my face and the words that struggle to get out of my lips. "Congratulations. I'm happy for you."

And I really am. My rational part is happy. It's my heart that can't keep up with all the emotions running through my chest, and it stays there, frozen, waiting to feel that happiness. The only feeling I can sense is guilt for betraying my friendship with Michael.

Damian comes over with his usual impetuousness, wraps his arm around Michael's neck, and drags him away, almost suffocating him. I turn around, walk to the closet by the front door, grab my jacket, scarf, cap, and gloves, and put them on one at a time, with a slowness that isn't me.

"Are you okay?" Evan's voice brings me to reality, but I don't turn to him this time. I'm afraid he'll read on my face all the shame I'm feeling right now.

"Yes, I'm just tired, and I need to go home."

"I'll tell the others."

He doesn't try to stop me, to make me talk, to reason, to tell me that I should slap a damn smile on my face and stay for my friend. Evan's like that. He protects us and fixes our messes when we can't. I nod and open the door without even saying goodbye. When I close it, the weight that lifts from my chest lightens my step and gets me home faster.

***

Three days have passed since my rough exit from Thomas's house. Everyone called me, making sure I was okay, since Evan justified my absence with a suspected flu and, not wanting to make a pregnant woman sick, I left without goodbyes.

I replied to everyone by reassuring them, saying that I was recovering since I wanted to prevent them from showing up at my house with chicken soup to keep me company during convalescence. Which is why, when the phone rings for the umpteenth time, I don't even check who it is before answering.

"Are you up for a meeting this afternoon, or would you prefer to postpone it for a few days?" Evan's voice sits me back down on the couch where I've been staring at the ceiling for three days.

"Good morning, Evan. You seem agitated." If there's one person who never starts a conversation abruptly, it's our manager.

I hear him inhale sharply and remain silent for a few seconds. "Forgive me, I'm inundated with phone calls, and I don't have enough time to answer all the emails, but that doesn't justify my rude manners. Good morning, Simon."

"Good morning, Evan. Did you call about something urgent? You seem to be rushing even by your standards."

"Can you come to the studio this afternoon? I have some news for the band." The emotion I sense in his voice makes me smile.

"I'll be there. Do you want me to call the others? To save you a couple of calls? I'll have them come at two, sound good?"

"Yes! You're my savior, thank you."

I laugh, amused. It's the first time in days I've felt light-hearted. "See you later."

I hang up and look down on my sweatpants full of chip crumbs, the only thing I've been eating since New Year's Eve because I don't even feel like cooking a decent meal.

By the time I make calls to my friends, tidy up the living room and kitchen, and take a shower, it's already time to head to the meeting. I must admit, curiosity about what he's about to tell us is making me feel more alive than ever. It's not every day that Evan gets agitated about something work-related. He's usually very calm and down to earth.

I enter the conference room and see Damian and Thomas sitting on the sofa. Evan is in the armchair while Michael is pouring himself a cup of coffee.

"Sorry I'm late."

Evan waves at me to sit, and my bandmates' faces look even more perplexed than mine at the smug smile of our manager. He's so pleased he's gloating; it almost scares me.

"Please tell us what's going on! You look like a teenager who got laid for the first time and can't wait to tell his friends about it," Damian urges with his usual impatience.

"We don't want to know the details of your sex life, Evan. We've barely managed to get rid of Michael's obscene stories. Please spare us," says Thomas, who earns a punch on the shoulder from my best friend.

We then get silent, watching our manager.

"If I told you that you can go back on tour, a real one, with tour buses, two stages, dates all over the United States, Canada, Europe, Asia, Central and South America, and Australia, what would you say?"

No one speaks. Everyone is suspicious about his question. Before Christmas, we didn't have the money for a world tour. We didn't even have money for one in the United States, with two stages alternating during the dates.

"Have you won the lottery, or are you going crazy and we have to get a new manager?" replies Michael.

"Or," Evan hints, "someone else pays for the tour."

"And who would be the fool to take on such an expense? What do they want in return?" I ask with more doubts than before this conversation began.

"A well-known streaming company may be interested in funding a tour in exchange for a documentary about the band, following you throughout the tour and doing exclusive interviews."

Silence falls in the room, and we all look at our manager with our mouths hanging open, eyes wide.

"*That* well-known streaming company? The one associated with the oldest television network in the country?" Damian questions, stunned like all of us.

The smile forming on Evan's face confirms his suspicions.

I'm perplexed. "Excuse me, but why are they asking us now that we've left the record label? They've had years to make a documentary about us."

"Apparently, the old label was asking for a crazy amount of money to exploit their name in the series, and it never went through."

"Sons of bitches," whispers Michael, and for a moment, our eyes meet, igniting the guilt that tears my chest.

"And how are you connected with them?" Thomas raises

an eyebrow, intrigued.

Evan smiles and leans against the backrest, crossing his fingers in his lap and tilting his head a bit. "If I reveal all my secrets to you, you won't need me anymore. I have to keep some hidden weapons to keep getting paid."

"You sly fox," Damian teases him.

"Are you interested, or should I cancel tonight's dinner with the producer who flew into town from Los Angeles this morning?"

A chorus of "Are you crazy? Of course we'll go!" rises into the room, and Evan smiles in satisfaction.

"When you say they'll follow us everywhere on tour to film, do you mean even inside the buses?" Thomas's question is as simple as it is uncomfortable. The idea of having someone following us all the time, having to be careful about everything we say, is frustrating even to think about.

"They want something authentic that gets to the heart of the band without filters, that shows who you really are, without the glamorous image the old record company promoted. So I assume that's part of the game, if that's okay with you."

We look into each other's eyes, everyone trying to discern what the other is thinking.

"Do you already know who they have in mind to assign us for the shooting? Can we get to know them first? If we have to live with this person twenty-four-seven, I'd like it to be someone we can trust," Damian said.

"They have guaranteed that everything about this documentary will have to be approved by you. We can also include the approval of the cameraman who will shoot if it makes you feel more comfortable."

"Yes, I'd also like to know at least a little bit about the people I'll be living with on tour, especially in a sacred space like the tour bus." Michael gives voice to what we all think.

An idea materializes in my brain and comes out of my mouth before I even think about it. "If you want, I can contact a person I know who's produced and directed several independent films and shorts of remarkable quality. It's not a famous name, but it's still better than a complete stranger, right? I don't know if this person is available, but it doesn't hurt to try."

Everyone's eyes are on me, perhaps waiting for some explanation I'm not ready to give. It may be the stupidest proposal I've ever made, but as soon as it crossed my mind, it seemed perfect. Now I'm not so sure anymore, since I've exposed myself to questions I don't know if I want to answer.

"And who the hell would be this person that we don't know? We're always together. How did you hide them from us?"

"I had a life before I met you, Michael. It just so happens that you don't know everyone in my life." The words come out harsher than I intended, and everyone looks at me surprised, as if I'd just insulted someone's mother. "Sorry, I'm just a little tired," I grumble awkwardly.

The truth is that in the last three days, I have spent more time on Nicholas's social profiles than I have being productive. Such as wiping a damp cloth on the leaves of the plants in the living room I've been neglecting.

I've been following him since the beginning of his career when I found him on social media after we became famous and he settled in Los Angeles. I've followed him from afar, never brave enough to contact him to tell him how proud I am of his work, of the awards he's received, of the high quality of his films.

I had a thousand opportunities to click that button on Facebook and ask for his friendship, or message him privately on Instagram to reconnect, but I never had the courage.

Since my best friend announced that he would be a dad, I wondered what would have happened if Michael hadn't taken me back to Manhattan that day, or if I had looked for Nicholas with more determination. If I had left the Jailbirds when we weren't famous yet, would I have felt as lonely as I feel right now? Would I have had Nicholas by my side?

Evan helps with my embarrassment, bringing the attention back to him. "Tonight, I booked a private room at Nolita. I want to avoid the Mandalay and going public with the paparazzi before I've signed the deal."

Michael is still staring at me with a frown and a stern look. Wanting to avoid him, I interrupt Evan talking with Damian, and get up from my chair. "Can you text me the time and name you booked with? I'll see you all there."

"Yes, of course. Do you feel sick?" Evan looks at me worriedly, and in those words, I read all the other meanings he infers.

"I'm just a little weak after the flu, is all." I smile and turn around, walking to the door.

"So we're going back on tour!" Thomas yells, clearly excited about it.

Well, we're back on tour. I should be happy. That's what I asked Evan on New Year's Eve. My wish came true and this was the change I wanted. So why do I feel so depressed about it? The idea of going on tour with my friends should be the most exciting thought in the world. Instead, I find myself struggling with the fear that my past and present may collide and sink into a sea of accusations and guilt.

I could always tell Evan that I heard from Nicholas and that he can't join us because of other projects. That would be the easiest solution. I'm afraid of what could re-emerge if I bring him back into my life.

Still, the part of me that wonders what would have happened if I had returned to my foster family after prison wants to try to mend a past I lost for years. A past that feeds on memories of rare moments of happiness, of faces, of caresses and hugs stolen in the dark.

CHAPTER 2
Nicholas

"Look where you're walking!" I turn to the person who just hit my shoulder, making my camera bag slide off it. I grab it before it hits the concrete while the woman, wearing a half-open backpack with fabric trailing out of it, doesn't even turn around. I don't think she even noticed me, nor do I think she realized someone rummaged through her backpack, and, likely, her wallet is gone.

Los Angeles is the city of sunshine, beaches, peace, love, and the laid-back life, at least until you're stuck in traffic on the freeway. But pick-pocketers have a field day with people who aren't paying attention to their surroundings, too busy enjoying the holiday. I see hundreds of these tourists in Venice Beach, walking along carefree, paying little attention to their belongings.

I turn to Haven and the intrigued expression on her face. "What?"

She shrugs her shoulders and shakes her head. "Nothing. It's just for years we've been walking this boardwalk bustling with tourists who bump into us all the time, and you've never complained. Yesterday you shouted at one in skates, today at that woman. Am I wrong, or are you nervous?"

I look down at the strip of asphalt dusted with sand,

clenching my fists in a grip that almost hurts. I was hoping she wouldn't notice, but if you've been living with your girlfriend for more than six years, maybe some of your mood swings are obvious even if you're careful.

She grabs me by the arm and forces me to stop. I look up at her hazel eyes, proud and determined to make me confess what's wrong. Haven doesn't like bullshit or people who sulk around for no reason. When Haven decides to find out what ails you, nothing gets in her way.

"I need to sit down for this," is my answer.

We walk on the sand of Venice Beach, past the skatepark bustling with skaters, and the palm trees, until we're almost to the ocean where few people are sunbathing. Although it's sixty-eight degrees and still January, the locals are used to much higher temperatures and walk around in jackets today as it's a bit windy. I sit down and put my camera bag between my legs.

"Okay, now you're scaring me. I've never seen you this down since we met. Are you sick? Has something serious happened?" The agitation in her voice convinces me to pull the phone out of my pocket.

I squeeze it firmly as I scroll through the emails to find the one I'm looking for. I open it, pass her the phone, and look at the ocean as I hear her snort in surprise when she starts reading. Several minutes pass before her voice reaches me again, penetrating the whirlwind of thoughts stirring in my brain.

"I had to read it three times to understand what it says, and I still have so many questions I don't even know where to start."

I want to answer that I also have many questions about that email, about myself, but I doubt that I'll ever have an answer. Because clarifying those doubts scares me, I don't know if I'm ready to deal with a past that almost broke me. With my thumb, I caress the leather bracelets that cover my wrists and I never take off. First the right, then the left. Right, left, right, left, as if brushing from one to the other can make them disappear.

"But the thing that most confuses me is that you've had this gloomy face for two days when this email has news that could change your life forever. And in a very positive way."

"I'm not so sure."

Haven pulls my arm and makes me turn toward her so I can't escape her stunned gaze. "They're asking you to make a documentary about their lives. It's the breakthrough you've been chasing for years!"

"That's the point! To make this breakthrough, I have to meet Simon again, and I don't know if I'm ready," I blurt out, almost screaming.

That silences her, but I don't think it's because I raised my voice. It's because of the bomb I just dropped without warning. I watch her as she closes her mouth and swallows. "You know Simon from the Jailbirds, and it never occurred to you to tell me?"

I shrug and look back at the ocean. "There was never an opportunity," I whisper like a coward.

I hear her snorting, shocked. "There has never been an opportunity? Are you joking? Not even when we listened to their albums and talked about how much they've improved compared to the first one? Or when the news came out that they were in juvie and I talked about it for days? Or when we were at the concert in Santa Monica last summer, it never occurred to you to tell me, 'You know, Simon and I knew each other when we were kids.' Has it never crossed your mind that something like that could be a topic of conversation? We've been living together for *six years*, Nicholas. Six years that we've followed the Jailbirds. There have been literally thousands of occasions to bring up the subject, but you decided to lie to me."

"I didn't lie to you. I just omitted details."

"Don't bullshit me! Omitting details of this magnitude on purpose and lying are the exact same thing, and you know it. Don't treat me like an idiot."

I don't want to treat her like a fool. I know I'm wrong, but it's hard to admit it out loud. The problem is, if I'd told her I knew him, it would have led to other questions I can't answer without falling into the same self-destructive spiral I struggled to get out of years ago.

"I don't want to talk about my past, okay?" I answer, sounding more annoyed than I actually am.

"I would never have asked you to do that. You know very well that I'm aware certain topics are better left where they were buried."

"Anyway, I'm not going to accept their offer."

"You have completely gone mad. It's the opportunity of a lifetime! You have a chance to get noticed for the work you do." I hear her inhale sharply, then continue in a calmer tone. "We've been starving for years, Nicholas. And not in a figurative way. This is Los Angeles, the land of dreams for every director or actor, but also the city where trains pass only once. If you don't take this one, you'll lose it forever."

She stands up and walks away, leaving me with my guilt

at the truth of her words. I should get up and follow her, apologize and explain what is happening to me and why I cannot accept the Jailbirds' offer. But I can't do it because I don't even know why I don't want to face Simon.

I hadn't spoken to him since the day the police came home to get him and put him in juvie. Since the day my heart broke in two and never stitched up again. Since the day I first experienced genuine fear, which freezes your stomach, takes the air out of your lungs, and keeps you from breathing.

I can't explain to Haven why I don't want to go to New York because there's no real reason, just a sense of helplessness that grips my stomach and makes my legs tremble. How can you mend a tear in your life so big that half of you feels lost? How do you fill twelve years of silence?

Two hours pass before Haven returns to me. Two hours spent staring at the ocean and imagining a thousand scenarios of how my meeting with Simon could go. None of them positive.

"Sorry for how I reacted earlier." She kisses me on the cheek as she kneels behind me and squeezes her arms around my neck. "I know this is your life and your decision, but it makes me angry and sad to see you throwing away this opportunity because of fear. You're the bravest person I know. You dared to say no to so many projects because they were not what you wanted. Because you thought they diminished your art and your work. But this time you're saying no out of a fear you don't even know is real."

I inhale and try to look for words to explain what is happening to me, but I don't know if I am capable of it. "Do you remember when you thought you were pregnant and waited fifteen days before telling me? I freaked out because those two weeks could have been crucial in evaluating all the possible choices we had. You said you were terrified that if you said it out loud, the pregnancy would become real, and you weren't ready to face it. The whole situation felt too big for you to even think about."

She nods with a stern look, frowning as she sits next to me. Her lips are tightened in a grimace that makes her face almost sad. I think it hurts her to relive certain memories about a life she decided not to give birth to.

"That's how I feel. I can't take that job because twelve years of fantasies and assumptions about Simon would become real. I don't know if I have the mental strength to accept anything bad I might find on the other coast in New York. In these twelve years, I have built countless walls that help me separate what my reality with Simon was from the rock star everyone knows. I don't think I'm able to put together these two versions of the same person in my head." It's such a convoluted explanation that it's hard to understand for me too, but it's the best I can do.

Haven looks for a moment toward the bracelets I wear on my wrists, then again to my eyes. She nods but says nothing, stretching out her hand to help me get up.

"Are you angry?"

"No, I understand your reasons. I'm sad because it's an opportunity that will never happen again, but I know there will be others. You're a great director, and that's never going to change, even if you don't work for them."

I nod and smile at her, even though the guilt settles in my chest like a concrete pour. We desperately need the money.

Accepting that job would mean breathing again without the nightmare of ending up on the street.

"Come on, Sady just finished his afternoon shift at the restaurant and brought us something to eat. He said something about lobster, if I'm not mistaken." She grabs my hand and smiles at me, dragging me toward the skatepark where I see the usual five desperate people we hang out with gathered.

Sady, the tattooed chef whose real name no one knows, is pulling out of the pocket of his trademark black hoodie a roll of paper napkins that he hands to Tom, Liv, Dan, and Rick.

Of all of us, only Haven, Sady, and I have a roof to sleep under. The others live sheltered under the cartons and tents located downtown. They come here during the day because more tourists are inclined to drop change into their filthy coffee paper cups. The faded names written on the cups with marker belong to the customers who have thrown their finished breakfast in the trash. They're also the names these people sitting in a circle in front of me use every day.

I have no idea who they are or what their story is. Over the years, I have tried to ask a little more about them. Although they're inclined to talk about their adventures, the story is different every time. Lies and reality mix, preventing me from really knowing these people.

I sit between Haven and Liv, who shows off a toothless but sincere smile. I pull out of my backpack a bag of chips Haven and I bought this morning and two bottles of water that I leave for the four homeless people. They look at it with such greed that I am afraid a brawl will break out for who gets to take the first sip.

I place them in the middle of our makeshift circle and

let Rick open the bag of greasy chips to share with everyone. When you have nothing, life is like that. You surround yourself with a few people to share what you find to survive.

Tom rummages into a pocket and pulls out a bag of peaches so red, ripe, and perfect that I suspect he stole them from the shopping cart of some supermarket patron. Sometimes you find fruit in the garbage cans behind supermarkets or restaurants, but they're usually bruised, imperfect, unsuitable for the demanding palates of consumers who pay through the nose for an off-season fruit.

"In that bag are lobster tacos. In the other, I put garlic bread with mozzarella and fried bread," Sady explains, pointing a hand covered in intricate designs, pale to the point of looking cadaveric. His face is hollowed out, dark circles contrasting with his pale complexion. Sometimes we make fun of him because, despite being born and raised in this city full of sun and beaches, he does not even have the shadow of a tan.

"Are you sure they won't fire you for everything you bring us from that restaurant?" Haven asks before biting into a taco and closing her eyes, savoring the delicacy that is also intoxicating my taste buds right now.

Sady shrugs and shakes his head. "The lobster is from a canceled order someone already paid for last night and we couldn't serve today. The others are just leftovers from some tables. They would have thrown them away anyway. Better to eat them, right?"

Sady works in one of the hottest restaurants in the city. He did an apprenticeship until he became a sous chef, working fourteen, sixteen, hours a day without a break, bowing his head and accepting whatever came at him from the raging chef. His dedication paid off because he's made a name for himself in the competitive environment of high-class dining in Los Angeles. If he left that place, more than a few would go out of their way to put him in charge of their kitchens, giving him the hard-earned promotion he deserves.

"Just don't get into trouble because of us. You're the only one with a decent job and can make a career out of it. I'd never want you to become penniless like us." I wink at him as I swallow the last bite of one of the tastiest meals I've ever eaten. That restaurant deserves the fame it has earned over the years.

We fall silent when we finish eating, huddling in our jackets and turning to the sea as the sky turns orange and pink and the sun sets on the water. They say that when you see the green ray—that optical effect of the sun meeting the water, creating a green flash that lasts only a few moments—you have to make a wish because it will be granted. A bit like shooting stars.

"Did you see it too?" Haven whispers as she snuggles up by my side and slips her hands into my jacket pocket.

"Yes."

"Well, at least there will be two wishes granted."

I don't think they will be very different. If I know her, she probably wanted the same thing I prayed for: a little stability. I would like, for once, to go to bed without worrying about how we'll pay the rent or if we have money for a decent meal the next day.

I wish I didn't have to knock on the door of every wedding planner in the city, begging to be recommended for the wedding shoot. People pay thousands of dollars for a wedding dress, but then skimp on the filming because "my cousin with the cell phone can do the same job for free."

I wish I could give Haven the life she deserves without always having to fight every day.

"I'm going to sleep. Tomorrow I have to get up at five-thirty," Sady announces as he gets up and cleans his black jeans of the sand. He lowers his hat over his brown eyes and pulls the hood over his head, looking like a faceless shadow that wanders the streets, sucking the souls of passers-by. I'm not surprised to see people steer away from him. If I didn't know he was a guy with a heart of gold, he'd inspire a bit of fear in me too.

"What do you say we go too?" Haven whispers in my ear.

I nod, get up, and help her stand up in turn. "Good night, folks." I wave at the four homeless people who kept us company, getting a few nods and another toothless smile from Liv.

Our apartment is not far from the skatepark, on one of the less busy streets in a two-story building with eight tiny apartments. The building's front door is difficult to open, and I always have to push it with my shoulder, scratching the concrete floor with a dull lament.

The walls in the dark lobby are caked with black grime up to the ceiling. No one thought of repainting them after a fire totally destroyed the stairs and wooden landings leading to the apartments a few years ago.

It's a miracle no one was killed by the flames and smoke that came up in a flash during the night. Firefighters said it was arson, but no one bothered to investigate in detail. The name of the culprit on the police report is "unknown." They were too busy trying to contain the crime wave in this area to spend time and resources on a fire that didn't kill anyone.

We climb the iron stairs replacing the charred ones up to

the second floor to our apartment. A letter stamped by a court and signed by a law firm is stuck to the door. Haven takes out her cell phone and lights it up, but I don't need to read it to understand we're in trouble up to our neck.

They're giving us until Friday to pay the three months' rent we're behind, or they will change the lock with all our stuff inside. Three days to find thousands of dollars that we couldn't raise in months. I rest my forehead on the front door, close my eyes, and inhale. Five minutes ago, I wished for some stability. Not even enough time to enjoy the sweet taste of hope before the umpteenth jolt kicks us to the ground.

Haven puts her hand on my shoulder and lays her lips on my temple, imprinting a kiss that can't lift my spirits. "We'll find a way," she whispers. "Tomorrow, I'll go back to the café and see if they'll hire me again. In the meantime, maybe we can ask Sady if he can host us until we find something else."

This doesn't solve our problems, not in the long term at least. The thought of getting help from a guy who kills himself at work because I can't find a solution to our economic situation makes me feel like a failure.

For so long, I've wondered if this stubbornness to chase my dreams is real passion or complete madness. Hollywood is ruthless. You can be crazy-talented, but sometimes you just can't break through. You have to have the courage to admit when it's time to throw in the towel and scale back your plans for the future.

Maybe I'm just a coward, feeling guilty for not being able to give us a life we dream and deserve. I don't want Haven to take responsibility for my mistakes, my inability to take care of her.

I barely swallow the lump that has formed in my throat, taking the keys from my pocket and opening the door, unable to look in her eyes.

While Haven is in the bathroom, I open the box I keep on the bedside table with the remaining money. Two hundred dollars. I count it once, twice, three times, in the vain hope that the number will magically change, but they are only twenty ten-dollar bills. It won't cover even a week of the three months of rent owed to our landlord.

I put the money in the box, and my eye falls on the fourteen-year-old silver cell phone. It's not a modern smartphone, there's no camera, just text messages and calls. It's what Simon gave me after his first robbery when I hugged him, terrified because I was afraid he would never come back. He gave it to me so he could assure me he was okay every time he went out, that he would come back. I lived clinging to that phone, convinced that one day, sooner or later, that message would not arrive.

I always kept it with me. I never dared to get rid of it, renewing it with a few dollars just to keep the number in existence. Even when, for two long years, the silence was almost unbearable. Still, I didn't want to give up the one thing I had left of the person who had broken my heart. Because, no matter how much it hurt, the pain was still better than the emptiness Simon had left.

Until the day the cell phone started ringing again. I never answered for fear that someone had the wrong number. Not knowing who was on the other side allowed me to bask in the idea that Simon hadn't forgotten about me, that somewhere, in his messed-up life, he had found a moment to think about me.

Every year, on my birthday, that call came on time, soothing the wound that had never healed. I never answered.

Sometimes it's easier to accept the fantasy that someone is craving your love, seeking you for ten long years without losing hope, rather than face reality and hear his voice.

If you live with the delusion, you're safe. In your imagination, people can remain close to you. They don't disappear into thin air, leaving behind silences so deep they hide your soul.

A voice different than the one that populates your memories brings you back to a reality you can't control, one that leaves you at the mercy of feelings that could break your heart. One more time.

***

I spent the night tossing and turning in bed without closing my eyes. Now, as sunlight finally starts filtering through the windows, the solution to our problems creeps into my chest.

I watch Haven sleep curled up next to me, her pink hair shaggy on the pillow, her lips gaping a bit, relaxed. An expression that will disappear as soon as she wakes up and worries slip back into our lives and thoughts.

I want to see her serene face not just when she sleeps, but during the day as well, with that smile that illuminates her features and lately has become so rare.

It's not difficult to decide to stuff what little we own into four large garbage bags and take our lives into our own hands.

Of course, nausea grips my stomach, but the idea of finding ourselves in the middle of a street terrifies me more than the unknown.

I knock on the door in front of me, and a few moments later, Sady comes to open it wrapped in a black bathrobe, the water dripping from his face. I wonder if he has any clothing in any other color than black. He has a bewildered look—I've never shown up at his house before.

"Sorry to bother you…" My voice trembles and I feel Haven's hand clutching my fingers in an encouraging grip. "We need to leave the city for a while, and I was wondering if you could keep our stuff until we come back."

Sady frowns and looks puzzled at our four black bags, the expression of someone wondering how it's possible to pack two entire lives into such a small space, but he's careful not to speak his thoughts.

"Of course, no problem." He recovers from the moment of bewilderment with a sweet smile that opens his face. "Come in, leave them here." He steps aside and points us to a built-in wardrobe just inside the entrance of his apartment that is much airier than ours, with white walls and a kitchen overlooking a patio we can see from where we are.

"Thank you! We'll come back to get them. We don't want to leave you with our mess," I try to reassure him, not daring to look him in the eyes. The defeat I feel inside is killing my pride.

"Don't worry, take as much time as you need. Where are you going?"

By the way he's holding his bathrobe firmly in place and staying in front of the door without asking us in, I understand that the question is more out of courtesy than a desire to make conversation.

"New York." My tone is so desperate it sucks all the happiness out of the room.

CHAPTER 3
Haven

We flew business class and a driver picked us up when we got off the plane. We're traveling in an SUV with tinted windows and leather seats so soft it feels like we're wrapped in a soft cocoon, pampering us. My gray sweatpants and worn Vans clash with the luxury surrounding us.

For years, I had not allowed myself to savor the glitz of celebrity life. Once, this was my world. I felt comfortable, powerful, and invincible as only a teenager in the spotlight can feel. I threw a tantrum if my mother bought water rather than Evian or I didn't have fresh strawberries every morning for breakfast.

Now it's a miracle if I get two meals a day and fill the worn bottle with water from public fountains. It's strange how a person's life can change dramatically overnight and how small details, like the soft leather of a car seat, can bring back memories you had set aside in the corner of your heart.

Stuck in the evening traffic entering Manhattan, I observe the skyline of one of the most famous cities in the world, getting lost in the twinkling lights of the buildings that appear magical. It seems an eternity has passed since we left our few things at Sady's house and turned our existence upside down. Again, from one day to the next, I find myself living a life that looks like someone else's.

Nicholas is huddled by the window staring at the city, and I have no idea if it's familiar to him. As a kid, he grew up in New Jersey with a foster family—it's the only thing I know about his childhood. I don't know if his nervousness is linked to his memories of this city or the person we are about to meet.

"Are you okay?" I ask him worriedly, looking at his gloomy face, his eyebrows wrinkled in a thoughtful expression, his lips clenched in a thin line that keeps his emotions hidden.

He reassured me that it was a difficult but conscious decision when we talked about it in LA. I tried to tell him it wasn't a problem for me to serve tables at a café until he finds another project to work on. He assured me with one of his sincere smiles that his nervousness was just a gut reaction to the email, insecurities he knows he can overcome. But the closer we get to our destination, the more doubts I'm having that this is the right choice for us. I've never seen him so nervous.

"Nicholas, are you okay?" I raise my voice a little when I don't get an answer.

I notice the driver, who introduced himself as Max, glance at the rear-view mirror. His impassive face doesn't show any emotion, but I think he's worried about having to clean my boyfriend's vomit from the back seat of his luxurious car.

Nicholas turns to me and tries to smile, but it never reaches his eyes. "Yes, I'm just a little tired. The plane always makes me nervous. I'll be okay."

He wants to reassure me, but the tremor in his voice reveals his insecurity. He never lies to make me feel safe. He knows I prefer stark reality to lies. But this time, he can't hide the fear that grips his chest.

I think the decision to come here was dictated by his wounded pride after the eviction. Suddenly, I have in front of me not a strong and determined twenty-seven-year-old, but a little boy afraid of what awaits him on the other side of this bridge.

I reach out my hand to grab his and squeeze it for the rest of the way, trying to instill the courage I cannot express in words. I always thought that I would be ready when the turning point of our lives came. Instead, I feel nervous after almost ten years away from this business. It's starting over in an environment that sometimes intimidates me, even if I face it head-on as I always do.

Half an hour later, we arrive in front of a house on the Upper Eastside that screams luxury, with its large windows that reveal an elegant décor. It's not tacky like what I've seen over the years in the homes of my mother's friends.

I can barely glimpse a fireplace under a light pastel-colored painting. It has simple and clean lines, highlighting the natural beauty of the wood, nothing like the massive, intricately carved stones of some fireplaces I've seen in LA, in the mansions hiding behind tall wrought-iron gates with the owner's golden tacky initials.

Nicholas wanted to stay in a hotel at first. He didn't want to stay at his old friend's house, but their manager, Evan, insisted that Simon preferred it that way.

Since we'll be spending the next few months in close contact on a tour bus, I agree that it's better to live under the same roof, share spaces, and get used to each other's presence. The tour bus can ruin even the closest friendships, let alone one that has been paused for twelve long years.

Nicholas was livid, ranting that Simon is a dictator, that fame has gone to his head and he cannot buy people with his money. But I understand Simon. I, too, prefer to know in advance what I'm getting into, to avoid discovering that a person gets on my nerves while I'm locked in a box of sardines I can't escape.

I turn to Nicholas, who observes the five steps that separate us from the front door as if they were the pathway to hell. I squeeze myself into my padded denim jacket, too light for New York's harsh January weather, and take the lead, knowing Nicholas would stay out here and freeze rather than ring the doorbell.

When the door opens, I am greeted by Simon's slender figure. I look up and stare open-mouthed at the young man with black hair and eyes so pale they seem almost painted. His lean figure fits into a pair of washed-out jeans that hug his long legs and a black shirt with rolled sleeves just below the elbows. Seeing he is barefoot, I lose my ability to speak. I've always had a weakness for men who walk barefoot around the house—it's so sexy.

I'm so embarrassed in front of the handsome guy I've seen hundreds of times on video, but never so closely, that I'm speechless. I didn't expect him to be so beautiful in person. His curious gaze rests on my face, studying my reaction.

I smile at him. "Sorry, I was bewitched. You should change photographers because official photos don't do you justice. And please, let your hair fall rebelliously like that on your forehead; when the stylist combs it, it looks like a cow has licked you."

The silence lasts for a few seconds too long, and I feel that I have been overly honest with a person I don't know, but Simon starts laughing. One of those belly laughs that makes him throw his head back and hold a hand on his stomach.

"You must be Haven. Nice to meet you." He extends a hand to introduce himself. His grip is firm and decisive, the way I like it.

"Nice to meet you too."

"I'll let Evan know your suggestions. Maybe that's why I'm the only one in the band who's still single." He winks at me and shows off a conspiratorial smile that almost makes my legs tremble.

His gaze shifts behind me to the sidewalk, where Nicholas silently waits next to the driver. The emotions that run through Simon's face are almost overwhelming: nervousness, surprise, the flash of a feeling I can't decipher. But then it softens as if memories that warm his chest take over, making his lips arch in a smile.

I have never seen so much sweetness in a man's gaze. It's like I'm witnessing a private conversation, consisting of looks and words never spoken. I almost feel like the third wheel standing here on these steps, waiting for someone to make the first move.

"Nicholas…" Simon's whisper is almost imperceptible, like a prayer escaping his lips.

I turn to my partner and find him motionless, a stern expression on his ashen face, and for the first time, I don't know what he's really thinking. A small nod of the head, almost a greeting, then he pulls up the shoulder strap of the camera bag that is slowly sliding down on his leather jacket. He doesn't say anything. He doesn't move. Next to him, Max studies the situation, unsure whether to carry our suitcases inside.

"Please, come in. It's freezing out here." Simon's trembling voice shakes me out of my embarrassment, and the electricity in the air dissipates but still leaves a bittersweet aftertaste on my palate. I am gradually more doubtful that coming to New York was a good idea.

I step inside Simon's house while he steps aside. Nicholas follows me right away after Max with our suitcases that he puts down near the doorway and then quietly leaves. The moment the door closes behind us, it's as if the air gets sucked out of the room.

"I ordered something delivered to eat. I thought you would be tired after the flight. I hope you don't mind. Leave your jackets on the bench, then I'll show you your rooms where you can put your suitcases."

"Thank you, but you didn't have to do all that." I try to intervene since my partner seems to have lost his tongue.

"Don't mention it. You're my guests." He beckons us to follow him.

We enter a formal living room packed to the limit with plants of all kinds. Some have giant heart-shaped leaves, others green streaks so pale they seem almost white, some long and pointed like swords, others with purple edges. I'm not an expert in botany, but I'm certain this vegetation needs meticulous care, and they are so lush that I assume that Simon spends hours nursing them. Or someone for him.

We enter the kitchen and find a table laden with every delicacy you could ask for, ready to welcome us.

"I didn't know what you liked so I ordered a bit of everything: pasta, chicken, vegetables, fish…"

I look at the table that looks set for a wedding luncheon with everything a person could want. As if Simon was nervous and doing everything to make us feel at home.

We sit at the table and begin to fill our plates, Nicholas maintaining a stubborn silence that is becoming embarrassing. And I, too, fall quiet, not wanting to start a conversation that seems forced.

I'm so hungry I could eat half the food on the table, stuffing my face, but the silence is so absolute that I move in slow motion. The sound of my fork resting on the plate is almost deafening and makes me feel like the center of attention, embarrassing me. I can feel the passing of time by counting the ticking of a clock in another room. Even my breathing seems to make too much noise, so I focus on my plate without ever looking up from the potatoes in front of me.

Simon speaks hesitantly, as if embarrassed to break the silence. "So, Haven, you're Nicholas's assistant? When he replied to the email, he told me that you're a team, that he wouldn't consider a contract without including you."

I'm swallowing a bite down with a sip of water when Nicholas decides this is the best time to intervene. "Haven is my girlfriend and business partner. She's not just my assistant," he barks, almost annoyed.

Simon seems to blush as he looks down at his plate. I turn to my boyfriend with wide eyes. He has never been so rude to anyone since I met him, especially in response to a completely harmless question.

"Forgive me. I did not catch this nuance from your email. I apologize for making assumptions without knowing the nature of your relationship," Simon says, embarrassed.

The pain in his gaze seems overly exaggerated for a minor misunderstanding generated by an impersonal work email. I can understand the embarrassment of two people who haven't seen each other for a decade, the difficulty in breaking the ice, but not all this tension.

Nicholas's irritable behavior and the extreme emotions Simon can't conceal make me think they're hiding something more profound than just a childhood acquaintance. A past that has hurt both or, perhaps, never been cleared up, bringing into this room a cloud of emotions.

I struggle to find a way to act as a mediator, to ease a conflict I had no idea even existed. I wasn't prepared for such palpable tension in this room. "It's not a problem, Simon. Really. It was also a surprise for me to be included in the contract. Your confusion is understandable." I try to reassure him, but I feel like a lawyer who tries to defend a murderer whose hands are still stained with the victim's blood.

I notice Nicholas close his eyes for a moment and inhale. When he reopens them, his face is much less tense than before, although sad, and the smile he tries to force does not light up his face like it usually does. "Forgive my unkindness. I didn't want to be rude. I'm just a bit tired from the trip. Thank you for this dinner. You didn't have to prepare all this."

The sweet Nicholas I know emerges, insecure from the onslaught of demons that has gripped him since the email arrived.

I look at Simon and find him softening, like when he first laid eyes on Nicholas, and I'm witnessing again a silent conversation between the two, made of glances and breaths caught in the throat, tenderness and regret, fire and ice that mix in a jumble of emotions. I'm an invisible spectator in this dance of feelings for a moment that seems endless.

I clear my throat, trying to push the feeling of discomfort back into my chest, and bring the conversation to a topic that can't cause significant embarrassment. "So, are you ready for this great documentary about your life?"

Simon bursts out laughing, and the atmosphere lightens a bit. "Absolutely not. It's a publicity stunt that Evan arranged to get us back on tour, but I don't know if I'm ready to show such an intimate part of my life to the public." He shakes his head and pours white wine from a bucket full of ice into our glasses.

"At least you'll have the chance to tell your truth and silence all the speculation the media makes." Nicholas's voice is sweeter and calmer than before, and a smile, though slight, forms on his lips.

For the first time since we arrived, the two of them look straight into each other's eyes, and the intensity of that gaze makes me almost run out of breath. If the emotions were palpable before, you can practically feel the electricity flowing between the two now. I have no idea when they met and under what circumstances, but now I'm sure that whatever feelings bound them before I met Nicholas haven't disappeared for either of them.

Simon smiles at him as he sips from his glass. "Yes. That's the positive side of this whole circus they're preparing. And then we have the opportunity to go on tour again, and that's a breath of fresh air."

"Are you excited to be back in front of a large audience?" I'm intrigued by this life "on the road." I've always loved concerts and bands, but I've never lived the life of a rock star.

"Oh, yes. I love playing in stadiums. But maybe the thing I like the most is falling asleep in a city and waking up in a different place. That's what fascinates me most about touring: in some ways, all the stages are the same, but they're always a little different. I know, it's a contradiction. You have to live it to really understand its meaning." He lights up as he explains it, keeping his eyes glued to Nicholas's, leaving me on the sidelines of a conversation I struggle to join.

From then on, the talk becomes fluid and light. Nicholas participates, although not with his typical small talk. And it's a little easier for me to analyze their complicated situation. It's as if there are ghosts from the past sitting at this table. I can distinguish their contours and presence, but I can't tell whether they're good or bad.

***

I close the bedroom door behind me and watch Nicholas sit on the bed and sink his face into his hands, inhaling deeply.

"Are you okay?" I've probably asked him this at least fifty times in the last two days, like a broken record playing the same song.

"Yes, Haven. I'm fine," he replies, annoyed.

"I wouldn't say that. You're barking at everyone." I'm tired of trying to justify his childlike behavior. He's an adult, he has decided to accept this situation despite not liking it, but he's not going to keep treating me badly and expect me to take it.

"I'm tired, okay? If we had the money, I would never have accepted this job, much less live here. I'm doing this to give you a roof over your head and decent meals."

His words hurt me, but I breathe deeply and sit next to him; I try to take his hand, but he avoids it. The dark stubble makes his face appear more hollowed out than it really is.

"Can you explain what happened with Simon? It's clear you two know each other well, not just a superficial childhood acquaintance. And it's also clear this thing makes you feel bad. I can't help you if I don't know what the hell happened before I met you."

Nicholas dodges my attempt to touch him, gets up, and takes the clean towels sitting on top of the bed. "There's nothing to explain," he snaps before entering the private bathroom and locking the door.

I watch the light filtering under the door where he has just barricaded himself, and take another deep breath, deciding not to press it any further, at least for now, and leave the room.

Going to the kitchen to get two glasses of water for the night, I find Simon doing the dishes and feel guilty for not offering to help him earlier. "You're doing all the work yourself." I approach and grab one of the empty containers, starting to fill it with leftovers.

"If I tell you it relaxes me, does that make me a loser?" He smiles and winks at me, pausing to gaze for a few interminable moments on my bare shoulder, left uncovered by the worn collar of a too-big sweatshirt that's fallen down on my arm.

I feel my cheeks heat up. While he's not as brazen as his other bandmates when they're on stage, he has a natural way of flirting. It's a side of him that doesn't come through in his public image.

"No, it doesn't surprise me."

He turns to me, resting his hip on the kitchen counter, fake horror painted on his face. "See? You do think I'm a loser."

I smile and shake my head. "No. It's just that of all the Jailbirds, you're always the most calm and quiet. Your home is immaculate, and your plants seem to receive a lot of attention... Basically, you seem like someone who loves to take care of the place where he lives. So I'm not surprised that you're putting the dishes in the dishwasher after dinner."

He nods and smiles. "You're a keen observer." There is admiration in his voice.

"I learned to study people before judging them...and I've seen the change in Nicholas since he received your email."

He stops for a moment, his eyes fixed on the plate he is washing. He stiffens and inhales sharply. "You mean he's not always this...difficult?"

"Nicholas always has a good word for everyone and would give anything to help others. What I see these days is a Nicholas I don't recognize."

I see him reflecting and nodding without adding anything else.

"Can I ask you a question?"

He turns and studies me with his intelligent eyes, carefully observing my face, taking time to caress with his gaze my hazelnut irises, the profile of my nose, descending to my lips and staying there for a time that seems endless. He swallows with difficulty, his nostrils dilate, his jaw contracts, revealing the agitation he struggles to conceal. He's having a hard time calming down before laying his gaze on my neck and resisting the temptation to go down further. He's almost not breathing when he returns to my face.

It's hard for me to remain neutral while he looks. When it takes several seconds to compose himself before answering me, I'm a little uncomfortable. Eventually, he beckons me to continue.

"Will you tell me what happened between you two? I found out a few days ago that you knew each other and your return into his life seems to have thrown him into a tailspin."

Simon frowns and leans against the counter, clasping his hands tightly on the marble edge. He's calm and composed on the surface, but the white knuckles tell me otherwise. "He never told you about me?"

I shake my head no.

"How long have you been together?"

"Six years. We came to your concert in Santa Monica last summer, but he never mentioned knowing you. He doesn't talk much about his past, and I never insisted. But right now, he looks like a beaten dog curling up in a corner, ready to bite anyone who approaches him. I don't know how to help him. I feel helpless," I confess.

I feel guilty asking Simon about something Nicholas doesn't want to admit to me. Still, the worry about what he's going through is stronger than the voice of my conscience. I can't help him if I don't know where to start.

I've tried to support him, but it's obvious it's not enough. For years, I've watched the leather cuffs he wears on his wrists, keeping an eye on every change in his moods in order to recognize his demons before they can drag him to the bottom. I feel him slipping away these days, and I don't know how to save him.

Simon looks at the floor and shakes his head before raising it again and nailing me with that deep look of his that lays you bare. "If he's never told you about me, he has his reasons. I don't feel I can betray his trust and tell you something that doesn't just involve me. I'm encouraged to know that the real Nicholas is not that angry and resentful man sleeping upstairs, but I can't help you by telling you his story. He's the one who has to do it. I can only give you my version when he's ready to share it with you."

His voice is calm and sweet, but his will is firm. There is a sense of honor and respect for an old friend in his words that I can only admire. I understand his position, the fact that he doesn't want to betray Nicholas, but this doesn't help ease the pain of the man I love.

We both go back to cleaning up the kitchen in silence, peeking at each other from time to time, trying to understand the other's thoughts. A thousand questions crowd my head as we work, but none of them ever cross my lips. They die in my throat, fueling a feeling of dread creeping into my stomach that the only third wheel in this house is me.

***

Jail Records' meeting room is one of those colorful, comfortable rooms that put you in a good mood as soon as you arrive at work in the morning. With its mismatched sofas and armchairs and fiery-red fridge, I don't mind being locked in here for a meeting.

The secretary, whom Simon introduced as Faith, is behind the reception counter with the phone earpiece pressed to her ear even though it's only eight in the morning. She greeted us with a smile and pointed out where to go, but there was no need. Damian's imposing size, Thomas's piercing gaze, and Michael's huge smile are hard to miss. Evan welcomes us, extending a hand to shake ours.

"Welcome! I hope the flight was comfortable."

"Traveling in business class has its perks," Nicholas smiles, making the others chuckle.

Last night's bad mood has been put aside, but he has not gone quite back to normal and, judging by the glances he throws at Simon, I don't think that will happen very soon.

"On the other hand, you made them get up at dawn and attend this meeting," Damian cackles.

"Do you have any idea how difficult it is to organize your life?" their manager reproaches him. "Thank heaven I didn't make you come here at six o'clock when Emily and I started listing the companies that provide the stages."

"Not one but two crazy people who get up at unthinkable hours to work," Damian teases, winking at him.

Evan rolls his eyes, but you can see he's used to their jokes.

"Haven and Nicholas, right?" Thomas focuses on us, distracting the other two from their bickering.

I nod.

"Nicholas, are you a friend of Simon? He never talks about his life before we knew each other," Michael pries with a serious look, far from the smiling, carefree face we see in all of their videos.

"Same foster family for a while," Simon intervenes, beating Nicholas to the punch.

I glance at my boyfriend and see him flash a tense smile. "Yep," he merely confirms.

"So, where do we start to create this documentary?" I speak and smile excitedly, but really I just want to change the subject before Simon or Nicholas explodes. The tension between them is so intense sometimes it's difficult to breathe when they're both in the same room.

"You tell us," Evan urges.

To my great relief, Nicholas has shed the role of the angry teenager and become the professional he knows how to be. "They didn't assign you writers to script the episodes, right? It seems to me that yours is a rather unique agreement."

"That's right, they say they want a genuine product, not artfully rehearsed with jokes written by someone who doesn't know the band's history. The truth is they're paying for a tour that costs millions, so they're cutting any other production expenses. Which is fine with us because we asked to make this documentary our way. We're comfortable going back on tour, but we're not willing to lose our freedom. Having left the old record company is a big step. We want to continue in that direction."

I like how Evan uses *we* when talking about the band. It took me five minutes of conversation and an exchange of emails to understand that he's the fifth member of the Jailbirds.

Nicholas nods, following Evan's logic. "I understand your point of view, and I share it. I thought I would follow you twenty-four hours a day, seven days a week. Take as many shots as possible of your life, of what you want to make public, and then alternate the live footage with interview moments."

"Can we approve the questions?" Damian worries about this aspect, perhaps because he is the one most exposed in the media.

"I thought I'd have you write them," proposes Nicholas, who takes notes in his ever-present leather notebook. "I don't know all the background to your story, only what was reported in the newspapers. I don't want to build an interview and questions based on facts that have been distorted by gossip newspapers. I don't want gossip. I can find that everywhere. I want to know the soul of the band. And I want to show it to the public without filters, without adding details that distract from what is most important: *your* truth."

"I like this guy," Michael intervenes, letting a smile light up his face. "I don't know why you hid him from us until this moment, Simon, but I'm glad you brought him here."

Evan nods. His face also seems to light up. "I have the right person for this job. Iris is the Public Relations Manager for the Jailbirds. You'll work together to fine-tune the questions."

My enthusiasm is genuine this time. "I love Iris! I followed her blog before it became your official source. I can't wait to get to know her." I sound like a little girl who idolizes her favorite actor, but I can't hide my admiration for a woman I respect.

Thomas bursts out laughing and proposes, "What do you say we order pizza tonight and eat it at our place together? Sooner or later, you'll have to get to know this group of crazies that keeps growing, you might as well face the lions' den right away."

And honestly, I can't wait.

The conversation from that moment on is a series of questions and answers that serve to fine-tune a lineup that helps us to outline the documentary's production. As the hours go by, the fear of finding myself in front of arrogant and capricious rock stars turns into enthusiasm for meeting genuine people.

When you live long enough in this business, between the parties, luxury, and snakes who try to exploit you in every way, it's inevitable you'll change. It's refreshing to discover that there are still people in the golden world of celebrities who value friendship and authentic relationships.

***

When we get back to Simon's and our bedroom, Nicholas lies on the bed, barely taking off his shoes. An arm covers his eyes while a sigh escapes from his lips.

"Busy day," I venture into a conversation, even if these days it is ever more difficult to relate.

It hurts me to see him like this, like he's torn between staying and making the money we need to survive and running as far as possible from Simon. I feel helpless witnessing his inner struggle.

"I thought it would never be over," he admits, with a look I can't decipher as I take off my shoes and jeans.

I approach the bed and crawl toward him until I straddle

his pelvis. "Do you need to release some tension?" I whisper into his ear as I kiss his neck, getting a sigh out of him.

His hands slide down my hips, reaching the flaps of my sweater. He sticks his fingers under the wool and caresses my skin with gentle movements.

"Maybe just a little bit."

"I was thinking of something more than a little bit." I kiss his neck while I make him sit up to take off his sweatshirt.

His slim physique is an invitation that my lips can't resist. I taste every inch of his skin, intoxicated by his scent, feeding on his choked moans. With a quick gesture, he pulls off my sweater and inhales sharply at the sight of my bare skin.

"I like it when you're not wearing a bra," he barely whispers.

I rest my hands on his belly and enjoy his gaze going through every slight curve of my body. I will never tire of the way he worships my body. He traces the dark lines of my tattoos on my hips, on my arms, as if to memorize them despite knowing them by heart after all these years. He rests his hands on my legs, caresses the skin of my thighs until he gets to the edge of my panties.

He tickles me through the cloth until I run out of breath. I bite my lip and enjoy when he sticks a couple of fingers under the panties and sinks into me, making me moan.

I get up on my knees just enough to unfasten his jeans and slide them with his boxers a few inches down, to free his erection exploding behind the layers of fabric. His fingers give me no rest, bending over and touching that point inside me that makes me reach the peak of pleasure.

I reciprocate, squeezing my fingers around his hot flesh.

He inhales and clenches his teeth, pushing his hips toward mine. I look him straight in the eyes when my fingers free his erection, and I sink on it slowly.

He gets up until he reaches my breasts with his hands and seals my lips with his. I move on him, dictating a rhythm that I know well, after years spent chasing a pleasure together that has never waned.

"Nicholas..." A lament escapes from my lips when I'm about to reach my peak.

"Shhh. Please, lower your voice. Simon might hear us," he whispers as he continues to push inside me.

My orgasm, however, fades away until it subsides completely. Nicholas is here, in my arms. He sinks into me and enjoys my flesh, but his mind is elsewhere. His brain and heart are inside another room of this huge house, and I can't reach him.

I stop, watching him as he continues to sink into me with his eyes closed and reach his orgasm without realizing I'm no longer involved.

I lie next to him, slip under the covers, and turn off the lamp on the bedside table. I close my eyes, giving my back to him. I hear him breathing slowly until he recovers from his pleasure, then he turns off the light on his bedside table, and in the darkness of the room, the silence between us has never been so loud.

PRESS *Review*

Hi, Roadies!

On New Year's Eve, we assured you great news was coming, and we are here to keep our promise. The Jailbirds are back on tour in the stadiums! You read that right. At the link below, you will find all the dates of the "Back to Jail" tour that will accompany the release of the album by the same name. A world tour that will reach all continents. Get your phones ready, because tickets go on sale next Friday at 10AM EST.

Be Kind and Rock'n'Roll,

Iris

82,386 Likes 78,604 Tweets 63,656 Shares 10,624 Comments

Simon

Fifteen years earlier

"Kid, come here and learn something useful." Tom's voice thunders behind me, and I turn around with a smile, ready to roll up my sleeves and help him.

I step toward him, but Liam passes me, bumping into my shoulder and reaching his father by the barbecue where he cooks burgers for everyone. For a moment, I believed he wanted to teach me how to use the grill, forgetting that he's not my father and that certain things are taught to your kids, not to your neighbors.

We're at the park a few blocks from where we live. There are a dozen families, all with stars and stripes flags and picnic tables set up with food everyone has brought.

We made the potato salad. Yesterday, Mrs. Margaret got all seven of us to peel the sack of potatoes she had bought that morning. She complained we were too slow, saying she'd have to get a few more orphans to make us finish the job faster. But she left us in the kitchen to do our job without bothering us too much.

It was fun because we laughed and joked for once without being scolded for making too much noise. But being the oldest, I had to teach Olivia to use a knife when she is only five years old, and I was terrified she'd chop her fingers off. If she had, Margaret certainly wouldn't have let us come to the Fourth of July picnic in this park.

For us kids who live in a foster family, that would have been a tragedy. These events make us feel like we're a real family—surrounded by our neighbors, fathers, mothers, children, and grandchildren who laugh, joke, and have fun.

I watch Nicholas play football with the older boys. At twelve years old, he is small and shy. He keeps his distance and runs after the others without ever getting too close to the bulky sixteen-year-olds. I suggested that he play with Olivia and the other little ones on the sand but he looked at me, offended as if I'd told him he should be wearing a diaper.

Randy throws the ball at Sean, who jumps to catch it, but barely gets to touch it as the oval ball pirouettes at great speed behind him. When I see Nicholas ready to catch it, my heart pumps into my chest. I rush toward him, but I'm too far away to reach him in time.

The ball slips through his fingers and slams into his slender chest with a thud that knocks the air out of his lungs. He ends up on his back, his face pale and his mouth wide open, trying to inhale as much air as possible.

I run faster, almost stumbling over my own feet, but Randy catches up with him, grabs him by the arm, and puts him back on his feet as if he weighs nothing.

Stopping me mid-run, the older guy makes sure Nicholas is okay and ruffles his dark curls with his huge hand as Nicholas nods. "Nice job, kiddo," he says, taking away the ball Nicholas still holds to his chest.

The wide smile on Nicholas's face shows his pride in the

compliment, and my stomach tightens in an annoying grip of jealousy. I can't make Nicholas smile like that when he comes to me and curls up by my side in fear.

"With that angel smile and face, they'll adopt him soon." Sally's voice by my side catches my attention.

When I look at the woman, Sean's mother, I notice the sweet smile on her face as she looks at Nicholas. The smile of a loving mother, like the ones you see in Christmas movies. Guilt invades my stomach. The mere thought of Nicholas being adopted makes me want to scream.

I look at him again, and my breath stops in my throat. It's true. Nicholas could be considered despite being twelve years old already. He's shy and innocent enough to attract the attention of potential adoptive parents.

When you look at him, you don't ask yourself, *What the hell did he do to still be in a foster family?* But rather, *Poor kid, what happened to him that he ended up in a foster family at this age?* It's a subtle difference I've come to recognize when people come for the kids who seem helpless and innocent.

"Yes, I hope so," I whisper. That's not true. While I want Nicholas to have a family, two loving parents who take him on vacation and give him presents on Christmas Day, I can't help but think that *I* am his family. No one will be able to take him away from me. Not even the kind of perfect family you see in the movies.

"If you stopped hanging around Roger, you'd find parents too. Nobody wants a kid who robs banks," she scolds in a low yet, somehow, loving tone.

I shift my gaze to the man sitting on the bench drinking beer. He's sneering as he talks to one of his boys in a way that makes you shiver. Someone like me, who goes around the city terrorizing bank cashiers with a gun. It's not an honest job, but it's the only one that allows me to earn money to provide for Nicholas.

I can give him gifts on his birthday. I buy him ice cream when it's summertime and the heat is unbearable, and hot chocolate when it's winter and our worn-out jackets don't warm us properly.

Roger gives me a chance to take care of Nicholas. Isn't that what a father should do? Provide for the kids? What does it matter if we don't live under the same roof and have to earn our money by being the lookout outside a bank?

"When I'm an adult, I'll have *my* own family, with a wife and a couple of children like you. I don't need someone to take care of me. I know how to make do on my own," I reply, angry and even a little humiliated by her statement.

Sally sighs and puts her hand on my cheek. My gaze is locked to her sweetness. "The problem is that if you continue on this path, you may never get to the age to make a family," she whispers to me in a broken voice.

Her words catch me by surprise, freezing my stomach. I don't know if it's because her eyes are clouded with pain or because of her insinuations, but I feel the tears rising in my eyes, and it makes me angry.

I don't cry. Not in front of others and not even in private, when Nicholas might see me. He's the one who's allowed to cry when he's scared. I'm the one who must be strong for both of us.

***

Fireworks fill the sky with colorful red, white, and blue lights. The air is thick with smoke, and the smell of gunpowder fills my nostrils, pinching a little. Nicholas is leaning on my chest. His nose is up in the air as is everyone's in the park and trembles a little with every explosion. I told him he could plug his ears if he wanted, but he replied that he's no longer a child.

A heavy hand rests on my shoulder, and when I turn to see who it is, I find Roger looking at me in a way that nails me to the ground, unable to breathe.

"Tomorrow, you come with me in the morning. I have a job for you. Bring your friend if you want." He nods his head toward Nicholas, who still has his nose in the air, not noticing anything.

"I'll come and do whatever you want, but don't touch him." I try to show as much bravery as possible. My voice is calm, even though I'm quivering inside my belly.

The grin that forms on his lips stops the blood in my veins. "Okay, whatever you want. But tomorrow you're coming in, not staying outside doing nothing. I'm tired of paying you to be the lookout. It's time for you to make a living."

Genuine fear creeps into my chest. That's why he taught me to hold a gun, because it's time to put a mask on my face and collect as much money as possible from the terrified women behind the counter.

"Who will stay outside?"

"Don't worry. That's for me to figure out. You just do what I tell you."

"Will you pay me like the others who come inside?"

Roger smiles and shakes his head. "Yes, I'll pay you like the others if you earn it. But if you try and pull some bullshit, you won't see a penny."

I nod, giving him my word. This may be the last Fourth of July I'll be allowed to be a kid, kick a ball, and watch fireworks. I squeeze an arm around Nicholas and watch him resting his hand on mine.

I swear when we grow up, we'll have our own families. A wife, a couple of kids, and Nicholas and I will celebrate the Fourth of July in the backyard of a house like the ones you see on TV.

We'll talk about how boring our office jobs are, but we'll fearlessly remember these years spent together. Because Nicholas and I deserve all the security and stability a normal life can give us.

CHAPTER 4
Simon

I walk down the stairs leading to the living area and hear their voices in the kitchen. I can't discern the words, but Haven's melodious laugh reaches my ears, warms my chest, and makes me smile.

Fifteen days have passed since our forced coexistence, and we've started a routine I still struggle to make my own. I'm not part of that well-oiled duo that seems to dance in the rooms of this house. It is a duet, and I am only a spectator.

Nicholas and Haven have their own way of communicating, with small gestures that enclose all the love they feel for each other. Like when Haven knots the scarf around Nicholas's neck before going out in the morning. Or when he warms her hands, clutching them between his and resting them on his chest under his jacket. Gestures I see among my friends with their women that make me feel more and more alone.

I turn the corner and stand still in the doorway of the kitchen. They haven't noticed me yet, and I watch them prepare the table for breakfast.

Nicholas is cooking eggs in a pan, his hands dirty with food prep. When a lock of dark curls falls on his forehead, Haven puts it in a ponytail on top of his head with a rubber band she's wearing on her wrist. They didn't even talk to each other, yet it's such a spontaneous gesture I can't help but wonder how often she's used the same care toward my friend.

A grip tightens my stomach. It tastes a bit like jealousy or envy. Once I was the one who moved his hair from his forehead, helped him with his homework, worried whether he had a hot meal on the table at least once a day.

"You're up!" Haven smiles when she looks up and sees me, embarrassed, in the doorway.

"I took a longer shower than usual. Sorry I didn't help you with all of this." I approach the table and notice there's nothing left to do. They've already arranged the fruit cut into pieces, yogurt, milk, bacon, and toast. I feel almost useless in my own home.

Nicholas turns off the stove, takes a trivet, puts the eggs on the table, and then sits next to his girlfriend. "You're hosting us in your home, and you won't let us contribute to the costs of food and lodging. Preparing breakfast is the least we can do."

Haven approaches him, pecks him on the temple, then begins to scoop her breakfast onto a plate. I feel my heart clenching in my chest.

When I thought of Nicholas for this job, I hoped I'd find that friend I left twelve years ago. The little boy with big, scared eyes who awakened my sense of protection. I never considered that he's now a twenty-seven-year-old man, and that he'd bring with him the woman he's been living with for a long time.

Seeing them together was a cold shower because I realized that he, like all my friends, went on with his life. He found someone to grow old with. The worst thing of all is that I understand why he chose her. Haven is a ball of energy. She's attentive, loving, and sexy as hell with those big, hazel eyes and short pink hair.

This morning, I came down later than usual because I had to take a literal cold shower, since I'd dreamed of taking her over the kitchen table, waking up with an erection so powerful it almost hurt.

And then guilt crept in. I felt dirty, like I was cheating for having desired, though unconsciously, his woman. A woman I am jealous of for the relationship she has with Nicholas, for the years she shared with him. The smiles she managed to pull from him, for all the times she wrapped her arms around a body that is no longer as thin as when he was a boy.

A mixture of feelings stirs in my chest, almost suffocating me. For a moment, I basked in the idea of leaving the band, giving up this life, and totally changing my future. After all, I can live for the rest of my life on the money I have. Why stay here to suffer in an inescapable situation?

Then I realized that whoever they chose to replace me could never be part of the group. The band has this harmony not because we are united by natural musical talent, but because our past links us beyond music and innate abilities.

We got so famous because we were always a solid group, determined to get out of that crap we ended up in. To leave would mean to kill my friends' dream, and that's a thought I can't even contemplate.

I was lulled into the idea of reconnecting my relationship with Nicholas instead, finding a friend, and starting again with him. But he showed up with Haven, her bubbly personality, her smiles, her beauty, her way of loving Nicholas. And so, my world collapsed again, with a thud no one heard but me.

"Simon?" Haven's voice brings me back to reality.

I was so lost in my thoughts I didn't hear their conversation. I look away from the girl to my friend and find him frowning, and then an intrigued smile appears on his lips. "What? Sorry, my head is elsewhere this morning."

Haven's sweet smile makes me feel even more embarrassed for not giving them the attention they deserve. "Are you in rehearsals all day? Evan talked about a possible last-minute radio interview, but he didn't call last night, so it probably didn't work out, right?"

"Yes. We didn't have high expectations anyway. It's not the first time they've messed up their schedules and skipped appointments."

"How can you miss appointments with the biggest band around? How do they survive?" Nicholas laughs.

"I don't know. They have a huge following because they don't advertise, and their host is so high he sometimes goes on rants that shouldn't even be public. They created a kind of cult around this broadcaster, funded by donations from listeners, and they actually play outstanding music. The problem is it's managed by someone who's not always in his right mind because of drugs."

Nicholas and Haven look at me with their eyes and mouths wide open, as if I were telling them about one of my bank robberies.

"Wow. Are you serious?" Nicholas's disbelief is almost comical.

"I swear. It's amazing how it's become the benchmark of alternative rock in the last twenty years, given how unorganized it is."

Haven laughs, resting a hand on Nicholas's arm and her head on his shoulder. An utterly natural and innocent gesture, but for that exact reason makes me lose my appetite.

"Excuse me, I have to hurry to the studio. Leave everything on the table, today they come to clean, and they'll put away the leftovers. You know how to get to Jail Records, so I think we'll see each other there, right?" I'm blabbering all in one breath, getting up, dragging the chair on the floor.

The problem is that, after fifteen days under the same roof, I can no longer watch their public displays of affection, reminding me that I, in the end, am as alone as I was on New Year's Eve.

"But you didn't eat anything." Haven seems almost disappointed by my exit.

"I'm sorry, but I really have to go."

It annoys me to death to feel like a guest in my own house. Maybe this idea of having them stay with me wasn't as great as I thought.

***

I open the front door of Jail Records and find Emily ending a phone call.

"Where did Faith go?"

"She was a little nauseous and went upstairs to get something warm. We have nothing without caffeine." She smiles as she walks away from the counter that should be occupied by my friend's fiancée.

"It was too good to be true to finally have a professional secretary," I complain in a low voice, but not low enough for Emily not to glance at me halfway between shock and reproach.

"Wow. You're talking about the future wife of your best friend. And it's not that she's not working because she doesn't feel like it, but because she's sick from the pregnancy," she points out in such a serious tone that I feel guilty even for thinking about such a thing toward Faith.

"I was just noticing that the timing of this pregnancy is not the best, don't you think? We'll have to find another secretary." I don't know why I'm being defensive rather than just offering a simple apology for my misplaced comment.

Emily arches her eyebrows and studies me with that somewhat arrogant attitude she only uses when we behave like perfect idiots. The point is she's never used it on me. I've always been the calm one with a good head on his shoulders.

"I have no idea what's going on with you lately, but maybe it's better if you take a deep breath and calm down a bit. The diva attitude doesn't go well with a documentary." She crosses her arms over her chest, and instead of feeling guilty, the anger mounts in my stomach like a wave I can't contain.

"Well, they'll just cut my scenes anyway. I'm just the bass player. If I disappear from the face of the earth, no one would notice, so don't worry."

I see her eyes widen and her eyebrows raise even more. A grimace of disbelief and indignation appears on her face. She's about to answer me, but is interrupted by the front door opening and Damian and Lilly, who enter laughing, followed by Nicholas and Haven.

"You should come to our apartment one night for dinner. Damian knows how to make tacos so good you won't even miss the ones in Los Angeles," Lilly proposes, continuing a conversation that began outside.

"No pressure at all! Now I'll have performance anxiety because I have to outdo the best tacos in California."

All four laugh.

"We'd love to. Maybe without a camera, what do you think? I'd like to meet you without having the screen in front of me," Nicholas suggests, and the grip of jealousy that presses on my stomach makes me tighten my jaw in a steel grip.

"I'm going to the recording room. If someone is still interested in working instead of standing here fucking around, you know where to find me."

I don't turn to them. I don't even want to see the expressions accompanying the stunned silence after my exit.

***

We've been in the studio for four hours now, rehearsing all the songs we'll play on tour again. Haven and Nicholas are in the room with us, each with a camera in hand, filming.

Nicholas wants to have a lot of footage even if it's repetitive, because he says that not having a script to follow, we can't redo the scene until it comes out exactly as he wants.

We want this documentary to feel spontaneous. Which means having them around all day, without a moment's rest. Today, in particular, I feel the cameras pointed at me, at my face, expressions, and gestures.

I close my eyes and try to ignore it, but it's as if every personal space is invaded by their presence, and it's not at all pleasant. I'm tense, unable to express what I want, all the frustration building inside. When Damian interrupts the song halfway, I already know the problem.

"Simon, do you want us to take a break? You came in late again." Thomas's voice seems almost perplexed. I open my eyes and find them all staring at me, waiting for an explanation for my inability to do my job.

Nicholas and Haven continue to film my moment of nervousness and frustration.

"No, I don't need a break," I mumble as I look down and fix the bass cable that doesn't need to be adjusted.

"Are you sure? Look, it's not a problem," insists Michael, who, sitting on his stool, is looking at me with no idea of what's going on.

He's had that look for days, and not being able to tell my best friend what upsets me almost drives me crazy. When I look up at Nicholas, I meet the gaze of my former best friend, with whom I haven't been able to speak in weeks. Or rather, conversations exist, but they're only superficial.

We never talk about our past, the feelings overlapping in my chest needing clarification. When Haven is with us, I feel embarrassed, and the few times we are alone, the distance between us is so great that the only thing in the room is a tense silence until one of us leaves it.

"I don't need a break. I need you not to always have the cameras pointed at me. I need to breathe but you're always on me, and it's driving me nuts. Do you really have to stick those things in my face? Do you like seeing me struggle?"

The silence that falls after my outburst is deafening. They're all stunned by my outburst, and no one dares to say anything. Even Damian, who would normally make a joke, stands and looks at me with his mouth wide open and disbelief in his eyes. When I move my gaze from my friends to Haven, I see her lower her eyes, embarrassed, while Nicholas has a harsh, almost scolding expression.

He's never looked at me like that. I can feel the shame flowing under my skin at my lack of respect for them. I take off the bass, put it on the rack, and leave the room without saying a word. In the backyard, even breathing the cold late-January air is not enough to calm the emotional torment that's overtaking me.

"If you don't want us here, just say so, Simon." Nicholas's stern voice reaches my ears and chest like a whip.

I shake my head and look down at my shoes, trying to calm down before bringing my eyes to his. I don't know how I'll react to his disapproval. "I gave them your name. I wouldn't want anyone else for this documentary." I realize that this is the absolute truth, and I go back to looking at my shoes.

"Really? It doesn't seem like it from how you're acting. For fifteen days I feel like I've been dealing with a robot. Even your smiles are fake! What do you have to say for yourself?"

I finally look up at him with the anger boiling inside me, ready to explode after days of repressing it and stifling my instincts to scream. I wanted to have a polite dialogue with him, not impulsively loosen the bridle on twelve years of silence. But I realize now it's impossible to channel these feelings into something peaceful.

"You showed up here with her!" I gasp with a fury I can't

contain.

Nicholas wrinkles his forehead and spreads his arms. "What the hell was I supposed to do? She's my girlfriend and the person I've worked with for six years. Should I have left her in Los Angeles? How could I possibly exclude her from this opportunity?" His question is almost a desperate prayer.

"You've all moved on! You've all made a life for yourself without caring about who you left behind." I know it's not right to blame him for what I feel. He's not responsible for my friends making a family while I'm still in limbo waiting for something I can't even name. At the same time, venting my frustration on him almost makes me feel better.

"We didn't care about who we left behind? Are you serious?" His face exudes anger and pain, feelings I'm not ready to see on the face of the most important person in my life. I watch silently as his eyes fill with tears. "You were the one who disappeared twelve years ago, leaving me alone."

"I had no choice!" I shout as I take a step toward him.

"And you blame me for finding someone who helped me put my life back together?"

"You never answered my calls." The pain in my chest, as I confess it, almost makes me short of breath.

"Because I wanted you to come looking for me! I wanted to have you with me again, in my life. If I didn't answer those phone calls, I thought you'd come looking for me one day. I thought you'd take me back." The broken whisper from his lips is like a red-hot blade piercing my chest.

"I came back for you when I got out of juvie, but you weren't there. You moved on like everyone else. You chose Haven, forgetting I even exist."

Nicholas pounces on me with a fury, his fists clenching around the collar of my shirt and rendering me speechless. He pulls me forcefully, a breath away from his face, so close I can see the green specks in the sea of his hazel eyes. God, how I missed these eyes!

"Forget about you? Really? You were my whole world, Simon! You were my everything, and they took you away right before my eyes. I shouted, cried, prayed for someone to bring you back, but you were swallowed up by a huge black hole that I couldn't reach."

The guilt at making such a huge mistake and leaving him alone makes me nauseous. "We were just two kids who knew nothing about love or affection. How could I be your whole world?" I whisper, unable to accept the harm I have caused to the only person I have ever loved.

"We knew nothing about love? I learned that day what love meant, Simon. Do you have any idea how much fear I felt when they took you away? How much I missed you so suddenly? Maybe I didn't know anything about love, but I knew how much I missed your touch, your smiles, your hugs. I missed feeling you lift the blankets and slip into my bed every night, in the dark, when no one could see us. I missed your hand slipping under my shirt, looking for contact with my skin. I missed your lips on my neck, near my ear, telling me everything would be fine when I was so fucking afraid of the world."

He moves away just enough to take off the leather bracelets he always wears. "You were my whole world, and without you, I didn't want to be there either," he whispers as he stretches out his wrists to show me two faded scars.

I look up in disbelief. No words are needed to confirm that he tried to take his own life because of me, for the pain I caused him by going to prison. Nicholas steps closer. He rests his forehead on mine and his hand reaches behind my neck, grabbing my hair, almost to prevent me from escaping.

"You were my world, Simon, and you took it away that day."

I reach out my arms and wrap them around his body, sliding my face into the hollow of his neck and trying to process what he'd just told me. I destroyed his world by making a terrible mistake. Haven found him and put together the pieces of the torn little boy I left behind. He tried to take back his life and fill the void I left.

Nicholas's arms wrap around me so tight it almost hurts, but I don't care. For the first time in twelve years, I feel like I belong to someone again.

CHAPTER 5
Nicholas

"Put it back on the plate, and no one will get hurt," Haven threatens with such conviction that I place the last taco on the serving dish Simon insisted on using. Apparently, my friend doesn't like takeout boxes. He says they make him sad.

"I've never seen anyone fight tooth and nail for a taco." He's amused, and I get lost looking at him and listening to his voice, not realizing how much I missed these moments until I set foot in New York.

Three weeks have passed since our fight, twenty long days in which the tension has dissipated, and we have begun to enjoy being together again. It's as if we somehow managed to resume the relationship we broke off twelve years ago. It's true. We have grown and changed. The difference between being a kid and an adult is cavernous, but I find it exciting to meet him all over again.

Simon is meticulous: he loves to eat in the kitchen and hates doing it in the formal living room. Each room is separate and has its own function. He never mixes them, except tonight, when Haven practically forced him to dine in the formal living room. The one full of plants and so absent of even a speck of dust I wonder if he keeps it vacuum-sealed when he's not in here.

Simon has never been someone to leave his stuff around. You're forced to be that way when you live in a foster family with six other kids who have nothing. They'd kill to get their hands on something of yours. This aspect of him hasn't changed as he's adapted to adult life; tidiness has remained part of his soul.

"Because you've never lived in Los Angeles. There's sort of a cult there for Mexican food, and anyone who doesn't serve above-average food closes within a few months," Haven explains.

"And how do you like this?" Simon raises an eyebrow defiantly toward my woman.

It's strange how the three of us managed to achieve a balance. At first, it seemed like Simon was jealous of her, but maybe he saw that she's impossible to hate over time. Haven is honest, direct, and has a heart so big she helps others without thinking about the consequences.

"Passable," she says with her mouth still full.

I look at Simon's horrified face and can't hold back a smile.

"Passable?" He is bewildered. "Passable? It's one of the best Mexican restaurants in New York, and you consider it passable?" he says, appalled.

Haven shrugs while she pushes the last piece of her dinner into her mouth with two fingers. Not one of her most graceful gestures, but very on-brand with the relaxed and no-frills girl I know.

"It's clear that you don't know how to make tacos here," she teases him, and I laugh heartedly at the two of them.

"Where the hell did you find her?" he looks at me baffled.

"In a garbage bin."

Haven bursts out laughing when I evoke our first meeting.

"He's not joking," she confirms, seeing Simon's curious gaze.

"Are you serious?"

"I was throwing a big bag into a tall dumpster. He passed by and gave me a hand because it was too heavy." She smiles at me and the memory of that day.

"In Los Angeles, right? When did you move there?" Simon's voice is calm and low, but I understand from his straight posture, sitting on the couch in front of ours, that this topic makes him anxious.

During these weeks, we've swapped a few stories of our past lives, but there's never been a direct conversation. I grab the fourth bottle of beer of the evening and let the alcohol dissolve the tension in me.

"At eighteen, after high school, I wanted to become a director. I didn't have the money and good grades to get into a university, so I simply moved to Los Angeles and started contacting people that make movies. Other independent directors, newbie actors. I started from there and then built a name and a reputation."

Simon nods, sipping his beer. It's strange how I know a lot about him, but he knows so little about me. "You managed to do really well, especially since you started from nothing. I like your work. You have a way of pulling the viewer into the story. I mean…I don't even know how to define it. When I finish watching, I can't pull out of it. For days I keep thinking about it, and I'm left with that underlying melancholy I can't shake."

The words of my former best friend creep into my belly and chest, warming me in a way I didn't think possible. I didn't know he had followed my career. I thought he called me every birthday because he felt somehow obligated or guilty. I had never contemplated the idea that he might be interested in my life. Sure, he found information about me on Facebook. Otherwise, he would never have asked me to work for them, but I didn't think he had bothered to check out all my projects.

"You've followed my work?" My voice trembles as I seek confirmation.

Simon wrinkles his forehead and tilts his head to the side, studying me with a stunned expression as if I had just said something shocking. "Of course. I've seen it all. Did you really think I had forgotten about you?"

"No, it's just…I'm not at your level of fame, is all." I take a sip to help relax my nerves.

Haven joins the conversation in a soft voice. "May I ask you what happened? I mean, I understood that you grew up together in the same foster family, but then out of the blue, you lost sight of each other and no longer looked for the other? Of course, it's your business, and if you don't want to answer, it's okay…but every now and then, I feel cut off from this world of yours, and I feel…incomplete."

Simon glances at me, silently asking if he can tell this story. It's nice how certain things don't change even though we've been apart for years. As children, we just needed a glance to understand each other.

When you live in a place where you have to be careful with everything you say because any word can be used as a reason for punishment, you learn to look into people's eyes and understand their thoughts. I nod and see him relaxing.

"We lived in the same foster family for five years. Being

more or less the same age, we shared a room right away. We were two peas in a pod. What one did, the other did too. Then I started with the bank robberies."

He looks first at me, then at Haven. I think he's a little ashamed of the decisions he made as a kid.

"When I was around fourteen, one went wrong. I had just started to go inside the banks with Roger and two older guys. During that robbery, the guard reacted by pulling out his gun. One of the two boys panicked and shot him. He didn't kill him, but all hell broke out. Roger ran away with the other two. Someone pushed me, another tore the mask off my face. I managed to escape, but the cameras had filmed me, and that night the police came to pick me up. They sentenced me right away to two years of juvie because I helped them get to Roger and the other two boys. The last time I saw Nicholas, I was handcuffed as they took me away. I only went back to that house once when I got out, but Nicholas was gone."

"Did they take you away from that foster family?" Haven urges me, eager to learn about the past I've kept hidden from her until now. A history that's not just mine.

"A few days after they took Simon away, I was so desperate that I tried to kill myself," I confess, looking at the bracelets. Haven knows this part of my story. It's Simon who has no idea what happened next. "Social services came and took away all the kids and put them in other foster families."

"Was it a good house? Did they treat you well?" Simon's voice is hoarse and broken with emotion. When I look up at him, I find him clutching a pillow tightly to his chest, as if needing to cling to something in order not to give in to his emotions.

"It was a great family. Cindy and Gregory were amazing people. I still have contact with them. When their children grew up, they decided to host orphan kids, mostly teenagers with little chance of being adopted. They treated me like a son, sent me to school, and cared for me financially and with affection. They made me feel like part of a family and not just a mouth to feed. It was great to spend those years with them." The relief I read in Simon's eyes is priceless.

"And you two…lost sight of each other?" Haven gently pushes for more of our story.

Simon speaks first. "More or less. At first, I couldn't find him. My only lead was social media, and Nicholas seemed to have disappeared. Then when I found him again, I had a career that kept me busy for long months, and I saw that he was doing well without me. I started to follow him from an artistic point of view, but I saw, from what little he shared on social media, that he was happy, and I did not want to barge into his life and annoy him with my fame and all the mess it brings with it."

"But you decided to call me for this job." It comes out more as an observation, although it's the question I've wanted to ask him since I received that email.

"They wanted to put a person on us for months, day and night. I wanted it to be someone I respect, and be in tune with. You heard Evan. We'll be sharing the same tour bus starting tomorrow for months. I don't want to spend it with a complete stranger I struggle to relate to. I know we were just kids when we met, but that doesn't change the affection I feel for you. It took years to build that trust. Two months under one roof are not enough to build the same kind of rapport with an adult."

His sincerity is disarming, and I don't know if it's because of the alcohol or his confession, but his cheeks are flushed. I just nod.

"But enough with all this nostalgia, or we'll be crying like three idiots. By the way, the alcohol is going to my head," he adds with a smile.

"Aren't you excited about going on tour? I still can't believe that tomorrow night we will sleep in the tour bus and not in this house." Haven's eyes shine with excitement.

I must admit that the idea intrigues me too. I've always worked with ridiculously low budgets, if not even losing money. With this gig, we have the best equipment and, from what I understood from the guys today, the best means of transport on the market. In all honesty, I'm not used to all this luxury and glitz.

"Eventually, even two mere mortals like us will see the underbelly of the life of a rock star," I joke.

"And when the tour bus starts to smell like dirty laundry and the spaces start to get tight, you'll enjoy the life of a rock star much less."

We all laugh.

"Why don't you take a plane? You have the money to do it. Why the hell do you travel by bus like a bunch of young kids?"

"It's my fault." Simon rubs a hand over his face, and I'm intrigued. "I'm terrified of flying."

"Really?" I'm incredulous. Simon was always invincible, standing up to everyone to defend me. I didn't think he was afraid of anything.

"So much so that not even anti-anxiety meds help. Of course, it's not that I never get on a plane, but a months-long tour where I have to take one every day is not manageable. They always told me that with time and habit, it would get better, but the truth is it gets worse and worse."

"And I thought it was about the band bonding, a way of feeling more united," Haven admits.

"No, in fact, when you struggle to sleep for several months, you tend to want to kill your bandmates," he snickers, getting up from the couch. "And speaking of sleeping, I'm going to bed. Tomorrow will be a busy day, and I need to sleep off the alcohol."

"Don't worry about dinner. We'll clean this up, you rest," I say when I see that he begins to collect the dishes.

"Thanks and goodnight." He waves his hand as he walks up the stairs to his room.

Silence falls while Haven and I finish our beers.

"You never told me your scars were over the loss of a guy." Haven's voice is almost a whisper. She gets closer and takes the leather cuffs I never remove in her hands. One of the first things I confessed to her was the suicide attempt. I wanted to be clear about my emotional instability right away, and she understood.

"Telling you something like that meant talking about Simon, and I wasn't ready. I've never talked about him with anyone but my psychologist. It's something I struggled to figure out, and it took me years to accept it."

"I'm glad you told me." She straddles me, caresses my face, and places a light kiss on my forehead.

The truth is, I didn't want to tell anyone until I told Simon. My psychologist has always advised me to address this topic with the person who caused it, even if unintentionally. I never understood how important this was until three weeks ago.

I closed a chapter of my past that affected my life in ways I never realized. For some time, I had accepted what had happened. I had learned to manage and overcome the sense of guilt related to my actions. I also learned that it's normal to be angry with Simon. I overcame this anger after so much time and so much therapy.

Haven reaches out a hand between us and begins to unfasten my pants, catching me by surprise. "What are you doing?"

"What does it look like?"

"Something we should stop right now unless you want me to take you here in the middle of the living room."

She kisses me on the neck, and some of my resolution and lucidity fly out of the window. "Why not? Simon went to sleep." She slowly slips her hand inside my boxers, and my decision to continue in the bedroom disappears.

"Because he could come down again."

"So what? You've shared me with other men and never worried about it. Are you jealous of Simon?"

A small chuckle slips from my lips as I stretch out a hand and grab her neck to lure her into a kiss. "That's not what worries me. It's that we're having sex on his immaculate couch! I'm afraid he'll have a heart attack."

Haven laughs as she gets up and pulls off her sweatpants and panties and then releases my erection before straddling my legs and moving sinuously, rubbing against me. The sensation of her skin against mine, of our most sensitive parts that meet and stimulate each other, is so overwhelming that I throw my head back and let out a small groan.

When I raise my head, my gaze rests on the doorway of

the living room where Simon stands looking at us. Our eyes meet, and for a moment, I forget everything. He's not angry, but it's as if he can't look away from us and, at the same time, can't move a step. He's not inside the room, but not quite on the stairs, as if he'd caught sight of us too late and had no time to turn around and climb back up the stairs.

"We have an audience," I whisper to Haven who is sliding down my erection until she envelops me with her warmth.

She turns her head toward my friend and we both look at him without stopping, without hesitating, and he remains there, observing as though hypnotized.

Haven turns to me, meets my gaze, and a silent question appears on her lips in the form of a smile. A couple of times another man took an active part in our relationship, and I don't even have to think about it to know that Simon is so much a part of my life that I want him to participate.

I turn to him again, beckoning him to join us. Haven gets lost in a moment of pleasure, clutching my body and burying her head in the hollow of my neck. Simon, however, seems to awaken from his slumber, lowers his gaze, and continues toward the hallway that leads to the kitchen.

For a moment, I'm disappointed, frightened at the idea he may decide not to continue the work collaboration, but then the mirror near the entrance wall reassures me.

Simon is there, hidden behind the wall, looking at me in the mirror as I look at him. He sees us. I see him. Our gazes meet through that reflection, and I am sucked once again into our world. Mine and Simon's, the one in which skin and caresses mix with our silent breath under the covers. A world I missed but I find again slowly without ever taking my eyes off him.

I watch him lean against the wall, his mouth open, his eyes full of a lust that matches mine. His chest rises and falls in rhythm with mine. His hand slides just below his belt. The mirror doesn't allow me to see where it goes, but I know he's touching an erection I'm sure is awakening.

The desire in his gaze leaves no doubt about how much he is enjoying this moment, and when I reach orgasm sinking between Haven's thighs, I make every single expression on Simon's face my own.

The head leaning against the wall, the eyes closing, the mouth opening wide, and the breathing becoming heavier. My pleasure mixes with his and remains imprinted in our eyes as if branded with fire when he opens his eyes and meets mine.

***

When Evan assured us we would have the best accommodation for the trip, he wasn't joking. The tour bus we share with Simon is like a hotel suite on wheels. Upstairs there are a couple of bedrooms, while downstairs is a common area with a fully stocked kitchen, two bathrooms, and a small living room with a TV and musical instruments.

I thought tour buses had tiny spaces and cubicles for sleeping. I could live my whole life in this place, not just a few months. It's bigger than our Venice Beach apartment.

"I'm beginning to appreciate the rock star's life," says Haven as she sits on the couch by the kitchen, the doors closing behind us.

"We'll talk about it in a month," Simon laughs.

It's the first time I've heard him laugh since last night when he watched us make love on his couch. I sit next to my girlfriend while Simon takes a side seat.

"Okay. Let's talk about it right away and get over this embarrassment," says Haven. "How long are you going punish us for violating the sacredness of your immaculate sofa with our naked asses?"

For a moment, the silence is so complete I'm afraid my friend will get up and leave offended. Then a laugh thunders from his chest. "You make me out to be a serial killer with plastic on my couches. I'm not worried about your naked asses on my furniture."

"But?"

Simon frowns. "There is no but. It's okay, it's not like you set fire to my house."

"But since this morning, you've been avoiding eye contact."

Simon shrugs and, for the first time, looks at our faces. "I didn't know what to do last night, honestly." He smiles, embarrassed. "As soon as I saw you, I wanted to apologize, but at the same time, I didn't want to bother you. Basically, I didn't want to come and tap you on the shoulder and say, 'I'm sorry to interrupt your intimacy. I'm going to the kitchen to get a glass of water. Don't mind me.'"

A smile escapes me, and even Haven can't hold back a giggle.

"But then when you asked me to join you…you caught me by surprise. Because you asked me, right? I didn't imagine that like an idiot."

This time I'm laughing. "No, you didn't imagine it. Forgive me if I misinterpreted you. From the way you looked at us, I thought it was a good idea." This time it's me who's embarrassed. I don't often misunderstand a situation, but it seems that I didn't get it right this time.

"No... Yes... I don't know. I didn't think you were an open couple, and, in all honesty, I've never done anything like that. It was out of the blue, so I didn't know what to do."

Haven opens her mouth wide, pretending to be surprised. "What? You're in a rock band, and you've never had a three-way? What kind of rock star are you?" She teases him a bit, trying to maintain a light tone for this conversation.

"Michael tried several times to involve me in the lascivious life of a rock star, but I never had an interest in his sexual activities." He laughs.

"Yes," confirms Haven. "He strikes me as someone who shares his adventures a lot."

"That guy has no limits and no respect for anyone's boundaries. You have no idea how many things I know about him that I wish I could erase from my memory."

"Is it a problem for you that we're an open couple?" I don't beat around the bush. I want any doubt, and possible source of irritation, to be clarified before we are too far from the city.

"No, why should I? I just didn't expect you to ask me. I mean...it's not like recently my sex life has been...how can I say...satisfying." He smiles, but he rubs a hand on his neck at the same time.

"Why shouldn't we ask you? You're a beautiful person

with whom we like to spend time. I wouldn't see anything wrong with it," Haven tries to reassure him.

Yes, why shouldn't we ask him? After all, he was the first person my heart ever beat for. Why should it be any different now that we're all grown up and more aware of our sexuality? My gaze rests on Simon's, and a shiver runs down my spine. Haven notices this and turns to me, smiling.

"Should I expect a lot of people coming and going from the bus?" Simon's question comes out as an embarrassed stutter. It's sweet how difficult it is for him to face this moment.

"No. For heaven's sake, don't even think such a thing," Haven says. "This place is sacred, and we would never dare to do such a thing."

"And anyway, we're not that kind of couple," I want to specify. "We're not swingers, and we don't just have random sex with other people and then never see them again. We're also not tied to a forced concept of monogamy imposed by society. If we both like a person and feel good with them, we don't see anything wrong with letting them participate in our life, even the intimate part. We don't feel the need to choose when no one prevents us from having both."

"It makes sense and flatters me that you thought of me."

The bus begins to move and enters the traffic. We shift our gazes and minds to the tour that is about to start instead of a topic that embarrasses Simon.

I wonder if he ever had someone with whom he shared both a friendship and physical intimacy. He's never been physically affectionate with people in general. I doubt anyone has ever been that way with him, apart from me.

When I ended up in the system, I was old enough to remember my parents. They both died in a car accident, but I remember my mother's caresses when she put me to bed, my father reading me a story to fall asleep.

I remember how they both hugged me after breakfast before taking me to school, how they played with me on weekends, putting aside everything important they had to do.

Simon had no one. He never looked for contact, and when I gave it, the first moments were uncertain and tense until he took a deep breath and reciprocated.

I watch him look out the window as he begins a new chapter in his life as a rock star. Everyone imagines this business is full of excesses, women, the drama of people around you all the time, opportunities to meet a lot of people.

Looking at this sumptuous but empty bus, I wonder if Simon's life is, instead, somewhat solitary, more than when he was a boy. My heart bleeds for him, for the kindness he has to offer, for the loyalty that binds him to those who stay with him a little longer than a brief stop from city to city.

CHAPTER 6
Haven

When the Jailbirds travel, they do it in a big way. There are four main buses, not counting the ones the roadies need to move from one concert to another. One for Simon, Nicholas, and me, one for Damian, Lilly, Thomas, and Iris, another for Michael, Faith, and Levi, and one that's a mix of operations center and home base.

In the latter, there are two bedrooms, one for Emily and one for Evan—when he is not in New York for work—a living area and a highly equipped office with everything you need to work on the road.

It's the second day of travel. Tonight, we'll arrive in Dallas, Texas, after stopping for a bit yesterday in Nashville, where the Jailbirds made a brief appearance on a couple of local radio stations to promote the tour and their upcoming album. It was not much different from New York during the couple of months we stayed there filming their rehearsals for the "Back to Jail" tour.

Today, however, is when the filming of interviews with the band's various members begins. We will start with Damian, but we want to ensure everyone is on board with how we want to proceed to facilitate the next few days. Which is why we're all crammed into Damian's bus and don't even know where to sit. There are ten of us. Only Faith and Levi are missing. They stayed on their bus to work and study, but otherwise, we're all in here, and the air is suffocating.

Nicholas is explaining the process. "My idea is to choose a seat in each of your buses where you feel comfortable answering questions and keeping that throughout the documentary. I want people to get to know your surroundings and feel at home as the episodes go on."

"There will also be backstage interviews, right?" Evan wants to know.

Nicholas nods. His face is a mask of professionalism. Whether he's engaged in a five-minute short, a one-and-a-half-hour film, or a twenty-two-episode documentary, his way of approaching work is always the same: professional, precise, and attentive to even the smallest details. When he starts a project, he knows how he wants it to look to the viewer.

I bet the moment he received the first email from Simon, his brain began to process all the details. It's something Nicholas does effortlessly, almost on autopilot. I have never seen anyone so passionate about his work that he thinks about it day and night.

"Of course, but those will be focused on the concerts, on the moments that precede or follow them. They'll focus on the adrenaline during the most exciting parts of the show, what the audience sees. Here, I want to create a more intimate atmosphere, suitable to sharing your life, your past. I don't want us to be interrupted all the time by people going back and forth, technicians moving crates, and things like that. I want it to be an intimate moment, almost a conversation with a friend. I want the viewer to imagine himself sitting on these sofas while you tell them your story."

All eyes are on him. No one breathes, hanging on his every word. Simon has an expression of admiration and tenderness that almost makes me want to move from the kitchen cabinet I am leaning on and hug him.

"I like the idea. They won't be easy topics to deal with, so the more comfortable we feel, the more it'll be like conversing with a friend," says Michael, who has been focused and silent the whole time.

He's one of those people who surprised me. He's always the clown in their videos, but since getting to know him, I find him to be one of the most professional people I have ever met. Of course, he's always joking, but it doesn't mean he's less attentive than others in his work. I expected the unpredictable rock star, but I encountered a real professional.

"Who will ask the questions?" Iris is worried about having her voice in the documentary. We discovered these days that for her, it's a walk in the park to be behind a computer, but she doesn't like being on screen, even her voice.

"I can do it," I explain. "It's just a matter of reading from the computer behind the camera pointing at you. Nicholas will manage the second camera and check that the shooting is optimal."

"Won't you be filmed asking the questions?" Thomas frowns.

I look at Nicholas, hoping that he'll support me on this point. "No. I'll just be the voiceover."

"Are you terrified of the spotlight too? I understand." Lilly winks at me.

I know from her stories that she didn't have an easy life

adapting to the limelight, and I get it. They're beasts—challenging to manage and keep at bay. When you're too young and inexperienced, you have two paths ahead of you: ride the wave, and hope you don't get too hurt or succumb and try to escape. There is no middle ground.

"No, but I don't want to appear on video."

This time Nicholas gives me a look that I understand: the time has come. We had this conversation in private when I thought I'd do the voiceover.

"Why not?" Damian proposes. "I honestly think it's a great idea to have you in front of us during our conversation. It will be less stressful for us to talk to a real person than to have you hiding behind the camera. In all honesty, when I have to answer questions, and the interviewer is behind the camera, I have to try much harder to isolate myself and not think someone is filming me. I vote to have you on screen, unless you have some really serious reason not to be there."

I inhale and try to gather strength for a conversation that I can't avoid, but that sucks all my energy every time. "You have no idea who I am, do you? You didn't recognize me."

All eyes are on me, perplexed, except Nicholas, who already knows my past and is staring at a point on the table in front of him.

"Does it ring a bell if I say 'The Space Girl?'"

"The teen show with the girl with silver hair squeezed into a silver jumpsuit?" Emily frowns.

"That's the one."

"Sorry, but I don't understand." Simon is as confused as everyone else.

"I was the girl squeezed into the jumpsuit."

The silence that falls is almost embarrassing. Everyone looks at me with wide eyes, and I don't know what to do. There are two types of reactions when people discover my past. Incredulity and silence, or the classic: "I knew you looked familiar. That's where I saw you!" That show was so much of a phenomenon that almost everyone's heard of me.

"Holy shit. I didn't recognize you with pink hair, piercings, and tattoos." Michael studies me, tilting his head slightly to the side and trying to see, perhaps, the resemblance to the girl of the past.

"Yes, let's just say that I decided to change my appearance so as not to be recognized. When I cut off my career as an actress and singer, it was a clean break."

"Wow, how old were you? Eighteen? Nineteen? May I ask why?" Simon gives voice to the curiosity on everyone's faces.

"Eighteen. Let's just say I didn't like what they forced me to do. I had to dress like a teenager but, at the same time, be sexy, appealing to the male audience. They couldn't have nudity because I wasn't of age, but they dressed me in clothes that were anything but innocent." I watch Lilly frown, and a flash of anger runs through her eyes. I can understand it. Not being in control of your own body and what others say about you is terrifying. "Do you know what happened once while I was inside that silver jumpsuit they squeezed me into?" I don't wait for them to answer, but they're all too interested in the subject even to move a muscle. "I ended up in the hospital."

"Are you joking?" Simon's voice is a mixture of disbelief and concern.

"They discovered from the data that thirty percent of the audience were men between the ages of thirty and forty who watched TV 'with their children.' Men aroused by a teenager in a silver jumpsuit. Men with stable jobs and a credit card they regularly swiped for posters and gadgets with my face and body. The producer wanted to milk this unexpected strand of the audience as much as possible, so he decided that the suit had to be as tight as a second skin. Everywhere. Especially in my most intimate parts.

"It was so tight I couldn't wear underwear. Only nipple covers, because in a children's show you can't show them, but down there, I was naked. The seams, after eight hours of shooting, rubbed against my skin until I bled. The wounds became infected, and I tried to disinfect them as best I could myself because I had to keep shooting each day. I went on like this three days, then I fainted on set.

"When I arrived in the emergency room, I had a high fever and an infection that threatened to kill me. The doctors said that if I'd waited a little longer, I might've ended up with an amputated limb or, worse, dead. And do you know how they explained my absence from the scenes for that week of filming and consequent loss of airtime? Stress from too much work—it was less scandalous than a vaginal infection. After that episode, it took me two years, but as soon as I could, I left and never looked back."

They all stare at me with their mouths open.

"Christ. Just when I thought I'd heard it all. Didn't you have a manager who could stop that from happening?" Evan inquires shocked, perhaps because he actually cares about his clients and doesn't exploit them.

A bitter laugh comes out of my lips. "He was my mother's manager and one of her many lovers. He did everything she told him, and if my mother saw an opportunity to boost my career, you could be sure she pushed me to do it, no matter how bad it was for me."

"Your mother must have gone crazy when you told her you wanted to quit," Simon says. "I mean, she's one of the most famous actresses of her era. She doesn't seem like someone people say no to."

This time my laughter comes out more sincere and, above all, amused. "I don't know. I left at night without telling her anything. I disappeared from her life. I cut my hair, dyed it pink, started wearing big sweatshirts, and hid from the paparazzi who followed me. It took me a couple of years, but in the end, I was able to give up that life and make a new one."

"So that's why you don't want to be seen on video? Do you think your mother could recognize you?" Damian tries to figure out the situation.

"No, I don't want to do it because the business sucks for me. It was a huge sacrifice because I like being an actress, and I like to sing, but industry people in Hollywood make me want to vomit."

"And that's why you should do it." Lilly's voice cuts like a blade through the silence that fell after my explanation.

I look at her, and the pride on her face takes me by surprise. She looks like one of those people in superhero movies, with a determination to change the world, alone if necessary.

"You shouldn't give up doing what you like because someone is stopping you. When I started, I was terrified of people's judgment. I almost blew up my career because an asshole had decided *I* was his favorite pastime. Until Damian made me realize that it's not right for me to put my dreams aside because others are assholes.

"It's *your* life, *your* career, *your* passion. You are giving up all this because someone forced you to do what you didn't want. Use this opportunity to show them that no one can control your life and body but yourself."

Her words come at me with a fervor I did not believe possible in Lilly.

"Hollywood is full of creeps who think women are just tits and vaginas to use to sell a product. Just look at all those singers and actresses who come out of kids' shows. If they're women, they're expected to wriggle suggestively over a piano or simulate oral sex with a microphone. They have to be sexy, provocative, squeezing into clothes bordering on obscenity. Compare that with the male actors who come out of the same teen shows. They're offered high-level projects to prove their skills and make a career in decent films. This is your chance to prove that you're not just tits and vagina for the use and consumption of the pigs that look at you."

Damian looks at his woman with such admiration and love they make me smile.

Nicholas encourages me with the determination of someone who truly believes in me. "She's right. You should show the whole world what you're capable of, not just me or those few who are lucky enough to work with you. You're an exceptional, talented person. Show everyone that you're not just a beautiful face"

"It's your rules, your job. Show everyone that you do what you want, and you do it damn well," Simon adds, and little by little, I find myself looking at the smiling and convinced faces of those who have chosen to believe in me.

"My rules? Can I choose how I want to project myself to the public?" I want to make sure I have total control.

"All decisions about it are made by you. No one will make you do what you don't want to do," Evan confirms.

"He never did with us either," says Michael with a grin.

"Michael, with you, I'm doing great if I manage to keep you out of prison," Evan scolds with a serious face but smiling eyes.

We all burst out laughing, but in the end, the excitement that expands in my belly and reaches my heart consumes me. I haven't been this enthusiastic about a new job in a long time. Sure, I like what I do with Nicholas, but this is what I love.

"Looks like you've found a face for your interviews," I say, my voice trembling with emotion.

***

The location for Damian's conversation is the room with the faux leather sofas and the TV at the back of the bus. With its elegant black and silver wallpaper, it could easily pass for the villa of a wealthy actor from Los Angeles, despite the landscape flowing past in the windows.

Before we started, we all got off the bus, except for Thomas and Iris, who retired upstairs to their room. Both Damian and I are wearing a microphone, but we still need a quiet place for the footage to ensure the audio quality you would expect from a documentary of this magnitude.

I reread the questions that Iris prepared for us while I wait for Nicholas to set up the monitors and computers in the other room.

"You can start whenever you want. We're already recording," my boyfriend announces.

The room is too small to fit all of us plus the cameras, so Damian and I were left alone, making the atmosphere even more intimate. He's wearing a pair of dark jeans and a gray V-neck shirt that offers a glimpse of his tattoos.

He's a tall muscular guy, and the way he locks eyes with me makes me almost forget about everything around us. Damian is one of those people who makes it impossible to look elsewhere when he devotes his attention to you. If I weren't used to hiding my feelings in front of a camera, I'd probably be blushing like a little girl by now.

"Can you tell me your name and your role in the band?"

The mischievous smile that appears on his lips almost shouts: *Do I really need to introduce myself?* But instead, he says, "I'm Damian Jones, the frontman for the rock band the Jailbirds."

His voice is calm and deep. One that makes women melt.

"Why did you choose to call yourself the Jailbirds?"

His face is smiling but not playful. This is one of the questions they insisted on including in the interview. Especially Damian, I think he has several things to get off his chest, and this is his chance.

"Because we've been hearing it repeated for months, some of us for years. Every day, several times a day, until we got sick of hearing it. Jailbirds are people who go in and out of prison all the time. The ones who never change, who are stupid enough to get caught again, again, and again. We were considered habitual criminals. We were fourteen, sixteen years old, and no one saw a different future for us. We were seen as lost causes and they had taken away all our hopes. So when we got out, we wanted to send a message to those who treated us like that every day: Remember the Jailbirds you thought were failures? Fuck you! We succeeded even though you never believed in us. Our message is a fuck you for all those who treat others as inferior beings. And every time we go on stage in a stadium, eighty thousand people help us shout that message even louder."

"But inside the juvie, there was someone who believed in you. How did they help you survive during your sentence?"

"Penelope, the psychologist, was the only one who helped us survive. At first, I was so beat down emotionally I didn't think I could ever be anything but a criminal. I would get angry with her because she saw someone redeemable in me, but I didn't believe it. By giving us a small purpose, like practicing a few hours a day with the band, she forced us to focus on something other than our failures. In those two hours a day, we were not jailbirds, we were musicians, and this isolated us from the hopeless reality that surrounded us."

His voice breaks a little from the emotion, and I wait for him to compose himself before asking the next question.

"Those two hours were possible thanks to a program for the rehabilitation of boys in juvenile prison. What do you think about cutting the funding for these programs, and other activities considered non-essential?"

Damian snorts with half a laugh. He shakes his head, turns his face to the ceiling, and then looks back to look at me. "Total bullshit. If you can't rehabilitate a fourteen, fifteen, sixteen-year-old boy, how do you plan to integrate an adult prisoner into society when he comes out after his conviction? Programs like this help prevent those kids from ending up in prison again as adults. Giving a purpose, an alternative to those inside, is very often enough to prevent them from returning to prison once they're released. That, together with the work of prevention and education in the communities most at risk, allows us to give a future to those who think they don't have any.

"How often have we made colossal mistakes, and thank heaven, someone gave us a second chance? Those kids made an epic mistake, and I can guarantee you that they understood it loud and clear! They don't need you to point a finger at them. They're the first to look inside and realize their mistake, but they're also the first to be aware that hardly anyone will give them a second chance. Without a person's trust, you feel useless and alone, and you see only one direction to take in your life. And it's not a healthy one."

His words remind me of the bracelets on Nicholas's wrists. Without Simon, without the only certain and positive person in his life, he felt so lost that he didn't think there could be a future for him. A lump forms in my throat because inside the bus I'll return to tonight, two people are linked by a bond so strong that one is lost without the other.

I might not have met Nicholas. The gratitude I feel for the Jailbirds bassist is so strong I want to sneak into the bus now and hold him tight until he understands how important he is to me.

***

After spending two hours alone with Iris going over the questions for tomorrow, I return to our bus and find Simon and Nicholas chatting, sitting on the couch drinking beer. I watch them for a moment, their sly smiles, tender looks, that way of touching their hand without even realizing it. My heart is filled with an affection I didn't know I felt.

I always thought that behind the veil of sadness that permanently follows Nicholas was his parents' death. But the more I observe him with Simon, the more I realize he is that wind that manages to drive the clouds out of my partner's heart.

Nicholas smiles at me as I approach after taking off my shoes. "You're here. We thought Iris had kidnapped you. We were ready for a rescue and recovery mission."

"That woman is pickier than you."

Nicholas unleashes a scandalized face. "Impossible!"

"Yes. She looks at every single aspect, weighs all the questions before deciding which ones to do. She takes her PR job very seriously."

I sit on Nicholas's lap after grabbing a beer from the fridge. Simon looks at us for a few seconds, then smiles and moves away a tiny bit from my leg that almost touches him.

"I'll give you some space and go to my room to read," he announces lightly, but I understand that he feels embarrassed.

"Stop." I grab him by the arm and take him by surprise. "You don't have to leave because of me. If you feel embarrassed by our affection, we'll dial it down." I don't want him to feel like the third wheel. This is his tour, his job. I don't want there to be any tension in here.

Simon shakes his head and smiles but remains motionless at a distance. "I don't feel embarrassed if the two of you hug or kiss. Hell, I saw you having sex on my couch!" He laughs. "I just don't want to get in the way. I don't want you to limit expressing your feelings because you don't want to embarrass me. Or feel obligated to invite me because I'm always around."

Nicholas stretches out an arm, places his hand behind his neck, and pulls him to his side with force. I move my legs just enough to rest them on top of his, and I curl up on Nicholas's chest.

My boyfriend gets closer to Simon, who seems nervous but shows no sign of moving. He approaches his ear with his lips, and I see Simon shivering and closing his eyes. "Don't even think you're getting in the way. You left once and almost killed me. I don't want to see you disappear from my life ever again, Simon. I don't want to miss another twelve years." The whispered words are like a cry in the silence of this bus.

Nicholas's hand squeezes Simon's neck in a grip I almost feel on my skin. The kind you do when you love someone, when you don't want to let them go, when you put all the strength you have into not losing that dream that has just come true.

Nicholas and Simon never told me about their relationship, whether they were a couple or best friends, but I'm sure my boyfriend's center of gravity just slipped onto this couch.

CHAPTER 7

Simon

Organizing a tour while launching an album is more complicated than you might think. Besides the concerts, you have to do promotional interviews, plus radio and television appearances. Everyone has to see our faces, remember the new album's name, and talk about it on social media. Emily, who's more hectic than usual these days, whether from too much caffeine or stress, says we must become a "trending topic," not just on Twitter—we have to be the main topic on everyone's lips.

So, after the initial concert in Dallas and two others in Las Vegas, we landed in Los Angeles for another type of tour: television interviews. Two a day for four days, on TV shows we don't even watch.

"Ready to stir up the hormones of every woman who watches *Hello America*?" Damian smirks behind the scenes of one of the most-watched morning shows in the country. A show that covers cooking, current affairs, entertainment, basically nothing relevant to our music.

"Remind me again why we're here?" I ask Emily who's focused on the monitor where the program is airing.

Emily turns around with a smile, her always-present iPad clinging tightly to her chest. "Because the audience for this show is mostly women between thirty-five and fifty-five."

I see Nicholas and Haven smiling as they film this inter-action. I don't know if it will ever end up in the documentary, but it is undoubtedly a testimony to how crazy our lives are.

"Who don't listen to our music…I assume."

"You assume wrong!" she smiles. "For many of these women, listening to your music is their guilty pleasure. They'll never confess it at their Sunday backyard barbecues, but you're definitely in their fantasies."

"No way! Judging by the people at our shows, I never would've thought that," Michael says, perplexed, and I can only agree with him.

Thomas surprises us all with an explanation. "The peo-ple who come to concerts are only a segment of those who buy albums. They're younger, without families, and have extra time to spend how they like, without having to worry about children. But download an album from the internet and you don't have to leave the house to listen to it. A lot of our fans who spend money on albums and merchandising are women of that age."

"And how the hell do you know that?" I ask him incred-ulously.

"I find it interesting to read the statistics on our website and social networks. I like to know who's interested in us, even if not specifically the individuals. It's nice to be able to put 'a face' to the people who helped us to get here." He shrugs, al-most embarrassed.

"We have statistics?" Damian is baffled.

We all burst out laughing, and when the assistant comes to call us to go live, he finds us bent over in hysterics.

"You can film from behind the scenes, but you have to be

absolutely silent," the guy says, casting a stern look at Haven and Nicholas. He's around twenty years old, with a headpiece set perfectly fitted on his skillfully combed blond hair.

The two seal their lips and nod, struggling to hold back a laugh. I think it's the twentieth time someone has repeated this to them. They usually don't allow other filmmakers to shoot on their set, but Evan called a guy from the production company who worked his magic. It must be someone very high on the food chain, but our manager usually doesn't disclose his sources.

"These are your headphones, so you can hear what's happening during the live show." The guy provides the two of them with headphones connected to a monitor that the technician focuses on to let us know when to go in.

Haven and Nicholas stand next to the technician. Emily, though, turns around and leaves the room with her phone in hand. I thought Evan was the busiest guy in our crew, with his cell phone glued to his ear, managing our lives, but that was before I met this woman. Not just Evan's assistant, she's a female clone of him. Sometimes those two together scare me.

"That's your cue," whispers the guy, beckoning us to get closer.

We can see what's going on in the studio from behind the scenes but we can't hear what's being said. Sitting out in front of the white sofas where the hostess and we will sit, the audience is mainly female.

A red light above our heads tells us we can't enter yet, but when it turns green, the assistant beckons us to take a seat. Damian, Thomas, Michael, and I parade along the white floor and under the blinding lights that prevent us from seeing the audience. However, we hear the clamor and screams very well. It's the same sound we hear everywhere when we make some public appearance.

The blonde hostess with a dazzling smile—Olivia—is tucked into an elegant pastel pink suit that makes her look too serious. Perhaps she wants to project a stern image to the naysayers that want her out of this job. At thirty, they say she doesn't deserve to replace the legendary Sharon Washington, who retired last year.

She waves at us to sit on the sofa for the final twenty minutes of the show. When we finally put our butts on the soft cushions, and the applause subsides, the part I like least about this job begins: answering the sometimes stupid, unoriginal, questions they ask us.

"Welcome to *Hello America*!" Olivia chirps with that fake cheerfulness that almost makes me get up and leave. I've never liked people who try to be overly-friendly. I struggle to understand where the genuine pleasure of meeting us ends and the celebrity obsession begins.

"Thank you, Olivia." Damian's persuasive voice catches her attention. "It's a pleasure to meet you again."

The smile she reserves for our singer is sincere and touched by a bit of lust she cannot completely hide. "A lot has changed since we last saw each other. You've been in juvie!" I wonder if the person who writes her script watches the show or is locked in a room with no contact with the outside world.

We all have our smiles plastered on, but I notice Michael's clenching his hand resting on his knee.

"No, nothing has actually changed." Damian takes the lead, laughing. "When we last came, we had already been in juvie, only no one knew. No change on that front. They didn't arrest us again, I swear."

My friend's response almost makes me laugh, and I struggle to keep a neutral face. Olivia giggles, showing her nervousness. Evidently, she didn't expect that answer, but we didn't expect to be ambushed in the first question. It's obvious Damian has decided to play just as dirty as her, giving answers that can be a bit thorny for those who have to manage the interview.

Olivia abruptly changes the subject. "So, do you like the new album?" Her smile never falters. What kind of question is that? We're here to promote the album. Does she think we put out an album we don't like?

"Of course, we're very satisfied with the work we've done," Thomas succinctly replies, in an attempt, perhaps, to prevent Damian from slipping into a wrong answer. "But even if it sucks, it's too late to change it now."

We all laugh at this answer that may seem like a joke, but is Thomas's way of shielding himself from people's judgment on our work. He's the most sensitive to negative criticism.

All the preparation for this interview went out the window with that first question, and we don't need to look into each other's eyes to understand that, at this point, every answer is fair game.

"But let's get to the most juicy news, the stuff our viewers have remained glued to the TV for: your romantic status. Is it true that you're all in love except Simon?" Her sly tone and the gleam in her eyes make me realize she's actually interested in the answer.

"And I thought I came here to promote our new album

and 'Back to Jail' tour," Michael replies sarcastically without getting any reaction from Olivia.

"Why, Simon, are you the only one left without a partner?" Her gaze penetrates my bones, and her words freeze me on the spot.

I'm usually the one they pay the least attention to. I'm not the life of the party, and during interviews, everyone turns to Damian or Michael, who know how to entertain journalists. I am mostly a spectator of my own fame.

"I haven't found the right person yet?" It comes out as a question while I sneak a gaze at the stunned faces of my friends. We promised Evan we wouldn't mess up, and we won't. Our career is still too precarious to play the part of arrogant rock stars. Getting up and leaving this couch is not an option. Nor is answering in a bad way, even if the hostess deserves both.

"There's no one who makes your heart beat faster than the others?" she insists, and I burst out laughing.

My friends look at me and smile because the situation is so ridiculous it's impossible not to laugh.

"That's actually a good thing! I'm not a teenager anymore so I don't have a lot of heartbeats and butterflies to waste. Anyway, no. At the moment, there's no woman I'm considering having a long-term relationship with. With the tours, the album coming out, and a new record company, I don't have much time cultivating personal relationships." The image of Haven, her smile, her eyes full of life make their way in an overbearing way to my mind and I struggle to find the strength to drive them away and focus on Olivia.

"You just have to find a woman who can keep up with you." Her tone is lowered a bit and makes her statement almost sensual.

"She'd have to be a marathon runner to be able to keep up with our schedule."

My friends laugh at the joke, and I keep my voice light, but looking her right in the eye, I try to channel the message: *Stop with the bullshit, let's do this interview.*

Michael comes to my rescue when he realizes my proverbial calm is about to go all to hell. "Olivia, what do *you* think of our album? I know you listened to it to prepare for this interview. Let's hear your opinion!" My best friend takes the woman by surprise. It's clear she hasn't listened to a single note.

"I loved it! Damian's voice is so husky." The smile she flashes at our frontman is so full of double meanings that even he is embarrassed. If we had a dollar for every time they called Damian's voice "husky," "sensual," or "poignant" to cover the fact that they haven't listened to our music, we'd never have to worry about the budget of our record company again.

Olivia's attention returns to Damian, the album, Michael's jokes, and I can detach again from this torture that will last another twelve minutes and twenty-nine seconds, judging by the big clock hidden behind the scenes in front of me. I stare at the numbers in red that go down, literally counting the seconds that separate me from the exit.

I occasionally shift my gaze to Olivia just to show interest. I nod, smile, and laugh when my friends laugh, but mentally I count, and when I look back on that clock, I check to see if I'm in sync. It's a little game I learned at the beginning of my career, to help me get through boring interviews.

***

When we finally get backstage and the assistants remove our microphones, the faces of Nicholas and Haven are both amused and amazed.

"Are all your interviews at these kinds of shows that stupid? Who the hell wrote the script for her?" Haven asks in shock when the technicians are far enough away not to record our conversation.

They've put their camera down, and we're enjoying the moment of rest before getting back in the car and taking refuge in the hotel waiting for tonight's party. It's hosted by an actor we don't know, but Emily has guaranteed it's a rising star with millions of followers on TikTok. She's the one who follows all the latest trends in social networks, and we trust her opinion.

If a party is trendy and puts us at the center of attention, we go without an argument. Even if we get bored or the people around us are not ones we enjoy hanging out with. It's part of the job, and in all honesty, there are far worse ones. To complain because we don't like a party is disrespectful to those who break their backs working three underpaid jobs they hate.

"I have no idea, but it's clear what tone they wanted to give the show since changing hostesses," I admit.

She smiles at me and nods. "They're giving the public something superficial and frivolous. They don't want people to start thinking about anything challenging, or they'll realize they don't actually need the latest ultra-tech, ultra-expensive sponsored gadget as though their life depended on it."

Sometimes I forget she knows how the entertainment industry really works. She's aware that behind every show are sponsors with money that replenish the production budgets. But this means if a brand invests money in a show, it expects an increase in sales proportional to the investment.

Shows like this focus on wanting people to disconnect from their everyday problems and enjoy a few hours of mindless pleasure. Because when a person doesn't think about their problems, they're more likely to spend money.

"Emily said the car is coming to pick us up," Thomas confirms.

"Here she comes again," Damian whispers with gritted teeth before putting on a smile as fake as a thirteen-dollar bill. "Olivia! You just can't stay away from us…" His expression looks almost flattered by the attentions of the hostess, but the irritated nuance of his voice reveals the opposite.

"I couldn't help but say goodbye before you disappear from the face of the earth again," she chirps with her unbearable good humor.

"This time, we're staying in Los Angeles for a few days."

"Are you planning any relaxing outings?" She looks like she's calculating what route to take to bump into us again.

"No fun, just business." I try to cut this conversation short and glance down the hall hoping Emily will appear to say the car has arrived.

"If you need company, just call me. I look good squeezed into a dress." Her attention has turned to me, as if she's just remembered I'm the only single in the band.

Out of the corner of my eye, I see Haven giving a slight elbow nudge to Nicholas, who stares open-mouthed at her brazenness.

"I'm sorry, no plus one for me these days." I look again at that damn corridor where Emily disappeared before we walked into the studio for the interview.

"What a shame because I'm really a *great plus one*," she insists with that sexy voice.

Damian can't hold back a half-laugh that comes out like a grunt, while Michael smiles like a madman. Thomas just shakes his head with a slightly annoyed expression. I think he's as upset as I am.

"I believe it, but I'm not interested."

Faced with my blatant rejection, her smile disappears, her back straightens, and she crosses her arms over her chest. "Si-mon, this failure at finding a woman almost makes me think you like playing for the other team." All her kindness disappears, and her icy look, with a grin and raised eyebrow, make it clear she doesn't like to be rejected, at least not in public.

It was her choice to hit on me and keep insisting when she could have accepted my first no. I can see my friends are all offended by her attack.

"Olivia, the fact that I don't feel any kind of attraction to you doesn't mean I'm gay. Maybe I just don't like you, have you ever considered that?" I answer, dropping the mask of courtesy I had maintained until this moment.

I look down the corridor again, and this time, I don't wait for Emily to come and call us. I turn around and walk like hell toward the exit, fueled by the anger that fills my stomach. Why people feel the need to put their noses between other people's sheets I'll never understand. Can't I sleep with whoever I like without giving an explanation to anyone? Maybe they *would*

stop asking me about my love life if I had a partner.

"Simon, wait!" Haven's voice makes me slow down.

"I'm going to see about our car." My tone is clipped, irritated by everything that is constricting my chest.

"Are you okay?" Her voice is sweet, the way I've come to recognize it in recent months. Haven never gets angry, never raises her voice, always finds a solution, and I usually like it. But this time, I need to be alone, to lick the wounds inflicted by a sore topic at this particular moment: my love life.

"I'm fine." I speed up again and open the studio door with so much force that it slams with a thud on the outer wall.

Haven doesn't follow me, and when the car arrives, Max and Emily get out. They only need one look at my face to not speak to me.

When I get to my hotel room, the anger hasn't faded. On the contrary, the comments and jokes of my friends made me snap during the trip from the studio to the hotel, earning me their side-eyes. When the door closes, Haven and Nicholas are behind me, eyeing me like a lion in a cage: not knowing how to approach me. This isn't their room, but they've decided that the day's mission is to let me vent.

"Do you have something to say?" I ask, frustrated when I turn around and find them standing still. I immediately regret the tone when Haven crosses her arms over her chest and raises an eyebrow, nailing me for my unkind manner.

"Can you tell us why you're so pissed?" she asks, and my friend puts his hands in his pockets, tilts his head, and studies me, as he usually does when he tries to understand my behavior.

"I'm annoyed by people who make insinuations or generate scandal where there is none."

They furrow their foreheads and observe me, both looking as serious as I have rarely seen them.

"Would it be a problem if you were gay?" Nicholas is puzzled.

I shake my head and look down, ashamed. "No, the problem is that she doesn't care. She just wants to create a scandal and then broadcast it on her show to gain an audience. Why can't people just mind their own damn business? Why do you have to explain your private life if you are famous?" I'm almost breathless with nervous agitation.

Haven softens her scowl, and her posture relaxes. A smile appears on her lips, and this helps me relax. They're not my enemies. I'm locked in my hotel room, safe, with two people who care about me.

"Simon, you rejected her in front of everyone. It was a reaction to what you told her."

"She didn't have to insist on slipping into my bed," I reply, annoyed and sounding a little like a brat.

"She was hurt. She reacted accordingly. It may not have been her best moment, but you struck her pride. I'm not justifying her words, but I can understand where they come from." Nicholas's voice is almost sweet when he explains this to me.

I lower my head and look at my toes, unable to meet their eyes. The problem is not Olivia. The problem is me.

"The real question is, Simon, *are* you gay? Is that why you felt trapped in there?" Haven gets straight to the point. Despite the sweet and understanding tone, her words pierce my chest with the harshness of their meaning.

I shrug and shake my head. The truth is I never asked myself the question and never answered it. I like men as much as I like women, but I've never felt complete in any relationship.

"I've loved only one boy in my life…" I gaze at Nicholas and find all the sweetness of when we were kids. "But I've also always been attracted to women." I turn my gaze to Haven's face.

"You're bisexual. You know there's nothing wrong with that, right?" Her expression and tone are so sweet it almost comes out in a whisper.

I shake my head and sit on the bed. "It's not that simple."

"Then explain it to us." Nicholas sits next to me and takes my hand.

"I've never felt complete with anyone. It's a constant search for something I don't even know how to explain. All the women I've been with since I became famous were wonderful at first, but then the enthusiasm faded just as quickly as it started. Men or women, there's always something missing. Maybe I'm the messed-up one. Maybe I should know how to be satisfied and live a peaceful life with someone without seeking perfection," I confess, exhausted.

Anger has devoured every residue of energy I have in my body. I'm tired of fighting for something I don't even understand.

Haven sits next to me. On the other side is Nicholas. She grabs my hand, and I feel at peace with myself for the first time since this morning. "Or maybe you have so much love to give that you need more than one person."

I look up at her, confused by her statement, but the certainty I find in her eyes calms me.

"You said you loved one guy in your life, and from how

you and Nicholas look at each other, it's not hard to understand who he is."

I look down at her statement. I didn't think I was so easy to read. I thought I had managed to hide the feelings that Nicholas unleashes in me.

My friend grabs my chin with two fingers and makes me turn toward him with a sweet but decisive gesture. His big brown eyes, the dark curls on his forehead, the stubble covering the cheeks I caressed dozens of times when we were younger, make me short of breath. The more I'm with him, the more I recognize the little boy I know is still in there.

He slowly approaches, giving me plenty of time to get out of this bed and leave if I want to. But he doesn't really know there's no choice. There will always be only Nicholas. To complete that piece of me I need to feel happy. There is no option. I can't back away from the only person who brings me home.

His lips rest on mine, shattering the logic that says he already has a girlfriend and therefore I can't want him. His fingers run slowly over my face, almost hesitant. I close my eyes and savor his tongue timidly taking possession of my lips. I open mine with hesitation, for fear an abrupt gesture could make me awaken from a dream that makes my heart hammer in my chest.

It's intense, more powerful than I've ever felt with anyone. His tongue caresses mine in a slow, sweet kiss. The kind that grabs you by the hand and takes you home, to the place where you have always belonged. Because Nicholas is home. He's that place where perfume reminds you of a stolen caress.

When we return to reality, his lips search for mine in two

small kisses. They are so light that if every cell in my body were not on high alert, I would believe I had dreamed them. I open my eyes reluctantly, knowing that as soon as our eyes meet again, the magic of this moment will become a reality.

Nicholas is there, ready to catch me when I feel the earth shake under my feet, with love in his eyes and sweetness on his lips. But when Haven squeezes my hand, reality fully takes possession of my mind.

I turn to her, prepared to suffer the consequences of my gesture, of the pain in her eyes for our betrayal. When I meet her gaze, I find the mirror of Nicholas's, open to all the love she can receive, full of everything she can give.

She closes the distance as slowly as he did, and I can't move. While Nicholas is liquid fire flowing under my skin, Haven is that calm that fills my lungs with all the air I need. They are like two chemical elements that, taken individually, cause diametrically opposite reactions in me, but together fill the void in the center of my chest that has always been there.

Haven's kiss is more decisive, vigorous. Without worrying, I let myself be carried away by what she has to give me— not thinking about the consequences.

When I open my eyes and meet her gaze, I am not surprised to find calm, sweetness, and the determination of knowing exactly where we're headed. I am so at peace with what's just happened that when the thought settles in my chest, an icy grip of confusion and fear makes its way into my belly.

For a moment, sitting on this bed, I lost control. I let someone else take over the reins of my life. It's happened only once before, and I ended up in juvie for that weakness.

"I need to go get some ice," I stammer as I get out of bed

and reach for the metal bucket above the table in my room.

"Simon…" Nicholas's voice is almost a prayer.

When I look back at the two of them, I find them studying my every reaction.

"I'll be back. I'm not running away…I just need to go get some ice." I grab the bucket, the magnetic room key, and leave before saying something I might regret.

I take a few steps, reach another room and knock vigorously, wishing to disappear from this corridor before someone decides to follow me.

"I need ice," I tell Evan as soon as he opens the door and looks puzzled at the bucket in my hand.

He steps aside as soon as he gazes at my wild eyes. I walk into his room in long strides and sit on the bed while he closes the door without making a noise. He sits in the chair in front of me, waiting for me to give him an explanation. I hold the metal bucket tightly in my hand.

"I kissed Nicholas. And then I kissed Haven too," I spit out before the fear of what I did grips my throat and prevents the words from coming out.

Evan looks at me, frowning. I don't know what he thinks of me, of my behavior, but I know for sure he won't say anything that could hurt me. And it is perhaps for this reason that I came to him before going to my friends. Because he's the problem solver.

"And are you worried that one of them will find out and it may ruin your relationship?" he questions with his usual clinical practicality.

"No, they were together, in the same room…I kissed Nicholas first and then Haven. They were well aware of it."

"Oh." I see the perplexity in his face, the effort he is making to help me, but I sit paralyzed, unable to manage my emotions. "And…you didn't like it?" he ventures when I don't speak.

The air leaves my lungs in a desperate half-laugh. "On the contrary, I really liked it, with both of them." I lower my head and stare at the bottom of the empty bucket, observing my deformed reflection.

"Simon, what's the problem? The fact that you kissed a man? A woman? Both of them?"

"I don't know. The problem is that I don't know. I'm so confused that I don't even know what the problem is."

Evan smiles and puts his hand on my knee. "Simon, maybe, if you liked it, there is no problem."

His answer makes me laugh. "They're a couple, Evan. They're a huge, gigantic mess."

Evan shrugs and leans against the back of the chair. "You're three consenting adults. If Haven and Nicholas decided to open this aspect of their lives with you, maybe they thought about the consequences, don't you think?"

What he says makes sense. They didn't have a problem with having sex where I could see them. I know for sure they've had other experiences like that. Maybe it's me who's struggling to handle this thing because I'm not used to it. But I can't convince my heart and brain not to make it a bigger deal than it actually is.

Suddenly, this situation sounds ridiculous. "Christ! I ran here to you to tell you about a kiss. Not even elementary school kids are so inexperienced that they rush to tell someone about a kiss."

Evan chuckles, amused. "At least you're not like Michael, telling me about more of his sexual adventures. From my point of view, that's a big improvement!"

We both burst out laughing, this time more relaxed.

"Sorry if I bothered you, but I needed a place to calm down."

Evan shrugs and smiles at me. "You know that I will happily help if I can."

"You don't have ice, do you?" Going back without the ice makes me feel, in some way, like even more of an idiot.

"Simon, I've learned to solve even your most absurd problems, but I still can't summon ice on command," he teases as I get off the bed and head to the door chuckling.

"Simon…" He stops me before I grab the handle. I turn to find him serious again. "If I were you, I wouldn't overthink this. Sometimes the best things in life are the things you don't plan."

I nod and open the door. "Thank you." My voice is firmer than my heart is.

My empty bucket gets heavier and heavier as I approach the door of my room. When I arrive in front of the dark wood, I take a deep breath, but, despite all my determination, I decide I need more ice. I turn around and walk down the corridor, totally unaware of where to find it.

Haven

Nine years earlier

"What the hell are you doing?" My mother's voice behind me almost makes me jump out of my skin. She stands in the doorway to my room, a martini in her hand, though it's not even five in the afternoon yet.

"I'm putting on nipple covers. I can't wear a bra with this dress," I explain. She should know. She bought me this piece of microscopic cloth when she learned that David Freewood wanted to take me to an exclusive party of one of his Hollywood friends.

"I bought it for you to impress David, not to cover your strong points." She approaches me, tearing the two small pieces of rubber from my hands, my only barrier against embarrassment.

"Are my nipples my strengths? And here I thought my intelligence and personality would do the job." I cross my arms over my chest and pout.

"Honey, at seventeen, no one expects you to talk about politics or have conversations about how to save the world. But you can use what nature gave you to get ahead in life."

She helps me slip into the piece of silver lamé cloth that doesn't cover any of my skin. Fastened behind the neck, it leaves the back uncovered, while a deep neckline descends to my navel where it joins with a short skirt that barely covers my ass. It's a pool party, so I assume there will be people in bikinis, but still, I feel naked dressed like this.

I look at myself in the mirror. The long brown hair descending on my shoulders in soft waves is what covers me the most. My mother looks at me like I'm the most beautiful thing in the world, and it makes me feel the weight of what I'm doing. I don't want to disappoint her, but I feel under scrutiny every time I go out with my boyfriend.

"I wish one of our dates was a walk on the beach or on the rides at Santa Monica Pier. I'm tired of these parties where there are only tiny appetizers and champagne to drink."

I try to fix the lace panties that slip between my buttocks with every movement. If I'm not careful getting out of the car, my nipples won't be the only intimate parts I'll show tonight. Thankfully, my mother takes me to her personal beautician every month. She says that the only hair a woman should have on her body is on her head and eyebrows. From the neck down, we must be so smooth men should want to touch us all the time.

Considering the many comings and goings of testosterone through this super luxurious mansion in the Hollywood Hills, I assume my mother is very smooth. When you are one of the most famous actresses of the moment, perfection is the minimum required of you.

My mother's face softens when she grabs me by the shoulders and turns me toward her. "Honey, those are kid's activities. You're a woman now, and when your boyfriend is forty-five years old, he expects you to behave as such. Let go of romantic dreams of boys holding your hand and making big promises. Men just want one thing from you: say yes with a smile and don't create problems. Go along with David, go to parties with him. You'll see, he'll boost your career way beyond that kid's show you're doing."

I inhale and try not to give in to the temptation to make a scene. "David is my boyfriend, not my employer. I love him. He loves me. And I like that kid's show! People recognize me when I walk down the street, thanks to 'The Space Girl!'"

I hate it when she belittles my first real starring role on my own show. I've been working continuously for eight hours a day on set for three years, and when I get home, I study and do my homework. I wish she didn't see it as a lesser quality show just because the audience is teenagers.

"Of course, honey. I've never doubted that you two are in love, but what harm is there in taking advantage of love's perks and doing something for your career? At the end of the day, if your boyfriend loves you, he wants the best for you. And trust me, David has a lot more experience than you have in this industry."

I breathe slowly, trying to swallow the lump in my throat that forms when I talk to my mother. She doesn't believe in love and Prince Charming. I was conceived during a summer fling with one of her bodyguards who moved to London when he learned of the pregnancy.

I never missed my father. My mother provides for me and my career, as my grandmother did for her. She drove her around the United States to win beauty queen crowns from the age of five. Men come and go in this house. No one stays long enough to get their own space for clothes in the closet. And that's fine with us, at least until David arrived.

He is my first great love. I met him four years ago, and for me, it was love at first sight. He teaches me about the producer's job, about how the world of entertainment works. He makes me feel important, even though he admitted to being my boyfriend just a couple of months ago.

From the standpoint of the law, our relationship is illegal, so we don't show up together in public except with his friends who understand that you can't put boundaries to love. The public wouldn't understand how deep our relationship is. He's waiting for my eighteenth birthday in a few months to leave his witch of a wife and start our life together.

"I have to go. David is here!" I cut her short when I look out the window and see the sparkling red Ferrari of the man I love in the driveway. I grab my bag and fly down the stairs, trying not to end up on the ground, tripping on the stiletto heels.

When I open the door, he is leaning against his car, his blond curls blowing in the wind. He's wearing elegant light trousers, a white shirt open at the chest, and eggplant-colored moccasins. Everything in him screams elegance and power, but what I like the most are those adorable dimples forming on his cheeks when he sees me and smiles. I run to him, and he holds me in his arms and kisses me on the cheek.

"How is my little mouse today?"

I love when he calls me by the pet names only the two of us know. "Good. How did work go?"

He rolls his eyes and smiles at me. "Let's not talk about negative stuff. Let's have fun, what do you say? There's a surprise for you in the car." He winks at me, and when I peek over his shoulder into the window, I notice a bag from my favorite bakery.

I squeal and wriggle out of his grip, leaning into the window and grabbing the bag from the seat. I open it and grab one of the sweets I love, stuffing it in my mouth, pushing it down with my fingers without even biting it.

"Oh my God, it's amazing," I mumble with a full mouth as he laughs.

"I hope those aren't chocolate-covered marshmallows!" My mother's voice thunders from the stairs. When I turn around, I find her with her arms crossed and a scornful look.

David laughs and grabs my waist. "Don't spoil the party as usual. She's got plenty of time to become like you and feed on celery and carrots," he teases.

The two always have this way of bickering that I can't understand. It's not playful, but it's not malicious either. It's like there's a silent conversation going on between their jokes.

"When you dump her because her butt is covered in cellulite, we'll talk about it. I'll tear your balls off if you hurt her."

David laughs again, and I glance at my mother. Does she always have to embarrass me in front of him?

"You know I like meat on my women. I'm certainly not going to dump her for a while…" He emphasizes his statement with a pinch to my ass.

My mother shakes her head but doesn't add anything about my physical appearance. "Bring her home before Monday's filming."

"What? No curfew?" my boyfriend provokes her, knowing that my mother never gave me a curfew even when I went to elementary school and went with friends to the park.

"Would you bring her back by eleven tonight if I told you

to?"

David bursts out laughing. "No."

"Then why lay down rules if we already know you're not going to respect them?"

"Because it's more exciting to break them." He says this while facing me, winking, and opening the door to get me in the car.

I smile at him and put another treat in my mouth before sitting next to him, preparing to be the perfect girlfriend and laugh at his friends' boring jokes.

CHAPTER 8
Nicholas

Living in contact with celebrities means constantly paying attention to details that you never thought you'd notice in your life.

After four days in a Los Angeles hotel for interviews and promotional appointments, we moved on to a mansion in the Hollywood hills. We're hosting the most exclusive party of the season, where the Jailbirds will showcase their album, "Back to Jail." There will even be a countdown at midnight when it will be officially available for download on the most famous sites.

I'm following Evan, Emily, and Iris, with the camera. Iris, being the expert, is looking for holes in the hedges where the paparazzi could slip through to steal some shots of this evening. All the popular celebrities will be here, including those who never considered me for their projects because I wasn't connected enough with Hollywood bigwigs.

"Iris, can you come down, please? You scare me when you jump from branch to branch." Evan's voice is as worried as his gaze, pointed over his head, where the redhead is making leaps that I struggle to follow with the camera.

"I don't want this documentary to become a horror movie, please," I add, helping the manager, who does not seem very successful in convincing her to come down.

Emily giggles as Iris finally puts her feet on the ground again.

"Of course, you men aren't very brave." She wipes her hands on a piece of paper towel that she removes from the back pocket of her pants.

"Are there any openings we should be worried about?" Emily asks as we make our way back to the pool.

"No, especially if we put a couple of security men on the outside of the wall along this side overlooking the street."

"Has everyone signed releases for filming?" I ask for the hundredth time, worried about having to cut scenes from one of the most critical moments of this documentary.

When I agreed to do this work, I hadn't realized the project's scope. I knew it would be a program with worldwide visibility, but I didn't quite understand the weight of responsibility. None of my films even came close to the magnitude of what I'm doing now.

This evening, to make sure I have enough material for the final editing, I requested the help of four other guys who will assist me, shooting at the various corners of this big place. Haven will help me coordinate the shooting in the multiple rooms.

"Yes, only those who have signed will participate. All the others have been removed from the guest list. Not that many have refused, but a few didn't want to comply," Emily confirms, making me breathe a sigh of relief.

Placing the camera on one of the deckchairs under the umbrella, I sit to admire the view of my girlfriend in the pool with the band members and their companions. I love watching the intricate tattoo designs on her back and arms. They are branches that intertwine with fish and give way to birds with outstretched wings. I asked her several times what they mean, but she always replied that tattoos must be lived, not explained, leaving me curious.

The hustle and bustle of the service staff setting up the large living room overlooking the pool has been nonstop. All the furniture has been removed to make room for modern sofas and tables for the champagne and appetizers provided by the catering company.

I watch the Jailbirds having fun, not paying attention to the people around them who could film or approach them to get an autograph the way I've seen their fans do dozens of times. But then I observe the people working, moving furniture and setting up drapes and tablecloths with their heads down. None of them notice the guys in the pool having fun. Who knows how many parties like this they've seen and kept their mouths shut because of the non-disclosure agreements?

Realization strikes me in the chest: I'm on the other side. I'm with the rich, the ones who don't care about what's happening around them because someone is taking care of their security and image. Damian, Lilly, Simon, and everyone else didn't have a care in the world when they jumped into that pool, having fun, laughing, and joking.

I realize only now I don't either. I relied on Emily, who took care of getting the contracts signed. It's strange how, until recently, these things stole a lot of my time. I had to take care of all the administrative aspects of the project I was working on. Today is the first time I thought about it when things are already done. It's incredible how quickly you get used to the luxury of having someone else do your work.

"Why the serious face?"

I was so deep in my thoughts I didn't notice Simon coming out of the pool and joining me. He grabs a white towel from the deck chair next to mine and wipes his face and hair. I lose myself for a few moments observing the wet lines of his physique.

He's not as built as Damian or Michael, and he doesn't even have the muscular arms and back that Thomas does. Still, those broad shoulders and outlined pecs make me want to run my tongue over him and dry all those droplets running down his chest. When I look up again at him, I find a mixture of embarrassment, surprise, and even a smug smile. My lust must have been obvious.

"Nothing special. I was just thinking about how quickly you get used to fame."

Simon sits next to me, keeping a distance that makes it impossible for us to make contact, even accidental. It's a good thing, because after the kiss the other day, the cells of my body seem to react disproportionately to his proximity. That dormant desire awakened, and I'm still unable to control it.

"Let's say that when you find yourself in this business, you either learn quickly, or you're mauled by jackals." His gaze rests on Haven and reminds me of what she had to go through when she was a teenager.

I wouldn't have had the strength to pack my bags and leave after what this world did to her. I think Simon is thinking the same because his expression darkens.

"Should we talk about what happened the other day in your room?" I ask him without hesitation. When he disappeared after the kiss, Haven and I waited for a while, but when we saw he wasn't coming back, we decided to give him space to deal with it. For two days now he's been avoiding us, and at this point, I'm afraid he regrets those kisses.

Simon looks at me and arches a corner of his mouth. He doesn't seem bothered, which is a good sign. "What do you want to talk about?"

Asking a question to delay the answer is not Simon's usual approach. Usually, he's the one who gets straight to the point without mincing words.

"Did you like it? Were you offended? Are you avoiding us because you feel embarrassed?"

A chuckle escapes his chest as he leans back on the deck chair and observes Haven, who's just been thrown into the water by Damian and Michael. I gaze at my old friend. I watch his strong, callused fingers, the pronounced veins that stand out on his pale arm. For a moment, I imagine those hands grabbing me in a moment of intimacy, but I nip the thought in the bud, aware of the complicated situation.

"Liked it? Yes, I liked it. No, I wasn't offended. I'm avoiding you because, in all honesty, I don't know how to deal with it." He shifts his gaze to mine and holds me with the look, making me short of breath. "I kissed you both, do you understand?" he whispers, perhaps for fear that someone might hear us.

"And is that a problem?" I want to understand what's going through his head, but he seems to be a more insecure, vulnerable Simon than I knew as a kid. He's always been my hero, and seeing him struggling fills my heart with tenderness.

"I don't know. You're a couple. You've been living together for years. I can't understand how I can be included in such a thing. You kissed me. It was an intimate gesture. You shared a private piece of your life with me, and I don't know how to handle it."

His sincerity lifts a weight from my chest. I thought his detachment was a nice way of telling us he doesn't want anything to do with our relationship. "I don't think there's anything to manage. Haven and I are aware of our choice, no one feels forced. It's a balance we've achieved over the years, and it's brought us together even more as a couple."

Simon seems to want to reply, but Damian's size shadows us and silences him, making him look away from me. "Sid brought us clothes to try on. Are you coming upstairs?" he interrupts.

Simon nods and gets up, not without glancing at me in a way I can't interpret. I want to clarify everything, to remove that sense of guilt I seem to have glimpsed in his eyes. But he follows his friend into the villa without giving me time to do so.

"Everything okay?" Haven's voice is a bit suspicious.

"I talked to Simon about what happened."

"And he's angry?" This is one of her fears. She thinks she crossed a line that Simon wasn't ready to cross.

"No. Confused, maybe, but not angry."

She sits next to me and squeezes her arm around my waist. Drops of cold water dampen my shirt. "It's important that he's not angry. You'll see, he'll make peace with his brain and understand that what happened isn't wrong."

I wish I had her optimism, but I'm afraid it won't be that simple. Simon is not a simple person.

***

When I used to imagine the launch of a rock album, I pictured a parade of industry insiders squeezed into elegant clothes, making polite conversation while holding glasses of champagne. I couldn't be more wrong.

The mansion has been abuzz with guests of all kinds for several hours. Besides the usual reps from major record companies, there are Hollywood stars, film producers, singers, YouTubers, and Instagrammers here enjoying the party.

They're all dressed like an after-party at the MTV Music Awards, with phones in hand to live stream or take selfies with other stars. *Glamourous* falls short in conveying the amount of glittering clothes and dizzying heels that roam the villa tonight. *Perfection* is the only word I could use to describe it.

Nothing is left to chance, from the white drapes descending from the ceilings to the makeup and clothes of the guests. Every person has carefully studied their clothing to look perfect from every angle. Even smiles never seem to lose their shine.

This afternoon I felt ridiculous when they put me in the clutches of Sid for a suit appropriate for the evening. But I'm thanking them now—I would have felt embarrassed dressed any other way.

My task tonight is to follow the Jailbirds, who seem to be doing a synchronized dance, moving around but never stepping more than a few feet away from each other.

My gaze rests on Simon. He is perfect in the dark jeans that wrap him like a glove, slightly torn at the knees to make him look even more the rock star. The black shirt showing off his sternum and offering a glimpse of his slim physique makes me short of breath. On his fingers, the skull rings I saw him wear only when he's on stage complete his transformation from regular guy to the god of rock.

The most absurd thing is that the Jailbirds are the only ones wearing jeans tonight, and that makes them stand out so much they make everyone else look like they're desperate to get noticed. So confident looking, no one can argue they're the undisputed main attraction this evening.

"If you keep staring at him like that, you'll miss the rest of the evening." Haven's amused voice pulls me to reality and takes my eyes off the object of my desires.

I lay my eyes on my girlfriend, wrapped in a golden dress that reaches her mid-thigh and leaves her back uncovered. The neckline plunges down to her navel and gives a glimpse of those full, perfect breasts that drive me crazy.

She's a vision tonight. I've always seen her wearing jeans and sweatshirts, far from the tight-fitting dresses of her teen-age years. But tonight, she transformed. She put on the role of the star she was and blended into this environment without any effort.

If she's uncomfortable, she doesn't show it, highlighting that part of her trained by years of parties like this. She is per-fect among these people, with the spotlight on her and the con-fidence of those who know how to dominate these situations.

"How can you not drool over that open shirt?" I throw a sly smile at her. I caught her a couple of times admiring Simon and his backside.

"Honey, I do it too, only I'm more discreet. Years spent as an actress teach you to camouflage your desires."

I smile. I would like to kiss her, but a laugh behind our backs draws our attention.

"Look who we have here." We turn to the person who slurs the words, clearly drunk.

The middle-aged man with white hair and a beer gut has a grin planted on his face that makes me shiver.

"David…" Haven's voice next to me is almost a hiss. I turn to her and see her go pale. I look back at the man and finally recognize him. David Freewood, the creepy producer who groomed her when she was a teenager.

"You grew up. I hardly recognize you with that hair and tattoos, but an ass like yours is not easy to forget. How about we leave this party and go to a quieter place to get reacquainted?" He tries to get closer, his steps uncertain. Haven extends her hand to stop him, and he looks at her almost fiercely.

"Do I need to call security?" I whisper so only she can hear me.

My question seems to bring her back to the present, to this party. She looks around at the people and gives me a slight shake of her head. I'm sure she doesn't want to cause a scene and ruin the launch party, but I feel the tension growing inside me.

This man gives me chills. The last ten years have not been kind to him. Clearly, the divorce has ruined his private life and his professional one. Ten years ago, he was a handsome man, but now he looks like one of those perverts who lures minors into online chatrooms.

"David, how about leaving the alcohol alone and continuing the evening with something lighter?" Haven's voice is firm and she's smiling, but I recognize the anger and pain in her eyes.

I wish I could punch this filthy pig.

The grin on David's face becomes more pronounced. "Why are you here? Did you find someone else to open your legs to? Did you fuck the whole band to get in here tonight? They must have had fun because I swear, I haven't found anyone who kneels down like you praying to suck it." He slurs the words, but everyone around has understood him very well.

Some have stopped to stare at us. Others are whispering with those next to them. Someone took out a cell phone to film.

"Enough is enough." My voice is firm, my tone loud enough to attract his attention and that of some people who hadn't noticed anything yet.

Haven's hand reaches mine and squeezes it. I don't know if it's to calm me down or if she appreciates my intervention. I'm not looking at her. I'm looking at the drunk pervert who laughs like a hyena.

"Who's this? Did she give you blowjobs too? Who did you fuck to get in here, honey? Him?" He points his finger at a guest who is smirking. "Him too?" He points to another who is filming.

"How about lowering your voice and walking to the exit?" Simon's voice next to me makes me turn around. All the Jailbirds are here, but Simon takes matters into his own hands like he used to do when we were kids.

The man snorts in disgust. "We all know she's a whore and would fuck everyone at this party."

Haven stiffens next to me, her features full of anger and her eyes veiled with tears.

Evan approaches with two security guards. "Come on, David, it's time to go home and get rid of this buzz. You're making a fool of yourself, and you're no longer welcome at this party."

I've never seen the manager's face so hard. At first, I wondered how someone who was hardly more than a teenager himself could have built a reputable career and reputation so quickly. But the more I'm around them, the more I understand this man. He's only a couple of years older than us, but he's got more competence and determination than many of his colleagues with decades of experience behind them.

David seems to be assessing the situation for a few seconds, his gaze wandering from Evan to the two security guards. He looks at the people around him filming and whispering then ultimately lets himself be escorted out, mumbling something that none of us can hear.

"Come on, guys!" Damian's voice thunders inside the living room. "The countdown to the launch is about to begin. How about moving near the pool's big screen and seeing if we can sell a couple of copies of this album?"

People laugh, amused, and disperse at the same speed as they stopped to witness the scene. Damian, Thomas, and Michael lead outwards while Simon approaches the two of us. Finally, I can breathe more easily.

I look at Haven who seems petrified. No emotion shows on her face.

"Are you okay?" Simon voices both of our concerns.

Haven smiles with her lips, but her eyes remain cold and

dead, masked from showing any emotions. "Yes, I'm sorry I caused this scene. I didn't want to divert attention from your party with my drama."

"Don't worry about the party. It's just promotional stuff. You're more important. Are you really okay?" Simon is worried, and I can't get a word out.

Haven shrugs, and this time her smile reveals the sadness that boils inside. The mask slips away just enough to let us glimpse the turmoil in her chest. "I just need to get a grip on myself for a moment. He caught me by surprise. I didn't expect to find him here."

"How the hell did he get in? I didn't see him on the guest list." The perplexity and frustration in my voice is evident.

Simon looks at me, and for the first time since he reached us, a sweet smile appears on his lips. "I think he was the *plus one* of someone here. We definitely didn't invite him. I'll ask Emily to pay more attention to the guest list. I'm sorry," he apologizes.

"It's not your fault. He's a filthy pig who should be in prison, not at a party." The anger in my voice makes Simon's head tilt. He seems to want to ask me something, but the guests' voices interrupt him.

"Ten, nine, eight..." they begin to chant from the pool.

"You should be out there with the rest of the band." Haven motions to the big screen where the Jailbirds are gathered.

"Seven, six, five..."

Simon's gaze rests on his companions, then returns to us. I watch Evan take two of the kids helping me and place them in front of the Jailbirds for footage that I was supposed to do. A sense of guilt grips my stomach.

"Don't worry, they'll do fine without me."

"Four, three…"

"But it's the launch of your album!" Haven's voice is full of guilt.

Simon smiles and gently caresses her face before looking at me.

"Two, one! It's online!" Everyone applauds enthusiastically.

"There will be other albums. It's not the end of the world. It feels more important for me to be here."

His gaze rests on my lips, then on those of Haven, and the air is charged with an electricity that vibrates under my skin. Everyone around us disappears, the noises seem distant, and the only thing left is the desire to explore this moment with all the unknowns that the new awareness brings.

He extends one hand toward me, the other toward Haven. Our fingers come together in a weave that no one has noticed but that represents our whole world. Simon doesn't understand what he wants yet, but the electricity flowing right now lets me know his heart has already chosen. It's heading in a direction he still can't see, free-falling toward us. It's up to Haven and me to catch him.

PRESS *Review*

People

Is it love between David Freewood and his former lover? Videos from the Jailbirds' album launch party captured a fiery exchange between Haven Lee, who once starred in "The Space Girl", and her former lover, David Freewood.

Witnesses say a proposal was suggested for a meeting to "catch up," but no confirmation of a possible reconciliation has yet been released.

However, we were all surprised by the physical transformation of the former child prodigy. Tattoos, piercings, and pink hair have replaced the girl next door we were used to. Given her inclination for transgression, it's only logical that her rebellious nature has led to this bad-girl makeover.

Who knows what projects she has in store for us after almost ten years of disappearance from the scene.

Rock Now!

New collaboration in sight? After videos emerged of the

confrontation between the two former lovers—former child prodigy Haven Lee and producer David Freewood—many have speculated about the girl's presence after ten years of total disappearance from the scene.

Some rumors suggest the Jailbirds need to revive their image and have chosen "Space Girl" for a collaboration. Losing her good girl image, tattoos, piercings, and pink hair hint at a possible transformation to a rock-n-roll persona. We await confirmation from those involved.

The Cat is Out of the Bag!

Hi, Roadies!

These days news gets around fast, and you asked us about the appearance of Haven at the launch party of the new Jailbirds album.

We wanted to wait a few more months and make a big announcement, with a trailer and some juicy videos, but the speculations being made about her presence force us to publish this post early.

A documentary about the life of the Jailbirds is in the making. You read that right. A secret project has been going on for a few months to bring the life, background, and latest tour of the most beloved band to the small screen. Haven Lee is the face chosen to accompany us on this journey, giving voice to the questions that will reveal the band's secrets.

Stay tuned for more news about this.

Be Kind and Rock'n'Roll,

Iris

97,556 Likes 88,072 Tweet 69,763 Shares 12,805 Comments

CHAPTER 9
Haven

"I'm going to Thomas and Iris's bus to work on the next round of questions. Do you want to come?" Nicholas proposes cautiously, perhaps because I've become unbearable since the launch party a week ago.

The media shared videos of the fight with David, making my humiliation go viral. Since that moment, everyone's been digging into my past, bringing to light skeletons that I preferred stay buried forever.

Paparazzi began lurking in front of the rented mansion, and since leaving on the tour bus, they haven't missed an opportunity to look for the trucks and assault us at every stop.

Today we're taking a break in the middle of a deserted road through Nevada to allow Nicholas to switch from one bus to another without being bothered. We even stop in different rest areas to prevent the guys from being harassed at every step with questions about me. Their return to the spotlight has turned into a media circus around a life that I abandoned more than eight years ago.

"No, I'm staying. Today Faith is with Michael in Thomas and Damian's bus. I don't want her to be harassed at the next stop. Being locked inside a bus in the seventh month of pregnancy is frustrating enough without adding a crowd of paparazzi with cameras pointed at their faces," I explain in a grumpy tone that reflects my frustration.

Nicholas nods and studies me for a few seconds without saying anything, then walks out of the tour bus. This situation is difficult for him, perhaps because he always knew about my past, but never realized how suffocating the morbid interest of the press was.

I went from being the sweet girl next door to ruining families overnight, and it was like putting a bounty on my head. Now that Nicholas is living in the eye of the storm, he realizes what hell our life can become. He has never seen me so nervous, and I know he is racking his brain because he doesn't know how to help me get through it.

"You know Faith doesn't care about paparazzi, right? She grew up so far from reality that this whole life of fame doesn't even bother her," Simon says from the back area of the bus.

I smile because when I found out where Michael's girlfriend is from, I was amazed, like a little girl seeing her first snow. I've never known anyone as honest and open as that woman, and when I think of how she made Michael, the biggest womanizer in the whole band, fall madly in love with her, I laugh.

"Were you eavesdropping?" I tease him.

Simon smiles and sits next to me on the couch in the living area. "I was relaxing with the door open." He motions to the back of the bus where we have a room with a TV and sofas as comfortable as the one I'm sitting on. "Not that this place is a palace. It's hard not to listen to other people's conversations," he says in embarrassment, and a feeling of tenderness stirs in my chest.

"I'm kidding you."

Simon leans his shoulder against mine, pushing me, but he stays next to me instead of moving again. It's the first time he comes so close on his own, especially when Nicholas isn't around. When he and I are alone, he almost seems to try and stay at such a distance that he can't even accidentally touch me.

I reach out one hand and caress his leg. When I see that he doesn't move, I look up. He studies me as if to convey all the emotions he's feeling. I smile at him and rest my head on his shoulder. His fingers caress the back of my hand resting near his thigh.

It's an uncertain gesture at first, then more deliberate when he sees that I don't move my hand. I watch him touch my skin, electricity running through me at such a simple and intimate gesture. I turn my palm upwards and let myself be carried away by the intoxication that invades my chest when his fingers draw imaginary lines on my skin, leaving sensations that run deep.

This is his way of telling me that he's with me, that he's looking over my shoulder.

One thing I've realized about Simon in recent months is that he feels the burden of protecting those he loves. Whatever he has to do to achieve it, the well-being and happiness of the people he loves come first, even before himself. It doesn't surprise me that he started robbing places without ever thinking about quitting: it was the only way he could take care of Nicholas.

"Faith's just an excuse, isn't she?" he whispers, resting his cheek on my head.

I nod.

"Do you want to talk about it? I can see you're hurting."

I raise my head and meet his gaze which softens. His hand glides over mine until he weaves our fingers. It's such a spontaneous gesture that a sense of peace runs through my chest, making me exhale a deep breath. His thumb caresses my skin in circular, slow movements that give me serenity.

"I'm tired that everyone remembers me as David's lover and not for my success. I was only eighteen years old and had an almost ten-year career behind me. I ran the show on my own since I was fourteen years old. I sacrificed my adolescence, going out with friends, living like a normal teenager to officially work eight hours a day on the set, but it was always more like twelve or fourteen. I learned to be professional and attentive to details. I always arrived prepared and had studied all my lines. I never once behaved like a precocious diva on set. I broke my back working when my peers went to parties and got drunk…yet the only thing they remember is my relationship with him."

Simon nods. A veil of pain runs through his eyes. He, too, found himself being judged for past mistakes rather than what he did to redeem himself. More than anyone, he understands the frustration of appearing to be someone other than his true self, branded without the possibility of redemption.

"You were a minor at the time, right?" he asks softly.

I nod without ever looking away from his eyes.

Simon rubs his hand over his face and shakes his head. "Christ! That jerk should be in jail. Who knows how many girls he's groomed, using his position as a producer?" The anger in his voice sends a shiver down my spine. Only Nicholas lashed out at him in this way. No one else has ever defended me.

"It makes you feel like a princess, grown-up, important. It took him years giving me gifts, earning my trust before he admitted to being my 'boyfriend.' It got to a point where he made me feel guilty if I didn't give him what he wanted. He told me I was sexy and it was my fault he couldn't resist me. On the one hand, it made me feel powerful because I could bring an older man to his knees. But I felt dirty because I was usually disgusted by what he made me do. It was Nicholas who helped me realize I wasn't in the wrong, he was a sexual predator."

Simon squeezes my hand and locks his eyes to mine without adding anything, leaving me time and space to continue. It's simple with him, much more straightforward than telling Nicholas because Simon knows this industry. He knows what people are capable of to get what they want. He had to lie about his past to please the record company for years.

"Nicholas explained to me that predators cultivate a relationship with their victims for years, tethering them psychologically until they do what they want. When I realized that, I also learned that sex doesn't suck. That if done with the right person, it's enjoyable and I shouldn't be ashamed. David made me feel dirty. I was not the one at fault. Nicholas taught me to seek my own pleasure and not be afraid to experience even what people think is unconventional."

"Is that why you looked for multiple partners at the same time? To experience what gave you pleasure?"

I shake my head. "That's not the only reason. I was trying to fill Nicholas's void, but we didn't know how. It's as if he's had this hole in his chest that I alone can't fill. I think he was looking for one person."

My words are lost in the air, letting them settle in his chest. When I met Simon on his doorstep for the first time, I realized that only he could fill that void. Those looks, that palpable tension, immediately clarified the intensity of the emotions that flowed between them.

He studies me with an intensity that makes my breath shallow. He's smart. He knows I'm talking about him.

The more I spend time with the two of them, the more I realize Nicholas has always been looking not for a third partner in our relationship but the piece of his heart Simon took when he was arrested.

The motion of the bus cradles us, and for the first time in a week, I feel I can relax because Simon is here to listen to me. He understands what I am going through because, in a certain sense, our lives are similar and overlap to some extent. We both have to live with a brand we carry with us and can't erase, and we both love the same person.

"Did you ever report him to the police?" His voice is hoarse, intense, full of unspoken words. I know he understood that *the* person Nicholas is looking for is him. I read it in his eyes, but he decided not to face it, and I respect that.

I shrug and shake my head. "What for? This is Hollywood. No one arrests a man behind the golden gates of his mansion in the hills."

Simon's mouth curls in a grimace with grief, and some of the anger that has resurfaced from the encounter with David slips away. There is an electricity in the air that separates our two souls. He rests his forehead on mine, closes his eyes, and inhales while he caresses my face.

I melt at his touch, my heart pumping into my chest at such a speed that I'm afraid Simon might hear it too. It bounces off my ribcage in an attempt to reach his. I reach out my hand and rest it on his chest, where his heart is also pounding furiously.

I slide my head into the hollow of his neck and inhale, imprinting a scent that makes me feel at home in my memory. His hands unravel from my grip, and then he wraps his arms around my body and pulls me in for a hug that melts our bodies. His lips leave small kisses in my hair and then go down to the skin of my neck. My hands cling to his shirt, unable to let go of that feeling of protection his arms give me.

Simon is calm, peace, security, trust. Simon is home.

Only when the driver knocks on the door that separates us do we realize that the bus has stopped. We sit up straight, putting some space between us.

"Come on in!" Simon's voice vibrates, full of emotions that have not yet dissipated.

Jason, one of the two drivers, looks in without entering. "I stopped to get gas. The paparazzi have decided to follow Damian and his bus, so you're free to get off without too much drama if you want to stretch your legs." Then he disappears again behind the door.

"Are you coming?" I ask Simon, who seems lost in his thoughts.

I need to get out of this bus, away from the electricity and intimacy that has been created between him and me. I want a breath of fresh air.

"No, go ahead. I have a few phone calls to make."

I think he's lying. I think he, too, has been caught off

guard by the intimacy we shared. I nod and get off the bus, heading straight for the gas station store. Before entering, I look around, seeing only five or six cars plus one that's parking right now.

The guy behind the counter looks up for a second from his phone when the bell above the door trills. He's maybe twenty years old, wearing a uniform and the bored face of someone who doesn't want to be locked up inside a gas station four hours away from the nearest town.

The boundless expanse of brown desert and dry shrubs is bleak enough to make me almost feel sorry for him. He doesn't pay much attention to me as I wander around the shelves, more to escape from the bus than to look for a snack to nibble on.

When the bell rings a second time, I look up, convinced I'll see Simon's smiling face. Instead, I study a man of medium build, dressed in beige pants, anonymous as the gray shirt. A hat lowered on his eyes prevents me from seeing his face, but the heavy shoulder bag suggests he's a paparazzo looking for photos.

Nervousness churns in my gut at the idea that this man has not only followed us, but he is in the aisle behind mine, watching me from above the shelves. I feel his gaze on my back.

I want to turn around and insult him, but don't want to cause a scene that could be filmed by the kid behind the counter and posted online, going viral.

I move along the aisle and notice that he's moving in the same direction. I can't see if he's pulled out his camera, and I wonder why all his other colleagues haven't already entered. They usually move in packs when they want to be sure to tear apart their prey.

I look at the shelf in front of me, and an exasperated snort escapes my lips. A row of gossip newspapers welcomes me with an image from the party video showing my confrontation with David in vivid detail. I'm facing him in a dress that, taken out of context, makes me look like some floozy. None of the other half-naked women of the party are visible. I'm the only eyesore.

Some of the magazines show smaller pictures of me as a teenager, squeezed into the silver jumpsuit that had become my second skin. Titles like "The Mistress Strikes Again" stand out in large letters, making me feel like a whore who's blown up an apparently perfect marriage. Nausea grips my stomach, almost making me vomit on the spot.

The bell above the door rings a third time, but I don't turn to look at who has entered. The shame I feel at this moment would be apparent on my face.

The chatter and giggles of a group of girls catches my attention, and I glance at the counter when one of them, a teenager with hair down to her waist, drops a key attached to a large key ring on the table.

"You should clean those bathrooms. They're disgusting." Her voice exudes disgust, and I feel sorry for the guy.

"Okay. I'll tell my boss." His answer is so annoyed that the girl raises her eyebrows, surprised and incredulous that someone can be so rude.

"Do you want anything else, or did you just need the bathroom?" he adds when the small group of seven girls doesn't move from his sight.

The girl who returned the keys snorts, disgusted, and without answering, turns around and marches to the aisle where I stand paralyzed. I instantly regret not putting on a hoodie to cover the pink hair, piercings, and tattoos that make me stand out like a sore thumb.

She passes me while I scrunch my shoulders, trying to make myself smaller, then she stops next to me, looks at the newspapers, glances at me, goes back to look at the photos, then looks at me again. I see the moment when her brain clicks and realization strikes her like a bolt from the blue.

"Oh, my God!" she squeals, attracting the attention of her friends who suddenly stop chatting. "You're Haven, aren't you?" She exposes me, grabbing the first newspaper that happens to be within range and slamming it next to my face to compare the two.

I don't answer. Denying is useless at this point. I turn around and try to avoid the small group that surrounds me and get back on the bus, but as soon as I try to move, they're all on me, euphoric and out of control.

"You're here with the Jailbirds, aren't you? Is their bus the one out there?" a blonde grills me, holding my arm. I try to free myself from the grip and glance at the cashier, who seems completely indifferent.

"I read that they travel in four separate buses! Who are you with?" another girl with blue hair asks me.

I try to wriggle out and get past them, but they have no intention of letting go.

"She can't be on the bus with Damian, considering she sleeps with married men. I doubt Lilly would allow her to sleep under the same roof," the girl with the keys, who looks like the boss, snorts annoyed.

I cast an annoyed look at her, and she challenges me to

contradict her, crossing her arms over her chest. I've always kept away from Jailbirds' fans because they can be very intrusive. Still, they're also teenagers, and I don't want to get the band into trouble with a complaint against me. This one, however—I'd like to tear out her hair.

"Excuse me, can you let me go? I have to get back on the bus." The request comes out harsher than I intended but doesn't seem to faze them. In fact, they seem almost energized by my request.

"Can we come with you? We'd love to see how the Jailbirds live," says another short-haired girl.

I don't even respond to their absurd request, I take a step forward to get out of this nightmare, but the group leader grabs me by the shoulder and pulls me, trying to make me turn around.

"We're talking to you. Are you deaf?" Her words are muffled because while I try to keep my balance amid the chaos, I lean one foot back, slam into the magazine rack, and fall against the shelves, dragging down the candy dispenser I grab to stop my fall.

The girls giggle as I hear the guy from behind the counter shout, "What the hell are you doing? Go out of my shop!"

A pair of big, calloused hands come to my rescue as I try to extricate myself from magazines and packs of gum. I look up and find a pair of blue eyes welcoming me.

"Simon!" squeak the girls in chorus, but he ignores them.

"Everything okay?" He helps me get back on my feet.

I nod as he grabs my shoulders and pulls me out.

"Simon, can we take a selfie?" one of the little harpies squeals.

He turns around, shocked. "Maybe you should have thought about that before you shoved my friend." His tone has a vein of rebuke and exasperation. Of the four bandmates, he's the only one who doesn't hold back when a too-aggressive fan needs scolding.

"She stumbled. We didn't push her," the girl tries to justify herself.

"Really? Because from the door, it looked like the opposite." His voice is so stern that the girls shut up, leaving us time to get out of the tiny space.

I look around to see if the paparazzo is still nearby to take some pictures of what happened, but there is no trace of the man. When we're finally on the bus, I breathe a sigh of relief.

"Are you okay? Did you get hurt?" Simon grabs my shoulders and forces me to turn to look at him.

"No, I swear. I'm not hurt."

"What did they say to you? You seem genuinely upset."

The girl's words come back to my mind, and so does the thickness in my chest, overbearing. "They said Lilly would never let me stay in the bus with her and Damian because, allegedly, I'm someone who steals husbands from good wives…"

I look down, full of shame, but Simon's hand wraps around my chin and forces me to raise my head. "You know they're just crazy fans, right? They talk like that because they wish they were in Lilly's place, and are jealous of all the women around us."

His eyes scan my face for an answer, his thumb caressing my cheek in an attempt to make me relax.

"I know, but it doesn't hurt any less to hear it." It's useless to hide my emotions in front of Simon; he's the kind who silently digs inside your soul until he pulls out the truth.

His eyebrows furrow with worry, and a veil of sadness falls over his eyes. He reaches behind my back with one arm and draws me to himself, clutching my hair with his free hand, forcing me to raise my face toward his, and then crushes his lips on mine.

It's a sweet kiss, full of affection. He doesn't push me to deepen it. He doesn't ask to savor my tongue. He remains there, leaning on my lips for a time that seems infinite but at the same time too brief.

He seems to want to free me from my pain, to swallow it and make it his own. When I open my eyes, I find those pale and tormented irises to welcome me. He rests his forehead on mine and then kisses me again.

My heart is pumping, restless. It wants our bodies to merge into one being capable of loving unconditionally. It would like me to take control of this moment like I usually do. Still, I resist my impulse, leaving Simon the space he needs to make me feel his emotions. They are overwhelming, almost primitive. Bleeding from him like a waterfall, making me breathless.

When his tongue touches my lips, I open myself to him. The moment of hesitation catches him unprepared but turns quickly into a frantic search for something we don't know how to describe. As his tongue explores my mouth, the barriers slip away, leaving only the vivid, exposed, vulnerable feeling.

CHAPTER *10*

Simon

The RingCentral Coliseum in Oakland is one of those stadiums equipped to host large events. Many of the fans who will occupy the sixty thousand seats have been in line since last night, waiting for the concert that will begin in a few hours. The sun will set on the San Francisco Bay, which Oakland overlooks, and give way to our stage lights, illuminating their sunbaked faces.

We arrived this morning in California and immediately camped out here, waiting for the roadies to finish setting up before the concert. I would have liked to take a tour of San Francisco, visiting the port area, even with all the tourists. I would have risked reducing my visit to a car ride to avoid being recognized. The large crowd my presence might create would be hard for our bodyguards to contain in an open space like the pier.

I don't know why, but this city has always attracted me. I find it colorful, with a lot of character, eccentric. The exact opposite of me, which is why I love to immerse myself in its peculiarity and take in all its oddities—something that doesn't particularly attract me while visiting other cities.

"Can we do 'Swing' again?" Michael's voice echoes in the empty stadium.

The burning sun makes us squint despite our sunglasses, but we don't want to give up our soundcheck, or at least part of it. The roadies take care of tuning and connecting our instruments, ensuring that everything works perfectly.

They've been doing this job for so long I'm sure they could set up with the sound engineers better than we do. But to be honest, you get bored to death when you arrive at the location in the morning and have to wait all day to go on stage. We could be typical rock stars and have fun around the city while others work for us. But after spending your whole life traveling from one town to another, you don't have much of a desire to be a tourist.

"You're a jerk, you know that?" Damian bursts out laughing, and so do Thomas and I.

"Why? This song is a pain in the ass for us." His fake innocence doesn't convince anyone, not even Nicholas and Haven, who snicker while filming this conversation.

"Liar. You're only doing it because you like to see Faith blush every time you sing it," I say, nodding to a chair just below the stage where Michael's girlfriend is sitting, her belly becoming bigger by the day. If it continues at this rate, it will explode before the July due date.

Michael bursts out laughing and shrugs. "I found out that since she's been pregnant, this song puts her…how can I say… in a good mood. I don't see anything wrong with taking advantage of it," he chuckles.

"Michael!" Faith shrieks. "Do you have to tell everyone on the microphone?" The embarrassment on her face is as comical as the disgust on Levi's sitting next to her.

"Sorry!"

We all burst out laughing, including the ninety-plus people who work behind the scenes all day to make every detail perfect for the show.

Thomas draws our attention with a slight hint of a drumbeat. Just enough to get our heads back to work and start with the first notes of "Swing." The song is about a woman who gets lost in pleasure with two men, shamelessly enjoying the attention that both give her.

My eyes skid over to Haven, next to Nicholas, and I find her singing every word of the song without ever taking her eyes off mine. Her lips move sensually while she keeps one hand resting on his back.

I'm hypnotized by those eyes, by those lips I tasted, and I wonder if this song does reflect myself a little. Would I be able to get involved with Haven and Nicholas? Sharing such an intimate moment with the two of them?

Maybe before kissing her a few days ago, I would have had doubts. But after savoring the desperate sweetness of that kiss, I'm curious to know more. I expected to be assailed by guilt for betraying Nicholas, but none of that happened. In fact, I understand why he chose to be with her.

My gaze gravitates toward the two of them all the time. People think I don't feel comfortable being filmed, that I don't want them around, but it's just the opposite. I need to have them close, feel their presence in my life. I want to know they're with me while everyone else is doing things that don't involve me.

They both want to include me in their experience, so what the hell am I waiting for? An official invitation? The thoughts crowding my mind make me almost stagger, and my heart hammers uncontrollably in my chest until my bones vibrate. Either I'm seriously thinking about getting into their bed or I'm having a heart attack.

The song ends, and I find myself almost breathless, not with the effort of playing it, but with the need to sink my fingers into their hair and savor what could become our forbidden fruit.

"Everything okay?" Michael's voice almost makes me jump out of my skin.

"Yes." I smile as I give the bass to John, one of the roadies looking at me as if I'm stupid. And maybe I am, since his hand has been stretched out toward me since we finished the song. I've been staring at Haven and Nicholas with my mouth open like a kid with his first crush.

"You seem off. Are you doing drugs?" My friend raises a puzzled eyebrow.

"No, idiot! I'm not on drugs. Just a little distracted is all."

He smiles at me and puts his hand on my shoulder, clutching it. "Come on, let's see if you can find someone to focus on at the meet and greet," he teases.

"They're teenagers, Michael. Do you want me to go to jail?"

"No, but the mothers who bring them are quite fuckable. I mean, you need to have sex, dude, or your dick will fall off!"

"You're an idiot," I mumble as I get off the stage and navigate the hustle and bustle of people moving crates and finishing the last preparations for the show.

"The girls are squealing more than usual," Lilly announces as she reaches Damian and kisses him. I look at them and wonder what would happen if I did that with Haven and Nicholas. I try to imagine the reaction of my friends, their companions, the guys who have been working with us, shoulder to shoulder, for years.

I can't do it. I can't imagine their faces seeing me do such an outrageous thing. Because for them, it would be just that: an outrageous gesture. So abnormal it would shock them, and I'd get uncomfortable questions, maybe even questioning my sanity.

"How old are they?" Levi's voice behind us makes us turn. Faith is with him and shakes her head.

"Why do you care?" Michael questions suspiciously, raising an eyebrow. Since he adopted the boy, his paternal instinct has been turned on, a switch that's given life to a part of him we never knew existed.

Levi shrugs. "So if they give me their number, I'll know if I can text them or not." His shy smile, the blond curls, and the angel face are in jarring contrast with this brilliant and horny fifteen-year-old boy.

"They give you their numbers?" Michael is dumbstruck while we laugh at his surprise.

"Sometimes, yeah. They say I'm cute." Levi alone can render my best friend speechless, his mouth and eyes wide open.

"You and I have to talk, kiddo." He points his finger at the boy as he nails him with a serious look.

"Not about the birds and bees, please," Levi complains as Damian thunders in laughter, Thomas shakes his head, and I watch them amused.

"No, my dear. We'll have a straight talk about sex, condoms, and how to use a banana to practice wearing one properly!"

"Oh, baby Jesus," Faith whispers, covering her face with one hand.

"Are you afraid of becoming a grandfather in your thirties?" teases Thomas.

Michael turns around with a serious look I've never seen on his face. "It's not a pregnancy I'm worried about. It's diseases that scare me shitless."

You expect practical topics like that from Thomas, not from Michael. He's come a long way from that teenager just out of juvie.

"Are you coming to meet your fans, or is it just Iris and I that have to go crazy?" Emily's voice down the hall distracts us from our chat, and I see Levi breathing a sigh of relief. I don't think this is a subject he wants addressed in front of all of us.

"Where the hell did your pass go?" Emily asks Haven, pointing her finger at the frayed cord attached to the piece of plastic that we always carry with us and that Haven keeps attached to her belt loop.

Haven looks at the piece of cloth that seems torn. "I don't know. Earlier, when we were all crowded at the entrance, I felt tugging, but I had my hands full with the camera, and I couldn't check. I pulled to free myself, and I must have torn it off," she admits with a bit of shame showing on her cheeks.

Emily smiles and puts her hand on her arm to reassure her. "I'll give you another one, don't worry, but maybe it's better to keep it around your neck. It gets stuck everywhere when it's fastened at the waist, and you might lose it again." She winks at her while the other nods.

We enter the windowless gray room set up for the meeting with the fans. There are about twenty people, including some legal guardians for minors. There are four boys and the rest are girls you can tell from a mile away have no idea how to act. They're all glued to the table where the catering has set up drinks and snacks.

These places have always made me sad. Cold concrete rooms, often used as storage without any color. Our guys try to make them more welcoming, covering the walls with posters of our sponsors, colorful plastic chairs, sofas with bright prints. But if you look carefully, you see it's all fake.

The impression it gives me is a room filled with temporary, shifting emotions. They last a few minutes then slip away at the same speed they entered your heart, leaving you with a feeling of emptiness inside.

As usual in these meetings, when we enter the room fills with shouts, and the girls launch themselves into a race to reach Damian, Michael, some even Thomas first. Almost no one comes to me, at least not in the first few minutes, when their excitement is fresh.

"I'm always surprised by the speed of those girls," Nicholas chuckles as he watches Haven wander around the room, filming the ecstatic faces of the fans.

"Why do you think we go to the gym every day? We have to work out to run faster than them."

Nicholas smiles and glances at me and then looks at Haven again. "So 'Swing' is a song you do a lot," he adds after a few moments of silence.

I never look away from the excitement in front of me, my back glued to the wall. I observe everyone around me, aware that this conversation could become uncomfortable, given the prying ears in this room. I look over at Evan, talking to Emily. Only he could understand, even from afar, the weight of this conversation.

"It's on our album. They expect us to do it live."

Out of the corner of my eye, I see him nodding almost imperceptibly. The ghost of a smile arches his lips. "And you always stare at your friends while playing this song?"

This time I turn toward him and observe his smile becoming more evident, even as his gaze remains focused on Haven.

"Only when my friends sing every word of the song while staring passionately at my lips."

This time Nicholas turns to me. He hadn't noticed what Haven was doing while he was filming us, but he doesn't seem upset. In fact, he looks intrigued. The excitement is quite evident in his eyes. His conscious smile awakens a massive erection in my pants. The air around us is charged with electricity. I want to reach out my hand, sink it into his hair, and kiss him until I get lost in him.

"Can I get your autograph?" The insecure voice of a girl makes me turn around.

A cascade of purple hair shrouds two hazel eyes that look at me shyly, full of excitement and expectation for the twenty minutes in our presence. It's like a cold shower bringing me back to reality. Lost in lustful thoughts toward my friend, I downright forgot about the people around us. I smile even though my heart is spilling out of my chest, aware that I have lost control. A pulsating erection in my pants reminds me that I've been so close to showing everyone my attraction to Nicholas.

"Of course! You bought the vinyl? Wow, you must really like our music," I tell her as I sign the album cover.

The girl blushes and shows off a shy smile. "My father has a huge collection of vinyl. He says it's the only way to listen to music, so I grew up old school."

I give her back the album, and she carefully puts it in her backpack.

"Your father knows how to listen to good music. I'd like to meet him. Next time bring him to one of our concerts." I smile at her, and she seems to melt with my words.

"I'll tell him for sure. He'll never believe it," she giggles.

"What's your name?"

She blushes violently again, looking down. "Janis"

I chuckle, amused. "Is your father a fan of Janis Joplin?"

She nods and smiles.

"So am I. Janis is a nice name."

The smile she flashes is contagious, and I can't help but imitate her.

"But I bet she's not your favorite singer," I keep the conversation going.

"I like her, but she's not the one that makes my heart beat."

"Who do you usually listen to? What album have you listened to so many times that you've worn it out?"

"Nancy Sinatra," she replies without even thinking about it. "'These Boots are Made for Walkin' is my favorite. I listened to her as a little girl with my mother while we danced in the kitchen, and whenever I'm down, I listen to it. It's my secret recipe for happiness."

"It's a good song. I like it a lot, too, even if it reminds me of *Full Metal Jacket* and stirs up somewhat contrasting emotions." I've never liked to talk down to our fans, so I enjoy discussing topics beyond just our music or a selfie and then falling into embarrassed silence.

"I never wanted to watch that movie. I want to associate this song only with my mother and our laughter every time we dance," she admits. "Do you have a song that puts you in a good mood every time you listen to it?"

I think for a moment. A lot of songs make me sad, but happy ones I have to think hard about.

"I don't know why, but Janis Joplin's 'Mercedes Benz' has always made me smile. Maybe it's the introduction she gives in the only a cappella recording of it, or maybe it's the final laugh. She recorded it four days before she died of an overdose, but there's more life in that laughter than in some healthy people I know. It's kind of melancholy, which should make me sad, but instead, it reminds me of life." I've never been as honest with a stranger as I am with this girl.

"You would totally get along with my father." She smiles at me with a tenderness that makes me want to hug her. "Would you mind if we take a picture together?"

"Of course." I lower myself to get closer and smile at the phone's camera.

"Thank you," she whispers when the one I assume is her friend takes her by the hand and drags her to Thomas.

I look up and find Nicholas and Haven smiling and filming me.

"That was a great moment you just shared with her," Haven says without ever stopping filming.

I shrug and put my hands in my pockets. "Damian and Michael attract fans because they have that rock star face that drives them crazy. The few people who come to talk to me are the ones who are really passionate about music."

Evan's announcement that our meeting is over is just what I need to take my eyes off the camera. The intense emotions running through my chest are overwhelming. Janis Joplin's song buzzes in my head, hiding a bit of the turmoil that stirs in my chest. If that girl hadn't interrupted us, I'm pretty sure I would have kissed Nicholas in front of everyone. I'm not sure I'm ready to face the consequences.

***

The concert is a blur of moments flowing so fast there's hardly time to think about it. My head is elsewhere, my eyes wander, searching for a camera I have come to love. When the first notes of "Swing" echo in the stadium full of people, my attention is totally absorbed by Haven's lips pronouncing every single word as if it were a sin. God, I would like to get dirty with those lips!

For the first time, I can't wait to get off stage and lock myself in the bus. When I set foot backstage, I'm happy when Evan announces we're leaving immediately. We'll shower in our tour bus because Portland awaits us tomorrow morning with a radio interview.

We don't have time to relax before hitting the road. Under normal circumstances, I would have felt the weight of fatigue. Today I can't run fast enough to get on that bus and avoid doing something impulsive I might regret.

I take off my clothes and slip into the cramped shower, looking down to see my erection still in full effect. Not even a cold shower can calm it down. When I finally manage to slip on a pair of sweatpants, I curse myself for not taking a single pair of boxers to contain the obvious agitation of my body.

"Hey, Simon, do you want to watch the conversation with the kid during the meet and greet?" Haven's voice catches my attention as soon as I get out of the bathroom.

She and Nicholas are on the couch at the back of the bus, transferring today's footage to the computer connected to the TV.

"I'm going to put on a t-shirt, I'll come back."

"No need." Nicholas's voice stops me on the spot. "Without a shirt, you look more like a rock star." He winks at me, and Haven smiles.

Maybe I'm not the only one who felt the tension grow almost to a boiling point this afternoon. The intimate vibe has not dissipated—if anything it's even stronger. When I enter and sit next to them, the temperature seems to rise by ten degrees. They've both changed clothes as well—Nicholas into sweatpants and a t-shirt, Haven a tank top and shorts that hug her ass. I clearly see she's not wearing a bra.

"It was a great moment with Janis today. Very different from what you see with Michael or Damian." Haven smiles as her gaze moves from the monitor to my face.

"Is that thing filming?" I point to the camera resting on the table, pointing at me.

Nicholas shakes his head, frowning. "Do you want us to turn it on and interview you?"

I look down on my pants, the obvious semi-erection under

the thin layer of cloth. "Not unless you want this documentary to be a porno," I laugh as they look at my crotch and smirk, but then their gaze rests on mine, full of questions I can't answer.

"Are you horny, Simon?" Haven's voice is suggestive, a defiant smile appearing on her lips.

"If you sing the words to 'Swing' in my face all day, you can't expect me to remain indifferent." I raise an eyebrow as I watch her snuggle up with her back against Nicholas' chest.

"You didn't complain." She raises an eyebrow in response.

My friend slips a hand inside her tank top and caresses her breast without ever taking his eyes off me. Her nipple stiffens, protruding through the thin fabric. They throw me a challenge, aware that I've been excited all day because of them. Now that the cards are on the table, it's clear I arouse them as much as they arouse me.

The desire to fuck them is reinvigorated in my pants, making it more than evident I'm enjoying the show. Nicholas takes it as an invitation to continue, kissing Haven's neck, sticking his other hand inside her shirt, and stroking both breasts. He plays with her nipples until her eyes squint and she arches her back.

Their breathing becomes shallow, their desire more intense with each caress, kiss, bite. It's so exciting to watch it's hard to breathe, and my heart speeds up the pace. Everything about this situation sends my brain into a tailspin. The excitement runs through my veins, almost boiling under my skin.

Haven opens her eyes and crawls on the couch toward me, reaching the corner where I took refuge. The low plunge of her tank top allows me a clear view of her firm breasts down to her navel. She's drop-dead sexy, and my erection twitches in my pants. Reaching me, she straddles my lap and lowers her face to kiss my neck. She is a sin. This woman is the sin that will send me to hell, and I'm not sure I mind.

"Haven…I'm not sure." My voice comes out as a whisper while I look behind her to make sure my friend is not angry. My body screams to dive right in, my heart hasn't been logical for a while now, my brain shouts, "What the hell are you doing?"—and that voice is louder than all the others.

Haven looks up at me, the tenderness in her eyes almost disarming. "You don't have to have sex if you don't want to," she whispers before kissing me.

Her tongue creeps into my mouth, causing my heart to explode. My hands search for her hips to drag her to me. It is a slow, sensual kiss, full of a feeling I struggle to understand. She's not in a hurry to get to the point, undress me, or fuck me. When I open my eyes, I meet her smile.

Nicholas is kissing her neck from behind. He pauses to take off his shirt, showing a slim physique with well-defined muscles, then goes back to kissing her neck, tasting her skin with his tongue.

He sticks his hands under her tank top and pulls it off her head. When Haven raises her arms to let the fabric slip off her body, Nicholas locks his eyes to mine and enjoys the moan that escapes my lips when Haven presses her core on my erection.

"I don't know if I'm ready," I confess with some embarrassment. My erection screams "go," but my doubts are stronger, despite the eroticism filling this bus with our breathing and groans.

Nicholas smiles at me sweetly as he gets closer to my face. He puts his hand in my hair and ruffles it softly. "We won't do anything you don't want to. You dictate the timing," he whispers in my ear, and I nod. "You can watch if you want. Would you like that?" I nod again as I close my eyes and shudder when he kisses my neck. "If you want, you can get off. We don't mind. Do you feel like touching yourself while watching us?"

His words reach my chest and stomach like hot lava burning inside me. I catch my breath. Excitement envelops my bowels and lungs, preventing me from inhaling the air I need to reason with clarity. "Yes…"

My answer comes out in a hoarse whisper and is swallowed by Nicholas's lips resting on mine before I let his tongue slide into my mouth. His beard tickles my chin, and it excites me to death. I never thought a man's beard on my face could trigger such intense desire.

I reach out a hand and run my fingers through his hair, squeezing firmly. He moans and I swallow before biting his lower lip. I search for Haven. She's looking at us with a smile. I reach out my other hand, sink my fingers into her hair and pull her in for another kiss. This time I'm even more excited, full of a passion I can't control.

She seems to want to devour my lips, dictating a frantic pace. I love her way of taking all the pleasure she wants, without excuses, without regrets. I wish I could be like her. Free from the mental restrictions that my brain refuses to break down.

I detach myself from her face and watch Nicholas's hands lower the elastic of my pants until he releases my erection. A sigh of surprise catches them both.

"Simon! The quiet calm one…a piercing on your penis?"

Haven looks at me with her mouth wide open, moving her eyes from my face to the Prince Albert I did years ago when meaningless sex wasn't enough for me. I needed to feel more, heighten my emotions and amplify my pleasure to fill the emptiness inside.

Nicholas looks up at me, and a grin appears on his lips. "Simon has a lot of little secrets," he whispers in Haven's ear before sticking his fingers into her shorts and pulling them off.

After getting rid of those, he gets up from the sofa. Without ever taking his eyes off mine, he strips off his sweatpants, freeing his erection. The show that welcomes me makes me breathless. We were kids the last time we were close enough to share the intimacy of a few caresses, kisses on the lips, whispers under the covers, in the darkness of a room.

Nicholas has grown up. He's no longer that helpless little boy. He's a man who sits on the couch and takes his woman by the hips to make her sit on him. Haven leans back against his chest, her buttocks sliding on Nicholas's erection pulsating with desire. His hands reach her breasts and play with her nipples until she groans his name.

When Nicholas sinks into her with a single forceful push, his eyes slide from my face to the erection squeezed in my hand. A smug smile confirms he's no longer the helpless little boy who didn't know how to get by. My best friend has grown up. He knows what he wants and how to get it. He wants me, he wants Haven, and he doesn't hold back by laying bare all that desire that devours his soul.

The sight of their two bodies grinding over each other, panting, sweaty, wet with that pleasure they don't spare themselves, is enough to make me come with an overwhelming orgasm. I grunt without being able to do anything to stop it. It's such an intense experience I'm trembling under the longing eyes of Nicholas and Haven.

My mouth is wide open, the breath struggles to enter my lungs. My eyes are fixed on the two of them, chasing pleasure as if their lives depend on it. The guttural moan that comes out of my friend's lips is so powerful that it vibrates in my chest, while Haven opens her mouth wide in a silent pleasure that makes her close her eyes.

I never thought an orgasm from someone else could give me physical pleasure. But the two of them got under my skin, taking possession of every fiber of my body, and showed me it's possible to enjoy the pleasure of others.

Silence falls in the room. Only the noise of the bus and our heavy breathing fill this place. I assumed the post-orgasm would be embarrassing, that sharing this moment with two other people would be challenging to manage. Instead, I just have to look at them to understand that the only thing I feel is the desire to do it again.

CHAPTER 11
Nicholas

I open my eyes, and the cream-colored ceiling above my head confuses me. After months on a tour bus, I feel disoriented, never having traveled outside the city where I've lived my whole life. Every day we wake up in a different place and walk through different streets and neighborhoods. For a creature of habit like me, it's frustrating to wake up and not know where you are and what's happening.

Today we're staying in one of the hotels in downtown Seattle. Last night the Jailbirds had a concert at the Climate Pledge Arena, next to the Space Needle, and tomorrow night they'll repeat it with a second date. Today is one of those rare days off, and Haven and I have decided not to work either.

This feeling of excitement, though, is familiar. Three days ago, I had the most explosive sex I've ever had in my life. With Simon's eyes on me and Haven's warm body moving sinuously over me, I almost caught fire. Since then, nothing has been the same. My erection hasn't gone away, but unfortunately, it's been three days full of work commitments. The few free hours we've had we used to sleep and recharge for the following day.

I look down at my erection and watch the sheet moving with the familiar figure of Haven below it. Her lips wrap around my flesh in the blink of an eye, and I find myself emitting a moan of pleasure.

"Honey, I don't know how long I can hold it if you continue like this."

The giggle out of her lips tickles the sensitive skin of my erection. I close my eyes and enjoy the sublime sensation of her mouth and hands on me. My orgasm mounts and explodes on her tongue with an embarrassing speed, surprising her.

Her head peeps out from under the white sheets, the mischievous smile curves her mouth, the pink hair messy on her head. She's wild in the most unrestrained sense of the word. No longer that scared, guilty teenager.

"I swear, I don't know what's going on with me. Even at fifteen, I wasn't coming so fast." I welcome her into my arms as she snuggles up with her head on my chest.

"Maybe because it's really like being a kid again. I keep thinking about the other night with the same smile as my fifteen-year-old self in love. Do you think Simon regretted it?"

The truth is I don't know. The rock star life is a continuous roller coaster of frenetic moments and days of silence spent inside a bus traveling slowly from city to city. The moment of intimacy with Simon happened just before one of those tumultuous periods, and there was no time to process how he felt after what happened.

"I don't know. I have no idea if his silence is due to his work obligations or the fact that he's avoiding us."

"He didn't seem angry when we sat chatting late into the night."

I nod, but I don't know what to say. With Simon, it's unlike any experience we've had with other partners. I think he's struggling to get his heart and brain aligned. Clearly, he's attracted to this whole situation, but I can't understand why his rational part restrains him. I don't know what his fears are.

A knock on our room door distracts me from thoughts about him. Haven gets up and puts on the hotel bathrobe. I put on the sweatpants I find on the chair next to the bed and a shirt I pick up from the floor. I need to wash it, the smell is terrible. I go to open the door while Haven hides in the bathroom.

"Simon!" I can't hide the surprise of finding him standing here. In all honesty, I did not expect him to come knocking on our door.

Haven opens the bathroom door wide, emerges still wrapped in the bathrobe, and throws her arms around Simon's neck when he enters. She takes him by surprise, and I notice he hesitates before returning the embrace. When she touches his lips with a light kiss, he widens his eyes and stiffens.

The moment Haven untangles herself from his embrace, I get closer to him and place a kiss on his neck, just below his ear. His eyes flash on mine, then on my lips, that arch in a smile.

"Good morning," I whisper before reaching Haven at the table by the window.

"Have you already had breakfast? I thought I'd order up room service," my girlfriend proposes, as she divides her attention between our faces and the menu in front of her.

"Okay, so I gather there's no embarrassment after the other night…" Simon rubs a hand on his neck like he usually does when he's nervous.

I study him for a few seconds as he sits on one of the armchairs at the round table between Haven and me. "We don't keep this part of our relationship secret. If we feel comfortable being intimate with someone, it doesn't change how we act in broad daylight. Do you feel embarrassed?"

Simon puts his hands on his face, snorts, and then smiles at us. "I don't know. I don't understand anything. I always avoided casual sex because I couldn't endure the awkwardness the next day. Not knowing what to say, what to do. Will there be a next time? Did they like it enough to do it again? I'm not good at small talk with people I barely know."

He inhales, looking at the ceiling, and then looks at us. "With you, there's not that problem. We're far beyond the small talk. But you're a couple, and I can't figure out how to get into the equation. On the one hand, I see it as a betrayal, but on the other, it isn't. Does that make any sense?" He laughs nervously.

Haven gets up from her armchair and sits on his legs, placing an arm on his shoulders. A sweet smile forms on her lips. "It would be a betrayal if you slipped into the relationship with one of us, secretly from the other. That would be mean. But we're both saying we like having you around, we like you as a person, we like the intimacy with you. In our society, a couple is the norm. Everything else is scandalous. Take the time you need, try to understand what you want and don't want, don't accept anything that makes you uncomfortable."

Simon looks at Haven, then at me, hugs her, and sinks his face into her neck, pecking her skin. "Okay," he whispers. "I'll try. I can't guarantee success." He chuckles as Haven clasps her arms around his neck.

"Can we order food now? I'm starving," I complain as I pick up the menu and the other two scoot in closer.

"Today, I thought we'd do something relaxing since we have the day off," Simon proposes once breakfast is over. "What do you think?"

I observe him carefully. I don't have the faintest idea of what goes on in that complicated and fascinating head of his. He goes from avoiding us to organizing trips, but he looks lovely with that confused look on his face.

"I'd love to! I need a relaxing day. What did you have in mind?" Haven asks excitedly.

"A movie?" The happy smile on his lips makes me smile.

"Can you go to see a movie without being harassed by screaming fans?" I ask him, perplexed. He usually goes out surrounded by bodyguards six feet tall and wide as a truck. I have difficulty imagining the logistics inside a crowded and dark place.

Simon chuckles, drops his head back, and rubs a hand over his face. "No. I can't do that. But I can rent a movie theatre just for us. One perk of this career is that there's no shortage of money—even for the most absurd things."

Haven looks at him with wide eyes and mouth hanging open. "Did you rent an entire screening room to watch a movie with us?" she says dumbfounded.

Simon shrugs, almost embarrassed. "Not really. That would have been too complicated. I rented the entire theatre. All three of its screening rooms are closed to the public this morning," he admits, and the two of us burst out laughing.

Until a few months ago, we were eating restaurant leftovers with the homeless, and now we have an entire public building rented for the three of us. Fate certainly has strange twists.

"Can we get candy, or are there no employees there either?" Haven's slightly mocking tone makes me smile, especially when Simon blushes.

"They'll be there. We'll have access to the snack area and a list of movies to choose from."

"Good. Because I can't watch an entire movie without candy to nibble on."

I smile. Haven can swallow her weight in gummy bears, and can't sit more than five minutes in front of a movie without munching on something. At first, before I knew her well, I was afraid I'd have to take her to the emergency room to pump her stomach.

"If you want, I'll text Max to pick us up."

"Give us time to change, and we'll be ready," I say.

Simon looks around, nods, gets up, and slips his hands into his jeans pocket. He looks like a fish out of water.

"You're leaving this room and waiting for us in the hallway, aren't you?" I ask him with a raised eyebrow when I sense his intentions.

"I want to give you some privacy," he mumbles.

"Simon, we had sex in front of you while you masturbated watching us. I think we're over the embarrassment of nudity, right?"

Haven chuckles at this as she slips into the bathroom.

I take my friend by the shoulders and make him sit back on the armchair he got up from, leaving him a light kiss on the lips and smiling at his embarrassed expression.

I use the bathroom myself to change into something decent to go out in. While I have no problem getting naked in front of the two of them, I don't like to make people I love uncomfortable, so I give Simon the space he needs to not suffocate. The last thing I want is for him to feel stuck in an awkward situation and decide to run away.

***

The cinema where we hide out is one of those independent ones with an old-fashioned marquee where the staff has to manually climb up and change the letters of each new movie title. It's located in the Queen Anne neighborhood of Seattle, near the Space Needle. Max drives us around the back of the building where one of the employees lets us in through the emergency exit.

He accompanies us to the entrance, where the girl behind the popcorn counter struggles to hold back an excited squeal at the sight of Simon. After the usual selfies, she fills Haven's container with candy, and we head toward one of the rooms.

The dark red velvet curtains, which cover the walls from ceiling to floor, give the place a retro vibe, the way I like it. The seats of the same color, old and worn, lend a melancholy feel to the vintage cinema. It won't be as comfortable as the high-tech multiplexes you see today, but it certainly earns points in terms of charm and character.

We choose a movie from the Marvel universe that all three of us have already seen. This date is not about watching the latest film release, but a moment of normality Simon wanted to give us.

I turn to him. Haven sits between the two of us, but I can

clearly see Simon's face illuminated by the screen lights. I always thought he was a handsome guy, fascinated by his angular features that give him an unconventional beauty. But seeing him grown, with that lived-in appearance he carries with him and without a trace of adolescence on his face, makes me breathless. I have never felt as much attraction to a man as I do to him.

As if hearing my call, he turns to me and locks me in with his gaze. We stay like this for a time that seems endless until Haven gets up, takes Simon's hand, and makes him sit with her. She snuggles up in his arms and resumes watching the film as if nothing had happened.

Simon pulls her closer, closing his eyes and inhaling the scent of her neck. When he reopens them, his gaze searches for mine again, his hand reaching out to my lap where I rest mine. He intertwines our fingers, squeezes them, brings them to his lips, and sweetly kisses them before resting them on his chest.

We both go back to looking at the screen, aware that this is the closest thing to ecstasy we have ever experienced. We have seen our naked bodies, we have tasted the pleasure of the flesh. But I've never felt so close, body and soul, to a person as in this cinema. Fully dressed, our eyes lost in the images before us, our bodies merge into an interweaving of feelings deeper than physical pleasure, more intimate than the contact of our skin.

The elevator doors open, and we enter to go up to Simon's room. Haven brings the pizza we stopped to buy after the movie. There's no one around the hotel at three in the afternoon, so Max didn't have to work overtime to escort us through the hallway that leads upstairs. Damian and Lilly were spotted at the zoo with Thomas and Iris, and the fan frenzy was unleashed in that part of the city. It's easy for Simon to move around. And Michael, who decided to take Faith and Levi to a spa for a relaxing day, has an easier life than the other two bandmates.

"Don't close the doors." Evan's voice from the hallway makes me stretch out my hand to leave him time to join us in the elevator.

"Thank you." He smiles at me before entering and leaning against the wall. His gaze rests on the three of us, and when I look at Simon's nervous face, my heart accelerates a few beats. Evan knows. He knows our secret. I don't know if Simon told him or if he just guessed it, but I'm sure he knows what happened. It's more than a feeling, it's a certainty. I gaze back at Simon to see if he's okay with this, but he doesn't seem to want to escape.

"Thanks for booking the theater this morning. It was fun to spend a few hours like normal people." Simon smiles at him, and I'm even more convinced he confided in Evan.

"Don't thank me, I told Emily to call. And let me tell you, I'm happy to be on the same side as that woman and not on the other end of her calls. I swear, I've seen grown men cry after her organizational fury hit them. She sinks her teeth in, tears them apart, chews them up, and spits them out with a mixture of terror and tears."

We laugh, amused because we were scolded several times by Emily when we made her work complicated. I can confirm that she is terrifying when she confronts you head-on.

"You're happy you hired her, though," Simon urges him.

"Yes. It was a real Christmas miracle. I never would have survived this last period of time without her." The smile on his lips seems to soften his usual stern demeanor. "Speaking of Emily, she's ready to pounce because there have been problems with your bus."

"Anything we need to worry about?" Haven's furrowed forehead mirrors mine and Simon's.

"No. Nothing tragic. We think some fans managed to sneak into the guarded lot where they're parked and tried to force open the door. They couldn't get in, don't worry, but we prefer to change the card keys for safety. We'll give them to you as soon as possible. I'll also give Max your new backstage pass. Emily went to pick it up this morning," he explains, looking at Haven.

"Thank you. And sorry again for the trouble. I'll keep it around my neck instead of on my jeans." A bit of embarrassment shines through her shy smile.

"Don't worry. It happens. Now enjoy the pizza. I'm going to see if Emily has finished tearing up the technicians who left a cable box from your concert in Oakland." He rolls his eyes and exits the elevator at the same brisk pace as he entered.

When the doors close, my gaze rests on Simon. "He knows, doesn't he?" The smile on my lips reassures him it's not an accusation. He knows what I'm referring to.

"I needed to talk to someone. I can't do that with Michael. His hands are already full with a family to manage. Evan's always been a practical problem solver." He's leaning against the elevator wall with his hands behind his back and a smile on his face. His eyes scrutinize me to see if I'm upset about his confession.

"Do you think it's a problem?"

He shakes his head and smiles. "No, but the mess I have in my head can become one. I needed a person with a clear mind to put things in perspective."

"Did it work?"

He shrugs and a guilty grimace appears, then stretches out in a smile. "It hasn't gotten worse," he admits.

"I don't understand what you're talking about," Haven says, bouncing her gaze from me to Simon.

"We'll explain it to you when we get to the room." I wink at her as I grab her by the shoulders and push her out of the elevator that has come to our floor.

***

The truth is that we couldn't explain anything to Haven. As soon as the door closed behind us, we placed the pizza on the table, where it still lies whole and cold, and Simon's lips crushed mine. Without warning, his hands wrapped my face, and his mouth descended on mine without a single word. In the end, I don't know how we ended up on the bed, Haven with us. The kisses became two, then three, and we're still here, with our clothes on, enjoying the tenderness of each one.

Haven's tongue makes its way through Simon's lips. I

watch them embrace each other and surrender to the moment's frenzy. His shirt rises slightly, and I can't help but admire his tight abs and dark hair disappearing under the belt. His skin draws me to him as if hypnotizing me.

I lower myself and savor his belly, my lips and tongue lost in the ecstasy of sensations flowing under my skin. I need to taste every little emotion I feel. A groan explodes between his lips, but it is swallowed by Haven, who then moves to kiss his jaw and his neck. I watch her devote herself to that part under Simon's ear that I discovered to be an especially sensitive spot for him.

He closes his eyes, bites his lip, squeezes the sheets in his fists, and his erection presses up against his pants. It's the sexiest vision I've ever seen. I settle between his legs and slowly lift his shirt, kissing, sucking, biting all along my path until I get lost for a few moments on his nipples.

"If you keep this up, I'll come in my boxers like a kid…" His words are almost a whisper, interrupted by small sighs. His breathing is shallow, excited, inebriated by the moment.

"Then maybe we should take them off, or they'll get dirty," Haven suggests in his ear before biting his lobe and making him groan.

Simon's eyes open wide when I touch his erection with one hand, and Haven's words settle in his brain. His gaze rests on mine, his chest rises at a frantic pace pressed against mine. I can feel his heart racing.

"Only what you feel like doing," I reassure him with a whisper.

Simon doesn't say anything, but a slight nod gives me permission to continue. I go down again to his chest, then belly. I take my time and make him enjoy it. Today only Simon counts. The erection in my pants doesn't matter. Neither does the desire I read in Haven's eyes. Today only he counts, lying on this bed, giving himself to an intimacy that terrifies and excites him at the same time. I want him to enjoy this moment, to feel it inside, all the way to his bones. I want him to carry it as the best memory of his life.

I lower myself between his legs, unfasten his belt and look up at him. His eyes are as wide and full of desire as those of my girlfriend. They both stare at me with an expectation that tears their chests with impatient sighs. I unbutton the jeans one at a time, slowly, anticipating every little expression of pleasure that appears on his face. I stick my fingers into the elastic band of his boxers, then pull them toward me along with his pants until they come down under his buttocks, releasing his hot, stiff erection. I savor it with my tongue, the whole length up to the tip, dwelling on its piercing. From the metal sphere at the base, I climb up to nip at the tip.

A moan pierces his chest. He raises his pelvis, arching his back slightly, unable to control his excitement. My chest fills with warmth to see him so vulnerable and helpless as he gives me his total trust.

I kiss him, tasting the saltiness of pre-ejaculation with my tongue, then I wrap my lips around his flesh and go down until it sinks into my throat. I enjoy every single sigh and groan of pleasure it releases from him, primal sounding inside this room.

Simon grabs Haven from the back of her neck and pulls her into a feverish, wet kiss, dirty with that sin he can't wait to taste. And I can't resist anymore. I grab the base of his erection and squeeze, pumping to the faster and faster rhythm of my lips, tongue, throat, ready to welcome his pleasure. In other circumstances, I would have slowed down, played with him, prolonged his delicious torture, but not this time. I want to give him that violent, deep pleasure you can't contain. I want him to lose control and feel every emotion in his gut, his lungs, unable to inhale enough air to make him reason. I want him to feel it in his heart. I want to mark him with a pleasure he won't be able to erase.

I am rewarded with an explosive orgasm between my lips, on my tongue, along my throat. The animalistic grunt that comes out of his chest is lacerating, primitive. He pushes his pelvis toward my face, and I am ready to welcome his impulses, his enjoyment. When he returns to collapse on the bed, he is exhausted, his mouth wide open, searching for that oxygen he seems deprived of.

Slowly I climb back toward his face. When his eyes meet mine, he grabs my neck and drags me into a deep, intense kiss. His tongue battles mine, the taste of his pleasure mixes with his breathing. I distance myself from him just enough to grab Haven's face and lure her in for an equally frantic kiss. I want her to be part of that flavor that will remain forever etched in the memory of my heart. From a man who dictated my life's joy and despair, the ups and downs, the emptiness but also the fullness. For better or worse, Simon has shaped every moment of my existence, and when I close my eyes and rest my head on his chest, I find the familiar rhythm of his heart that cradles me until I fall asleep.

Haven

Seven years earlier

"Do you realize how badly you messed up?" My mother's shouts bounce between the living room walls, making me curl up deeper on the white sofa I've been sitting on for more than two hours.

The two bodyguards she pays to be on my back twenty-four/seven are standing, motionless, with unreadable faces. They're paid to protect me, be discreet and keep their mouths shut. I'm an actress, not a government spy, but my mother has become paranoid since some fans climbed over the wall and evaded security by leaving me gifts at the front door.

"Do you have any idea what the publicists have to do to solve this mess?" she shouts at me rabidly. She walks back and forth like a wounded, angry animal wrapped only in a silk robe over her white micro-bikini that leaves nothing to the imagination.

"I..." Words die in my throat when her furious look tells me to shut up.

"You what, Haven? You what? You got caught by the paparazzi at the pool with your tits out, and David's hands tucked into your underwear. You *what*, exactly?"

I look at the two bodyguards. They're stiff as marble statues, but they're still human beings who see, listen, judge. I lower my face, embarrassed. I didn't even want to be in that house, by that pool. But David wanted to do something special for the two of us. He had bought the most expensive champagne, told me to relax, that there was no one around, and he wanted to see me naked in the sunlight because I was beautiful. The deck chair we made love on was uncomfortable, the wooden slats pressed on my back, but the champagne had a strange effect and I felt euphoric, uninhibited…drop-dead beautiful, like he always tells me.

It didn't even take us long. When David is in one of his moments of uncontrollable excitement, he doesn't do foreplay. He gets straight to the point, and after his orgasm, he gets dressed and takes me home. Sometimes I wish I could try an orgasm myself, but I suppose this is how busy adults have sex—no time to waste on stupid details. My mother always tells me that men who make women climax exist only in books or movies. If I want pleasure in a relationship with a man, I have to make an orgasm happen myself because they don't have the patience to learn how a woman's body functions.

"He's my boyfriend, I'm of age, and sex before marriage isn't a scandal. I mean, we're not in the eighteenth century!" I try to justify myself with a trembling voice.

My mother's laughter freezes me on the spot. Her look of mockery and pity is like an icy hand that slips into my stomach and squeezes it until it hurts.

"Do you really think you're his girlfriend? That he will leave his wife to be with you?" The questions hang in the air before settling like a boulder in my chest. "You're a dumb little girl. When a producer asks you to kneel in front of him and give him a little service with your mouth, you do it. When he bends you on his desk to fuck you, you move aside the contracts where you rest your tits, grit your teeth, and shut up. You're nothing more than a piece of young meat to have fun with in exchange for a career. When you're twenty-five years old, you'll be old news, he'll dump you, and you will have to drop your pants for his seventy-year-old boss if you want to keep working."

Tears run down my cheeks, and nausea grips my stomach so violently I have to run to the bathroom to vomit up my lunch.

I hold the phone in my hands in a grip so hard it hurts. My mother is wrong. David always treated me like a princess, always gave me gifts, took me to the most exclusive parties, and constantly bragged to his friends about how beautiful I was. Our relationship is different from the ones he's had in the past. I know. I feel it.

This morning, I had to mute my Twitter notifications because after those pictures came out, I was flooded with hateful messages from anyone with access to a phone or computer. They say I'm a homewrecker, that I should be ashamed, that they should shut down my show and never let me work in Hollywood again. Everyone blames me, forgetting there are two people in that photo.

Sitting on the white marble floor of the guest bathroom, I look at the Twitter icon, undecided whether to open it or not. On the one hand, I want to know how bad it is, on the other, I'm terrified of reading the nasty comments about me. I decide to set aside the press and the fans for the moment and take refuge in the comforting voice of the one who has always held me tight in his arms for the last year.

"What do you want?" David's voice is harsh. He seems almost annoyed that I called him.

After a moment of hesitation, I find the courage to respond. "Have you seen the pictures?" I whisper.

I hear some background noise, a door closing, then silence. "Of course, I saw the photos. My wife has been shouting at me since this morning. Not even our lawyers can keep her quiet," he growls savagely. The few times I've heard him this furious have always been business calls.

"Maybe now's the time to talk to her, to finally tell her about us…" I manage to get the words out despite the lump in my throat that almost chokes me.

The few seconds of silence on the other side of the phone seem to last for years. "Do you actually think I would leave my wife for you?" There is anger and disbelief in his voice. "You're just one of the many sluts trying to make their way in Hollywood by opening their legs to anyone who gives them a job. Between you and your mother, I don't know who gets fucked more in exchange for fame. Do you think you had your contract renewed because you're the next great thing? You got signed because your ass looks good squeezed into that jumpsuit, and you give great blowjobs. Don't fool yourself, honey, and most importantly, don't call me. Never again. I already have enough shit to fix without your whining."

When David ends the call, my sobs are so violent they turn my stomach until I cling to the toilet and vomit again. I try to inhale air, but it's almost impossible. I feel a hand pick up the long dark strands of hair that run down my face, while another massages my back until I calm down enough to catch my breath.

When I look up, I find Steve, the oldest bodyguard, the one with photos of his three children in his wallet. For once, there isn't a blank mask on his face but a smile of compassion that softens his features.

"For what it's worth, I don't think you've done anything wrong. Your only 'fault' was to fall in love with a filthy pig who treated you like you didn't deserve. You can count on my testimony if you want to go to the police, because you were a minor when he put his hands on you." His words are whispered, but they slam straight to my chest as if he had shouted them.

I wrap my arms around his neck and sink my face against his chest, crying all the tears I can no longer hold. I have never felt so alone in my life.

***

I've been staring at the reflection of the pool water on my bedroom ceiling for hours now. It's late at night, and the silence is deafening after hearing the shouts from my mother and the questions of my publicist who came by to save a situation that, basically, can't be saved.

Public apology, leave the show I've been starring in since before I was a teenager, therapy at one of the best rehab clinics in Los Angeles, and flying under the radar for a while. This is what they want me to do. I asked if David would go through the same ordeal to save his reputation, and they laughed. He's a man. He doesn't have a reputation to preserve. It's a given that men have extramarital escapades. A slap on the wrist, some jokes about his wife making him sleep on the couch, and his life will go on as before. Mine, on the other hand, is ruined forever.

I can't tell if the thing that hurts most is David's words and the realization that our whole story was just in my stupid romantic teenage head, or the anger rising inside me for how I'm being crucified by everyone, even my mother. The humiliation is so intense I want to disappear. The idea of apologizing in front of the world for an intimate moment with a person I trusted blindly and who betrayed me, and was publicized by a stranger, makes my skin crawl.

Paparazzi have been lurking in front of the gate for hours. The thought of passing through it in the car to go to a press conference is as terrifying as jumping from a plane without a parachute. Tomorrow the stylist will come to find a modest and suitable dress for my public appearance, and a hairdresser will have to create a conservative hairstyle that highlights my girl-next-door face.

Because I have to defend myself, I'm guilty. I'm the one who opened her legs and stained herself with sin. I just wanted to love a man who has given me his attention since I didn't even have breasts. But I'm the wrong one. Everyone says so.

I get up and enter the bathroom, rinse my face and pause to observe the dark circles under my eyes. A lock of my sinful hair slips down my cheek, the same hair that until yesterday was treated with products worth thousands of dollars so the set light could bring out the nuances, adding an eye-catching touch to my image. I grab the small scissors I use to cut the cuticles around my nails and start cutting, strand by strand until nothing remains of the hair my mother always brags about. I look at the mass of dark hair inside the sink with a hatred that I've never felt for anything or anyone. I grab and throw it all into the toilet, flushing several times until every trace disappears.

I go back to look in the mirror and smile. When the heroine's cathartic moment in the movies is resolved with a drastic haircut, the result is always perfect. Mine is not. It looks like an animal chewed the strands, cutting them off at different lengths. It's horrible, and it attracts me. It's so different from what everyone expects of me that I like it, even though it makes me look like I just escaped from the asylum.

I get out of the bathroom, put on a pair of sweatpants, my Vans, and a loose hoodie my mother thinks she threw away, but I hide under the bed for those days when I don't feel beautiful enough for this world. I take out of my wallet the five hundred dollars my mother gave me the other day to have a coffee, and I climb out my bedroom window, the one on the corner, where the alarm hasn't worked for years.

I run through the patio where the pool is until I reach the shaded area of the garden. As soon as I breathe easy, thinking I've gotten away with it, a hand grabs me by the elbow and pulls me.

"Where do you think you're going?" Steve's voice makes me spin around. "Haven? What are you doing out here? It's three in the morning. What did you do to your hair?" As soon as he recognizes me, the questions following one another have a tiny hint of panic.

My eyes fill with tears.

"Does your mother know you're out here?" His tone softens.

I shake my head, and he closes his eyes and inhales.

"You can't run away. You'll make everyone worry like that." He frees my arm.

The anger rising in my stomach is almost overwhelming. "Who? The only person on my side is here in front of me right now. Is it my disappearance they'll worry about or their reputations?" I hiss with anger and tears running down my cheeks.

Steve closes his eyes, inhales, then pulls his wallet out of his pocket where he keeps his children's photos.

"I only have a hundred dollars on me, but keep my credit card. It doesn't have a high limit, but use it if you need it, okay?" He sticks it in my hand and closes my fingers around them.

"What will your wife say?"

He smiles at me and wipes a tear from my cheek with his thumb. "That I did the right thing."

I look down, ashamed of what he knows about me, of the most intimate aspects of my life that I should not share with anyone.

"Climb over the wall at the back, we just took a look, and no one's over there. The paparazzi are all at the front gate."

"Thank you," I whisper before taking a step toward the fence.

"Haven?"

I turn to him. His sweet expression warms my heart.

"You are a beautiful person outside, but most of all, inside. Never doubt it, okay?"

The tears begin to fall again before lowering my head,

turning around, and running toward the darkness that will make me disappear from this house.

CHAPTER 12
Haven

There are certain mornings when you wake up and know your day will be all uphill. For no particular reason, nothing bad happens, no news to put you in a bad mood. You just open your eyes and get a feeling in your stomach that doesn't leave you alone, a feeling you can't shake off. You blame a nightmare, a piece of news that's troubled you lately, but nothing's really wrong. Sometimes it's just the universe trying to warn you that a catastrophe is about to hit your life.

"You're awake." Simon's hoarse voice reaches my side while I continue to stare at the ceiling of his bus room. Next to me, Nicholas sleeps.

Since falling asleep in Simon's bed two days ago in Seattle, we haven't stopped sleeping together. There hasn't been another particularly spicy moment, but we established this pleasant cuddle routine before falling asleep.

"I think something awful is going to happen today," I say out of the blue, making him rise on one elbow, looking confused.

"Do you want to give me a clue, or do I just wait for it to happen?" He smiles at me, but there's a thread of concern on his face.

I shrug and turn to him, gently kissing him on the lips.

"Just an impression. Call it a sixth sense."

"So we have to keep our eyes open, waiting for something to happen?" He draws me into a hug.

I stick my nose into the hollow of his neck and nod. It's the same feeling I had that morning when pictures of David and me came out in the newspapers.

Behind me, Nicholas stretches and turns, resting his chest on my back and wrapping an arm around Simon and me. I hear the snap of a kiss, and when I look up, I find Simon's tender look on Nicholas. As much as he may still be undecided about this type of relationship, it's clear what direction his heart has taken.

"What are you talking about?" Nicholas's hoarse voice tickles my neck.

"Haven's bad omen."

"One of those you can't explain?"

I nod.

"Then we'll wait for the catastrophe to come," he whispers before kissing my neck and pressing his erection against my butt.

"Okay, now you're worrying me. You seem sure that something tragic will happen. Do I have to start looking over my shoulder?" Simon asks.

I smile and put my hand on his chest. "Don't worry. If something's going to happen, it *will* happen, whether you worry or not. So why ruin your day with a bad mood before something *really* ruins it?"

"You're not reassuring me, you know that, right?" He raises an eyebrow.

I laugh, amused, and Nicholas behind me laughs, making

my back vibrate.

"Are you awake up there?" Damian's voice thunders from downstairs.

"We'd better get up before he comes to pull us out of bed," sighs Simon almost resignedly.

Today is a travel day, as we're heading to a particularly far-away city. We take the opportunity to stay on the same bus and do some interviews. Damian has decided to dictate the timing of the day; it's only seven-thirty and he's already telling us to get out of bed.

"We're coming!" Simon shouts as he walks out of the room and closes the door behind him, giving Nicholas and me time to put our clothes on.

I grab my phone from the table at the foot of the bed where it was charging, and my heart sinks a little. Fifteen un-answered calls from a stranger. Considering that only a hand-ful of trusted people have this number, I pray with all my heart it's someone who's made a mistake. Fifteen times. The feeling that something bad is happening comes back into my stomach, and these missed phone calls make the hair on my arms stand up. The phone lights up with a call from the same number. I ignore it and put it in the pocket of the sweatpants.

"Everything okay?" Nicholas's voice is perplexed, and when I turn to him, I find him studying me carefully, not miss-ing a detail of my expression, so I put on a smile and push aside the thought of those phone calls.

"Yes. I was thinking about what to wear for the interview. Getting in front of a camera means I have to dress up every day." I roll my eyes.

He smiles and kisses me on the lips. "You're beautiful in

anything."

"I'll wear a burlap sack and see how it goes. Maybe even without makeup, what do you say?" It's a half-joke, but he knows I sometimes miss wearing a sweatshirt and jeans every day. After eight years of carefully avoiding dressing up, it's hard to go back to the old habits of wearing makeup all day.

An hour later, I'm sitting on a small section of sofa in the back of the bus. The rest of the space is occupied by the imposing bodies of the four Jailbirds. When they're all together on a sofa, the room becomes small and stuffy. Fortunately, their partners decided to stay in their buses. Otherwise, it would have been impossible to breathe.

"Today, the questions are much more personal than they've been. Are you ready?" I ask the four faces who are watching me, relaxed. Iris has already given them the list of questions, so they know what to expect.

"Ready to be crucified again," laughs Michael amusedly, and everyone else follows.

I notice Nicholas is already filming. "Are you worried the audience won't like what you'll say?"

Michael shrugs and abandons the playful expression he always wears. "People are afraid of someone who's served time. No matter how much you've changed, there's always that doubt surrounding you. We're used to it, but this doesn't mean we don't notice the tension in our presence. But the time has come to open up about our past, to talk about our families. There's been a lot of speculation about us, and we want to clarify once and for all the way things really are."

I nod as he gives me the look to direct the conversation where Iris wants to lead it.

"Damian, there's been a lot of talk about you and your father lately. How do you feel when people ask you about him?"

The smile on his lips is a mixture of melancholy and tenderness. His imposing size and hoarse, scratchy voice give him the appearance of a straight-shooter, someone who doesn't take anyone's bullshit. However, during this documentary, he's dropped his guard several times, giving a glimpse into the vulnerability that makes him human.

"Detached." It's a dry answer I didn't expect. He looks me straight in the eye and continues his explanation. "For me, my father died the night he killed my mother. The monster that was put in jail is someone I feel nothing for, not even anger, hatred, or disgust. In my heart, my father no longer exists."

"Have you ever visited him in prison? Has he ever tried to look for you?"

His gaze lowers to the hands in his lap for a few moments, almost searching for the right words, or trying to compose himself while emotions are gripping him.

"I never saw him after that night," he admits, looking up again. "I know he tried to contact me when we became famous, but our manager took care of it. I didn't want to know anything."

"Do you have any memories of him before that night?"

His lips curve in a melancholy smile, and complete silence falls inside this bus. Even the engine's hum in the background, a constant reminder we're traveling, seems to have fallen asleep.

"He took me to the stadium to watch baseball." His voice is almost a whisper, as if he remembered a particular episode. "I was little. I must have been five or six years old. We didn't have much money, but my father knew the guy in charge of maintenance. He let us in for free, and we stayed in the tunnel area where the players enter and leave the stadium. He wasn't always bad, a monster. Everything started falling apart when he lost his job and started in with the alcohol. Before that, he was smiling, he played with me, he went with my mother to the grocery store. I have several memories of him as a normal father, even loving...or maybe I was too small to notice the cracks in a man who later turned into a murderer. I don't know, and maybe I'll never find out."

I pause for a moment before moving on to Michael. They're all looking downward, Thomas torturing the zipper of his sweatshirt, Simon clenching his fists rhythmically, channeling his stress into a gesture that calms him.

The air fills with emotions we're all struggling to manage. I feel my own eyes pinching, the tears pressing to get out. I struggle to swallow through the lump in my throat and recognize it's part of this work I hate and love at the same time. I hate it because it tears your chest apart and makes you bleed empathy, but I love it because it brings you closer to the people in front of you like nothing else can. It's as if I have Damian's heart in my hands, and I can see it inside his soul.

"Michael, you also have no contact with your family anymore, if I'm not mistaken. Your father was in prison, right?" My voice comes out calm, but I keep it low for fear of ruining this moment when we're all alone with our thoughts.

Michael nods and tilts his head to the side. "Yes, let's just say it wasn't my passion to rob homes as a teenager. I was... urged to stay in the family business." His usual irony makes this moment seem less heavy than it really is. Michael's family story is perhaps the worst of them all.

"Would you tell us a bit about how you went from being a studious kid to breaking into houses to rob them?"

He shrugs and smiles. "I've always been curious to understand how things work. As a child, I loved taking things apart to study how they were made and then trying to reassemble them. I didn't always do it right, which resulted in beatings and punishments from my father. He had a heavy hand, so I started to prefer books to home experiments. I became more interested in computers and alarms, things my father didn't have the slightest knowledge of, so it was harder for him to blame me for breaking them."

"How did he find out that you could turn off alarms?"

A bitter smile appears on his lips. "In the motel he managed, the room where he kept the safe was protected by an alarm. One day, the burglar alarm went crazy. It kept ringing and not unlocking the door. The technicians weren't there yet, and my father had begun to lose his mind and blame my mother. To keep him from beating her, I went to the alarm panel, and five minutes later, it was turned off. From then on, he never left me alone. He would have beaten me to death if I hadn't done what he said."

"Your testimony put him in prison for three years for what he made you do."

"Yes, we didn't win the award for the best father-son relationship that year." He laughs bitterly. "He had too many important friends to stay behind bars longer." He lets the words die, and I know to stop with this line of questions.

Continuing would lead to uncovering other illicit activities of the man whom Michael would be forced to face in a court as a witness. This would have all too serious consequences. The media exposure this documentary will shed on Michael's family is enough to worry him about his possible future involvement in the affair.

"Simon, you grew up in a foster family, right? Did you ever know your parents?" This is the information most often rumored about when it comes to his past. Everyone builds stories and theories about what happened to his biological parents, but he's never told his version of the story.

"My mother had a drug problem. She was in and out of rehab. I never knew who my father was. I'm almost certain she didn't know either. Social services entrusted me to my maternal grandmother, but as much as she loved me, she couldn't take care of me. So at the age of seven, they put me in a foster family."

My heart clenches in my chest. As much as my mother has not been able to raise a daughter, at least I have always had a roof over my head and the semblance of affection, something Nicholas and Simon never had.

"Is it while living in that house that you started robbing banks?" I ask him with a lump in my throat.

Simon's past is like a punch in the stomach because it is inextricably linked to the person I have been living with for six years. I glance at Nicholas, who's looking at the monitor in front of him with far too much attention. His desire to avoid anyone's gaze at any cost is evident. Especially Simon's, who looks at him then lowers his eyes to his hands, squeezed into a vise when he is not reciprocated.

"Yes and no. The person who looked after us in the foster family was not a bad person. She always fed us, bought us clothes, and we could have gone to school if we wanted. She just never had the energy or the desire to raise all of us—sometimes five or six, other times as many as nine kids inside that house. She was always too tired to raise us properly, to give us direction."

"So it wasn't there that you met the people who introduced you to that life."

"They were neighbors. I always tried to ignore them, but when they started to set their eyes on the younger guys…" He looks again at Nicholas, who stubbornly refuses to return his gaze. "I decided to do what they said as long as they left the kids alone. I never thought my life could ever change. I thought that was my future until Michael helped me see another way."

He leans on Michael's shoulder and pushes him while his friend gives him one of his most sincere smiles. It's such an intimate gesture I can't help but wonder if there was anything between the two of them. I choose this moment to glance back at Nicholas, and I notice his gaze fixed on the two bandmates, pain running through his eyes that he can't hide. My heart clenches in my chest for him.

"Thomas, there's been a lot of speculation about your family's role in getting you in jail. Some even insinuate that they weren't able to raise such a problematic kid. Can you tell us your story?" My voice trembles a little because Thomas's is, perhaps, the saddest story of all. The melancholy smile on his face reveals a vulnerability that makes you want to hug him.

"Mine was the typical 'good family.' We weren't rich, but my parents gave me everything. They taught me what was right and wrong and to earn the respect that an honest man deserves. I betrayed their trust in the worst way and broke their hearts."

His voice trembles with emotion. He takes a moment to swallow, inhale thoroughly, and compose himself.

"My father died of a heart attack a few days after my sentence. My mother followed him shortly after of cancer. They were sweet people who gave me all the affection a child needs. I didn't have a childhood as hard as my bandmates. I had no justification or compulsion to make those choices. I knew what I was doing was wrong, but in my head, it was a heroic gesture for the girl I was in love with. I didn't want her to leave me, and I never fully understood the seriousness of my actions until they arrested me."

"Did you think it was just a kid's stunt?"

"I didn't think it was so bad I'd end up in jail. I knew the sentence drug dealers got was prison, but I didn't sell it. I didn't give it to addicts who then died from it. I transported it to rich people who didn't use it. In my naivety, I thought my sentence would be much milder than drug dealers who sell to addicts, endangering their lives. Plus, I wasn't the son of criminals. I was a kid who went to school, had excellent grades, and studied every day. I never thought I could end up in juvie. For me, the worst thing that could happen was losing my girlfriend. I didn't realize she'd never leave me because I was never her boyfriend in the first place. She used me."

I nod and let him take a little break before the question which I'm sure is like a punch in the gut.

"You also have a sister, don't you? You don't talk about her much. Do you want to tell us about her?" We discussed this question with Iris for twenty minutes, trying to determine if it was appropriate to include it since the topic upsets Thomas so much. In the end, we made him decide.

"I wish I could tell you that we have a beautiful relationship, that we have remained friends even as adults, that our families meet and celebrate on Thanksgiving, but that's not the case. She moved to another continent when our mother died, and I never heard from her. I hired a private investigator and found out that she's married and has three children. She wanted nothing to do with me anymore. I don't even know if my nieces or nephews are aware of my existence. I can't blame her. I destroyed our family, and there's nothing I can do to remedy the pain I've caused them."

At the end of his confession, no one breathes. No one says a word, only Damian, after a while, smiles sadly and breaks the silence. "And you, Haven, what kind of family do you have?" There's no malice in his voice. He knows who my mother is, he knows what happened to me, and he seems concerned about me.

"The kind you run away from…" I reciprocate his smile before looking away and staring at Nicholas as he turns off the camera.

**

"You have pizza?" Damian approaches Evan when he gets on our bus after we've stopped in the middle of nowhere. There's not even a rest area, only a parking lot in the mountains somewhere I have no clue about.

Their manager holds up the boxes before putting them on the table where we're sitting. "The charge to deliver these forty minutes outside of town cost more than the pizzas," he smiles.

"So? Did you do the interview?" His voice is calm, scrutinizing our faces. He knows today was one of those days when our hearts were put on the line.

"Yes, and I don't want to relive that for a long, long time," Damian admits. "I have no intention of being seen as that emotional all the time. I have a reputation, for fuck's sake." His tone is mocking, but his look is heavy with the strain everyone felt on this bus today.

"Did he cry?" Evan winks at me.

"Of course, he cried. After all, he's just a big teddy bear!" I tease him a little, trying to lighten the melancholy mood.

They all laugh and sit around the table, opening the pizza boxes, stuffing their faces as if they hadn't eaten for weeks. Evan sits with us and loosens his tie.

"Evan, forgive me for asking, but we've been in the middle of the mountains and locked in a bus since last night. Did you put on your suit and tie just to pick up the pizzas?" I ask and everyone else bursts out laughing, including him.

"No, today I had video calls and had to dress well, at least on top. I also had to wear pants, since I don't live alone on that bus."

Michael laughs again. "That's not true. You dress like this even when you're home alone watching TV. Emily's not shocked by seeing you walking around in your underwear. She sees us half-naked all the time without batting an eye. Admit that you're a die-hard," he teases him, and we believe Michael more than Evan's explanation.

"Stop looking at me like that. I don't change how I dress just because you're a motley bunch with no taste in clothing," he replies before grabbing a paper towel, opening it on his knees, and grabbing a slice of pizza. A gesture that makes everyone burst out laughing while he rolls his eyes.

Then Evan turns to me and says, "Haven, I almost forgot. Today your mother's manager contacted me and asked me for backstage passes to one of the concerts. I told him I'll let him know. It seemed strange that he hadn't asked you directly for them." He drops the bomb like it's nothing, but his look tells me he wants to know my relationship with her.

Nicholas and Simon's eyes are fixed on me, and they've stopped chewing their pizza.

"My mother doesn't even have my number. We haven't spoken to each other since I left home." At least, I don't think she has it. But the calls from the unknown number I've been receiving today now make much more sense.

"So if she contacts us, you don't want to see her?" Damian is actually interested.

"I prefer not to. I decided to cut off contact with her after the scandal with David broke out," I admit in a firm voice, but my heart hammers in my chest.

Everyone is watching me, perhaps hoping that I will explain more, yet no one dares to ask the question. Nicholas observes me carefully, knowing how delicate this topic is for me, but today, everyone has opened up to my questions, to the audience that follows them. It seems fair to explain why they have to protect me from my mother.

"I've never had a good relationship with her. She always pushed me toward career, work, parties with the big names in Hollywood, but she never acted like a mother. She pushed me into David's arms, making me believe that it was normal for a forty-five-year-old man to be interested in a seventeen-year-old girl. I always felt exposed, like an object to own, and she was the one who put me in the window. She told me I was a beautiful face, a beautiful body, that I didn't need to rely on my intelligence to survive, that I just had to say yes and open my legs, and everything would be fine. When she didn't defend me during David's scandal, I saw she had no interest in me as a daughter, only as a shiny jewel to show to the world that at that moment had lost its brilliance."

"Speaking of dysfunctional families…" Damian snorts in disbelief. "Welcome to the club. You can rest assured that your mother won't set foot in any of our concerts."

I smile and nod. "I know. I figured I'd found the right strays to tag along with." I wink at him, and he bursts out laughing, filling the bus with the lightness we needed.

They all go back to eating pizza, focusing on other topics to spare me more embarrassment. Evan studies me for a few seconds and then winks at me and bites into his slice. I wish I'd had a manager like him when I was younger. Many of the things I had to endure would never have happened.

I look at Simon and Nicholas, who are watching me with apprehension, but neither of them dares to speak, to ask questions. I know they'll leave them for later when the bus has emptied, and everyone returns to their families.

***

"Explain this thing you have with the sixth sense and the catastrophes because today was nothing short of scary." Simon smiles at me as he sits next to Nicholas and me on the back sofa. We just got back from dropping off the others at their buses.

I burst out laughing and welcome him in my arms when he snuggles up by my side.

"I don't know. I wake up some mornings and have a premonition. That's it. It's not something I can explain."

"I know, but your mother got in touch today, just when you had that feeling. Let me tell you, it's disturbing." He stretches out his hand and rests it on my belly before leaning out toward me to kiss my cheek.

"See? I'm not the only one who thinks so! At first, it freaked me out." Nicholas laughs.

"Drama queen," I retort.

"Does it happen often?" Simon is worried.

"Too much." Nicholas's eyebrow raises.

"Can you predict earthquakes too?"

Nicholas and I smile.

"I wish! Living in California, I would have become a millionaire."

Nicholas holds me in a hug and makes me sit on his lap while Simon gets closer and wraps us both in a hug. His face sinks into Nicholas's neck, and he kisses him delicately.

"If you had been a millionaire, I would never have met you. I'm glad you can't predict natural disasters." There's a hint of relief in his voice that tells me he's thought of such a thing.

Nicholas and I haven't had an easy life, but I'm grateful to have faced the difficulties and come this far, on this bus, with the two people I want to have in my life. Nicholas is the part of me that challenges me to take control of my life, while Simon has become the one who stands between me and my fears when I don't dare to ask for help. Both have become so important I can't even imagine life without them.

I close the distance with Nicholas and kiss him on the lips, then I lean out and lay my lips on Simon's. "Thank you for always being attentive to what happens to me. I'm glad to have someone who cares about me. Although I don't often say it out loud."

Nicholas sinks his face into the hollow of my neck while Simon moves a lock of my hair and caresses my cheek. They don't say anything, but being squeezed between the two of them is enough to make me forget my mother and the reason she got in touch with me again after almost ten years: to have a front-row seat in the glamorous life of the most popular celebrity at the moment.

CHAPTER 13
Simon

The fifth of July, with the scorching sun roasting our heads, is not the best time to be strolling the streets of Manhattan, but after months of tour buses, hotels, and precarious accommodations, at least we got to sleep in our own beds last night. We paused the tour for a few months because Faith is getting close to her delivery date, and we wanted to give her and Michael time to enjoy it without the stress of trying to find a hospital to give birth in on the road.

She followed us everywhere on tour, with her huge belly, never complaining, not even about the inconvenience of going to the bathroom or taking a shower on a bus. It's our turn to give back to the woman who made our friend the happiest man on the face of the earth.

And Michael is delighted to be a dad. You can tell by how he takes care of Levi that he'll be one of those hands-on parents who would do anything for their children. It's true that the family you grow up in can teach you what kind of adult to be, but it can also open your eyes to what kind of man you *don't want* to become. A valuable lesson in both cases.

I enter the building in Midtown and approach the list of names and floors of the businesses here. The security guard at the entrance glances at me but doesn't get closer, only checking my pass when I walk by his station next to the elevators. He smiles at me, motions for me to go ahead, and I step into the elevator, enjoying the slow scrolling of the numbers on the display as I go up for the radio interview.

The silence that surrounds me in this narrow space is almost pleasant. This morning when I got up, I told Nicholas and Haven to go ahead, that I would walk here when it was time for the interview. As much as I love being with them, I needed time alone in my house to check my plants and resume my morning ritual of watering them while I think about the day's appointments. It's a routine that helps me relax, put things in perspective, and recharge amid the chaos and emotions that sometimes overwhelm me on tour. If we hadn't had appointments in the city for the album's promotion, I would have retreated for a few days in Connecticut.

"Welcome. We thought you decided to abandon us!" Robert Harvest, the radio broadcaster of *Rocking America*, the station hosting us this morning, welcomes me with a smile. It's one of the most popular stations in the country, playing all kinds of rock music, from classics to newcomers like us. Because let's face it, we might be on top of the charts, but Mick Jagger is the undisputed God of Rock.

"I took my time walking here." I reach out to shake his hand.

Michael chuckles next to me. He knows the first day home after months on tour, I need to get back into my routine. I've always been like that, ever since we started touring.

"I bet you left late this morning because you watered the plants," he teases, giving me one of those smiles he hasn't flashed me in a long time.

"Of course!" I laugh and put my hand on his shoulder, squeezing it, a familiar gesture I've missed for too long.

I glance at Haven and Nicholas filming our exchange, and I can't decipher their expressions. They're both relaxed, but the smiles are missing from their faces. It's strange how now that we've returned to New York, and we're no longer forced into the bus together, things have become uncertain between us. I stayed home this morning; they came to work. Just one day in real life, outside the small space of the tour bus, seems to have put a distance between us and feels heavier than I expected. This is real life out here, not the fantasy world on a bus where anything's possible, like a three-way relationship that actually works.

"Shall we sit down? We have time to settle in before we go live." Robert's voice distracts me from my thoughts.

I follow them inside a studio with a glass wall that looks out into the hallway. A semicircular counter with four microphones is positioned in front of the console. It's a simple set-up, no frills. On one side, you're looking at a hallway where passersby get a glimpse of the show; on the opposite wall, a large window faces the street and a similar building to this one made of concrete and glass. No spectacular views of the city from this studio.

We take a seat around the table: Damian in the middle, Thomas and Michael on either side of him, and me next to Michael, my back to the hallway where Haven and Nicholas are filming behind the glass. I almost breathe a sigh of relief because today it would be difficult to stay focused on this live broadcast if my thoughts wander to the questions filling my head since this morning. *What the hell are we doing? Where is*

this relationship going?

After a few minutes of small talk, the "On Air" sign above the speaker's head lights up red, and all my attention is focused on the microphone suspended in front of my face.

"We're here this morning with the Jailbirds, the biggest rock band of this generation. Welcome, guys."

A chorus of greetings rises from our side of the table.

"You've been in juvie, you've come out of it, you've signed with one of the biggest record companies in the world, you've left, you've founded your own record company, and now you're on a world tour with a television crew shooting a documentary about your career. You're not even thirty years old yet. Who did you sell your souls to get all of this?"

The amused smile on Robert's face puts you at ease. He's sixty years old and wearing a Rolling Stones t-shirt with a black leather vest and ripped jeans. He looks like he walked right out of one of those rock movies where all the characters are exaggerated caricatures of themselves. But somehow, the outfit works on him.

We all smile. Damian chuckles and responds first. "We've always been ambitious kids. I mean, not everyone ends up in juvie so young." He pulls a laugh from our host, then continues. "This business moves at the speed of light. One day you're a complete stranger, and the next, your YouTube video is viral, and a hundred million people know your name overnight. We had some good songs at the beginning but no way into the music industry. We lucked out meeting our manager—he's the key to our success. He knows this industry well and has guided us through all the noise toward a single goal: becoming the greatest. It's to his credit that we've come this far, because these days making good music isn't enough. You also have to have the right connections."

Robert nods, interested in our stories. It's a breath of fresh air to find someone in his line of work with a genuine passion for music. "It's true—the ones behind the scenes are often just as important as the ones on stage. But the story behind your first meeting is extraordinary. Will you tell us how it happened?"

Thomas smiles and takes the question. He's more attached to that event than all of us because just before meeting Evan, Iris fell into his life for the first time.

"It all started when the band he was supposed to check out gave him the wrong address and wrote West instead of East 145th Street. Instead of ending up in the Bronx, he ended up in Harlem, where we were playing. We've always called it destiny because what are the chances that in a city like New York, two places with the same address have a band playing live at the same time—one in the east, the other in the west?"

Robert is fascinated by our story and shakes his head in disbelief. "Did you ever learn which band your manager was supposed to go and listen to? They must have kicked themselves for that mistake."

Michael nods and smiles, no doubt remembering the day we ventured there to find out who we'd stolen the place from. "It was a band of kids that eventually broke up. We tried to contact them, but they used stage names, and we never managed to reach them. Evan was supposed to go to a small rehearsal room in the basement of a house. We tried to ask the owner if he remembered who was there that day, but he said at least seven or eight groups at a time go in and out of there and he didn't remember everyone's names. Some of them he never even saw in person. When Evan tried to contact them a few years later, the band had broken up."

The man shakes his head and smiles, a little amused, but there is a vein of disbelief in his expression. "That's why I tell my kids to check even the smallest details before doing something important, because a tiny mistake can change your whole life. Today you're here to promote your album, 'Back to Jail,' released a few months ago, and from day one, it's been number one on the charts without a hint of going down. Did you expect this for your first album released on your own record label?"

Damian inhales deeply and crosses his arms over his chest. "In all honesty, we didn't know what to expect. Of course, we had a PR team monitoring the promotional campaigns, verifying the data around the public's response, but they're just theories until you go live with the release. We felt like the fans appreciated what we were doing, but we were cautious in predicting the charts and the success our album would have. For us, the most important thing was to put out an album with *our* record company. It was already a success because we had full control over our careers for the first time ever. We decided on every single aspect of this album, and it's been the biggest hit ever for us. But dreams don't pay the bills, and I confess we were a little worried about how much it would keep us afloat in terms of income after the leap of faith we took. Thank goodness, our fans are the best and have shot our music way up in the rankings."

Robert watches us for a few seconds in silence, then smiles and nods in approval. "Finally, someone who's open to talking about these things. Everyone always tends to emphasize the artistic side without ever speaking honestly about the economic aspects of an album's flop."

I smile and nod and, for the first time, respond. "The artistic aspect is important. If fans don't like an album, it definitely makes us ask questions. You spend months giving your best in the recording studio. No one wants to put out an album that sucks. Refine the details, emphasize the exact sound you have in mind, work with the producer to bring out the best in the songs you've written, sweat, and cried over for weeks. A review that crushes your album hurts. You get angry because others can't see what *you* see in your work, but you survive. If an album is a flop, especially for a young record company like ours, it can mean that there will be no other releases. The production of a record is an expensive process, and at some point, you have to set aside the romantic side and think about the accounting."

"Long live honesty!" laughs Robert and my companions with him. "But speaking of the romantic side, you paused the tour for a few months to give birth to a new life. And this time, we're not talking about music but about a real baby. Michael, is it true that you are about to become a dad for the second time? Is it a boy or a girl?"

Michael's eyes light up with sweetness every time we talk about this pregnancy. He transforms completely. "Who would have thought I'd be the first to start a family? Everyone thought it would be Simon, but he's the only single one left." He winks and smiles at me. It's a joke my bandmates always make, but the truth is it kills me. I smile, look down, and glance behind me where Nicholas and Haven are. It only takes one glimpse at their faces to understand that not even Michael would believe this relationship could work.

"Joking aside, we don't know if it's a boy or a girl. I can't wait for these next five days to pass quickly, so I can meet my other kid. Levi is thrilled to be an older brother." He's delighted, sitting across from the smiling face of the host while my mind leaves this topic and jumps ahead to my future, where there are no children, marriages, or indescribable happiness like my friend's.

***

"Evan, what are you doing here?" Michael's voice is agitated.

We're all worried when we see the smiling face of our manager as soon as we leave the studio where we did the broadcast.

"A car is waiting for you. Levi called me fifteen minutes ago, saying Faith was having contractions. We took her to the Manhattan Clinic, and now he's there with her. I think she's in labor," he explains with a calm that none of us can believe.

Michael pales and leans on me for support. It's the first time I've seen him at a loss for words and utterly unprepared to handle the situation.

"But there are still several days before the due date..." Damian seems as agitated as I am. I glance around and find everyone looking disoriented. The only one at the height of his mental faculties is Evan, who seems all too reserved for the situation.

"I think this is one of those things not even Emily could have planned." He chuckles and pushes us toward the elevators. "There are three cars ready to take us to the clinic."

When we get into the vehicles, I'm not at Michael's side to encourage him for the first time in my life; I'm in the third car with Haven and Nicholas. My friend doesn't even seem to notice, and on the one hand, I feel relieved.

"Everything okay? You seem shaken." Nicholas takes my hand and squeezes it as he looks at me with concern.

"Yes." I hope the smile plastered on my face seems sincere enough.

***

The private clinic that welcomed us has rooms large enough to hold a rock band and our whole crew. While Michael and Levi are in the room equipped with a tub big enough for Faith to have a water birth, all of us wait in the next room in complete silence for two hours. In addition to the band, there's Evan, Emily, Iris, Lilly, Nicholas, Haven, and even Max. Even though it's a private clinic where the visiting rules are a bit more flexible, the head nurse frowned at the sight of all these people until Damian opened his wallet and bought three different cases of snacks and drinks for the nurse's break room. They let us stay only if we remained silent and didn't wander around the building.

It was two hours of poorly-stifled cries from Faith, "Oh

my God!" from Michael, and "I can't look! What the heck?" from Levi. At one point, Iris went in to ask if he'd rather leave the room since it's a very delicate, intense time and might upset him, but he stayed by Faith's side, clinging to her hand with eyes full of that pride rarely seen in such young people. Since the adoption was finalized, all his insecurities have slipped away, and he's become a kid who's determined to do great things in life. Staying close to the one who became a real mother to him is one of them.

"I will never give birth. I swear." Lilly's whisper leaves her lips after a slightly louder cry from Faith.

In all honesty, we're all tense and wondering if it's normal for a woman to shout like that when giving birth. The footage Haven and Nicholas are getting right now would be perfect for a commercial about condoms. No one would dare have sex without a condom if they heard those ear-splitting cries on the other side of this door.

Damian tightens his grip on Lilly and pulls her to himself, kissing her forehead. I don't think he can even imagine inflicting this torture on the woman he loves. He seems to be traumatized by this experience.

After a last miserable wail followed by an endless moment of silence, we hear the cry of an infant who's come to life. Weak by comparison to the mother's screams, but strong enough to hear through the door. The silence we've managed to maintain until this moment is interrupted by sighs of happiness and shouts of joy. Everyone is standing, excited, except me.

As soon as it settles in my brain that this moment is real, that Michael has become a father for the second time, a grip tightens my stomach until it hurts on a physical level. It's as if an explosion in the center of my chest is spreading to all my internal organs, hitting them one by one. Without even thinking, I turn around and leave, walking quickly down the hallway until I reach the doors that open to the fire escape.

I inhale deeply, but the warm Manhattan air struggles to get into my lungs. A desperate hiss escapes my lips as air comes out of my mouth and hiccups shake my chest. I'm not crying, no tears are running down my cheeks, but emotions come out of my body with such violence I have to bend over until I collapse to the ground, resting my forehead on the cold concrete of the wall in front of me.

A warm hand on my back is my only foothold with reality. "Breathe." Evan's whisper barely reaches my ears. "Breathe."

A breath of air enters my lungs and it's like coming up to the surface after a long sleep.

Evan stays silent, continuing to massage my back with slow gestures until my breathing becomes regular. "Can you sit?"

I realize I'm on my knees with my arms and head leaning against the wall in front of me. I nod and accept his help to turn around and sit on the concrete landing.

"Do you want to talk about it?"

I shake my head and stare at the closed door in front of me for some time until I regain some clarity. "And say what? That I'm a bastard for feeling suffocated because my best friend has a child instead of being happy for him?" My voice is hoarse.

Evan sits next to me. "You're not a bastard. Everyone reacts to the birth of a child differently. You're going through a period where you don't feel you belong to anyone, and this baby coming takes from you the one person who's been your constant friend for years."

"They're all moving on without me. I feel stuck in the present while they're all thinking about the future. They're walking away and I can't move."

Evan remains silent for a long time, and when I turn to him, he's frowning and thoughtful. "Are you sure you're stuck in the present? Because it seems to me that with Haven and Nicholas there could be a future."

An exasperated sigh leaves my lips as I rest my head on the cold concrete behind me.

"What future is there for a relationship like ours? It works inside a bus while we're on tour, but it can't survive in the real world."

"Why not? Of course, it won't be a conventional relationship, but I don't see why that's a problem."

I study him. Does he honestly think so, or is he just reassuring me? "Can you imagine if Haven ever gets pregnant? Who would be the father? Who would enter the delivery room with her? Do you really think people wouldn't have something to say about the whole situation? They may decide to take our children away from us, and I know what it's like to grow up in a foster family, without real love, feeling abandoned every minute of my childhood."

Evan shakes his head and smiles. "For one thing, you don't even know if you want to spend the rest of your life with these people, if you're even compatible. Second, if Haven becomes pregnant, you'll think about who goes into the delivery room when the time comes. Unless she has a difficult pregnancy, she may simply give birth at home like many women do, in the comfort of your home, with both of you supporting her and no one judging you. Third, they gave a son to Michael, a former drug addict with a juvie background and the wild life of the rock star. Do you genuinely believe they would take a kid away from a loving family? Social services wants the child's well-being, not necessarily a two-parent family." He sighs and places a hand on mine, squeezing it.

"Is it so wrong to want a normal family without so many complications?"

"Simon, you're obsessed with the idea of a traditional family because you've never had one. For years, your dream was to have a father and a mother who loved you, and you're having a hard time separating yourself from that idea because you think it betrays the dream you had as a kid. Don't you realize you're already moving on with Nicholas and Haven? Don't you realize how happy you are with them? You've been lucky enough to meet not one but two people you can imagine a happy life with. Enjoy the moment and see if this can really be your future. The longer you wait, the more you'll regret all the missed moments you spent mulling over whether it was right or not. You can't get back lost time."

"Can you imagine what people will say?"

Evan smiles at me and nudges my shoulder. "That you're a rock star and live like one. You're lucky to have a job where unconventional behavior is considered part of the territory. Imagine if you were the President of the United States and fell in love with them. You'd have to choose between your career and private life."

I watch him get up, and I feel a little lighter. Evan can make you see things from a point of view you hadn't considered. "Thank you."

He shrugs and smiles at me as he grabs the door handle, ready to go back in. "Stay out here a bit longer until the color comes back to your face. Otherwise, you'll make everyone worry."

An hour later, the door opens again and Michael walks out to sit next to me. "Evan told me where to find you."

I nod, swallowing before I say anything. "I needed air. Emotions took over."

He smiles at me and nods. "I sensed that."

"So? Boy or girl?"

Michael bursts out laughing and throws his head back. "Girl."

I burst out laughing too. "She's going to drive you crazy. You know that, right? You're going to go batshit on every guy who hits on her," I tease.

"I know." He laughs, putting his hands on his face. Nothing could take that smile away, so vulnerable and at the peak of his happiness.

"What did you call her?"

"Liberty."

I smile. I knew they would choose a meaningful name.

"I'm terrified," he whispers to me after a long silence.

"You'll be a good father." I'm sure of that. Seeing him with Levi gives me this certainty.

"How can you say that?"

"Because I watch you every day, and maybe you don't realize it, but you already are a good father to Levi."

"He's grown up. He knows how to care for himself. Liberty is…microscopic, defenseless. I'm afraid I'll break her."

I shake my head and smile at him. "The fact that Levi doesn't depend on you for the most basic things doesn't mean he doesn't need your support. That kid's been deprived of affection for so many years that you're reviving him with all your love now. You're shaping his character, his future. You make him feel loved and give him the confidence he needs to become a decent adult. You'll learn to change Liberty's diapers. That's not so hard, but the love she'll get from you, Faith, and Levi will make her a wonderful adult."

Michael smiles and looks down. "Do you know how wise you are?" He looks back at me.

"Someone has to be. You're all half-criminals," I tease him with an old joke that dates back to the days when Joe scolded us because we were always in some kind of trouble he had to fix.

He smiles and studies me for an infinite time, perhaps trying to understand what's going through my head. There was a time when we understood each other without speaking. Now I'm not so sure anymore.

"Are you okay?" he asks after an eternity.

No, I'm not okay, but I need you to figure it out for yourself because I can't talk about it. "Yes."

He gets up, dusts off his pants, and walks to the door. Before opening it, he turns to me again. "I miss you, Simon."

My heart hammers in my chest. "I miss you too," I whisper before seeing him disappear behind the door, which closes again, taking all the air from my lungs.

CHAPTER 14
Simon

Getting back on tour almost six weeks after Liberty's birth is so intoxicating it almost makes my head spin. We arrived in Charlotte, North Carolina this morning and immediately locked ourselves in the stadium, without taking the time to enjoy the views of the city. The excitement is almost like returning to school after summer break. The roadies have all spent time with family or taken a vacation, and all have something to share. They're gathered in small groups, laughing and joking, invigorated by a break that provided a short rest from the stress of the tour.

"Twenty minutes and we'll be ready for soundcheck," John, the technician who takes care of my instruments, tells me when I pass him in the hallway pushing a crate.

"Thanks, has anyone told the others?" I ask as I can't find anyone, not even Haven and Nicholas.

He shakes his head and shrugs. I smile, wave at him, and try to call Evan, who doesn't answer.

The stadium for tonight's concert is enormous, the hallways and rooms running all around it resembling a labyrinth. Some of the doors have signs, but most don't, complicating my search. The third time I open one full of crates labeled with our band name, my frustration becomes more evident, and I slam it.

"Nervous today?" Nicholas's voice makes me turn toward him.

I rub my face, aware that even the most stupid things make me irritated lately. "Do you have any idea where everyone is? I can't find anyone in this maze," I explain more calmly.

"I think Liberty wouldn't stop crying, so Faith called Michael, who panicked and made the others nervous. They're all on their bus trying to figure out what's going on." He smiles, shrugging his shoulders, and a sarcastic laugh escapes me. I can't hide my irritation.

"She's a six-week-old baby. Crying is what they do, right?" My question comes out more annoyed than I meant it.

I tried to advise Michael that a newborn should stay at home, where it's quiet, not in a bus driving across the country, but he won't listen to reason. He wants his family with him and threatened to leave the tour. I understand he wants to see his children grow up, but Levi is one thing, he's fifteen and finds this life exciting. A newborn who needs constant care and attention is a whole other can of worms.

Nicholas frowns and narrows his mouth in a hard line. He grabs my hand and drags me into a hidden corner behind some crates by the metal staircase that leads to the stage. You'd have to bend down and look this way from the stairs to see me leaning against the wall, him resting a hand on my face, gently stroking my cheek.

I close my eyes and enjoy the contact with him.

"Will you please tell me why you've become so short-tempered since that little girl was born?" He gets straight to the point, forcing me to open my eyes and get lost in his.

"Have you noticed that you know where all my friends are while I'm wandering around like an idiot looking for them?"

Nicholas frowns. "I was in the same room, that's why I know. If I'd been somewhere else, I'd be asking the same question."

I shake my head and look down. He can't understand what I'm feeling. "But I'm part of the band. Did anyone call or text me? We have a soundcheck in less than twenty minutes, and no one told me about this delay. It's like I don't exist." The last sentence comes out in a whisper.

Nicholas reaches out his hand and puts it around my waist, getting closer. An all-too-close distance. If someone saw us, there'd be no doubt about the kind of relationship we have. My heart hammers against my chest.

"She's the first baby girl born into this group. None of you has a clue how to handle her. Every little worry is magnified in the frenzy of these first months. Everyone will come to their senses and settle into a new routine, things will return to normal." He tries to reassure me, but he doesn't know his words hurt me even more.

Like before. "Do you know what my life was like before you and Haven?"

He shakes his head slightly, and I notice the worry making its way into his eyes. I never told him that while he and Haven were playing tourists around New York during the tour break, I never got a single message or call from my friends. When I said no to their invitations to join them sightseeing, it wasn't because my band wanted me in the studio, like I said, but because I was waiting, hoping Michael would call me to go see his daughter. I'm not like Damian or Thomas who can just show up without an invitation. I need to feel welcome when I ring a friend's doorbell. I desperately need him to reach out to me.

"Until less than two years ago, we were all single. The four of us were the first people we thought of when we had to make a phone call or send a message. We hung out together, we were at one or the other's house, it was just us, and we were enough. Then out of the blue, they all found a partner, Michael even has two children, and I became last on their list. I'm not saying I can't stand their families. On the contrary, I love them. But do you have any idea how lonely you feel in this business? I don't blame my friends, I would behave the same way if I were in their shoes, but that doesn't change the fact that I sometimes feel sidelined."

Nicholas's eyes keep me glued to him. His hand slips under my shirt and touches my skin. He gets closer and rests his forehead on mine. "You have me, and you have Haven. Aren't we enough for you?" he whispers on my lips before kissing me gently.

My hands rest on his hips, and I drag him in. I need to feel his body against mine. His warmth envelops me and erases the emptiness I feel inside.

"You have Haven. I'm just the third wheel," I answer breathlessly.

Nicholas does not respond to my provocation, not in words. He pushes me against the wall and grabs my face with both hands before reclaiming my mouth, sliding his tongue in, and possessing mine. A moan escapes my lips, but he swallows it and returns one of his own. The kiss is frenetic, one of those that turn your senses upside down and shake you to the core.

I squeeze his hips and pull him to me as if afraid of him suddenly disappearing. I'm terrified of waking up one day and not finding him again, like that first night in prison, when I called his name, but there was no one to answer me, only kicks and punches waiting for me. I didn't do it again. I never again pronounced his name within those walls.

My erection presses against his, and the sensation is so intoxicating I can't stop my hands from slipping under his shirt in search of his skin, the muscles that move under my fingers. I love everything about Nicholas's body, every single inch of him excites me so much that he sends me to heaven...or hell, depending on your point of view.

His hands slip into my hair and squeeze it in a grip that's both painful and pleasant. His chest presses against mine, his beard tickles my lips as one kiss becomes two, then three, and I start to miss the air, but I don't care. I'd rather die of suffocation than let go of his taste, heat, and this electricity between our bodies.

One of his hands slips over my erection and grabs it over my jeans. A growl of pleasure escapes my chest, rises in my throat, and turns into an animalistic grunt that bounces between the concrete walls and the crates of this cramped place. Nicholas takes it as an invitation to get closer and presses his body against mine, making me feel the man behind the clothes in all his glorious presence.

Nicholas pulls his mouth away from mine to catch his breath, but I'm not ready to let him go. I bite his lower lip until his hand slips from my hair to my neck, grabbing it in a firm grip that makes me let go. His thumb slides over my jaw and caresses me. His eyes are on fire, the desire burns in his chest as much as mine, and I'm sure I'd have no escape if we were on the bus. If we were alone, he would take everything from me, body and soul, and I would let him.

During the break from the tour, I distanced myself from him and Haven, taking time to be alone and figuring out what I wanted. I needed to be on my own to put my thoughts in order, but the truth is, when I got on that bus again, everything became confused again. I can't think logically when I'm with them, which scares me to death. I went so far as to make a list of pros and cons of the three-way relationship, and, as long as I was locked in my Manhattan room, I found logical and valid justifications both to continue and to let it go, without coming to a clear conclusion. But in the tight spaces of the tour, everything has become chaotic and full of feelings so strong they bring any reason I have to its knees.

A slight knock on the crates and someone clearing his throat is the bucket of icy water that brings me back to reality.

I shift my gaze and meet Evan's. "Sorry to bother you. Simon, we're ready for soundcheck." His words are firm, there is no rebuke or even judgment in them, but the wave of shame that engulfs me is devastating.

"I'm coming. Give me a minute."

Evan nods, smiles at me, then turns around and leaves.

When I look back at Nicholas, I find him confused. His hand slips from my throat to my chest, and with a sharp gesture, I push him away. How did I get to the point of letting myself go like this in a public place where anyone could see us? When I pass him to go to the stage, he grabs my arm and makes me turn around. The wounded look on his face is a stab in the chest.

"Aren't you even going to say anything to me?"

"We're lucky it was Evan who discovered us. Can you imagine if someone else had? Do you have any idea of the rumors it would've started?"

"Are you ashamed to be seen kissing a man, or is your disgust specifically about me?" His stern expression reveals all the anger he's feeling.

"I don't have a problem being caught kissing a man. It's being caught kissing an engaged man while his woman is nearby. Do you really believe people think Haven's okay with this? They'd brand me as the guy who sabotaged your perfect relationship to take you away from her. I'd be the bad guy," I hiss between my teeth as my anger grows and his gives way to guilt.

It's hard to look at his suffering face without my chest contracting, making me want to hold him in my arms. So I give him my back and leave without turning around.

***

For the first time since we started filming this documentary, I find myself not looking for Nicholas and Haven during the concert. The show is a succession of songs, jokes by Damian, and Michael behaving like an idiot and making our fans laugh. The usual show that's been comforting for years and tonight I can't stand it.

The moment the last song ends and the lights go down, I pull off my bass and hand it to John, who looks at me in confusion. I'm always the last one to leave the stage, but this time I can't get off fast enough.

Damian grabs me by the shoulder, forcing me to turn around. "We're stopping to have a beer just outside the city. You coming?" His expression is cautious, as if trying to determine if something's wrong.

"No, I'm tired. I have a headache. I'm going to sleep." I don't even try to smile at him. All I want is to be alone.

"Don't you want to stop to take a shower?"

"No. I told you, I have a headache and I want to go to sleep." Damian raises his hands, and his eyebrows arch in surprise. He doesn't say anything, but it's clear he didn't expect such a rude answer.

I turn around to leave and find Michael and Evan watching us along with Nicholas, more distant and secluded with Haven, who casts a worried look at me. When I pass by our manager, our eyes meet and I see obvious concern on his tense face, but I don't stop to give explanations. I'm suffocating in here.

Once on the bus, I strip off my clothes and slip into the shower. I inhale with my mouth open, trying to open the lungs that feel so constricted inside my chest. I feel like I'm choking. I've never felt so vulnerable in all my life. The magnitude of what happened today presses on my chest and prevents me from breathing. I'm terrified of someone finding out what we're doing, not so much because I'm having an affair with a man, but because if a scandal breaks out over this relationship, I'd be alone again.

"Simon, are you okay?" Haven's voice invades my thoughts until I open my eyes and realize I haven't moved an inch, the water falling down on my body isn't washing away the fear.

"Go away, please."

"You know I won't. We're forced to share this space for a while. Let's clear this up before the air gets too heavy, okay? We're not kids anymore." Her tone is calm but firm.

She's right. I can't hide in this shower for the rest of the tour like I did during the break in Manhattan. I turn off the water, grab a towel that I tie at my waist, and step into the living room. Nicholas is sitting on the couch and doesn't even look at me. Haven is leaning against the small kitchen on the opposite side, arms crossed over her chest and a serious look on her face.

"What do you want to talk about?" The irritation in my voice is a clear sign I already know the answer.

Nicholas smiles, baffled, shaking his head and raising his face to the ceiling. Haven scowls even more. "Really? Do you want to play this game?" Her voice is tense, her hand nervously pushes a lock of pink hair behind her ear.

"What do you want me to say? Tell me what you want from me."

Nicholas bursts into a sarcastic laugh and, for the first time, looks angry and hurt. "Today, you almost got me to fuck you in a corner near the stage and then you threw me aside like I was your dirty little secret. Want something from you? What do *you* want from us? We welcomed you into our relationship, showed you we want to have something more with you, and you're *ashamed* of us? You disappeared during your break in Manhattan, so we stepped back and gave you room to clarify your feelings. Decide what you want, Simon," he finishes, yelling, and his words make me feel both angry and ripped open.

"I don't want to let everybody know, okay? I don't want it to be public domain. Is that too much to ask? I don't feel ready for that step," I reply, just as angry.

Haven moves from the cabinet and approaches a few steps. I can see she's hurt, and it's making me sick. "Because you're ashamed of us? Of the relationship? Of what?"

A vein of despair in her voice breaks me, and a wave of emotions pours uncontrollably from my chest.

"Because when the shit hits the fan in the media about this story, you'll see how hard it is to have a relationship under that kind of scrutiny. Our relationship will fall apart, and you'll have Nicholas, he'll have you, and I'll be alone again. I'll be left behind like all the other times in my life. First my father, then my mother, then my grandmother, Nicholas, and now my friends. No one stays in my life, everyone always leaves, and I'm tired of being alone!" I shout with all the breath I have in my body, the feelings I've been carrying explode out of my chest and give voice to a void I've not been able to fill for years.

I collapse on the couch, emptied, with my chest ripped apart by pain and my stomach twisted into a knot I can't untangle. I'm tired of fighting.

Nicholas and Haven approach, eyes shining with emotion and determination on their faces. They don't say anything but sit next to me, holding me in a hug that makes me tremble.

Their hands caress my chest, my face. With their lips, they savor my skin until they reach my lips. Haven breaks that silence with a whisper next to my ear. "We're not going anywhere, Simon. We're not going anywhere. We're here with you every single step of the way. You're not alone. You won't be ever again, you have us, never forget that."

Her lips move along my jaw until they get to mine, and she sinks her tongue into my mouth. It's a kiss that nails you to the spot, not letting you escape. Nicholas's rough hands slide toward the knot of the towel and open it, leaving me naked and vulnerable once again.

It's like this with the two of them: they strip off my clothes and all the layers of protection I've built around myself over the years to survive. Every day it's a struggle to protect my heart from being more and more exposed, vulnerable, and at the mercy of the feelings these two bring out of me. It's an experience I'm not used to. As a child, I was never hugged or caressed, no gestures of affection that lasted more than a few moments.

In the darkness of our room, Nicholas was the only one who gave me the human warmth that only a thirteen-year-old boy can give: sincere, inexperienced, genuine, vulnerable. As soon as I got used to that heat that warmed my nights and made them less terrifying, it was torn away from me, and with it my ability to open my heart to another person.

Their hands, their lips slip on my skin, their tongues wash away some of my fears, but it's not enough to convince my heart that everything will be fine. I'm here, naked on this couch, while they're dressed. It's not just a layer of cloth that separates us. It's six years of a solid relationship they've built together, to the point of allowing another person to join it without endangering it. They're the strong, confident, tenacious ones. I'm the naked one who steps in between, occupying a space that doesn't feel like mine.

I close my eyes and abandon myself to their attention, to their tongues that alternate in my mouth, but I feel millions of miles away. I'm on another planet, looking down on a naked, helpless, vulnerable boy who's being pleasured by two people entirely clothed. Two people in tune, who love each other, know each other so well they don't need language to understand each other. They have a silent conversation I don't understand, I'm a stranger to it. Like a tourist in a foreign country whose language I can't speak and whose beauty I can only admire without really being a part of it.

CHAPTER 15
Haven

Nicholas and I get off the bus early in the morning without crossing Simon's path. After last night, however, we don't know if it's because he's still sleeping or if he's avoiding us. After confessing his fears yesterday, and our attempt to make him feel included, Simon got up from the couch saying he was tired and wanted to go to sleep and then locked himself in his room. For the first time in months, we didn't sleep all together. Even during the break in Manhattan, although he preferred to be alone during the day, we still went to sleep together in the evening, savoring the intimacy of cuddling and respecting his will to not go any further.

I knock on the door of Thomas and Iris's bus, which is parked like ours in a service area for a break. The redhead, Thomas's girlfriend, opens it and welcomes us in for the interview we're doing with Thomas and, in this case, also with her.

"Come in. We just finished having breakfast. Do you want coffee?" She smiles at us as she steps aside to let us in.

Their bus is very similar to ours, with the living area on the first level and the rooms upstairs. Thomas is already sitting on the couch, ready for our conversation, his eyes fixed on the phone. Damian and Lilly are in Michael's bus to give us the space we need to shoot this interview.

"A coffee would be perfect, thank you." Nicholas's response beats me to it.

"Good morning." The drummer's curious eyes rest on us.

"Good morning. Ready for today's interview? It's the first time we've included Iris." I sit across the table from him while Nicholas mounts the cameras and Iris hands us our coffees before sitting down next to Thomas.

"I don't know if I'll ever be ready for this. I'm used to being on the other side of the lens." The grimace on her face is comical, and Thomas bursts out laughing, wrapping his arm around her shoulders and pulling her in for a hug.

When Nicholas has the cameras ready, I start with the questions we've all agreed on and discussed. She wasn't happy about appearing in the documentary, but she's a smart girl and knows she'll have to give her version of the facts to paint a complete and honest picture for the fans who will watch it.

"Why did you decide to be a paparazzo? How did you get started?"

She smiles at me and looks down, almost intimidated by the red light that indicates we're recording. "One day, I was out and about in Manhattan taking pictures of people, of artists performing around the area, and I came across a group of photographers who were taking pictures of some actresses on a break on the set of a movie. Nothing special, but it was rumored that one of them had left her husband for another actor who worked with her on that film. The photographers were stationed there to capture the evidence of the affair."

She stops for a second, looks up at Thomas, then lowers her gaze to her crossed fingers resting in front of her on the table. She feels ashamed, and it's not an emotion you often see on Iris's face. She's a proud, determined woman. It must not have been easy for her to choose that path. Thomas smiles and encourages her with a nod, and she inhales and then continues.

"One of the guys stationed there saw me with the camera in my hand, unsure of what to do, and encouraged me to try. In the beginning, I was hesitant. I didn't like what they were doing, but I gave in to curiosity. I tried and got one of the best photos of a stolen kiss I've ever taken. I had proof of that betrayal. The photographers teased me, calling it beginner's luck. They said if I submitted it to one of their contacts, I'd get paid—a lot. And I did. I received fifteen hundred dollars, which I desperately needed and accepted. From then on, when I needed money, I would go out and take pictures of celebrities."

She clenches her lips between her teeth in a grimace that's not a great look for the camera but obviously shows her discomfort.

"How did you take the news that she was a paparazzo? You already had a relationship at that point, right?" I turn to Thomas, who nods and smiles.

"Very badly." He laughs and rubs his hand over his face and then glances at Iris, who is blushing. "When you're a celebrity, you're always questioning why people are around you. Whether it's because of your fame, your money, or because they're actually interested in getting to know you. When I found out, I felt stabbed in the back. I had opened my heart to her and believed she'd used me. Those weren't the best times." He still laughs, nervous, but then breathes and gets a hold of himself.

I almost see remorse in the way he looks at Iris. I don't

know the details of their story, but if I had to guess, I'd say he didn't treat her well when he found out. I think back to how I spoke to the paparazzi when I encountered them, and a sense of guilt toward Iris stabs in my chest. It's hard to believe this was her job for so long. She's sweet, sensitive, and in my mind, it's incomprehensible that she used to do something so distasteful.

"But Iris was able to regain your trust, yes? After the video in which she took all the blame went viral. How did you react?"

Thomas laughs and shakes his head. I believe he still hasn't gotten over what his girlfriend did. "I was terrified. On the one hand, I was sure she hadn't betrayed us, and I watched her career collapsing with horror. No one had ever done something like that for me, and I was ecstatic and terrified at the same time. I wanted to stop it, to make that video disappear from the Internet, but our old record company had already made it viral. I've never felt so helpless," he admits, looking at Iris as she shrugs and reciprocates his loving gaze with a shy smile.

"Iris, were you aware that this video would blow up years of work on your blog?"

"Yes. It was a conscious decision to destroy my career to save theirs."

"Was it a difficult choice?"

She shakes her head and smiles. "It was the easiest step I've ever taken in my life. If they hadn't made it public that they'd been in the juvie, there was a reason, and it wasn't my job to reveal their past. It was for Thomas and the others to decide when to tell their story to the world, and I had to respect their timing. The only way I could remedy the damage I couldn't control was to undermine the credibility of that news, and the most effective way to do that was to spin a story about how I had made the whole thing up. I knew that video would destroy my credibility."

I nod and study her for a few moments. How could such a selfless person do such a disgusting job?

"Thomas, your confession saved Iris and the blog."

He nods seriously. "We needed to come out with it. It's difficult to live everyday life when you're hiding news of that magnitude. You can't have serious relationships with a partner, you can't have deep friendships with anyone, because those relationships are all based on a lie, and when it comes out—because it's not a question of *if* but *when*—they're bound to fall apart." He glances at Iris and breathes a sigh of relief.

"Iris, how did you take Thomas's confession? Was it difficult to accept such a troubled past?"

Iris wrinkles her forehead and thinks about it a bit. I don't know if she's ever stopped thinking about the answer to this question. "Honestly, I never gave much weight to what happened during his teenage years. I've known a caring, generous adult who knows how to love without holding back. Discovering that, as a teenager, he made mistakes never undermined my trust in him. He explained to me why he hadn't told me, I understood his point of view, his reasons, and I accepted his explanation. People make mistakes, I know something about that, but not necessarily because they're bad. You've come to know the band in recent months. You can confirm that none of them would ever hurt a fly."

"Absolutely. I would put my life in their hands without

even thinking about it," I confirm, and Thomas smiles shyly. "And you, Thomas, have you started to see the paparazzi differently?"

He breathes and shrugs. "I've learned to live with them. My grudge against them was related to Michael's old story, but the anger I harbored inside faded when he forgave the ones who took the photos. I don't feel hatred toward them. I just don't care as much about their invasion into our private lives as I did before I met Iris."

His answer digs into me like a worm. I wish I had the same ability to detach myself from the plague of paparazzi in my life. But I can't. I'm not able to forgive what gossip newspapers and photographers have done to me.

"Everything okay? It looks like you've eaten a lemon." Nicholas's voice brings me back to reality, and I notice all three are looking at me, brows furrowing. My partner even turned off the cameras.

"I can't understand how you can do that." I smile and shake my head. "I can't accept, even after all these years, what they did to me. They consciously destroyed my life. They took an eighteen-year-old girl and plastered her all over the media. Don't they have a conscience? Don't they have daughters they want to protect? Would they take those kinds of pictures of their daughter, sister, or mother?"

I realize I've raised my voice a bit when Iris squeezes her shoulders and looks down, embarrassed. I'm sorry, but for me, it's not so easy to separate the good guys from the bad guys. And in this case, she was one of the villains. "Forgive me. It's not an attack on you, personally. I know you did it because you had to take care of your mother, but I can't believe that all paparazzi have a similar tragic reason that justifies their bad behavior."

Iris smiles and nods. "I understand your anger, really. I can only speak for myself, not for others who do this work. They definitely have different stories that I don't know. But maybe I can help make things right for you. Let me make a few phone calls." She gets up from her seat, and we watch her go upstairs to their bedroom.

"I have no idea what she has in mind," Thomas admits when I turn my perplexed gaze on him.

***

It's just past two in the afternoon when we arrive in Tampa, Florida, the next stop on the "Back to Jail" tour and Iris told us to be ready because she arranged a meeting for Nicholas and me. Half an hour after the bus has parked in the parking lot outside the concert venue, we enter a bar inhabited by only a few very drunk patrons at this time of the afternoon.

Two men in their fifties catch our attention, sitting at a secluded table with cameras in plain sight resting in front of them. Iris has not told us what she arranged, but the closer Nicholas and I get, accompanied by the redhead, the more we realize these guys are paparazzi.

"You're Fred's friends, right? I'm Iris."

The two nod and cast a puzzled glance at Nicholas, filming with the camera. She arranged a meeting with people who could give me answers.

"Do you mind if we shoot for the documentary we told you about? You have to sign these if you want to continue." She gives them the non-disclosure agreements.

The two look at each other, a silent conversation passing between them.

"It's paid," Iris says when she sees them hesitate.

The two sign quickly after the mention of money. Blood boils in my veins.

"Is it really all about the money for you?" I ask as I sit next to them.

They study me for a few seconds.

"Not everyone was born in a Hollywood mansion surrounded by money, so if we can make a few bucks from this interview, we'll take it," the grizzled man sitting next to me says, confirming that he recognized me.

"Why can't you get a normal job like everyone else?" I'm upset and it shows, all the venom leaking through my words. Nicholas puts his hand over my leg and squeezes it, conveying his calm to me.

"I have four children between the ages of five and fourteen. I didn't get a diploma. I dropped out of high school in the second year. I work as a temp for a construction company that calls me only when it needs labor. This job allows me to feed my family. Why shouldn't I do that?"

"There are other jobs that don't require special qualifications. Working as a bartender or bouncer, for example. Why the paparazzo?"

The man smiles at me and shakes his head as if I were a little girl who doesn't understand adults' motivations. And maybe I am.

"Because this job pays more, and there's no risk of being replaced overnight by an intern just out of high school with pimples who's easier on the eye." His tone exudes sarcasm.

I look at him carefully, and I realize he's right. He's a big guy with two massive hands full of calluses, his face aged by time spent on a construction site in the sun. Thinking about the kids behind a coffee counter, I wonder how the hell someone like him would do serving me a cappuccino.

"You do realize that you ruin people's lives, right?"

The blond across from me, who appears a little younger with a surfer vibe, looks at me and smiles. "Do you know what I was doing when I got out of college?" Without waiting for me to answer, he continues, looking me straight in the eyes. "I worked for a medical insurance company. My job was to sift through claims for reimbursement of medical expenses, and to refuse any benefits that weren't what they considered standard. I had to look for loopholes that would allow the insurance company to refuse to pay. I was sending people out into the streets, suffering with diseases that were killing them. I sentenced them to death. *That's* ruining people's lives, not taking a few pictures of celebrities who crave media attention." His tone is cold, and his words reach my belly and tighten a grip that makes me uncomfortable.

When you think of jobs that ruin people's lives, you think of illegal things like drug dealers or ethically questionable ones like the paparazzo. But there are so many jobs that happen behind the closed doors of reputable companies and cause more deaths than the ones you see on the streets.

"Do you think an eighteen-year-old girl needs to attract attention with stolen photos of an intimate moment? On private property, no less?" I reply with more vehemence.

"You're lucky they only published the photos where you still have your underwear on because there are definitely others showing you having sex," he snorts with a half-smile, making me feel like a naïve and stupid girl.

I'm nauseous just hearing these words. I look at the other paparazzo for confirmation, and he does nothing but nod. The shame that creeps into my chest is almost suffocating. The idea that there are pictures of me with my legs open by the pool while David fucks me is so repulsive I have to swallow several times to keep from vomiting on this table.

"For sure. But either the newspaper he sold them to decided not to publish them, or the paparazzo had a stab of conscience and decided not to sell the most explicit ones," confirms the older man.

Next to me, Nicholas stiffens. "What crap," he whispers loud enough for all of us to hear it.

The two turn to the camera, shaking their heads. "Don't blame us. Blame the people who buy that crap. We just take pictures. We don't decide what gets published or not. Complain to your fans who keep clicking on the links of gossip sites or buy copies of newspapers with you on them. If no one were interested in these things, we'd be unemployed. We're not the bad guys."

On the one hand, they're right. Those gossip sites and magazines wouldn't exist if there weren't a morbid curiosity to know celebrities' most intimate details. After all, these days everyone has a camera phone and anyone can take a picture and post it on social media.

"I never messed up once. You never caught me drunk at

a party or in a position that could be compromising. I was always the model girl. I worked hard for years, giving up all that bullshit a teenager does because I knew I was under the public's watchful eye. Why climb the wall of a private home to take pictures? Wasn't there someone more interesting than me to photograph?"

The blond responds with a guilelessness that makes me feel like I'm the one at fault here. "Because you have that girl-next-door image, that's why the paparazzi follow you like vultures. Indecent photos of you are worth much more than some actress who's always in the media for some scandal. Think of the band you're with, the Jailbirds. Everyone expects bad boy behavior from Damian—a betrayal, a kiss with someone who's not his woman. It's Damian. He's always on the front pages of newspapers. But you know how much they'd pay for a picture of Simon…I don't know, snorting coke in some club? That would sell for months."

And suddenly I understand Simon's words, his fear of unleashing an uproar, the onslaught of journalists if our story were to come out into the open. What relationship could survive that hell? How the hell do you defend yourself against those kinds of jackals?

I look at Nicholas and see that he, too, has come to the same conclusion as me. Simon already had to endure the meat grinder of journalists when the scandal of their past broke out. He knows how tough this situation is, and if this conversation didn't make me change my mind about the paparazzi, it certainly opened my eyes to Simon's point of view on our story.

***

When we enter through the door of our bus, Simon is sitting on the couch in the living area, scrolling lazily through the news on his cell. He looks up at us and smiles, no trace of anger.

"I looked for you all afternoon, but Thomas told me you went out with Iris."

A sigh of relief fills my chest that there's no tension between us after last night. He gets up, approaches me, and then leans on the small kitchen counter, hands clasped to the countertop. I think he's nervous, but attempting to get closer after last night's rude behavior.

"Iris arranged an interview with local paparazzi," Nicholas explains as he leans his camera bag against the table near Simon, who looks at him with wide eyes.

"And how did it go?" His face expresses all the curiosity and fear he has just talking about it.

Nicholas looks at me and motions for me to continue. I'm the one who knows what it's like to have your life turned upside down by photographers. Nicholas can support me if I need it, but he can't fully understand what it means to feel exposed to the entire planet without being able to erase what happened. A part of me has been violated in the most brutal way, and I'll never be the same. Even if you try to overcome that kind of humiliation, it changes you forever.

"We understand why you don't want to expose yourself by talking about this relationship," I confess. "The media would have a field day, and the paparazzi wouldn't leave us alone until they've bitten, chewed, and spat out everything good between us. They would sniff out scandal, perversion, and maybe it's better to let a new relationship mature before feeding it to the jackals."

Simon reaches out a hand and grabs me by the waist, pulling me to himself. The other hand sinks into my hair while he slides over to my ass and pushes me against his erection. He dips his tongue into my mouth without leaving me time to react. For the first time since we met, he's the one initiating the intimacy. A moan escapes my lips as he squeezes my ass with a strong hand.

My surprise is so evident when I pull back that a half-laugh escapes him. "I needed to hear you say that."

"If that's the reaction, let me talk next time!" Nicholas teases us.

Simon reaches out his hand and gently grabs behind Nicholas's neck, pulling him in and kissing him with the same passion and intensity he had for me.

"That's better," smiles Nicholas, as we all sit on the couch, huddled together.

"Did you change your mind since last night? You didn't seem to want to stay in this relationship..." I ask to make sure this change of mood is not temporary.

"Can you give me time to get used to it?" He looks at both of us, but Nicholas beats me to the response.

"Today's conversation with the paparazzi shed some light on what our lives would be like if the press knew. I'd say giving it time is a must if we want this to last. Let's start here, with what we have, figure out what works for us, and then decide together when we're ready to tell people."

Simon nods and gently kisses Nicholas on the lips, then turns to me and repeats the same gesture.

"Okay, can we talk about the hard-ons you both have? Because in all honesty, it's difficult to have a serious conversation with the two of you in this condition," I tease them, looking down at their massive bulges.

"Can you give us a hand getting rid of them?" Simon raises his eyebrow in a challenge.

"Are you sure?" My voice carries all the excitement that's been building for months and is about to explode.

Simon nods, smiling pointedly at me.

"I don't want to ruin the mood, but the condoms are upstairs," Nicholas warns when Simon grabs me by the butt and pulls me in.

I've never seen human beings run upstairs as fast as the three of us do, almost killing each other to get to my and Nicholas's bedroom.

"The fact that I don't have any proves just how active my sex life is. If you're wondering, I'm clean. I haven't even seen the shadow of sex since the last I got tested." Simon smiles in embarrassment.

"We are too…and we haven't had any other partners in quite a while," I admit.

Nicholas approaches Simon from behind, pulls off his shirt, then leans on his back, kissing his neck and grabbing his erection over the thin layer of cloth. "How about getting rid of our clothes before we think about whether or not we need condoms? I can't wait to watch Haven come on that magnificent Prince Albert," he whispers sensually.

Simon closes his eyes and raises his arms to sink a hand

into Nicholas's hair and hold him next to him, his lips savoring his neck and making him groan. At least until he looks at me again, lying on my bed.

"Take off your clothes." Simon's voice is hoarse, full of excitement, the command reaching my belly and making my legs tremble.

Both of them stand there looking at me as I take off my shirt, unfasten my bra and drop it on the floor. I take my time pulling down my shorts, and, before taking off my panties, I get lost watching them.

"I said, take off your clothes," Simon repeats more forcefully. I like his way of commanding us in the bedroom, it's so drop-dead sexy. Nicholas also appreciates his strong side, and I watch as he pulls down his pants and boxers and kneels in front of Simon, taking his erection between his lips.

Simon looks down for a moment at Nicholas, then looks up at me as I watch, enchanted by the sight of my boyfriend's head of dark curls moving on his erection.

"Take. Off. Your. Clothes," he growls, his eyes devouring every inch of my body.

When I slowly pull off my panties, Simon's eyes fill with a desire I've never seen. I dare to spread my legs apart, to give him a peek of what awaits him, and he holds his breath. With one hand, he grabs Nicholas's hair and, with a decisive gesture, lifts him up to kiss him with a desire and a frenzy that leave him breathless.

"Undress," he orders, holding the grip on his hair until an excited smile opens on Nicholas's lips.

Only then does his gaze rest on me again, and his desire almost makes me come without even touching me. With a quick gesture, he pulls off the pants around his ankles, kneels on the bed, and approaches with a predatory crawl that makes me squeal. I've never seen this side of Simon. It's a sexy surprise that leaves me breathless.

He grabs me by the ankles and pulls me to himself, eliciting a scream of surprise from me. He caresses me with his hands until he reaches my knees, and with a decisive gesture, he opens them wide, exposing me to his gaze full of lust. His eyes run over every inch of my body, from my face to my breasts, descending to my belly and further down, between the folds of my pleasure that implores him to touch me. The ravenous smile on his lips is so sexy that when he sinks his face between my legs, licking and sucking voraciously, the roar that comes out of my chest is almost animalistic. I arch my back and press my pelvis against his mouth while he tortures me with his lips, tongue, teeth. It's as if he's wanted to savor me for years and can't hold himself back.

Nicholas joins us on the bed, his hands and mouth feasting on my breasts, bringing my pleasure to the limit of madness. They devour my body as if I were a dish they can't resist. They lick, suck, bite until I run out of breath. When Simon sinks into me with two long, strong fingers of a musician who knows exactly which strings to vibrate, my orgasm explodes so violently that the cry from my lips rises and hovers between the narrow walls of this room.

The moment I finally catch my breath and open my eyes, Nicholas's lips are looking for Simon's, eager to taste me on his tongue, on his mouth, their tantalizing erections in full view. I reach out a hand, grabbing Nicholas's and clutching it at the base the way he likes it. He interrupts his kiss with Simon, and with eyes full of lust, approaches my lips but instead, I wrap his flesh with the warmth of my mouth and suck. With one hand, he searches for Simon, but he never looks away from me, chained to my soul by a thin thread that doesn't break.

"Don't let him come. I want to finish him off myself when I'm done with you." Simon's voice comes like a burst of eroticism through my body.

I've always preferred to take the reins in my relationships with Nicholas after my experience with David. But the truth is, with the two of them I feel safe, even when Simon surrenders to his most commanding and animalistic self.

Simon lifts my pelvis and slips between my legs with a decisive gesture, sinking with a slow push but never stopping. His Prince Albert tickles every inch as he makes his way inside me. The moan escaping my throat almost makes Nicholas faint as he sinks more deeply into my mouth.

"I don't know if I can hold it much longer. You're killing me here." Nicholas's voice is a panting gasp full of effort.

He bends forward and rests his elbows on the other side of my body, too weakened with desire to kneel. I hear Simon chuckle as he sinks into me faster and faster, holding my hips firmly with his strong hands. His thrusts make our bodies resonate, the sound of our skin touching mixed with Nicholas's groans and Simon's wheezing breaths. The position I'm in and his piercing that stimulates my most sensitive parts with every thrust make me quiver, and another orgasm shakes me, spasming around his erection. My pleasure triggers his, and he fully gives in to his most primitive side.

Nicholas pulls out of my lips when Simon lets me slide back down on the bed, kissing my belly, breasts, lips with a delicacy that makes my head spin. The guy giving orders disappears between these sheets. His tongue caresses mine with a quick kiss, then he gets on his knees while next to me. Nicholas is still panting, his erection threatening to explode.

Simon kisses him slightly, caresses his chest, and wraps his fingers around his erection. The moan that comes from Nicholas's lips vibrates in his throat, and he closes his eyes as he pushes his erection between the fingers of his first true love. Plunge after plunge, his orgasm mounts until it explodes in Simon's hand, who, not for one second has looked away from the face of the man in front of him. The tenderness of the love that shines between them brings tears to my eyes.

When all three of us finally slip under the covers, exhausted, the only thought that crosses my mind is that the feeling binding us together is so precious it must be protected from anything that could break it.

CHAPTER 16

Simon

I've spent my life teasing Michael about his wild passion for sex, which I always thought was overrated. I mean, sex is great, but not something to die for if you don't have it. I've never been so wrong in my life. Sex brings you back to life when you're having it with the right people.

I look toward the middle of the bed where Haven is sleeping between Nicholas and me, covered up to mid-back by a light sheet tented now by our morning erections. I can't hold back a smile that soon turns into a cackle. It looks like the Golden Gate Bridge in San Francisco.

Nicholas opens his eyes, raises his head, and looks at me perplexed. I say nothing, pointing to the work of art our pelvises created, and he bursts out laughing too, then climbs over our girl and lies on top of me. Our erections touching gives me a strange feeling, different from what I'm used to but equally as pleasant.

He leans up on one elbow while his other hand caresses my face. His gaze is different from last night's excitement and passion; this morning it's loving, almost tender. He hesitates when he lowers himself to touch my lips with a kiss. I expect to be enveloped in that next-day discomfort, but it doesn't happen. Rather, I feel the need to put my hand in his hair and drag him to me to deepen the kiss, while with the other, I squeeze his ass tight and push my hips against his.

A groan escapes his lips while my tongue moves from his mouth and descends toward his neck, savoring the skin, biting it, experiencing that frenzy that lingers from last night.

Haven's warm body joins Nicholas's, clinging to my side while her tongue flicks over my shoulder, my chest. What started as a laugh soon turns into a tangle of limbs, groans, sweat, and pleasure. I've never been awakened like this, with an orgasm that makes my body and heart tremble.

"Is it crazy that I don't want to leave this room, even to eat?" My voice comes out panting.

Haven giggles with her head resting on my chest while Nicholas kisses my neck on the other side.

"I don't know if it's crazy, but I know I'd stay here with you," Nicholas says as he stands and looks down at his lower belly. "It's not often that I come and then two minutes later have a hard-on like I hadn't fucked in months."

We all laugh again. Haven's the first to break this idyllic moment, sitting up in bed. "I'd like to repeat this, but we're already late for the interview with Michael." She gets up, putting on a t-shirt she finds on the floor. It's Nicholas's, and I can't help but wonder if she chose his because he's her boyfriend or if it was just the closest. I chase the thought out of my mind, grab a pair of boxers, and leave the room.

"Do you want coffee while we wait for Haven to get out of the shower?" I glance at Nicholas, who is still lying in bed.

He nods and gets up, his erection still evident and inviting. For a moment, I'm tempted to kneel and free him from that embarrassment, but the mere thought makes my heart bolt in my chest. I'm not sure I'm ready for that. When I look up again at him, he's smiling tenderly as though reading my thoughts, and I'm a little ashamed.

He gets closer and kisses me on the cheek. "Don't be in a hurry. One step at a time," he whispers in my ear.

I pause for a few seconds to enjoy the warmth of his body, then I go down the stairs to make coffee and take a deep breath. But a vigorous knock on the door distracts my thoughts and I go to open it in my boxers, hoping it's not someone who's overly modest.

Michael enters without so much as a glance, and all my worries slip away. "It smells like sex. Are you having orgies in here?" He sniffs and looks around as he walks to the coffee machine.

I feel myself blushing like a little boy just as Nicholas joins us, and I decide to ignore his question. "How the hell can you be so awake at seven in the morning?" I grill him as he pulls out slices of bread and sticks them in the toaster.

"I'm on my fourth coffee. Do you know how often a new-born wakes up at night?" His words come out so fast that I suspect he's overdosing on caffeine.

"Maybe it's not such a good idea to drink the fifth?" I grab the cup in his hand and put it back in the cabinet. "Do you want to die of a heart attack?"

"Do you want me to fall asleep during the interview?" He raises an eyebrow.

"Whatever, do what you want." I give up arguing with him.

"You're different this morning. What happened?"

I turn my back as he asks the question. My gaze slowly

rises on Nicholas sitting on the couch in boxers and a t-shirt, hiding his face behind a glass of orange juice he's just poured. He looks equally tempted to tell him the truth and terrified at my reaction. There's an urgent desire in my stomach to get off this bus and run far, far away.

"I'm in a hurry. I have to change and get out of here so you can do the interview in peace."

"Stay if you want..." He frowns as if he'd assumed I would be there.

I laugh. "No, Michael, I'm not going to stay here all day watching you pose for the camera. I have my limits." This isn't the real reason, but the lie is an easy one.

I don't wait for his answer, but head straight to my room looking for something to put on and get out of this bus before I suffocate.

***

The moment Evan comes to open the door of his bus, I slip inside without an invitation. He's dressed in elegant sand-colored trousers and a white shirt. I wonder if this man has anything else in his closet. Does he even own pajamas, or does he sleep in dress shirts?

The bus he shares with Emily is a bit different from ours. It has two rooms upstairs, but downstairs it's pretty much an office with a small kitchen. There's a soundproof room for phone calls and conference calls in the back. Basically, it's our record company on wheels. To be honest, his presence here isn't necessary. We have a tour manager who takes care of our concerts. But since the record company is run by the five of us and is still too new to run itself, it's more practical if we're all in the same place. We can discuss important topics that are difficult to deal with on the phone while traveling. Meanwhile, Evan takes advantage of the travel to reach out to local artists who may be interested in signing with our label.

"I had sex with Nicholas and Haven…at the same time… and now I don't know what to do," I blurt out as soon as the door closes behind me.

"Oh." The voice behind me makes my blood freeze.

Emily. She wasn't in the room when I entered, and I totally forgot she lives on this bus.

Evan grimaces with an expression that seems to say, *Sorry, I didn't have time to warn you.* I close my eyes, breathe, and collapse in the armchair. No sense denying it, like a kid caught with his hands in the cookie jar.

"This can't leave this bus, okay? I'm not ready for this conversation with other people." I open my eyes and find them sitting in the chairs in front of me with serious but relaxed expressions.

"I don't talk about my sex life, let alone someone else's," Emily reassures me with a smile.

"Okay. You went from kissing to having sex. Sorry, but I don't see the problem." Evan frowns.

Emily turns to him with her mouth and eyes wide open. "You knew?"

Evan frowns at her. "Of course, I knew! I'm their manager."

"Oh, so you manage their sex lives as well as their careers? You must have been really busy with Michael." She crosses her arms and raises an eyebrow.

"No! I solve their problems, and if fucking is going to cause drama, I want to know first. Not about the fucking part… just the drama. I mean, I don't want to know about their sex life…Christ! I'll never win with you." He rubs a hand over his face, desperate, while Emily smiles and turns to me.

I can't hold back a half-smile.

"Back to us, you had sex with Nicholas and Haven. At the same time, so I assume you were all consenting. And your problem is?" Emily inquires with a smile.

"I don't know. I feel euphoric and terrified at the same time," I admit as I look up at the ceiling. When I look back at them, they stare at me with that professional look they always have when they focus on solving a problem. I feel like a lab rat.

"Okay, let's focus on the terrified," Evan suggests. "Euphoric is a good thing."

Emily looks at him with a raised eyebrow. This woman makes me anxious. "Euphoric is a good thing with Michael. This is Simon. He doesn't have extreme emotions, even if you slapped him."

Evan sighs, exasperated. "Can we call you *moderately happy*? Do you like that description?" He sighs again while I can't hold back a laugh. At least they're helping me get through some anxiety.

"Moderately happy represents quite precisely what I feel," I tease them, and Emily nails me with a look that makes me understand I don't have to say anything more.

"Seriously though, Simon, I can't understand what's

wrong. From what you told me, they're more than happy to have you in their lives. Why are you terrified?" Evan's voice is calm and somewhat less harsh than usual.

"It's hard to explain because it's more of a feeling than a real problem. They've been a couple for six years. They live together. They have shared memories, good and bad. I come into their lives like this, out of nowhere. If this were to end, I'd be cut off. They can always salvage their relationship. I have nothing to go back to."

"You have Nicholas. Your story began long before Haven entered the picture. Do you think if he had to choose, he would pick her over you?" Emily expresses my fears out loud.

I'm sure he would. No one has ever chosen me. "We were two young kids who supported each other. We've grown. We've changed a lot. We're two different people now."

"Talk to them about it." Evan studies me. "I'm not joking. Talk to them about it, express your fears openly."

"Evan's right."

"Really?" Our manager is genuinely surprised, but Emily rolls her eyes and dismisses him with a wave of her hand.

"Only they can give you an answer, and from there, you decide if you want to continue or not."

"I don't even know how I'd approach this conversation." I put my elbows on my knees and drop my head in my hands.

"Have they had relationships with other people, or are you the first one they invited into this kind of thing?" Emily's sweet voice makes me look at her.

"They had others, but it didn't go well. I don't know the details."

"Then they'll be able to advise you better than we can in

this situation." Evan smiles at me.

"Yes, ask them why it didn't work. Some people like to spice up their relationship from time to time but prefer to grow old with just one partner. Ask clearly what kind of relationship they have…" Evan looks at her with wide eyes as if he wasn't expecting this kind of knowledge about couples from her.

"Can I stay here with you today?" I beg. "I can't face Nicholas, Haven, and Michael all together."

"Of course, you can stay, honey!" Emily puts her hand on my leg, and I turn to Evan for his approval. I know how protective he is of his workspace.

"It's her decision." He raises his hands as if surrendering to the fact that he has no say in the matter.

I laugh, amused, but the weight I carry in my stomach is heavy. I have a thousand questions for Nicholas and Haven, but I'm not sure I'm ready to hear their answers.

***

We're sitting in a private room of a restaurant in Tampa, where we have a show tomorrow night. It's just the band, their partners and children, Evan, Emily, Nicholas, and Haven. I watch my friends sitting around the table laughing, making jokes, and seeming relaxed, at peace with themselves.

Michael and Faith have dark circles under their eyes for lack of sleep, but the truth is they're happy. Next to them, Haven and Nicholas chat quietly about something I'm not included in. When we walked in and found our seats, everyone settled next to their partner and assumed Haven and Nicholas would sit together as well. No one would think to leave extra space for the other member of that relationship. In conventional society, something as simple as a seat at the table creates essential discrimination that no one even notices. It's like when you walk into the supermarket to look for a ready-made meal and find single packs, two packs, then the family size of four or more. No one imagines there can be a family of three people.

At that exact moment, I wondered what my friends would think if I sat down with them, if I declared that I was part of that relationship. I'm sure they would have been surprised, maybe even made some jokes, but I can't go beyond imagining the initial moment of embarrassment and disbelief that would have come with that news.

Nicholas gets closer to Haven and kisses her on the lips. Next to them, Faith observes the scene and blushes, looking down. I smile at the thought of her face if I were to get up right now and kiss both Nicholas and Haven. She'd probably frantically make the sign of the cross. As much as she's learned a lot about life outside her community, it's difficult to imagine she'd readily accept such an unconventional relationship. Still, she is the fiancé of one of my best friends. I'll have to deal with her looks of embarrassment every single time we all meet.

"Hold her for a bit. Enjoy our little Liberty." Michael's voice behind me makes me turn around.

He hands me a peach-colored bundle that encloses the most peaceful face I've ever seen. Her eyes are closed, her mouth is frowning, and her nose is so delicate it makes her perfect. She is the sweetest child I've ever had in my arms— when she sleeps and doesn't scream like a possessed bundle of joy.

"Because you want me to enjoy a few moments with her, or you're about to collapse with exhaustion?" I tease when he puts her in my arms.

"Both." He laughs as he sits in the chair that Evan vacated next to me. "You're quiet tonight."

I shrug and take the opportunity to look at his daughter and avoid his gaze. "I'm a bit tired."

"Were you also tired this morning? When you rushed out of the bus as soon as I got there?"

"Yeah, I was. You woke me up at dawn."

Michael remains silent for a while, staring at me until I feel uncomfortable and look up at him. "Would you tell me if there's something bothering you?"

How can I tell him that I feel abandoned by everyone, him most of all? I smile at him. "There's nothing, Michael. Rest easy."

He pauses to look at me for a long moment, perhaps to decide whether to believe me or not, then he also smiles and shakes his head. "I wish I could rest. I don't give a shi…pping bag about the quality. I just want a few hours of uninterrupted sleep."

I burst out laughing, eliciting a cry from Liberty, and, before she wakes up and starts screaming, I give her back to her father. "What the hell's wrong with your speech?"

"Faith kills me if I curse in front of her."

"She's right. Levi already swears like a sailor."

Michael grimaces halfway between guilt and resignation. "With Levi, there was no time to get used to it gradually. I hope she'll learn much less quickly." He looks at Liberty with so much love I bet if Faith asked him to cut off his tongue, he probably would.

It's the most normal conversation I've had with Michael in a long, long time, and when I look up at Nicholas and Haven watching me, I realize I haven't thought much about him or the rest of the band in the last few days. Somehow, the problems of my love life have distracted me from those feelings of inadequacy and abandonment I've struggled with for a couple of years now around my friends. The relief lightens my chest.

"We'll have to go out for a beer when things settle down. Like we used to, yeah?" I ask him.

Michael looks up in surprise at my proposal. He studies me carefully, like he wants to say more, but then he smiles and nods. "Yes, I'd like to. We haven't done that in a long time."

The conversation fades away between a promise I don't know if we'll ever keep and a distance between us filled with unspoken words. When Evan returns to take back his place, Michael goes back to Faith again, and the evening leaves me with a bittersweet taste I can't wash away.

When we get to the hotel again, in the single suite Emily has booked for the three of us, I turn to Nicholas and Haven and look them straight in the eye. The conversation with Michael, the distance that separates us, digs into me like a worm.

"Why did your previous relationships with other people end? Is it something you still do occasionally, or did you want a normal relationship after all? And why did you two stay together, instead of one of you ending up with someone else you brought into the relationship?"

Nicholas and Haven study me closely until I motion for them to sit on the couch.

"The only two people we were involved with weren't looking for the same things we wanted. One thought he'd found an easy way to have orgies, the other a shortcut to show-biz in Hollywood. In both cases, neither was interested in a long-term relationship," Haven explains

"Okay, so it wasn't like a swinger thing, where everyone goes their own way afterward. Do you think it's possible to have a long-term relationship with three people?"

Nicholas smiles, and Haven settles in my arms.

"Are you asking us if we consider your part of this relationship as more than just a short-term fuck? If that's what you mean, the answer is yes," Nicholas says.

"I know these are ridiculous questions, but sometimes I think about them and wonder if it's just me who's paranoid about the future."

Haven reassures me. "They're not ridiculous. They're reasonable doubts. But I never would've thrown myself into this with you without considering it might lead to a longtime future. I want to grow old with you."

A half-laugh escapes my lips. "I know it sounds cheesy and stupid, but today I was thinking when we return to New York, I'll have to buy a bigger bed to fit all three of us...but then I realized I haven't even asked if you want to live with me. And that led to wondering if you've even thought about taking that step with me, or if you assumed that, after finishing the documentary, everyone would go back to their own homes."

Nicholas smiles at me and scoots closer to grab my hand. "I haven't thought about after the tour because it's so far away, and I don't plan my life like that, but I assumed that once the topic came up we'd talk about it and figure it out. It never crossed my mind to leave you behind."

A smile forms on my lips, and the torment inside begins to dissolve. It's a long process, making my brain and heart agree, but today I discovered something vital about myself. That emptiness, that sense of restlessness I've felt lately, didn't start after my friends settled down. It's been there for a long time, but the background noise of fame was louder than what my thoughts and my heart were shouting.

When I asked Michael if he wanted to go for a beer tonight at dinner, I realized that I've always felt like that in their company: wanting to be part of something that filled my loneliness. But it wasn't until I looked at Haven and Nicholas that I realized that my huge empty hole was reduced to a shadow. I've always been afraid my friends would abandon me, and when they found their mates and built a life outside the band, that fear and emptiness amplified. But they weren't the source of my discomfort. I carried with me wounds so deep I didn't know how to stitch them back together.

Nicholas and Haven, though, came into my life when I had lost all hope of having someone beside me forever, and they filled that void, sealed the cracks so permanently that I can no longer even see it.

Nicholas

Four years earlier

The songs coming from the kitchen have the unmistakable sound of Christmas. I put on a sweatshirt, sweatpants, grab the towel from the bed and dry my hair as I reach Haven in the kitchen. She's focused at the stove, her back to me, wearing my gray hoodie that reaches almost mid-thigh with the sleeves rolled up so many times it looks like she has water wings. I smile seeing her so carefree and cheerful as she dances to the beat of the sweetest Christmas songs.

"One day, I'll take you to New York. Venice Beach has nothing on Christmas on the east coast." I kiss her neck while holding her in a hug.

She turns around and kisses me on the lips. "We should start another box where we can put money away for the trip."

Our boxes. It makes me smile because we have a box for money for new equipment for work, one for emergencies, one for bills and groceries. The truth is that most months, we empty out all our boxes just to pay rent or to survive until the next time we get paid. But it's nice to have dreams. That box will undoubtedly remain empty, but it will inspire us to keep moving forward when we don't even have the money to buy food for our two meals a day.

"We'll set it up after opening our gifts," I suggest.

She smiles, nods, and kisses me again. "Help me make these pancakes, and then we'll sit in front of the tree and the fireplace to eat."

I laugh as I grab the plates and help put our food on them. Our Christmas tree consists of a now dried palm leaf decorated with colored Christmas decorations cut out from pizza cartons. And the fireplace is just my laptop playing a video of a fire, framed in a cardboard design of a fireplace decorated for Christmas.

"You used chocolate chips! We're celebrating in style this year." I kiss her head as I take the two plates to the small living room and place them on the coffee table.

Haven follows me with the coffee and sits next to me on the floor. "Since we can't afford a turkey, I thought it would be nice to overdo it with chocolate."

I pull her in for a hug. How I wish I could give her the life she deserves. She never complains, but sometimes I wonder how much she misses the luxurious life she ran away from. "This breakfast is perfect."

She sticks a piece on her fork and puts it in her mouth, enjoying it. I don't know if the little groan she gives is due to the delicious chocolate chip pancakes or because we haven't eaten since yesterday at lunch and she's starving. I reach out my hand under the sofa where I hid my gift for her last night. When she opens her eyes, I put it in front of her.

"You didn't have to. You know I don't mind not getting a Christmas present."

"I know. Which is why you deserve it more than everyone else."

She grabs it and looks at the Christmas card for a few seconds that the girl in the store insisted on attaching. When she opens it, and sees the book's cover about the history of cinema, she bursts out laughing, and I'm a little dumbfounded. She loves cinema. Sometimes we spend whole days discussing and dissecting old films. Her eyes light up every time, but seeing her laugh now, I wonder if she just pretends to like it because I like it. Is it possible she's lied to me for more than two years to not disappoint me?

When she looks up and sees my perplexed face, she stands and runs to our bedroom and then returns with a gift with the same paper as mine. She hands it to me, I open it, and I burst out laughing. It's the exact same book.

"Okay, I thought my gift was ridiculous for a second."

"No, if this isn't telepathy, I don't know what is."

"Perfect harmony? Love? Maybe we know each other more than we know."

She looks at me smiling, then gets closer and kisses me again. "Thank you very much for the gift. It's perfect," she whispers on my lips.

I hug her before sinking the fork into my plate and eating a bite. My stomach makes a desperate growl as soon as my taste buds make contact with the chocolate.

"Can I ask you a question?"

I nod as I swallow a sip of coffee.

"Did you buy a gift for Tom?"

Even the name of the guy who was part of our relationship until a couple of weeks ago sends an unpleasant shiver down my spine. Tom was our first experience. He seemed like a regular guy, with aspirations to be an actor and the desire to make our relationship exclusive. He turned out to be a person who wanted to make films with us, but actually had sex with half the people in the Hollywood movie industry. As soon as he found a bigger fish to drop his pants for, he never looked back.

"No. I had no idea what to give him. I would have gone for a belt."

"Same here. Only I would have chosen a polo shirt instead of a belt." She smiles at me. "Let's put it this way: good thing we didn't waste our money."

I laugh. "Yes…"

"Do you think you'll ever find what you're looking for?" Her question is not an accusation, just a simple curiosity that springs, perhaps, from her concern.

"I don't know," I admit, feeling that emptiness in my chest bigger than ever.

CHAPTER 17
Nicholas

I watch Haven come down from the concert stage in Dallas, Texas. She looks beautiful enough to take your breath away, and she's finally alone. Simon's still on stage. Since meeting, these two have begun to discover they have a lot to talk about, and it's difficult to get either alone, except when Simon deliberately avoids us, but from that standpoint, at least we're improving.

"We need to talk." I grab her by the arm and drag her to a corner where the crates can hide us.

"You know when you say that to a woman, she starts thinking about a thousand horrible scenarios that could happen, right? Even catastrophes that have nothing to do with you."

I laugh and hold her in a hug. "But you're not like other women."

"True. If you tell me something I don't like, I'll kick your ass." She crosses her arms over her chest and arches an eyebrow. I love it when she challenges me.

"I wanted to invite Simon out. Just me and him." I pause to study her reaction.

We've never talked about this. There are so many factors to consider when you're in this type of relationship. Like how to go on dates. In everyday life, commitments lead to seeing more of one person than the other. Sometimes, though, you feel the need to spend more time with one than the other. This is one of the most delicate balances to maintain because the other person should not feel excluded. It's not about loving one more, but about wanting to focus more on one person at times. And when that happens, little acts of love toward the other will help them feel part of the relationship. These harmonies are difficult to maintain when two people are involved, and can be potentially destructive when there are three and they don't talk about it openly.

The smile that appears on Haven's lips reassures me. "Finally. The two of you need to reconnect a relationship that has worn you out for centuries. Go fix what broke years ago, and come back to me."

She squeezes her slender arms around my waist and lays her eyes on me. That's all I need to feel brave enough and accomplish what I hope will show Simon that we're serious. I smile at her and move away to search for Evan, who is the only one who can help me without asking too many questions.

"Nicholas."

I turn to her.

"Have you finally found what you were looking for?"

I shrug and smile. "I hope so."

She nods and returns my smile.

***

The concert is, as always, a spectacle that takes your breath away. The Jailbirds have charisma, sex appeal, music that grabs the audience and transports them to another world. Every time they take the stage, thousands of sweaty, tired, screaming boys and girls are caught and thrown into a parallel reality where the rest of the world does not exist.

This is the effect they have. They make you forget you have a life, a reality, problems outside the walls of this stadium. You're happy here. You feel safe among people who accept you and understand what you're going through. It's the most beautiful and authentic experience a person can live, and it causes me the same feelings of euphoria as when I see Simon.

Haven is filming tonight. I wanted to be presentable when I ask him to come with me on a special date. Standing in front of him in my sweaty work shirt is not how I want him to see me. I don't know why, but I wanted to change out of my usual sweatshirt and t-shirt and give this date more significance than a simple reconciliation between two old friends. It isn't enough for me to find the Simon of when we were kids, I want to experience the adult Simon to the fullest. I want a taste of how it will be from now on.

"The room keys."

Evan catches my attention by handing me the magnetic card of the room he booked in the hotel we'll be staying in for the next four days for the two concerts in this city. I couldn't arrange anything big, but considering his celebrity status, it was difficult to find a place to be alone without prying eyes interfering and disturbing us. I need a night just with him, for him to be entirely mine, to convince him he's no less important to me than Haven.

"Thank you very much."

"I set up everything you need for the surprise," he continues with a smile.

"I owe you big time."

Evan shrugs and looks at me intently. "You don't owe me anything, but I'll tear your balls off if you hurt him." And he emphasizes his threat by placing a hand on my shoulder and clutching it.

"You have my word. I lost him once, and it didn't end well for me."

The manager nods but says nothing. He goes back to watching the show, paying no attention to me. I'm glad Simon has so many people watching his back. When we were kids, he was the one who looked after us, and I was afraid that, even as an adult, he had no one to count on.

When they finally get off the stage, my stomach twists to the point of nausea. I've never been so nervous, even for a date with Haven.

"Shirt and jeans? Are you going out?" Simon slips into the green room they use to catch their breath after the show. His bandmates are busy laughing, making jokes, and groping their partners, but he, as usual, is more secluded, sipping from a bottle of water.

"I hope so," I admit with a smile I pray didn't come out as a grin given how nervous I am.

Simon frowns. What was perhaps a joke turns into curiosity. "Let me guess. Haven is angry with you, and you have to make up for it?" His tone is amused, but I find a vein of healthy interest in his expression.

"It's not Haven I'd like to spend the evening with." The rush of pleasure that comes from uttering these words is almost overwhelming.

"Does she know?" I don't miss the worried nuance of this question.

"She gave me her blessing."

The words seem to have a disruptive effect on him. He widens his eyes and swallows with difficulty, hope veiling his gaze almost as if doubting he's the one I want. Who else could I want? Who could take his place? He doesn't understand how I've tried to fill that void with other men, but no one ever managed to make me forget him.

"If you want, there's a car waiting for us," I add when I see he's somewhat speechless.

"I didn't even take a shower."

"I didn't have a lot of options to keep you away from the crowds. I wanted something secluded, intimate…so I thought a hotel room would do. I promise I won't take advantage of you." A half-smile curves my lips. I'm a bit embarrassed, afraid he'll think I just want to take him to bed.

"I never considered that was your only agenda. Go ahead, I'll meet you in a few minutes."

I nod and walk out feeling like everyone has their eyes on me.

The wait inside the car is eternal. Less than five minutes pass, but the fear that Simon will change his mind makes me a bundle of nerves. When the door finally opens and he sits next to me, I am so nervous I sit frozen like a cold fish. He's the one who reaches out his hand and squeezes my fingers. He does it discreetly, without the driver noticing, lightly stroking my skin with his thumb. The windows are darkened, but when we pass among the fans waiting outside the gates, my heart bumps in my throat. What would happen if someone took a picture of the two of us, our intertwined fingers? Would Simon retreat into himself again if that photo became public? I realize I'm holding my breath when we finally manage to get into the street and away from the mob of concert-goers.

We remain silent as the car goes down into the hotel's underground lot for service vehicles, then take the private elevator closed to the public to the floor indicated on my key card. Neither of us gets close and speaks for fear that someone may hear us, but the palpable tension between us is almost exasperating. I want to reach out for him, tear off his clothes, and mess up his shaggy hair from an evening spent on stage. I want to stroke his stubble and kiss it until I get my fill of it.

When I finally open the hotel room door, we are greeted by Evan's setup. I must admit, when you give him directions, he follows them to the letter.

"Wow. Are those camping chairs and a bonfire?" Simon's eyes widen when he looks at the patio where Evan's managed to remove the couch and put two horrible folding chairs in its place. There's even a portable cooler, like people bring to picnics.

I laugh and close the door behind me. I'll have to thank Evan for going this far. The patio isn't very big, but the wall surrounding it on both sides makes it secluded. I believe the manager personally checked and made sure no one would disturb us, even though the neighboring rooms are occupied.

"The best memories I have with you are from when we were kids, in that pigsty backyard eating s'mores on those uncomfortable, worn-out chairs. We had nothing, but the smell of marshmallows roasting over a fire still stirs up happy memories to this day."

I watch Simon smile as he sits on one of the two chairs and drags the other close to his. He has that glassy-eyed look of someone remembering the past. "It's one of my favorite memories, too" he admits. "Along with the Fourth of July when we all went to the park."

"The potato salad and sandwiches. It was the one day we could gorge ourselves without being scolded."

Simon nods and smiles but says nothing. That was when he was committing robberies, and at night he'd sneak me something to eat under the covers. He grabs one of the marshmallows, puts it on a stick, and then passes it to me so I can roast it. It's a gas bonfire, not as good, but who cares. It's enough just to be here with him, to relive those moments while the whole world spins around us.

The first bite of s'mores makes me groan with pleasure. Simon swallows his and smiles at me. "You've always been a sucker for sweet things."

I nod. "I haven't changed. I love sugar, and wouldn't give it up even under torture."

"Does it help compensate for the bitterness life has brought you?" He observes me as he utters those words.

"Actually, as hard as it was, I found people who loved me and can't say it was all crap. Of course, there were times when I thought I was suffocating, but I met people worth living for. You're one of them." I can no longer hold back the need I have to tell him.

"Why am I here, Nicholas? The real reason you brought

me here without Haven." His face is serious as he studies me to understand what I'm hiding, not realizing I can't hide anything from him.

"Because I'm in love with you. I was as a kid, in an immature way and unable to prove it, and I still am. With Haven, I've always been missing something, a void I tried to fill with other men, but the truth is no one could. The emptiness I feel inside has your shape."

The words all come out in one breath. The same breath that Simon is holding back. I rush on, not wanting to stop now.

"I don't know why life decided to give me two people who complete me, but I'm lucky enough to have met them both at the same time, and I don't want to give up my happiness for some stupid social convention. You are *my* person, Simon, in the same way Haven is, yet in such a different way. Maybe it's selfish of me, but I'm not giving up on you just because someone said being with only one person is the rule."

The silence between us makes me fear I've crossed a line, that I've frightened him, and when he gets up from his chair, I'm sure. At least until he gets closer and extends his hand to help me get up. When I'm in front of him, he lays his hand on my cheek and covers my lips with his. His kiss at first is tender, but when I rest my hands on his hips to drag him to me, it is as if a dam overflows, and the feelings we have kept inside for all these years pour into this contact. Our tongues collide in a frenzy that takes our breath away.

We grope at the door before being able to open it and slip into a room lit only by the flame of the bonfire. I grab his shirt and pull it off. His desire penetrates me to the bones, so much so that when I take off my shirt, I unfasten one button at a time, slowly enjoying his gaze trembling with anticipation. As soon as it slips to the ground, I don't give him time to react. I take off my shoes and move on to my jeans and boxers. My erection is stiff under his longing gaze.

I'm surprised and entirely unprepared when he kneels before me and his lips envelop my flesh. I close my eyes, hold my breath, and let my chest release an almost animalistic grunt when his tongue tastes the most sensitive part of me. I sink my fingers into his hair and guide him in his movements. His hands grab my ass, giving me the freedom to dictate the rhythm and depth of the thrusts. When I look down, I find his blue eyes staring at me, showing all the love he has to give me.

I grab him by the hand and make him stand, tasting myself on his lips. "If you keep this up, you'll make me come right away," I whisper in his ear as I reach the buttons of his pants and unfasten them. "And I want to keep you here all night."

"Do you promise?" He moves away slightly to look me in the eye as he asks me. His question refers to tonight, but his eyes are asking for much more. He's asking if I'll be here tomorrow, the day after tomorrow, and the day after that until I no longer count the days.

"I promise." I kiss him gently, taking the time to savor his moans.

I push him on the bed, pull off his shoes, pants, and finally free him of the boxers. He lets me do it all without looking away from me, and I can't move my eyes from his magnificent naked body. I grab the bag I asked Evan to bring, with a box of condoms and a tube of lubricant. I didn't come to this room assuming we'd have sex, but I hoped it could happen. I toss them on the bed and watch him as he sees them fall.

I lie on top of him, my erection against his. Skin against skin and the desire to feel more. But I can't go so fast. I need to know what he thinks, what he wants. "You know if you don't want to do it, we can stop, right?" I whisper before kissing him.

Simon smiles and looks at me determinedly, without lust to blur his gaze. "Are you serious? If we don't finish, I'll explode."

I laugh as I lay beside him so as not to crush him. "Okay, whatever you want. Have you ever had sex with a man?"

He shakes his head, and I almost feel my legs shaking, honored to be his first. "How do you want to do it? How would you feel most comfortable?" I ask, not knowing how to have this conversation.

He furrows his brow. "Are you asking me what position I like?"

I smile and rest my forehead on his chest. "No. I'm asking you if you feel more comfortable giving or receiving."

He doesn't think much about it, as if there was only one answer for him. "I want to feel you inside me. I want to experience every single emotion you have to give me."

I'm surprised. It's not often when a guy experiences sex with another man for the first time that he wants to be on the bottom. Simon is giving me much more than his body. He's offering his vulnerability. In a physical and intimate way, he's putting his whole self into this story. He's opening up the part of his heart he's kept sealed for years and giving me the power to nurture it but also to kill it. The weight of this responsibility rests in my chest, but it doesn't hurt me, it expands until it almost explodes. After tonight, there is no going back.

I sit on my knees between his legs, watch him put a condom on me, then lie down. He looks at me as I grab his ankles and raise his legs until I rest them on my chest and shoulders. He never leaves my gaze, not even when I use the gel to release his tension and not even when I slide forward and lean on his opening, pushing. I penetrate slowly and stop when he closes his eyes and clenches his teeth. I kiss his ankles, stroke his legs, and stay still until he relaxes.

It is a game of small movements, waits, sighs, and held breaths, but when I am completely lost in him, that moment of tension turns to pleasure. The moans out of his lips as I sink passionately make me lose my mind to the point that I can no longer understand anything. I've had other men. I looked in them for that warmth I lacked, but only now do I realize I wasn't looking for just any man. I was looking for Simon, his skin, his breath, his warmth, and his hands clinging to my arms as I grip his erection and guide him to pleasure. He closes his eyes, and a scream pierces his chest as he trembles in the grip of an orgasm that makes him short of breath.

That sight: his lips parted, his eyes closed, and the muscles of his neck tense with pleasure, make me sink one last time, emptying me of my feelings and fears. I slump over him, my head resting on his chest and his semen covering my belly. We are sweaty, dirty with his pleasure, short of breath, and without strength, but I have never been so happy in my life.

"I knew it would be intense. But I didn't think that intense," he whispers before kissing my head.

I find the strength to lean on one elbow and look him straight in the eye. "Do you regret it?"

His gaze softens at my fears. "No, but give me ten minutes to recover before repeating that."

I chuckle and rest my head on his chest again. "Even fifteen. We have our whole life ahead of us."

"Is that a promise?" There is a mixture of hope and concern in his voice.

"It's a promise."

I kiss him on the chest before closing my eyes and letting myself be lulled by the crazy beat of his heart.

CHAPTER 18
Haven

One of the mundane and unglamorous activities that no one talks about, even in the most detailed documentaries, is doing laundry. The Jailbirds have someone to take care of their clothes, which appear clean and perfectly ironed in their closets. We mere mortals, however, have to do it by ourselves. Which is why I'm late this morning. After washing two changes of underwear, I'm now drying the panties I need for today. I believe the most irritating things on earth are wet socks and cold damp underwear touching my skin.

"Okay, I thought I'd seen everything in my rock star life, but never anyone drying panties with a hairdryer." Simon is leaning against the jamb door of my and Nicholas's room, which we no longer use, watching me with an amused grin.

"This is what happens when you have the organizational skills of a carrot, and you forget to wash your laundry for weeks."

He laughs. "What I don't understand is why you're warming them up with the hairdryer. Don't you like them at room temperature?"

"I don't know if you noticed, but I'm naked from the waist down. Do you have any idea how annoying wet underwear feels?"

Simon's gaze descends from my eyes to the piece of skin between my legs, exuding lust. Everything has changed since he slept alone with Nicholas a week ago. Simon threw himself into this relationship body and soul, and if I thought his way of loving was intense but sporadic before, I was wrong. Simon is like a switch: on or off. Those little flashes of love he gave us before were nothing compared to what he delivers now, physically and emotionally.

"Impossible not to notice that you're naked." His voice is hoarse, and when he slowly moves from the jamb to get closer to me, my heart picks up speed in my chest.

I drop the hairdryer and everything else in my hand and drag myself across the bed until I slam against the headboard. I watch Simon crawl toward me with a look that would have set my panties on fire if I had any on. He grabs me by the ankles and pulls me toward him, spreading my legs and turning my scream into a groan when his mouth sinks between my thighs, devouring me as if he were starving.

I sink my fingers into his hair, push him closer to me, and arch my back when his hands make their way under the thin tank top and grab my nipples, clutching them between two fingers. The mixture of pain and pleasure makes my orgasm mount until it almost explodes. Simon, however, notices it and raises his head with my cry of protest, abandoning my most sensitive parts to feel empty and cold as a winter day.

"You can't leave me like that…" My panting voice is almost a whisper.

The smug smile on his face challenges me. "Trust me, you'll be shouting my name in two minutes." He takes off his shirt and unfastens his jeans, pulling them down to the middle of his thighs along with the boxers. His hard-on adorned with piercing welcomes me like a heavenly sight. I love that Prince Albert, who stimulates parts in me that take me to heaven.

He grabs me again from my ankles, dragging me toward his hips and making me giggle at his roughness. I'm like a rag doll in his hands. Kneeling between my legs, he grabs my ass and lifts me up to his erection. My shoulders still resting on the bed give me the right angle, and when he penetrates me in a single fluid movement, I arch my back and groan with pleasure.

"Keep it up, Simon, please." My voice, hoarse with pleasure, comes out almost in a whisper.

I look at him and find him smiling and mischievous. His expression is mock evil, as new as it is irresistible. He draws back almost pulling out of me and then sinks in again with one strong push that tears another cry from me. His eyes never leave my body arching under his thrusts. He repeats the slow gesture a couple more times until he can no longer resist and then he increases the pace until I explode with pleasure and shout his name in one last gasp before collapsing, panting, on the bed.

His thrusts continue undaunted, and when he comes too, I stare at him as his neck muscles strain, his arms and strong hands drawing me into a grip against his hips. He throws his head back, his eyes close and his mouth opens as the orgasm overwhelms him.

He sits on his own heels and bends forward to kiss my belly and breasts when he relaxes. "I told you I would make you shout my name."

I prop up on my elbows and kiss him on the lips. "I like it

when you keep your promises."

He smiles, and when he stands up, with his pants mid-thigh and his erection now dormant, it hits me how beautiful he is. Not as flashy as Damian or Michael, but he's one of the most handsome guys I've ever met. I bite my lip to keep from smiling too much at my luck. Simon studies me with an amused look, but doesn't say anything if he notices my smile.

"I need to shower before going back to meet the others. They sniff the smell of sex like dogs. Do you have to take a shower too?" he asks as he pulls up his boxers and pants.

"No, go ahead. I have to finish drying my underwear first." And I also have to recover from an orgasm that left my legs like jelly.

He laughs as he goes down the stairs to get into the shower. "Is it normal that there's more of your underwear hanging in here?" he shouts from downstairs, and I burst out laughing.

"Yes! Move them as well. I'll put them back to dry after my shower."

I hear him chuckle before closing the door behind him.

***

It's almost two o'clock in the morning when we finally manage to get back on the bus before leaving for a new town and another concert. Tomorrow, luckily, the Jailbirds don't have another gig, and we can sleep a little more while traveling from Houston, Texas to St. Louis, Missouri.

"I need a shower. Can I go first?" Nicholas yawns.

"Yes, wait. I left the underwear to dry in the shower. I'll take it to our room." I beat him to the bathroom while Simon chuckles.

I open the door, and am puzzled when I see no trace of my panties. I try to rummage on the floor and in the drawers, but they've disappeared.

"Did you take my underwear?" I ask when I return to the living room.

Simon frowns as deeply as Nicholas. "No, we haven't been on the bus since this morning. And they didn't even come to clean it..." He points to the basket in the kitchen still full of garbage.

I look at him, perplexed. "You were here with me. You saw that I hung them in the shower, right?"

"Yes, did you look on the floor? Maybe they fell down." His voice is worried as he gets up and goes to check.

Realizing that my panties are gone sends an icy wave down my spine.

"Okay, this isn't some kind of joke, is it? Because if you two are kidding around, now's the time to say so. I'm getting scared."

Nicholas frowns, gets up from the couch, and approaches me and Simon, who's joined us again. "No, we wouldn't play idiotic jokes. We're serious—we didn't take them. What scares me is your terrified face over a pair of missing underwear."

I breathe and try to think about something that's just now dawning on me. "This isn't the first time my underwear has disappeared."

My sentence seems to have frozen the two of them, who stare at me with wide eyes.

"Another couple disappeared during the tour, but I never noticed because I thought they were lost in the laundry. Like when a single sock disappears in the washing machine? I thought it was something like that."

"Why didn't you say something?" Simon's voice is full of concern.

"Because I didn't think about it until just now."

Simon seems agitated. "If you thought the washing machine had eaten them, it's because you know you put them in, right?"

Nicholas frowns, trying to understand.

I shake my head. "No, when I do the laundry, I empty the laundry bag inside the washing machine without checking what I put in it."

"So you're not sure they were in the bag, right?" insists Simon, increasingly worried.

I shake my head again.

"What are you thinking?" Nicholas looks at him with that frightened look that makes me uncomfortable.

Simon looks at me. "When you go and do laundry, you never leave your stuff unattended. You always bring a book and read until it's done, so you'd notice if someone opened your washing machine and took your underwear. That means someone took them from here, like this morning."

The realization freezes all three of us on the spot. "Are there people who regularly enter this bus? That's a chilling thought."

"Let's find Evan. I don't think their bus has left yet…" Simon glances out the window to the parking lot that surrounds us, almost running toward the front door. Nicholas and I follow him closely.

We find Evan talking to Michael in front of the door of his vehicle. As soon as they see all three of us, their faces go from smiling to worried.

"Have you been locked out?" Evan is puzzled.

"I wish that was it. I think someone got into our bus and stole Haven's panties," Simon cuts to the chase.

Evan and Michael rest their worried eyes on me for confirmation.

"Yes, and I think it happened a couple other times. Always underwear."

Michael shakes his head. "Another stalker, Simon?" He studies him with a serious look, as though worried but not frightened. It is, however, an expression that makes my skin crawl.

"What do you mean, another? Have you had this problem before?" My gaze rests first on Simon, then on Michael, and finally on Evan. All three have the same contrite expression on their faces.

"Not quite like this time, but she spent months leaving me love letters and gifts that were...how can I say, 'inappropriate' outside the bus."

"How inappropriate?" Nicholas seems disgusted.

"She left him her used underwear. Honestly, it's disgusting for me too, and I've had some freaky fantasies," Michael explains.

"The last straw was when she was found naked in my hotel room covered with red rose petals," Simon grimaces.

My eyes bulge and I try to swallow to calm down my heart that's now jumping into my throat. "You mean she managed to get that close to you? That's disturbing." My voice comes out like a squeak.

Evan puts his hand on my shoulder, getting my attention. When I look at him, I find a reassuring smile.

"It's a familiar scenario. The girl has been sued, and she's no longer allowed to get close to them. There was no danger to Simon or the others. Sometimes fans let themselves get caught up in the excitement and try to take home some trophies. Once, we caught one rummaging through the basket of dirty towels backstage, sniffing them all to find the one Damian used."

"You're not helping," I stutter insecurely.

Michael smiles and puts a hand on Simon's shoulder. "Worst case scenario, you'll go back to sleeping in my bed for a month, like the last time," he teases.

Simon turns to us. "It's not what you think."

"You want to try out the full package, I get it…" Michael massages his groin, and the four of us can't help but smile, aware that he has no idea how close this comment is to reality. In other circumstances, I would say something, but he's trying to lighten a mood that terrifies me a little, especially in a dark parking lot in the middle of the night.

"I'll have two security guys come and check your bus to make sure no one's inside. When we leave later, they'll have no way to enter."

"Thank you," I whisper, even though I'm not so calm now that I know someone has invaded our personal space.

"I'll ask to put more barriers around your buses so the fans don't have access to your private areas. We'll solve this situation." Evan looks me in the eye as he tries to reassure me.

***

An hour later, the three of us are lying on Simon's bed, staring at the ceiling. The bus moves slowly toward the next stop. No one had hidden in here. Nothing was broken or vandalized. But we're in a state of total frustration and discomfort.

"Do you think they were lying on this bed?" The very idea that someone has used our stuff gives me chills.

"Should we change the sheets?" Simon whispers.

I shrug. I don't even know what I want.

"There's something about the thought of someone else lying here that gives me the chills. It's an even deeper violation of our privacy than the photos stolen by the paparazzi," I admit, as Nicholas and Simon hold me. "At least they didn't invade my physical space. Sure, they had telephoto lenses, but they didn't break into where I lived. What would have happened if we had returned to the bus while one of the fans was peeking into our stuff? Would they attack us? Would they have asked for an autograph? What?"

"I'm sorry," Simon whispers.

"It's not your fault."

"I'm the one who attracts this kind of deranged people. I should be more careful."

Nicholas leans on his side and looks first at me, then Simon. "Don't even think that. They took Haven's panties. It may have nothing to do with you."

The silence that falls after this statement freezes my stomach as the discomfort expands into my bowels. What was supposed to be an ordinary trip to the next stop turns into a night staring at the ceiling, riddled with doubts and unease. We're incapable of making rational assumptions about who it might have been.

A faceless person appears in my mind, and every little detail of the last few months in here, every misplaced object or noise we haven't been able to explain, fills our heads with doubts. Even that slice of pizza we were convinced had remained in the fridge but was never found is a cause for concern.

This happy little bubble, where the three of us could be ourselves, has been violated in such a vile way we no longer feel comfortable between these walls. We lived with intensity and passion every single intimate moment here, and now that memory is stained by the awareness that this space was not just ours.

CHAPTER 19
Simon

The following days go by in a whirlwind of so many concerts and appointments that the break-in to our bus fades into the background. The only moment we remember what happened is when we approach the vehicle, climb over a couple of extra barricades and enter cautiously, looking over our shoulders and peeking into the darkness of the rooms.

"Did you close the door when you left?" Haven grills me when I go backstage for the concert.

"Yes," I smile at her.

"Did you check it?" She giggles.

This has become our joke since everyone thinks we left the doors open because there was no sign of burglary on the lock. I grab her by the hand and drag her to a secluded corner near today's meet and greet room.

"Yes, I checked…" I kiss her gently on the lips, savoring the feeling of intoxication I get every time I'm with her. I sink my fingers into her hair, deepen the kiss, push her against the wall, and enjoy the little groan when I touch her breasts.

Her fingers slip under my shirt, taking my breath away. I want to take off that sweatshirt she's wearing to savor the skin of her belly until I get lost in her. Her taste, along with Nicholas's, has become a drug I can't resist anymore, and sometimes

I wonder if you can become addicted to people.

Her tongue caresses mine with such lust that the desire to give up everything and drag her on the bus to make love until it consumes us seems the only possible solution. My lips and tongue explore her neck in a series of kisses that make her sigh and cling to my shoulders. My erection presses against her belly, and when my hands slide toward her butt, her teeth bite my shoulder to not scream.

"Simon…" Her panting whisper almost makes me come in my pants.

I press her against the wall with my hips and enjoy her excited moans, savoring the tiny pushes she gives me, looking for pleasure against my erection.

Voices coming from the hallway remind us we're in a public place, and we step apart, but not before I give her a little kiss on the tip of her nose.

"It's not fair distracting me so I won't worry," she chuckles.

"Did it work?" I raise an eyebrow.

"You should do it again, just to be sure."

I look around. Too many people could see us. "Don't tempt me, or I'll turn into a caveman and drag you into one of these little rooms to punish you." I wink at her.

Haven gets closer, placing her hand on my chest and tip-toeing up to my ear. "Promise?"

I burst out laughing as she walks down the hall toward Nicholas, who's filming the arrival of the girls who bought backstage passes to spend some time with us. Meanwhile, I stand still for a few minutes leaning against the wall, hidden from view, trying to make the bulge in my pants disappear. It's like flaunting my total loss of control. I rub my face and laugh, then smile like an idiot because I already know that my arousal will stand at attention as soon as I set my eyes on Nicholas or Haven. I can't help it. I've been living for weeks with a constant hard-on.

When I finally get a hold of myself and enter the meeting room, I'm so lost in happiness I'm smiling from ear to ear.

"Did you just get laid or what?" Michael calls out.

"No. What makes you think that?" Lying to my friends makes me feel a little nervous and guilty. They haven't noticed anything, too busy with their lives, but maybe the smile plastered on my face for days is finally betraying me. For someone who was so relieved to come clean with our past, I'm a master at keeping secrets about my private life.

"You have that smile on your face." Damian laughs.

Apparently, they're ready to make fun of me now that the girls are about to enter, and I can't defend myself with jokes that aren't appropriate around minors. Everyone except Thomas, who's giving me looks that could kill, which doesn't suit his peaceful personality.

I raise an eyebrow at him, silently asking why the hell he's so grumpy, but there's no time for conversation because the sound of ecstatic screams reaches us, and twenty girls rush into the room. Smiles, photos, autographs, small talk, automatic answers to the same questions follow one another smoothly, but my gaze keeps flickering to Thomas, who reciprocates with icy stares. I can barely stay focused on their questions and give coherent answers with the feeling of discomfort growing and unnerving me.

"You suck, you know that?" His hiss hits me like ice water freezing my chest. When I turn around, his face is a mask of disgust, and I'm speechless.

One of the roadies catches Thomas's attention as the girls straggle out of the room. The pre-concert frenzy is set in motion, and we're surrounded by technicians who put in our earpieces, people who walk around us with instruments, guests who expect you to smile and take pictures with them. I try several times to approach Thomas and ask him what's wrong, but there's always someone who cuts between us, draws our attention, and keeps us apart.

Paranoia creeps into my head. I'm afraid he's found out what we're doing and disapproves. I can't think of any other reason he might have attacked me like that. I spend the whole show thinking up a thousand possible scenarios. I'm lucky the setlist of songs is secured at my feet with duct tape, or I wouldn't even know what to play during the two hours we're on stage.

All my certainties begin to falter at the first hint of difficulty. Which is why I wasn't convinced this was such a good idea—not even my friends can understand my choices. When we get off the stage after the last song, I'm so deep into my world of catastrophic thoughts and apocalyptic scenarios that my mood is shot and nervousness flows through my veins.

"Did you swallow a dead mouse? You were smiling like an idiot until three hours ago. Now you look like you want to kill someone," Michael says as we walk to our buses. Nicholas and Haven are already inside while we took some time to shower. Thomas ran to the exit without giving me time to approach him.

"I'm just tired." I try to smile, but I'm aware that it looks more like a creepy grimace.

My friend's worried face confirms that I'm not convincing him. Luckily, Faith saves me from having to explain when she calls him because she can't open the bus door with the sleeping baby in her arms. I've never appreciated the birth of Liberty so much as at this moment.

When I get to my bus, I notice Thomas leaning against it with his arms crossed at his chest. I waited all day to clear the air with him, but now that I see his stern face, I lose my courage. Fear, disgust at myself, guilt, and shame overlap in my chest, leaving a rancid taste in my mouth. I wish I could keep living in the bubble we've created without reality interfering, obliterating that dream I thought we could live in.

"What the fuck are you doing?" His direct words hit me like a punch in the stomach.

"Living my life?" I know it's hard to understand, but I was hoping they'd at least support me in this choice. How will I deal with other people's judgment if I don't even have the support of my own bandmates? The disappointment at discovering that Thomas can't accept our relationship is a stab in the chest I didn't see coming.

"Sticking your tongue in your friend's girlfriend's throat? Don't try and deny it. I saw you today. What the hell were you thinking? If Nicholas finds out, do you have any idea what a mess that would be? Life on tour would be hell. Did you think about the consequences before stabbing him in the back?"

The wave of emotions that hits me is so unexpected and sudden that it tightens my stomach in an icy grip before expanding into a feeling of relief. I'm stunned. My head is spinning. If he had slapped me, I'd be less shocked. I burst into laughter so loud that Nicholas looks out the door of the bus.

"Everything okay?" His voice is filled with the same confusion as his face.

Thomas frowns, not understanding.

"It's best you get on the bus if we're going to have this conversation."

My friend looks at me with a mixture of perplexity and concern but doesn't open his mouth as he enters the doorway of our vehicle. Haven is sitting on the couch and watching us in surprise. Nicholas sits next to her.

"Thomas is worried because he saw me kissing Haven this afternoon."

"Oh." It's the only answer I get from Nicholas as they both look at me with wide eyes. At this point, the truth is the only way forward, and to my huge surprise, I find it a relief to tell someone.

"We're together," I blurt out, not knowing where else to start.

Thomas frowns and watches Nicholas. "So you're okay if your ex is with your childhood friend?" The doubt in his voice matches his expression.

The embarrassed faces of Nicholas and Haven push me to explain the situation.

"No, Thomas, all three of us are together. Nicholas is part of our relationship...I mean, we all...sleep in the same bed." I have no idea how to explain our situation.

My friend looks at us first with a confused expression, then surprised, and finally bursts out laughing like we've told him the funniest joke ever. I would have predicted a thousand other reactions, but not this one.

"Sorry, I didn't mean to laugh," he manages to say as he inhales deeply to calm down. "I just didn't expect this from you, Simon. From Michael, maybe, but not you. So, you have sex with both of them? That's why you've had an idiotic smile plastered on your face for days! You're overdosing on sex."

This time it's our turn to laugh.

"Yes, we all have sex," I admit.

Haven is amused by my friend's reaction. "Why are you so surprised? I mean, this is someone who got his penis pierced. I wouldn't call him old-fashioned, that's for sure."

Thomas's head snaps in my direction, and I feel my face blaze with embarrassment. I don't often blush like a little girl, but his wide and shocked eyes make me want to disappear.

"No one knew about my piercing but you two," I confess to Haven.

"You have a piercing on your dick?" Thomas is stunned.

"It's not a big deal." I try to downplay it, but his face tells me he has no intention of letting up.

"How? When? Where?" he stammers, not knowing where to begin. The confusion on his face is obvious, and I'm struck speechless that this conversation has turned to my private parts.

"A Prince Albert," Nicholas intervenes, trying to ease my embarrassment.

Thomas shifts his attention to him with such a bewildered look Nicholas may as well have been speaking elven. Recovering, he pulls the phone out of his pocket. "Wait, I need to google it."

Nicholas shakes his head slightly, amused, as I move to stop my friend, standing with my hand in mid-air while he looks for the kind of piercing I have.

"Christ, seriously?" He puts his hand over his crotch with an expression of pain just imagining it. It's so comical I can't help but smile. "Did you really do that? When? You, who spend your days in a greenhouse pruning plants! When the hell did it enter your mind to do such a thing? Were you drunk? High? Possessed?"

He's getting all worked up and I rub a hand across my face, exasperated. "Can we move the conversation from my penis to the reason we asked you to come on this bus?"

Thomas seems to calm down at this. "Sorry for what I said before the concert. I was furious at you."

I shake my head and look down. "It's not your fault. You couldn't have known. It hurt like hell, though, to hear you say it," I admit, and take in the confused faces of Nicholas and Haven. I'll have to explain later.

"What bothers me most about this whole thing is that you didn't tell us. How long has it been going on? Months? Don't you trust our friendship enough to tell us something like this?"

I shrug and shake my head. I don't even know where to start. "No, it's just that we decided to keep it quiet. It's already hard to make a two-way relationship work…with three of us, we needed to find our balance within the relationship before facing the world's criticism."

The kind smile forming on his face warms my heart and also makes me feel guilty. "We're not the world, Simon. We're your friends, and we're on your side."

"When was the last time we went out and talked like the old days? Just the four of us, without bringing the families."

Thomas's eyes lower until they reach his fingers fiddling

with the zipper of his sweatshirt, guilt running over his face. Nicholas extends his hand over mine and squeezes it as if to give me courage. It's the first time I've openly addressed the discomfort I've had with my friends in a long time.

"We tried to invite you, to include you in the outings, but you refused most of the time. We thought you were tired of hanging out with us."

"I felt like the spare tire," I confess honestly. "You have your companions, your lives, and I felt excluded from the conversations. That's why I stopped going out with you. Because I felt sidelined."

Thomas's eyes lift to meet mine, and the veil of sadness I see is a punch in the stomach. I didn't want him to feel bad, but I also can't continue to ignore this pain because I'm afraid of hurting my friends.

"I'm so sorry. I didn't realize we had excluded you. There's no excuse for that." He keeps his eyes glued to mine despite the evident discomfort that fills his chest. I appreciate the gesture.

"It's my problem. You can't do much about it. It's me who feels this way. I have to solve it within myself. It's not a solution anyone can impose on me from the outside."

Thomas nods and smiles. The heaviness lightens just enough to be able to change the conversation. "But whenever you're ready to tell the others, I swear, I'll tell them about your piercing. I will definitely distract their attention to that detail, trust me." He laughs as he gets up and walks toward the door.

"Thomas." He turns around. "Thank you, and if you want to tell Iris, I get it. Just don't go flaunting it around, okay?"

I know how important it is for him to be honest with his

partner. I don't want him to feel obligated to lie to her to keep our secret.

He nods and waves as he gets off the bus.

When I turn to Nicholas and Haven, they're smiling at me.

"I never thought a piercing could take center stage over a three-way relationship. You learn something new every day." I laugh as the other two move closer and hug me.

"The real question is, why did you kiss Haven today and leave me without the slightest display of affection?" Nicholas raises an eyebrow, pretending to be offended.

I smile at him, sitting by his side, giving him my most innocent look. "Is there still time to make up for it?"

"You're going to have to work really hard. Why don't you start by kneeling down and apologizing?" He spreads his legs apart, and I can't help but smile at his proposal.

Haven snorts. "Wait, he just kissed me. He didn't fuck me backstage." She crosses her arms, acting offended.

"Honey, we'll fuck you good tonight. Don't worry." Nicholas winks at her and what started as a joke soon turns into an erotic game that excites me.

The bus begins to move out of the parking lot, and the swaying of the movement cradles me as I slide my partner's pants and boxers to the floor. I move closer to his erection and savor it with my tongue while Nicholas sticks his fingers through Haven's hair and pulls her in for a kiss that makes her moan while he slips his other hand into her sweatpants. She leans on him, trying to slip her fingers under his shirt to pull it off. When he moves from her to take it off, his eyes rest on mine, and my lips descend on his erection. I never stop looking at him as I go up and down with slow movements, teasing him, using my tongue to increase his pleasure.

He is so full of lust that when he grabs my hair to drag me to his mouth for a kiss, his grip almost hurts. His tongue sinks between my lips to claim the kiss I gave to Haven today but denied him. He takes everything, my breath, my groans, my desire to be one with them. Thomas said I'm overdosing on sex, but it's actually the opposite. I can't get enough of it. When I'm not with them, not having it is so strong it almost hurts physically.

Haven's hands slip into my pants and boxers, sliding them to the ground as Nicholas's lips possess mine with a frantic kiss that marks my soul. There's no doubt who my heart, body, and soul belong to. When Haven's lips envelop my erection, I inhale instinctively and pull back to enjoy the view, but Nicholas is not done with my mouth. He holds me still with one hand behind my neck and squeezes my lower lip between his teeth. A mixture of pain and pleasure sends an electric shock down my back. My erection sinks a little deeper into her throat when he lets go of my lip.

"Holy shit," I whisper because I don't know if I'll be able to resist for much longer.

Nicholas gives my chest a slight nudge and I back up to take off my sweatshirt and watch him as he pulls off Haven's sweatpants. Her firm, round ass that drives me so crazy shimmers in the soft glow of the street lights we pass on the road. I grab her hair with a gentle grip and lift her up.

"Undress," I whisper before kissing her and taking the opportunity to get rid of the pants and boxers around my ankles. Nicholas does the same.

One glance at my friend and lover confirms what we want. Haven looks at us with a mischievous smile that promises to fulfill our wishes then gets on the couch, her tongue teasing my erection and playing with my piercing. Nicholas is behind her now and he sinks a couple of fingers inside her, making her moan with pleasure. It's such an erotic sight I can't resist reaching out my hand to slip it into my woman's hair and guide her to my pleasure.

I sink between her lips, looking into her eyes the moment she makes room for my erection in her throat. It's a beautiful vision that takes my breath away. Her eyes, full of desire and love, look at me with such intensity it's like touching her soul. I've never experienced this with any other woman. I've never wished so hard that this moment could last forever, that my orgasm could wait long enough for me to enjoy the sight in front of me. When I see her trembling with pleasure, I look up at my friend, whose face is turned upward as he sinks into her with a disarming slowness, savoring every inch of the conquest of the heat that surrounds him.

Nicholas looks at me, and my whole world is sucked into the lust in his eyes. Thrust after thrust, moan after moan, I watch him possess Haven with a passion so intense that I can't resist any longer, exploding with an orgasm that takes me by surprise, emptying my pleasure in her throat. The moment I pull out and sit on the couch, my hands reach for her breasts, and her tongue makes its way into my mouth, sharing the salty taste of my essence. I swallow her moans, supporting her while the orgasm catches her and makes her arms give out. I hold her close and look up at Nicholas, who, with a last deep, strong thrust, lets himself go to his pleasure, closing his eyes, and groans.

Haven kisses my naked and sweaty chest as she curls up in my arms, welcoming Nicholas into hers. At this moment, in the calm and bliss that surrounds us, I accept the idea that no one ever, in my future, will be able to complete me like the two people I hold near me tonight.

CHAPTER 20
Nicholas

The thing I like most about this job is that every day is different from the previous one. Today we're at the zoo. And I'm not speaking metaphorically about the noisy chaos that usually surrounds us during the shows. I'm talking about a real zoo with animals, fences, and cages. The Cincinnati zoo, to be exact, is the fifth oldest in the United States and currently in a period of economic difficulty. The Jailbirds are guests for a day with their families and will be attending a charity lunch in the adjacent botanical garden to raise funds for renovations.

"Sweet Jesus! Are those bats?" Faith hides in Michael's arms while Levi, who pushes the stroller with his little sister inside, snickers with glee.

It's a constant discovery process following them around and shooting. Even though months have passed and I've gotten to know them, I'm still amazed at the naivety of that girl. I'm often tempted to ask her if I can make a documentary about her and the cult she grew up in. She insists on calling it a religious community, but the more I interact with her, the more I believe it's a real cult.

"They're flying foxes, it's a kind of bat." Michael hugs her and chuckles as he explains what they're looking at. She occasionally peeks between the fingers covering her face but closes them as soon as she sees the big bats.

"If they escape from their cage, they'll kill us all, leaving us without a drop of blood in our bodies," she says.

Michael frowns at her observation with a mixture of perplexity and fun. I have no idea how two such different people could have ended up together and started a family.

"Wait, they eat fruit. They're not bloodthirsty beasts," he reassures her.

"I told you not to let me watch movies that scare me," she complains, never moving her forehead from his chest.

"What the hell kind of movie did you show her to terrify her this much?" I ask him, amused, as he turns around and flashes me a guilty smile.

"An old vampire movie. I thought it was harmless, but she got scared. And don't get me started on Disney movies. They make her cry all night and even a little the next day."

Faith raises her head, scandalized. "In *Bambi,* the hunter kills his mother. In *The Lion King,* they kill his father. In *Snow White,* they order a hunter to tear out the heart of a little girl. Those are violent films!"

We both burst out laughing as Simon joins us. Levi is bent over, laughing at Faith's catastrophic telling of children's movies.

"When you put it like that, she's not wrong." His voice makes me quiver like a schoolboy with his first crush. I wish so badly I could leave my camera back at the bus and enjoy the day like them, to tell everyone that I'm Simon's family, but I realize this is just wishful thinking more than actual mourning. The truth is Simon's been by my side and Haven's all morning, walking around with my, or our, girlfriend's camera. It still seems strange to call her "ours." Although we haven't put a label on this relationship, it's clear that the three of us are one.

"See? Someone else agrees with me!" Faith says.

"Faith, when we go back to New York, come to our house, and Nicholas and Haven will show you movies that won't scare you."

Our house. For everyone else, this phrase seems normal. After all, we camped out at Simon's house at the beginning of January, and we didn't move out. But to me, it feels like someone's taken electrical wires and shocked me all the way through to my heart. Those two words slipped so naturally from his lips that I have no doubt he really thinks of it that way, he considers that our home. When I turn my gaze toward Simon, I see him lowering his eyes and glancing sideways at me, as if seeking my approval for something he may not have intended to say out loud before knowing what we felt about it. I nod, and a smile spreads on his lips. A smile that makes my legs tremble.

"If you'll follow us, lunch is ready in the botanical garden." One of the zoo staff guides us to where a long table has been placed in a small open space, among the tall plants with colorful flowers, and other smaller tables scattered around, covered with elegant white tablecloths.

About fifty lucky fans who paid four hundred dollars for a lunch with their idols will have the chance to sit here with them and say they hung out with the band. A local TV station will shoot and share the footage with us for the occasion. Being a delicate environment, the risk of having too many people walking around with cameras and cables amongst the priceless flower beds was too high, so we gladly set down our cameras for the lunch.

At our table, there are no assigned seats, but when everyone starts to sit, Haven clings to my arm and waits with me for the band to sit with their families.

"Damian, can you move down a bit farther?" Thomas intervenes when almost everyone is seated, and Simon looks at the table to figure out who to have lunch next to.

The singer looks a little puzzled but eventually slips into the space left free between Lilly and Michael as Thomas turns to us and winks.

"Thank you," I say quietly when we manage to sit all together for the first time. Haven slips between Simon and me, and all three of us exchange conscious glances that make Thomas smile, sitting across from us.

In the confusion of the moment, no one even noticed what happened, but for us, this is an achievement that makes our hearts swell.

"That's what friends are for, right?" He casts a knowing glance at Iris, who smiles at us.

The waiters slip between us, bringing us the first appetizer of the day, and as soon as they leave, my hand slips under the tablecloth, looking for Haven's leg. When I finally reach her, I find Simon's fingers. I glance at him, surprised to find him studying me casually, stroking my fingers like nothing is happening. Haven, in the middle, straightens her back and stiffens. I look up at her. She has a tense smile printed on her face and is staring blankly in front of her.

"If you keep stroking your fingers between my thighs, I will come before finishing our appetizers," she says in a whisper, never looking into our eyes but staring at an indefinite point behind Thomas.

We're dumbfounded by her confession, but Thomas bursts out laughing, Iris follows, and we can't hold back. We take both our hands from under the table and cover our faces with napkins. When we finally regain composure, we see the amused and confused faces of the others. In particular, Michael is studying us with concern in his eyes, or maybe it's pain. Since coming back into Simon's life, I've come to understand that Michael's been his best friend since they met in juvie, but I've also seen the distance separating them in recent months, and I believe Simon isn't the only one hurting from it.

***

Lunch was a succession of smiles, shouts, photos, whispers, more photos, Damian's jokes, and videos. In short, a typical day with fans in the life of the Jailbirds. When we finally return to our buses to leave and stop outside the city for dinner, we're all a little tired and want to relax. I always thought that life as a rock star was just luxury and pampering, but I soon realized it's a lot of hard work and not much down time.

"Simon, I swear you have to do something about your flying phobia. I'm tired of being in a bus instead of planes and hotels like normal people," Haven teases him as we open the door.

"Young lady, let me remind you that you can have us all to yourself without sneaking into other people's rooms thanks to this arrangement." He steps back to give her space to climb into the bus.

"When you strut like that, you look like Michael." I laugh as he just glares at me.

"Guys, come here!" Haven's panicked voice snaps us to attention and we jump into the bus.

We stop still when we see a pair of Haven's panties and a yellow envelope on the table, one of those large and anonymous ones used for documents. The grip that tightens my stomach almost makes me vomit.

"Have you looked inside?" Simon questions as Haven shakes her head.

"I didn't dare, but those are the panties I left drying in the shower."

Simon comes forward and grabs the envelope, opens it cautiously, either for fear that something dangerous is inside or because he's terrified of finding out what it is. I grab Haven's hand and hold it tightly. His eyes widen as soon as he peeks at the photo he pulls out. He turns it toward us, and my heart sinks into my stomach.

It's a photo taken from the outside of our bus, moving, since you can see the frame of a car window. Simon and I are bare-chested and kissing, while Haven stands in the background in a bra, looking at us. It's a bit blurry, but we're recognizable without a doubt.

I turn to Haven, her eyes wide and shiny.

"There's a message inside too. We have to get to Evan before he leaves." We don't think twice. None of us want to stay on this bus longer than necessary.

Evan's bus has already started to move; the door is closed. Simon stands in the middle of the parking lot to stop it, and all the other buses behind Evan's stop. They all empty out in less than a minute, everyone worried when they see our faces.

"We found this envelope with Haven's stolen panties inside our bus. I don't think it's a crazy fan this time. Haven has a stalker with access to our bus." Simon's words remain in the air for a moment, suspended in between looks of disbelief, before everyone hurries toward us to make sure we are okay.

Emily speaks first. "I'll call a hotel and book the rooms. Tonight, we'll stay here. I'll inform the radio station that tomorrow morning's appointment fell through and that we have to reschedule." As she walks away with the phone already at her ear, Evan starts talking to the drivers and security.

The turmoil and confusion surrounding us in the following minutes do not help to ease the fear gripping my stomach. Everyone asks us questions, hugs us, tries to make us feel safe when, in the middle of this parking lot, I feel exposed and naked and unprotected. It's a subtle fear that gets under your skin and makes your blood vibrate with a terror you can't shake off. There are thirty people around us. Whoever wants to hurt Haven can't even think about approaching without one of us knocking him out and immobilizing him, but something in my brain is telling me we're not safe.

An hour later, we're all sitting in one of the rooms of the Summit Hotel in Cincinnati—the whole band plus their families, except Levi, who they didn't want to worry, Evan, and the three of us.

"So this person has been stealing your panties for months?" Damian is confused.

"Three times, but I only noticed the last one because it was hanging in the shower to dry. The other times I thought I'd lost them doing laundry." Haven's voice trembles and I reach out to reassure her. I know she's terrified right now.

They all nod, but no one dares to speak except Thomas. "What does he have against you? If we're all here instead of in a bus, it means he's threatened you."

Simon gets up holding the envelope we found. "A picture of the three of us."

Thomas nods. Among Simon's friends, I think he's the only one who might know what the photo shows.

"What picture? Can we see it?" Michael requests.

Simon turns to us, seeking silent approval. We both nod. When he hands it to Michael, everyone else huddles around him. It's almost comical when, once they realize what they're seeing, their heads snap up at the same time.

"Are you gay?" Damian asks what everyone must be thinking, looking at Simon with wide eyes.

"Not exactly. It's more that…I like both men and women." Simon shrugs and puts his hands in his pockets. I reach out my hand and rest it on his, letting him know I'm here. He gives me a glance, a small smile, and leans a little toward me.

"Unbelievable," Michael snaps, offended, and we all turn to him.

"What's unbelievable? That I like men? Get over it, Michael." Simon's voice is a bit annoyed, and I get it. Of all of them, I thought Michael would be the most chill in accepting the situation.

"No!" He looks at him, outraged. "That I spent my teenage years masturbating in the bed next to yours when we could have just fucked."

The silence that falls for a few seconds is deafening until

Faith's voice screeches, "Michael!" Obviously scandalized.

Damian rubs his hand over his face. "Only you could think about sex at a time like this," he whispers, pulling a smile from us.

Evan gets up and grabs the envelope from Simon's hands. "Okay, all kidding aside, what does this person want?"

"This is where it gets crazy. He says if Haven doesn't leave the two of us to go back to doing the show she left when she was eighteen, he'll release a video of the three of us having sex."

"The three of you have sex? All together?" Damian's eyes widen, his comment earning him an elbow from Lilly, who is curled up on the couch between her boyfriend and Iris and Emily.

I burst out laughing, and everyone turns to me with a surprised look.

"Okay, let's clarify this, or we can't move on. Haven, Simon, and I are in a relationship. We sleep together, we have sex, we do everything you do in a romantic relationship. I don't know how else to explain. It's like being a couple…only there's three."

"Wow, and I thought I'd seen everything with Michael," Damian says in amazement. "Anyway, back to the problem: this person is clearly crazy. What do we do? Can we track them down or get the video before the media gets it? Obviously, Haven can't go back to her show. I mean, it's not like we can go ask the station to dig up a show they canceled almost ten years ago."

"Can I just say this terrifies me?" Lilly's voice trembles with anger, fear, or I'm not sure what. "How close did this person get to you if they had access to your bus? What if that's not the only place they have access to take those photos? They could've been near us every single day and we didn't even know it."

The words settle in my chest like a boulder. We all stare at her, understanding all too well the implications of her thoughts. Such a person does not behave like normal people. They don't reason with common sense as we all do. We can't expect them to stop until they get what they want.

"Do you think they planted hidden cameras? Do they have actual footage?" My words travel in the room shrouded in silence.

"The photo is from a video taken outside the bus, but we can't know," says Michael.

"I've already had it emptied of all your belongings. To-morrow, they'll send another one to replace it, but in the mean-time, we'll stay at the hotel. If cameras were hidden inside, we'll eliminate the problem at its root," Evan said.

"This problem is still here, though. How do we get a hold of the video? When it comes out, it will make public a relation-ship that, clearly, they don't want the press knowing about," Thomas explains. "Can't we stop it somehow? Threaten the media?"

His gaze rests on the three of us, studying our faces with a look of helplessness that both mirrors my own feelings of inadequacy and strengthens the awareness of having an ally.

"We can't. We'll make the relationship public." Simon's calm voice makes us all turn to him. I study his face to look for traces of indecision or a hint of uncertainty, but the determina-tion I see surprises me.

"Are you sure?" I ask him, aware of what a massive step this is for him.

He turns to me, smiles, and kisses me on the lips before bending down and kissing Haven. "I'm tired of hiding. I've been doing this for years, and it's exhausting. The only opinions I care about are the ones inside this room; the others, if they accept it, great, otherwise, not my problem. I'm tired of always putting my public image before my happiness."

I hug him and feel Haven's delicate arms clutching us. I inhale his scent and close my eyes to enjoy it to the fullest. When we turn around, we meet the bewildered faces of the others.

Damian's voice breaks the awkward silence. "I'll just say it. We just came from a zoo and entered an alternate universe where Michael has a family and Simon has sex like there's no tomorrow. Am I the only one freaked out by all this?" He laughs, and the others smile with him.

"And that's not all! Simon has a penis piercing!" From the gleam in his eyes, it's clear Thomas couldn't wait to drop his bomb in the presence of everyone.

All heads turn at the same time toward Simon, a gesture so synchronized it's almost comical. Simon's face heats up with embarrassment as he rubs a hand over it nervously. "Could this day get any crazier?" he whispers as he looks up.

I cross my arms and count down the seconds to the avalanche of questions. I don't get to five before the "hows," "wheres," and "whens" hit from all sides.

"Haven, please. Tell me it's a Prince Albert." Emily looks at her dreamily, and I smile because I'm guessing she had a partner who had one.

"Yes." The delicious grin on Haven's lips is comical, while Simon presses two fingers on his eyes, unable to find a way to end this conversation.

"Lucky woman…" Emily sighs.

"Christ, you did this to your dick?" Damian is horrified as he looks up from his phone where he undoubtedly googled the name.

"Can we stop talking about Simon's dick? Now I can't help but imagine it full of surgical needles," Michael shouts, disgusted.

"You're the one who wanted to fuck him until five minutes ago," Thomas scolds.

"Thomas!" Faith's shrill cry pierces the air.

And here it is, the zoo I'm used to.

"Can we stop talking about Simon's genitals and come up with an action plan before bedtime? I'm drained." Evan's stern voice silences everyone.

"Do we wait for the news to break, or do we anticipate it with a post?" Iris raises the practical question, addressing mainly Simon.

He shrugs and shakes his head. "I'm not going to hide it, but I also don't want to flaunt it. I wouldn't want to set off this psycho and put a target on Haven's back." He looks at us both, and we nod at his reasoning.

Emily makes a suggestion. "It would be outside of your usual press policy. The blog's never published gossip, which this would seem like without the story's context. If the news comes out, we'll prepare press releases to confirm the relationship."

"Will you take care of it?" Evan requests. "And I'll try to

find out who we're dealing with. In the meantime, everyone stay in your hotel rooms without putting your noses out. I want security to be on board with all of this before showing your asses in public."

Their manager is a war machine, and I'm increasingly amazed at how he manages these things with an almost surreal calm. Now I understand why these guys trust him completely.

"Finally, a forced day off to stay in a hotel in our underwear, watch TV, and eat crap." Damian is relieved. There is no trace of mockery in his voice.

"I'm glad some fool started stalking me so you can take some vacation time," Haven jokes.

"Thank you, sweetheart. You'll get an even better Christmas gift now…"

"So I'd be getting a crappy gift if a psychopath weren't on my back?" she challenges him with a raised eyebrow.

Damian bursts out laughing, and Simon shakes his head, amused. "Simon, I like this one. Hold on to her. Both of them, because from the looks you two throw at him, I'm thinking you guys make fireworks in bed." He laughs again. "*Now* I know why you're so drained these days."

We all laugh at the umpteenth joke, but I pause to observe Damian, who looks at me, gives me a slight nod, and winks. Within minutes, we went from being friends you don't know where to put at the table to part of Simon's extended family. We're not just here for work but we're sharing the problems and concerns discussed only in the close circle of family members.

I struggle to identify exactly what's changed, perhaps their looks or their jokes, but out of the blue, it's as if a light turned on to a reality that makes me feel like I belong to this tight-knit group. I'm no longer just a spectator in this strange family, I'm one of them.

CHAPTER 21

Haven

Two days after leaving the bus and locking ourselves in the hotel, Evan came to tell us the new vehicle is ready. It has two levels of security and locks, with a code and a key. But this doesn't reassure me one bit.

"Are you ready to get back on the road?" Thomas, sitting next to me at the restaurant eating breakfast, looks at me briefly before returning to his plate.

I should mention that since they learned of our relationship, the dynamic of the group has changed. Before, Nicholas and I were two friends, well-liked and always involved in their talks, but now that we're Simon's partners, a deeper bond has formed with them too. Almost like a switch turned on their protective instincts toward all three of us. The only word that comes to mind to fully describe this change is *family*. Or at least what a family should be. I've never had a decent one, but I've seen some that looked normal.

"Can you ever be ready to lock yourself in a bus again after what happened?" I ask him.

Thomas shrugs and thinks about it. "Probably not, but at least this time it's a new bus, checked from top to bottom, and we're sure no one else has been in there."

"The problem is I can't shake off that feeling of being invaded in our personal space. He rummaged through our stuff. Every time I take something from my suitcase to wear, I wonder if he touched it, if there are traces of him on it…or her. Not being able to give a face to that person drives me crazy."

Thomas nods, it's just the two of us left at the table, but near the door stands one of the security people Evan hired for extra help. On the surface, everything is normal, but the reality is that we're constantly being watched, whether with good or bad intentions.

"Have you talked about it with Simon and Nicholas?"

I shrug and shake my head. "They feel it too. Adding my paranoia doesn't help."

He frowns and looks at me for a few seconds. "It's not about whether or not it's helping, but whether they feel cut off from your life."

It's not a rebuke so much as concern after years spent protecting each other. They fight shoulder to shoulder against any threats, but this time I feel I'm the cause of all their problems. It's not a bully, the record label, or paparazzi they're fighting. They got pulled into this because I'm with them. That stalker doesn't care about anyone else, they're just pawns he'll use to blackmail me, to make me do what he wants. If I surround myself with other people, he'll use them instead, leaving the Jailbirds alone.

Maybe cutting them off is the only solution to this enormous problem. If I leave the tour, they can live peacefully without the nightmare of someone attacking them while traveling. After all, I'm not dumping them. It's not even like I'm taking a break. Our relationship can survive the distance. Besides, knowing they're safe would make me happy.

"Thank you."

"For what?" Thomas looks at me bewildered as I get up.

"For giving me the solution," I say and wink at him.

"Really?" He's more confused than before.

I kiss him on the cheek and leave him dumbfounded at the table, alone with a half-full cup of coffee.

***

Cincinnati International Airport is not very big, at least not like the ones in the big cities I used to travel to. The first available flight to Los Angeles is at four o'clock this afternoon, and after visiting all the shops in the terminal, I'm convinced I'll die of boredom while I wait five more hours. My bag, filled with the few things I collected from my room, lies at my feet. Before sneaking out like a thief without being seen by anyone, I grabbed a jumble of clothes, a book, my phone, and the boarding pass. I'm tempted to turn on my cell, but I'm sure I'd find missed calls and messages from Nicholas and Simon going crazy.

I left without saying anything, leaving a note explaining that if I leave the tour, the stalker will stop following them, and they would be safer. If I'd told them in person, I'm convinced they would have done everything to stop me, including tying me to the bed or dragging me onto the bus.

I pick up my boarding pass and look at it. I haven't decided yet what I'll do when I land. The apartment in Venice Beach was leased to someone else. I could ask Sady if I can stay for a few days until I find other lodgings. I think he'd say yes if it's only a couple of nights. Or, there's another option I hate but have begun to consider. Going back to the house where I grew up. I haven't heard from my mother in almost ten years, but I'm sure that after her initial outburst, she'd take me back. There would be security cameras everywhere, and once she sees my piercings and tattoos, she won't leave me alone for one second, swearing for hours about how I disfigured my body.

"Are you going to just disappear like a criminal?" The voice behind me scares me so much I drop my boarding pass.

I turn and find Evan studying me with a kind expression. "How the hell did you find me?"

He shrugs, passes by the row of uncomfortable seats I'm perched on, and sits next to me. "I tried the bus station first, then came here."

I study his smile and the almost relaxed attitude he carries with him. I've never seen him lose control once since I've known him. He faces every problem with all the calm in the world, carefully dissecting them until they disappear. It's strange how everything seems to fall back into perspective around him, even my fears.

"So? Are you going to disappear?" he asks me again when I don't answer.

I inhale and turn my gaze to the ceiling before bringing it back onto him. To someone else, I would have replied it's none of their business, but with him, I can't.

"If I leave the tour, the person obsessed with me will leave you alone. Clearly, he's crazy, and I don't know how far he'll go in his demands. Michael has two young children with him. What happens when he realizes we're not giving in to his threats? That we don't care if our story ends up going public? If he decides to use Liberty or Levi to make me do what he wants? If something happened to them because of me, I'd never be able to forgive myself."

Evan listens to me without batting an eyelash, without interrupting me, giving me all of his attention, sucking me into his calm without letting me escape. "You're right. You can't know how he'll react if you stay with us."

I wait for him to add more, but he doesn't. "Why do I suspect there's a *but*?"

Evan smiles. "No but. Your logic does make sense."

"So you're not here to convince me to go back on tour?"

He shakes his head and leans against the armchair crossing his arms over his chest. "You're free to do what you want. I won't stop you."

"Okay…" His way of dealing with things makes me feel insecure.

"Do you know for sure that he won't use Simon or Nicholas to blackmail you if you leave? Or Liberty and Levi? I ask because you seem confident in your plan, and I want to be prepared for any possibility. If you leave, you're still my responsibility."

I look down at my bag and feel my stomach tighten because of guilt. "No. I'm not sure."

"So I'll still have to increase security and make sure that the people on tour with us are safe. Whether you're with us or not."

"I guess so." I look up hesitantly at him.

"So what you're doing, actually, doesn't make anyone

safer on the tour, right? But now, we'll have to monitor two distinct situations and anticipate where he'll show up next—on tour or wherever you decide to settle."

I grip my fists in a vise. He can't just waltz in here with his know-it-all attitude and undo all my efforts to do the right thing. "I guess you're right," I hiss through gritted teeth when I see a smug smile appear on his face.

I don't know if anyone has ever dared to slap him, but I swear Evan is so close to being hit right now. I grab my bag from the floor when I fully realize the situation: my plan sucks and doesn't solve anything. There's a madman out there who must be stopped.

"See? There wasn't a *but* in my question at all," he teases me.

"Fuck you, Evan."

"With pleasure. Would you like to accompany me?" He smiles as he hands me the arm I cling to after collecting all my stuff.

When we head toward the exit, I look at him perplexed. "How did you get through security and find me?"

"I bought a plane ticket that I will deduct from your paycheck," he announces smugly.

"Sounds about right," I mumble between my teeth as we leave the airport.

***

Nicholas and Simon looked disappointed with me as they

lounge on the couch inside the bus. They did not take it well when I left and, after hugging, scolding, kissing, and scolding me again, they retreated into a conspiratorial silence that makes me roll my eyes. I know it wasn't one of my brightest ideas, but at least I'm not behaving like a child.

"Are you going to be pissed off with me until next year?"

"You're the one who took off, leaving us in a panic. Give us some time to cool off." Simon gets up from the couch, followed by Nicholas, and they sit next to me.

"What are you doing?" Nicholas picks up the notebook I'm writing in and reads the rows of dates, places, and times.

"On the third of August, I was in New York at a Starbucks at twelve fifty-seven." I list more dates and places, looking at the Internet pages on the laptop in front of me. "On the twelfth of June, in a laundry room at four twenty. On the sixteenth of May, I was in a restaurant at six thirty-five in the evening."

Simon and Nicholas get closer, perplexed.

"Are you keeping track of your movements?" Nicholas is puzzled.

"I'm not." They look at me as if I'd gone crazy, unable to follow the thread of reasoning I'm rattling off. "These are all the times someone recognized me, took a picture of me, and tagged me online. Not paparazzi, not people at concerts, but normal people who post about me online."

"Wow. How many are there?"

"Dozens, maybe hundreds. Every date of the tour plus anywhere we stopped to eat or refuel. My private life, my trips, and even how often I've done my laundry are available to everyone on the Internet."

"This is crazy. I don't pay attention anymore to all the

times people recognize me and takes pictures of me. I've never even looked up my name online, but it's really disturbing now that you point it out," says Simon.

I shake my head and stare at the screen, the anger growing inside me. "You know what bothers me the most? No one asks my permission. They think it's okay because I'm a celebrity, and my life is public. They don't realize that being a public figure doesn't mean my private life should be available for all to see. But if you look at the profiles of these people, you see dozens of photos with their friends, even embarrassing ones. How many of them asked permission from their friends to put those photos online? They think they can just post people's private moments whenever they want to! They don't care that those photos will never disappear from the web, whether the people in them want it or not."

Nicholas leans on the table and observes the computer, flipping through the profiles of perfect strangers who have taken the liberty of making a private part of my life available to everyone.

"People don't realize the positive and negative power of social media. They provided your stalker with the times and places of your every movement. He could have had a Google alert with your name, and then followed you when you were most vulnerable," he whispers in a low voice, without being able to take his eyes off the screen.

"Maybe that's what he actually did, the thought gives me the creeps…" Simon holds me in a hug.

"You have to talk to the fans, make them understand that what they're doing is not only wrong, it's also dangerous," Nicholas suggests.

"Do you have the camera handy?" Simon demands.

Nicholas nods and grabs it from the couch, turns it on, and points it at Simon's serious face. None of us breathes until he starts talking.

"This is not one of our usual videos we post on our blog. This isn't about a show or the documentary or any other gossip about us. This video is a personal appeal I'm making to you and that I hope will reach your hearts and your consciences."

He grabs the notebook I wrote the dates in and shows it to the camera. "On the third of August, Haven was in New York, in a Starbucks at twelve fifty-seven. On the twelfth of June in a laundry room, at four twenty in the afternoon. On the sixteenth of May in a restaurant at six thirty-five in the evening."

He takes a breath and puts the notebook back on the table.

"These dates were taken from photos some of you took and posted on social media. Any person with an internet connection can access this information. While most of you don't have bad intentions for Haven and would never use that information to hurt her, others don't feel the same way."

He takes another breath and looks me straight in the eye, an unspoken request to make the news public. Despite my nervousness, I nod.

"There's a person who's obsessed with Haven. It's a threat we're taking seriously, and we've contacted authorities to ensure the safety of all the people with us on tour. But this isn't enough. We need your help. From the bottom of our hearts, we beg you not to take photos and videos of Haven other than at our concerts. If you do, you're giving this person the opportunity to know exactly where she is, what she's doing, and who's with her, aiding their intent to hurt her. Please help me, help all of us to keep her safe."

No one says anything for a few minutes when the camera turns off. We are trying to wrap our heads around this exhausting situation.

"I'll send it to Iris and Evan, ask them to upload it to the blog," Nicholas announces, getting up and going to the back of the bus to transfer the video to the computer.

"Thank you," I whisper to Simon, getting closer and placing a hand on his shoulder. He smiles at me, reciprocates the hug but says nothing. I think he also feels the weight of being back inside a bus that, although new, makes us uncomfortable.

I enter the bathroom, turn on the sink faucet, and raise my eyes to the mirror in front of me. I open the cabinet, looking for I don't even know what. Wires? Antennas? Red lights indicating someone's filming me? This place has been checked from top to bottom, it's new, but I can't shake the feeling that someone is watching me, which makes my skin crawl.

PRESS *Review*

Important Plea!

Hi, Roadies,

We're back with a little different post from the usual but no less critical. Simon has a strong appeal to make. Please watch the video below and spread the word. Help us in this challenge. Use social media, this time, for a good cause.

Be Kind and Rock'n'Roll,

Iris

92,486 Likes 88,698 Tweets 98,672 Shares 11,572 Comments

People

The "Back to Jail" tour doesn't seem to be a very safe place, at least for the Jailbirds who find themselves dealing with a stalker. In a video appeal that appeared on their website this morning, they're asking fans not to post photos of Haven, one of the documentary's film makers, on social media. While the request is entirely reasonable, more than one person wonders if it's appropriate to have her continue on with the tour, rather than preventing other people from being targeted by this deranged person.

The "Back to Jail" tour is full of twists and turns. It appears that a stalker targeted Haven Lee, forcing the band to ask fans not to photograph the documentarian outside of official events. A request that made several people who would have preferred she leave the tour question the band's motives in keeping her on.

We look forward to seeing if there will be any further requests in this regard.

Rock Live

Life as a rock star is not easy, and having a stalker is every celebrity's worst nightmare. The target is Haven Lee, who is accompanying the Jailbirds on their "Back to Jail" tour. In the video below, Simon's heartfelt appeal asks not to photograph the woman outside of official occasions. We invite all our readers to watch the footage and spread it so that we can reach as many people as possible. Let's use social media to make something useful go viral for once. Haven's safety is our responsibility.

ERIKA VANZIN ∘ Showtime – Roadies series | 345

CHAPTER 22

Simon

When I realized that making our relationship public was not going to end in disaster, I felt relieved. The simple fact that my friends are aware of it gives me the peace of mind to finally behave with Nicholas and Haven the way my heart dictates. I've thought several times about giving an interview or posting on our official blog about it before someone else does, before some stolen photos appear on the web and people start speculating.

But waiting for the "right moment" maybe wasn't such a good idea. Ten days after our appeal, someone knocks briskly on the bus door while we're having breakfast. I get up from the table meeting the perplexed looks of Nicholas and Haven. We have a meeting in less than an hour, so it must be something that can't wait. When Evan's face appears in the doorway, I know it's not good news. I invite him in, and when Nicholas and Haven see him, their sleepy expressions turn alert and attentive.

"It's bad news, isn't it?" Haven voices our thoughts out loud.

"Yes and no. I mean, we expected it. The person who sent you the first photo released another photo from what, at this point, we know is a video. It's public."

"How serious is it?" I ask, sitting next to him, across from the other two.

"It shows the three of you having sex," he calmly explains. "Nothing obscene. You and Nicholas are kissing…Haven is hugging you. You don't see anything explicit, but it's obvious what you're doing. It's on all the front pages of the gossip magazines."

"Fantastic." Nicholas rubs a hand over his face, clouded with disappointment.

"In all honesty, I think it's great." Everyone turns to me, trying to figure out if I'm being sarcastic. "I'm not kidding. Hearing this news, I feel…relieved. I've spent years of my life hiding. First with the robberies, then when the record company buried our past under layers of lies. It was my idea to announce we'd been in juvie, and I never regretted it. Let the world know I live with a man and a woman! Why should I care? I'm tired of hiding."

Haven has a half-smile I can't decipher, Evan nods, and Nicholas frowns, saying, "So you're not afraid this will wreck our relationship? That the media pressure will break us?"

I get it. After all, it was one of my initial fears when I wasn't sure I was part of this relationship, when I felt like a third wheel. "I have no doubt about the strength of our relationship. Not anymore. Every worry I had at the beginning has dissolved, and I don't feel threatened by what people might think."

My tone is calm, and I smile when I see them slowly smiling in relief.

"So? We don't care about what the world thinks?" The excitement in Haven's voice lights a fire in me.

"We don't care about the world," Nicholas confirms with more certainty in his voice.

I look at Evan and find him smiling.

"What will the situation be when we get off the bus?" I ask.

Evan's lips arch in a sorry grimace. "You'll be besieged by paparazzi and fans who want to know more. It's better for now if you don't go out anywhere near the concert venues, even when we're forced to make stops along the way. I'm sorry, but the head of security doesn't want to take unnecessary risks, especially with that psycho still out there."

"Did the private investigator you hired find out anything?" I ask, knowing that if he had something important to tell us, he would have done so immediately.

"I have a phone call scheduled in the morning with him for an update, but at the moment, I have nothing important to tell you."

"I imagine it's not so easy to find out anything. Even the police said that without much evidence it's like finding a needle in a haystack." Haven doesn't seem particularly frightened by the situation, which encourages me.

"That's why we hired a private investigator," Evan reassures us. "The police are overworked, and unless someone is hurt or dies, they can't invest too many resources on a person who, as far as we know, is no longer nearby. We have increased private security. We know everyone who works with us. If someone we don't know gets close, we'll identify them immediately,"

"We totally trust you." Nicholas smiles at him, and I see a note of relief and, perhaps, pride in the face of our manager, who gets up to go out.

"I'll let you finish breakfast. The meeting at eight o'clock is still on. We'll find a way to get you to the location without being harassed." Then he greets us, waving, and walks out the door.

"Is it normal for him to be dressed in a suit at seven in the morning, or were those his pajamas?" Haven's question makes us erupt with laughter, changing the topic so naturally that no one feels the need to continue it.

***

When Evan said there would be chaos, he wasn't joking. The whirlwind of fans and paparazzi who try and get our attention is almost deafening. Which is why, when we get off the bus that's hidden between the others, all of my friends are there to escort us into the stadium. When I say all, I mean my bandmates, their girlfriends, Evan, Emily, and even Levi. The only one staying on the bus with the nanny is Liberty. The fact that Faith left the baby to someone else to be by our side is a gesture that warms my heart.

The emotion is so overwhelming I can't speak, only nod and smile to show them I'm grateful for the help.

"You know tonight on stage I'm going to make fun of you for this story, right?" says Damian with a half-smile.

"Thank you." I nod, and there's no irony in my voice. I'm grateful because it's his way of helping me play down the story with the public without forcing me to do it myself.

Because the truth is that the news has blown up so much it's impossible to hide or minimize it. Our fans feel like they're part of our family and certain things in the family are talked about, especially since we've decided never to hide again. It feels like a betrayal to confirm this relationship with the press before doing it with the people who have always supported us. It's like letting relatives know you got married via the newspaper rather than a phone call.

We all march together toward the stadium, Haven, Nicholas, and me at the center of a group that leaves no opening, protected as we've never been before. All the way up to the doors and concrete hallways, where the roadies have been at work since before the sun rises to get everything ready. No one says anything to us. No one looks at us with curiosity or anything else. We've been living together for so long that something like this isn't all that exciting. Only Steve, one of the oldest technicians who's been following us since we were inexperienced kids, comes up and puts his hand on my shoulder.

"I knew you were the smartest of all. They talk and talk, but they don't get laid. You, though…" He pats me twice on the back, and I watch him leave, stunned. My bandmates snicker without hesitation.

"You've become his new hero." Damian laughs as we approach backstage.

Today we decided not to do the soundcheck in person, but to show up when it's almost time to get on stage. The meet and greet, for safety reasons, was also refunded, and the girls were given an invitation for an all-expenses-paid event in New York that we'll organize after the tour. I don't even have time to get nervous, thinking about what awaits me out there, when the technicians put the earpieces in us and motion that it's time to take the stage.

When Damian told me he would make fun of me, he wasn't kidding. During one of the most surreal concerts of our career, where all the attention is on me, the loser bass player no one even thinks about, Damian jumps off the stage and grabs one of the signs in the front row.

I can't see what's written on it until he comes up again and shows it to me: "Simon, marry me." It's the first time in my life that a sign has been dedicated to me. The strangeness of it makes me smile. How are you supposed to react? I feel the embarrassment make my blood rise to my brain and whistle in my ears. I look at Haven and Nicholas behind the scenes, chuckling at my inability to process it.

I laugh, and Damian lifts a corner of his mouth in an accomplice smirk. "I'm sorry, honey, but I think Simon is already taken," he explains to the girl, then takes off his headset and leans down to hear what she's saying.

I find myself curious to hear this exchange of jokes.

"You're not jealous?" Damian repeats to me and the whole audience. I've never heard a stadium of sixty thousand people more silent than it is now. "It's a good thing you're not, honey, because your wedding bed could get pretty crowded."

The roar of laughter that rises from the crowd vibrates inside me so that even I can't hold back a laugh.

Damian turns to me, smiles, and winks. I give him a slight nod to show him what he's doing doesn't bother me.

"And to think I've been living like a rock star, trying to keep the standard high. Only to find myself changing diapers and raising two children, while Simon's quietly living the dream for all of us!" Michael intervenes, making the audience laugh even louder.

"You've always been someone who talks more than he fucks," I tease, and the audience supports me by applauding and whistling.

Michael bursts out laughing, throwing his head back and showing me his middle finger.

"I think this is the perfect time for 'Swing!'" laughs Damian, playing the hook for the next song.

As soon as the first notes start, the audience bursts into a roar, and just like that, with a few simple jokes my friends manage to normalize a situation most people would find scandalous.

Evan's words come to mind, about being lucky to have the kind of job where I can get away with something like this, rather than one where I'd have to choose between my personal life and my career. I do feel lucky. If I'd been in any other position, I could not have been in this relationship so openly.

I know there will be many who snub their noses at us, someone will always have something to say, but I'm fortunate to have what many people don't, and I feel a little guilty. Who knows how many others are out there in my situation, but who are forced to hide because of work, family, or the simple fact that the town where they live would not understand. I'm a lucky bastard, and I haven't even realized it yet.

At the end of the concert, we find ourselves in total chaos. Our buses were mobbed so much the drivers had to move them to a safer place during the show, leaving us here at the stadium. Our companions have already been on the bus for hours, while the band waits in a room backstage for the green light from Evan and security to use a back exit to the car that will take us to our buses.

"It's the first time a stadium's completely empty, and we're still here. I think they've almost finished taking down the stage," complains Michael, sipping from the water bottle.

"Drama queen. We've been in here for two hours, not six days." Thomas throws his empty bottle at him.

Michael dodges it and flips him off while Damian laughs and says, "I thought Michael would bring on something like this, not Simon. Do you realize we've been sitting on these uncomfortable plastic chairs for hours because Simon scandalously likes to stick his dick into men *and* women ?" His laughter becomes even more hysterical.

"Why is that so strange? Do I look like a priest?"

"Given your previous sex life, yes." Michael raises an eyebrow.

"You don't know anything about my life," I mumble, looking at Thomas and immediately regretting it. Guilt runs through his gaze.

Michael's reply is sharp. "You're right. I don't because you like hiding everything instead of talking to your friends. You know everything about our families, but I guess you think we're too stupid to accept your relationship."

The anger boiling inside me erupts with a fury. "No, it's not because I think you're stupid! It's because all you talk about is your families, and you don't notice the people around you who feel lonely and abandoned. Why do you think I turned down your invitations to hang out all the time? Because I felt like an intruder in my own band. Once you all found a companion, you forgot about everyone else."

Michael rolls his eyes, Thomas looks down, and Damian raises a surprised eyebrow, then breaks the tense silence that follows my outburst. "It's because this family thing is new for us too, and we don't know how to deal with girlfriends so we exchange advice. But it's not the only thing we talk about," he says to justify himself.

"Simon's right. We do talk about them a lot. And if we don't talk about them, we bring them everywhere," Thomas says. Obviously, he's thought a lot about the talk we had some time ago. He looks me in the eye as if to apologize, and with a slight nod, I thank him for defending me.

"Is that why you avoid my family? You never want to hold Liberty, not unless I ask you to. Do you hate her like you hate us?" Michael's words reveal all the pain he is feeling right now.

All the anger leaves my body, leaving me exhausted. "I don't hate her, and I don't hate you, Michael, but the moment she was born, I knew our friendship would change forever. Didn't you notice it?"

He doesn't say anything, perhaps because he realizes it's true.

Damian speaks instead. "You've never been a talker and you're not exactly what I'd call affectionate. I thought you were cool with everything, that detaching is just your way of dealing with things. Christ, sometimes I wonder if you'll break my nose if I go in for a hug!"

I look down at my hands and take a breath before looking up at him again. "I don't know how. No one ever hugged me as a kid, and I don't know how to do it." My voice comes out in a whisper. "The only person who ever tried to hug me back then was Nicholas, and I never knew how to reciprocate. When he disappeared from my life, I just stopped trying. I don't know how to show affection to people, or to tell them I'm lonely. I don't know how to tell people that when they get on with their lives, I feel abandoned again, again, and again."

Tears cloud my eyes, but I don't let them fall because I stopped crying years ago.

Michael kneels in front of me and hugs me, sinking his fingers into my hair and pulling my head to his shoulder. Thomas moves to my side and grips my shoulder, and Damian joins us on the other side. I sit there, motionless, arms at my sides, accepting this lesson from my friends about how to love, how to feel less alone, how to heal a friendship that was slipping between my fingers without holding it too tightly in my fist. The warmth and strength they surround me with are helping me hold the pieces of a life together that I struggled to do on my own.

PRESS *Review*

People

Those who thought Michael was the sexual deviant of the Jailbirds were mistaken. Apparently, Simon has a kinky secret he's kept hidden all these years, which has only come to light now. Hot images of a ménage à trois involving the bassist and the former child prodigy leave no doubt about the relationship between the two of them and a mysterious guy. Sources close to the band confirm that Simon made room for himself in an already existing relationship by offering much more than the documentary material the three are shooting. Maybe those cameras are also on in the bedroom!

Gossip Now!

Let's face it, at first glance, we all thought those pictures were Photoshopped. Who knew Simon could have such a sexy life? Apparently, Haven Lee, the former child prodigy who made headlines in the past with her own sex scandal, managed to corrupt even the quietest of the Jailbirds. Is this just a wild phase or will we have the opportunity to see the bass player take over the bad boy role of the heartbreaker? Sooner or later, even Simon will have to overcome his indecision and choose who he really wants. Will it be the girl with tattoos and pink hair or the mysterious and sexy curly-haired guy in the photos? We're waiting for confirmation from Simon's entourage.

A Different Post than Usual.

Hi, Roadies!

Today it's not Iris writing to you. It's Simon, and I have something to tell you. For days now there have been speculations flying around about me, my love life, and, let's face it, even my sex life.

I asked Iris to give me this little space to tell you my story, my truth. Yes, I have a relationship with Nicholas, and yes, I have a relationship with Haven. Many people have asked me if I switch from one to the other, if we are friends who have fun with some healthy sex, if they are my little dirty secret or if I'm a homewrecker. The answer is no to all of these.

Haven, Nicholas, and I are in a relationship. Nothing more, nothing less than a normal and regular family of three people. We behave exactly like other partners, with all the ups and downs that come with a relationship. We eat together, sleep together, watch TV together, and, in our case, work together.

Why did I choose this space to make such a private thing public? Because I'm tired of reading online that we're something dirty and perverse. I was lucky enough to meet not one but two people to love and who reciprocate my feelings. I don't see why I have to choose one, hurting the other, simply because society has a one-track mentality about relationships.

I love both of them, and I chose not to compromise my feelings just to silence the gossip. It would not be fair to Haven and Nicholas and the strength that binds us—a deep, intimate affection that doesn't break down because of outside pressures.

I hope this message encourages other people to live their lives and feelings authentically and freely. There is nothing wrong with loving, and no one should tell you who to share your life with.

Be Kind and Rock'n'Roll,

Simon

86,442 Likes 71,823 Tweets 83,496 Shares 9,761 Comments

CHAPTER 23
Nicholas

The moment Simon confirmed our relationship, both at the concert and with a heartfelt blog post, our lives were completely turned upside down. Mine, perhaps more than the others, since I'm not used to being in the spotlight. People at concerts recognize and greet me as if they know me. It's strange to have to smile at complete strangers who call you *a friend*. I've never had so many friends in my life, but I've noticed the word gets thrown around in this environment until it has almost no meaning.

The Jailbirds and their families never use it. They *are* all friends, but that's not how they see themselves; they consider themselves a family, and the more I live with them, the more I discover what it means to be part of this family and enjoy the attention they reserve for you.

Today, it was difficult to convince everyone to stay at home while Simon, Haven, and I headed to the *Hello America* studios for an interview that Simon himself requested. He wants to discuss the relationship in the same studio where he was targeted by Olivia, the host who tried to slip into his bed. I don't know why he agreed to an interview alone with her, the woman who insinuated not too covertly that he's gay, but surely he has something in mind. If there's one thing Simon never does, it's make impulsive decisions. Of course, some things even he can't control, but this was a choice he made with eyes wide open. One that made Evan shake his head in confusion.

His bandmates wanted to be there, ready to intervene and block any blows Olivia might try and throw at him, but Simon just wanted the two of us. Maybe because he doesn't want to be overshadowed by the big personalities of Damian or Michael, or because he's used to getting by on his own, but either way, he was adamant about it.

"Can I say that I was excited the first time I walked in here, but now I'm just annoyed at seeing her face again?" In the silence of this dressing room, Haven's question brings me to reality.

Simon turns to her and smiles. "You'll see, it won't have the same effect on you after this interview. There may never be an opportunity to enter another studio, but at least it will be worth it…"

"You won't tell us what you're going to say, will you?" He smiles at me, reaches over the armrest of the chair, and leans in to kiss me gently on the lips.

"Don't worry." He caresses my cheek. "I know you're asking yourself a thousand questions inside that head, but you have to trust me."

I trust him. I always have, ever since I was a kid who couldn't defend himself. I never thought he'd disappoint me, not even when they forced him out of our house. I was scared, but I knew he'd never intentionally hurt me or not consider me before doing something impulsive. Simon has always taken care of others. I'm sure he won't let me down now.

"You know I trust you." I reciprocate his smile.

The knock on the door and the assistant's voice announcing five minutes until the live broadcast gets our attention. When we get up, my heart jumps in my chest with all the nervousness and emotions overwhelming me. This moment will completely change our lives. Until now, the official status of our relationship had only been made known to fans of the blog. After this morning, we'll be the talk of even those who have no idea who the Jailbirds are but who love to gossip. Nothing in our lives will be ordinary again, and I'm scared and excited at the same time.

We hold each other in a hug. Simon kisses Haven, then me on the lips. "Will you be backstage listening to the interview like last time?"

"Yes, and if you need encouragement, just look at us." Haven speaks for both of us.

The walk to the set is thick with a tense silence. When we get to the guy with the monitors, he hands us our headphones without even looking at our faces. He seems bored with his work, and I can't blame him. This is one of those shows where gossip and lies blend together, creating the kind of fake news only conspiracy theorists believe. No one I've met behind the scenes so far is smiling.

"You're up." The assistant brings Simon closer to the divider that separates us from the studio.

Olivia introduces him as the "bad boy of rock," earning an annoyed sigh from Haven, and when the light turns green, the assistant literally pushes Simon into the studio. I watch him walk with his head high, his broad shoulders wrapped in a black short-sleeved shirt that's purposely ripped, and a pair of dark jeans that hug his perfect ass. He walks so proudly that my chest swells with pride.

"How sexy is he when he walks like that?" Haven whispers, never taking her eyes off him.

I smile, crossing my arms over my chest as I enjoy the view while he sits casually on the sofa. "I would fuck him in the middle of this studio," I whisper back, grinning and making the disinterested technician smile.

Our attention, however, is immediately diverted to the host's voice in our headphones. We both move our eyes from Simon's back to the monitor in front of us that shows a frontal view of the two sitting in the studio. Compared to what we saw the last time we were here, Olivia's gaze looks almost snake-like. I used to see her as a woman trying to make room for herself in a boys-only industry. Now that I've seen how she behaves behind the scenes, I think she's just a bitch.

"Simon, these days, you're at the center of everyone's attention for a hot affair that came to light thanks to stolen photos. You also confirmed it in the *Rocking in New York* blog. What can you tell us about it?"

My stomach writhes in a shudder of disgust. I observe my partner's peaceful expression, and when he smiles and tilts his head, watching her as if she were a rare animal to study, I sense that he'd already predicted the tone of this conversation before setting foot in here.

"If you'd read that blog and not had an intern to do it for you, you'd know there's no affair and nothing hot. I'm in a relationship with two people I love. Same as any other relationship."

His calm reply stirs up an intrigued murmur from the audience. The technician next to me goes from a bored slump in his chair to sitting up straight, listening with interest. This is the Simon I know, *my* Simon, the one who can stand up to anyone.

Olivia seems surprised but immediately recovers from the undiplomatic response. Her smile promises revenge. "Yet, when I asked you to go out for a drink a while back, you said no. Was that because you were already in a relationship or because you're really a bit gay? You denied it on that occasion."

Her attempt to make him appear fickle and wishy-washy, even at the cost of asking questions that don't follow a logical thread, is so evident that the guy next to me shakes his head and crosses his arms over his chest.

Simon bursts out laughing, crosses his legs, and leans against the back of the sofa with his fingers crossed in his lap. He's the portrait of serenity. "No, I wasn't in a relationship, and I told you no because you really aren't my type. I'm not attracted to you."

The forced smile on Olivia's face remains intact, but her eyes seem to want to throw flames. Being rejected on live TV must be embarrassing. "But then you must be a little gay," she insists.

Simon shakes his head and smiles even bigger, satisfied with the direction of the conversation. "There are an infinite number of nuances that identify a person's sexual orientation, a whole morning would not be enough for me to explain them all, but there is no such thing as 'a little gay.' I identify as bisexual...you know what that means, don't you? When you like both men and women." His tone is that of a teacher trying to explain a difficult concept to a small child.

"And what do your friends think? With all that testosterone on tour...I mean, did something sexual happen with them too?"

Her attempt to find the scandal at all costs causes a murmur from the audience that I can't tell is approval or disbelief. How can anyone with one iota of intelligence try to talk about someone's sex life on live TV on a Thursday morning?

Simon tilts his head, like he's asking himself the same question. The guy next to me rubs his hands on his face and then sticks them in his hair.

"Olivia, I'm bisexual, not an animal. I don't need to mate with everyone in my path. My family took the news with a smile and a pat on the back. They're happy I've found not one but two people to love. Isn't that what families do, families who love each other?" My chest swells with pride again listening to his words.

Olivia, on the other hand, begins to sweat. I'd feel sorry for her, but I can't find a shred of empathy for that woman. She had an opportunity to take the show in two directions: something innovative, with moral depth or tasteless gossip. She chose the easiest way to gain an audience rather than make a name for herself by producing interesting content.

"I was just curious. You can't blame me. There's something a little indecent about this relationship since Haven is someone who ended up in the spotlight for having sex in a public place with a married man. Isn't that why she chose this...promiscuous life...with two men? It was the inevitable next step, given her past."

The icy grip that tightens my stomach almost makes me vomit. I look at Haven and she is petrified. I grab her hand as I look at Simon and find his expression serious for the first time.

"You mean that time a paparazzo broke into a private estate and took pictures of a sexual predator taking advantage of a teenager? Because your insinuations are downright disgusting. It's almost like you're taking the side of the criminal, not the victim."

The buzz rising from the audience this time is much more insistent and hard to settle down. Olivia drops any semblance of a smile and looks like she's about to take Simon's head off.

"Holy shit…" the assistant next to us murmurs while Haven and I hold our breath.

"That's a very serious accusation. You're taking a big risk going out on that limb without any evidence," Olivia snaps back through gritted teeth.

Simon flashes a bitter smile. "I have the testimony of the victim who admits to having been groomed from the age of thirteen, until it resulted in a series of sexual intercourse episodes at seventeen when she was still a minor. That's what sexual predators do: they cultivate a relationship with the victim. They distort their perception of reality until they surrender and feel guilty at the thought of telling anyone about what's happening. They make the victim feel guilty for provoking them, for luring them into their trap when in fact it's the opposite."

He says this to the hostess with an almost surreal calm and then turns to the camera with the red light on and looks directly into it.

"If I had a teenage daughter who wanted to make it in the entertainment business, and *that* producer got close to her, I'd have packed my bags and gone as far as possible. And if I knew a woman who had the misfortune of meeting *that* producer everyone is talking about, associating him with this story, I would tell her to come forward because she's not alone. Someone like him doesn't have one victim. He doesn't make just one seventeen-year-old girl believe she's his girlfriend. I would tell those women to speak up, because what happened was not their fault."

When he looks at Olivia again, the woman is speechless. His appeal to the female victims of David Freewood is so blatant she can't ignore it. The air leaves my lungs in a hiss so loud it pulls me from my paralyzed state and makes me look at Haven. She's staring at Simon with a smile on her face and tears in her eyes.

The guy beside us mumbles in disbelief, staring at the screen. "Holy shit. The director must have been petrified with all of us, because he didn't even try to switch the shot, cut the audio, or go straight to a commercial."

"Or he thought a scandal would gain more of an audience than something interrupted by a commercial break," Haven says while I look at Simon.

"Did he really tell you he was your boyfriend?" The disbelief in the man's voice is sincere.

Haven looks at him and nods. "At thirteen, he was my best friend. At sixteen, he groped me. At seventeen, he fucked me," she admits blatantly. There is no anger or shame in her voice. Just the awareness of being the victim and carrying those wounds with her head held high.

"Holy shit, what a disgusting jerk. If he did that to my daughter, I'd kill him with my bare hands."

Our attention is brought back to the studio when Olivia tries to backpedal. "I didn't want to imply that Haven was a promiscuous teenager," she says smiling, embarrassed.

Simon raises a hand and interrupts her. "Yes, that was your intention. You insinuated that Haven is a slut who goes from bed to bed and needs two men to fulfill her perverted desires. You tried to ridicule her for having a relationship, making other women at home feel guilty for liking sex. Why didn't you make lewd remarks about Nicholas and me? We're in the exact same situation. Because a woman who experiences pleasure is considered a slut, while a man who behaves the same way is an alpha male. What's worse is you're a woman hosting a TV show aimed at other women."

The signal on the monitor tells us that the director decided to cut to commercials after all. But Simon doesn't know it and continues to roll that boulder off his chest.

"You had a chance to ask me questions about how this relationship makes me happy, how I found love with my oldest and dearest friend and the woman who's been by his side for six years. You could have let the audience witness sincere, intense, solid love. You could have asked me how lucky I feel to have found love not in one person but in two, but you decided to push the scandal, trampling anyone in your way. So please don't insult my intelligence by trying to convince me otherwise."

He gets up, takes off the microphone, and walks off the set with his head high and to the sound of the audience's thunderous applause. People are not stupid, they know when a person is trying to manipulate them.

When he gets to us, he draws Haven into a hug and kisses her passionately, as though trying to wash away all the terrible experiences of her past. When he pulls away from her, he grabs my face in his hands and gives me a kiss equally full of feeling and promises no one can steal.

I turn to Olivia, pale-faced as a technician crouches in front of her saying something. She doesn't look in our direction when we turn around and take a step toward the exit. To our surprise, the technician drops his headphones and gets up from the chair.

"I think I need to go home and have a talk with my daughter," he explains with a smile.

When we look again toward the exit, we're even more surprised to find Michael, Thomas, Damian, and Evan leaning against the wall with satisfied smiles on their faces.

"We knew you'd be great," Michael tells him proudly, putting his hands on his shoulders and drawing him in for a hug.

Damian and Thomas cling to them in a gesture only they understand, something so intimate and linked to their connection that not even Evan dares to interrupt.

When we all get in the limo and head into the Los Angeles traffic, Evan is so busy with his phone, I'm worried Simon's accusations have stirred up legal problems. Even though he didn't name names, his accusation was clearly about what happened years ago with Freewood.

"Is there a problem? Have Freewood's lawyers seen the interview and want to take off his head?" I ask, stopping every conversation and attracting the manager's attention.

Evan looks up from the screen and smiles at me. "Actually, no. It's the other way around. Since Simon's appeal, other women who fell into Freewood's trap over the years are coming forward on Twitter and Instagram, tagging the Jailbirds' profile. Some are commenting anonymously on Simon's post on *Rocking in New York*. I'm asking Emily to contact our lawyers and see if there's any way to help them...maybe we can set up legal action against the guy." He looks at Haven. "If it's okay with you."

Haven smiles at him and shrugs. "I've been hoping to see him behind bars for years, but it's always been my word against his. My bodyguard at the time told me he'd help me if I decided to testify. He was the one who drove me to many of the dates I had with David."

Evan nods and returns to text on his phone while the others watch us, smiling when I stretch my arm behind Haven's shoulders until I reach Simon's neck and grab him in a firm grip.

He turns around, smiles at me, and winks so sweetly that even Michael, sitting across from us, sighs like a girl in love. "I still can't believe you never tried to fuck me," he says with such sincerity we all laugh.

"Never even entered my mind—get over it," Simon teases, and we laugh our heads off.

***

When we get to the hotel room where we're staying, we look at the bed and, without even a word to each other, take off our shoes and collapse on it, emitting a long sigh that's a combination of relief and fatigue.

"I wasn't planning to bring up your past today." Simon turns to Haven, lying between the two of us.

She smiles at him and puts her hand on his cheek. "Don't worry. This story would've ended up in all the gossip magazines sooner or later. As soon as I got back into public life, everyone started to dig up the past. He just got what he deserves."

A weight lifts from my chest when I hear these words. It took years for Haven to stop feeling guilty for that affair, and I was afraid bringing it up on live TV might devastate her. Sometimes I forget how strong she is and maybe worry too much about her.

"There will probably be a lawsuit against David, or Simon for defamation. Are you worried?" I ask.

They watch me closely, perhaps to understand how much this concern has crept into my brain.

"It's not like we have to be silent just because this is Hollywood. Does he want to sue me? Let him do it, but other victims are raising their voices from what Evan says. How will he defend himself from those?" Simon says, appearing just as calm as Haven.

"And then there's my testimony. Simon didn't say anything I can't confirm. He told the truth, and I have evidence of what happened." The serenity on her face reassures me.

I snuggle next to Haven and stretch out an arm to reach Simon, who gets closer and wraps her in a tight hug.

"And I have the two of you. If you're with me, everything else takes a back seat," Simon whispers as he kisses her neck and draws me closer.

Hearing this, I let my fears slip away, just like I chased them away when the blankets of my bed rose in the dark when we were kids and Simon reached out his hand to let me know he was there.

Although we're independent adults now, capable of taking care of ourselves, the peace I feel knowing my hero is here with me makes me smile like I'm thirteen years old again. No matter how many years pass, or how many cracks I see under his hard surface, Simon will always be the one who saved me from my fears and protected me when I was most vulnerable. I know with him I'll feel safe even when we're old, and the passion that overwhelms us now will be a distant memory, but the bond that binds us will be stronger than ever.

CHAPTER 24
Haven

Simon's appearance on TV created such a stir that the fifteen days we had off from the tour to return to New York and relax turned into two weeks in Los Angeles for interviews with the Jailbirds and Simon in particular. Many shows have asked for my perspective, my testimony in the case of David Freewood, but Evan has used all his power to shield me in a situation that, by now, we're almost certain will end up in court.

After Simon's accusation, many other women came forward to denounce what David did over his thirty-year career. What happened with me was not just a one-time offense where he got caught with his hands in my panties, he got away with it with many other girls, some barely fifteen when they first had sex with him.

"What are you thinking?" Simon wraps his arms around my waist as I bask by the pool.

"That it all started by a pool like this. My whole life, from that moment on, fell apart. Everything I worked for, all the sacrifices I made instead of enjoying my teenage years, evaporated with a single photo that ended up in the newspapers."

"Did you like working in television?"

I love that Simon doesn't treat me like a helpless victim. He doesn't pity me. He's curious to learn things about me. He sees behind the tattoos, piercings, and pink hair.

"I loved it. I liked acting and understanding what was going on behind the scenes. I was interested in production, shooting, everything required to bring the finished product to the audience. That's how David lured me in. He exploited my curiosity, explained the details to me, made me feel part of something other actors couldn't care less about. I felt important. That's why I immediately found myself in tune with Nicholas."

"Do you want to go back to doing that kind of work?"

He sits behind me and wraps me between his legs. I lean back on his chest and enjoy the hug, thinking about it for a bit. For so long my main concern has been survival that I stopped nurturing my dreams.

"I gave up when I was still a teenager. I hid. I cut off all contact with that world. I don't even know if that's in my future or if there's something else that might interest me more."

Simon nods and gently kisses me on the shoulder. "What work do you like so much that you'd even do it for free?"

The question leaves me bewildered because only one answer comes to mind without even thinking about it for a second. "Acting. But I don't like the Hollywood environment. Besides David, who's disgusting, it's exhausting to constantly feel the micro-aggression of people who want to take your place or rule over you. There's no healthy competition. Everyone smiles at you while they stab you in the back. Maybe I was too young at the time to react to what was being done to me, but in hindsight, I realized that the environment was toxic for a teenager who still had to grow up and learn to defend herself."

Simon squeezes me a little tighter. "You needed someone

to protect you, to shield you."

A bitter smile curls my lips. "My mother pushed me into David's bed to give me a career. In the end, the same thing happened to her: my grandmother put her in a beauty contest when she was five years old. They toured the United States, competition after competition, and if she didn't win, she faced weeks of hell on a strict diet, repeating the dance steps or songs that weren't perfect and caused her to lose the first-place title."

"Seriously? I had no idea her life was like that."

"Do you know why my name is Haven?" Simon shakes his head and lets me continue. "My mother never went to school. My grandmother made her study at home just enough to pass the tests, but her whole life was always spent preparing for one contest or another. When I was born, she wanted to call me Heaven because she said I was her corner of paradise, but she didn't know how to spell it, and she registered my name without the *e*. Haven. I'm named this because my mother can barely read and write."

"Wow. That's…I don't think I have words to describe what I'm feeling. From the outside, your life seemed perfect. Two successful women who had Hollywood at their feet. How does your mother learn lines for movies? Did she learn to read over time?"

I shake my head, and a bitter smile forms on my lips. "I don't know if anything's changed in recent years, but her assistant recorded all her scripts when I lived with her. They always considered her a diva for this. They thought it was her way of throwing a tantrum. In reality, it was just ignorance in the most basic sense of the word."

The sound of steps behind us draws our attention. We turn

to see Nicholas coming out the patio door of the mansion they rented for everyone. I like how the Jailbirds are always together. They could have rented hotel rooms. Instead, they chose a massive estate with enough rooms for all of us, a dining room that accommodates twenty people, and gathering areas that bring us together. Like a family, a real one, the kind you choose.

Yesterday I watched Levi cuddling Liberty while Faith and Michael watched, along with Lilly and Damian. Those two kids are learning what it's like to have a real family, one that loves you no matter what and would do anything for your happiness and beyond, not just their parents but all the Jailbirds.

"The private investigator's here. I think he has news about your stalker."

Nicholas's words fall on me like a cold shower. Simon's arms tighten protectively around my body, but they don't calm my heart hammering inside my chest.

Nicholas extends his hand and helps me up, and so does Simon. I feel the arms of both wrap around my back, one on each side. I've never felt as protected as right now, squeezed between two wings of support.

We approach Evan in the light, airy living room and wait for others to join us. The serious face of the investigator scares me a little, but I don't know if it's his way of maintaining a professional appearance or because he has horrible news to give us.

We're all seated on the sofas, only Levi and Liberty are not in the room. I think Michael and Faith don't want to scare the kid and tasked him with watching over his younger sister.

"Do you know the name of the person who broke into our bus?" I ask impatiently.

The man hints at a half-smile but shakes his head, and the mixture of hope and fear dies in my chest. I hoped to finally put a face to my tormentor. The wave of emotions that hits me almost makes my head spin, relieved that I don't have to face it and annoyed that this saga won't end today.

"We don't have a name yet, but we're getting closer," he replies.

"Okay, but I don't think you came here to just tell us that, right?" Michael inquires. "And most importantly, why are we all here?"

A murmur of general assent follows.

Evan beats the investigator to the answer. "When we asked for the services of the investigation agency, we wanted to know if this was a die-hard fan who wanted a souvenir or if we had to worry about something more serious."

I don't like the direction this conversation has taken at all.

"Apparently, this is not an isolated event, but it's better if he explains it to you," Evan adds.

Nicholas and Simon, sitting next to me, grab each of my hands.

"Did you know that when you were fifteen, your mother filed a complaint because someone had broken into your house?" He gets straight to the point.

I wrinkle my forehead and think about it a bit. At fifteen, my life was hectic, but I remember a day when I came home to find police cars in the driveway.

"I remember some fans had managed to get into the back-yard and leave a gift in front of the door of our house. My mother wanted the police to intervene, but it ended there. She hired bodyguards from that day on, more out of paranoia than real danger." The last words come out in a whisper because I see his face getting serious again.

"They weren't fans. The person who entered your house was not limited to the backyard, he was in your room. He left a package with a gift and covered your bed with red rose petals. That wasn't the first time it happened, so your mother had your bodyguards follow you. She was really worried about you."

I feel nausea taking hold of my stomach and sour bile rising in my throat.

"She never told you about this?" Nicholas whispers.

I shake my head.

"Do you think it's the same person? After more than ten years?" Damian breaks the silence, sounding hopeful.

The man crosses his arms and nods as if expecting that question. "There are all too obvious similarities to what happened before. In fact, it was a breakthrough when I spoke to the police and found out there'd been an investigation in the past."

"Be honest, what are the real dangers here for her?" Simon is worried.

"With the security you hired, I think it's difficult to get close to her, but I would avoid going out too much until we learn more. Having no idea what he looks like, it's hard to keep a safe distance from anyone suspicious. From his behavior, we're almost positive he's a man, driven by sexual desire, but we can't completely rule out a woman."

Absolute silence falls, broken only by the indignant whisper of Faith. "What animal would feel sexual desire for a fifteen-year-old girl? She was just a child."

It's the first time I've heard her take such a firm and disgusted position toward a subject that doesn't concern her.

Damian answers her question. "The kind who want to see her squeezed into a skin-tight jumpsuit that leaves nothing to the imagination. All the show cared about was not showing a bra, or a nipple, or cleavage, but they'll feed a teenager to the beasts if it means gaining an audience. And unfortunately, a lot of men are beasts." He leans back on the sofa and hugs Lilly tight.

His words bring to mind my mother and how she pushed me toward David to see those TV ratings rise with every new episode.

"I hate her." My words come out so full of anger that everyone turns to look at me. "My mother, I hate her. She didn't tell me anything. A man broke into my room, violated my sacred space, and she didn't tell me anything."

"Maybe she did it to protect you. So you wouldn't be frightened," Thomas says as he grips Iris's hand.

I smile at him but shake my head. "I really wish it were like that, but my mother is not the kind who cares about her daughter. She's the kind who bought me sexy clothes for my dates with David and scolded me when I got caught by the paparazzi. Trust me, she did it to protect my image, not me. I had no idea and ran away alone in the middle of the night. On foot. What if that man had been out there waiting for me?"

I feel Nicholas and Simon's hands squeeze harder as Thomas looks down, embarrassed. I didn't want to make him uncomfortable, but I can't stand it when anyone tries to justify my mother's behavior.

"What happens if you don't catch him? If you can't find out who he is?" Nicholas's voice is full of tension. I turn to see him staring at the man with a mixture of anger and resignation. I know he wishes he could do more to protect me, but he's as powerless as I am in this case.

"Usually, with people who stalk their victims for so many years and aren't arrested, the outcome is typically one of two things: either the victim dies, or the stalker dies. These people are obsessed with the idea of owning and controlling the person who's the object of their fantasies."

His words are like a punch in the stomach. Will this story only end with the death of one of us?

"But why now? Why didn't he continue to follow her all these years?" Lilly asks, perhaps in the hope of discovering they're really two different people.

I think I know the answer. "Because that night I really did disappear. I disguised my appearance with heavy makeup, piercings, dyed hair, and clothes that hid my body. At first, people would say I looked like someone, but they couldn't say who. Everyone was looking for the girl next door with long hair and a wholesome face, not someone out of a Tarantino movie. I disappeared from the stalker's radar, evidently. It was too sudden a change for him to follow me."

The investigator nods as if to agree with my hypothesis.

We all remain silent for several minutes, digesting the information we've just received. From the living room doorway, Levi's voice makes us all turn toward him.

"So tonight we order takeout, right?" No one noticed his presence until now, and it's clear he witnessed the conversation. He's too smart not to understand what we're talking about.

"I have a better idea," says Nicholas as he gets up and picks up his phone on the kitchen counter. We all watch him, the curiosity to know what the hell he has in mind distracting us from the worries that trap us inside this room and make us not want to face the outside world.

I observe all the tense faces, and I feel guilty for what's happening; when I get to Michael, he nails me with a stern look. "Don't even think this is your fault, got it?"

His tone is so strong I curl up on the couch. "You're all forced to be here because of me, because we don't know what that person might do. It *is* my fault."

"Do you think things like this never happen to us? That we never have to hide because some fool decides we're his favorite pastime? We once spent a month in a cottage in Vermont, surrounded by acres of nothing but trees because we found a fake bomb at our record label office left by a religious extremist group that thought we were the devil incarnate. We're public figures, and with the fame comes the crazies," he replies.

Well, I feel a little relieved at that.

"It's not like we're locked up in prison. We're in a Hollywood mansion with a swimming pool. It could be much worse," Damian chimes in.

"And tonight, our friend Sady is coming to make us dinner and spend some time with us," Nicholas adds, returning to the living room.

"Really? I can't wait to hug him again!" I'm surprised at how excited I am to see him. I didn't realize how much I've missed him, and how it seems like light years ago that we ate lobster in Venice Beach. Our life has changed so much that one evening will not be enough to catch him up on all the news.

***

The sight of Sady at the stove is a spectacle that has enchanted everyone, especially Damian, who seems to want to steal all the chef's secrets. At first, our friend was a bit intimidated by the band, but when he saw how easy-going and humble they were, he started to smile and joke around. He even began explaining to Damian and Thomas what he was doing, answering their most complicated questions. I've never seen him at work, and I must say it's fascinating to observe his skill in preparing food.

He cursed Nicholas for only giving him a few hours to get the ingredients and prepare a dinner that wouldn't disappoint, but I must say, he did great. He served mixed tacos with lobster and crab for appetizers, risotto with prawns and saffron, clam chowder in little bread bowls, salted sea bass with steamed vegetables, and skewers of Alaskan halibut that made Levi groan with pleasure. Even though he would have preferred takeout burgers and fries, we convinced him to sit at the table just to taste the main courses and the lemon mousse with strawberry compote Sady prepared for dessert.

"Are you really a sous chef?" Damian's expression is incredulous.

"Yes." I've never seen Sady as proud as he seems right now with all eyes on him.

"Why the hell haven't they promoted you to chef yet?

You're better than a lot of big names in five-star restaurants we've eaten in all over the world," Michael insists.

"Maybe because I'd have to kill the current one to become a chef, and I think murder is still illegal."

Everyone bursts out laughing. I've always liked Sady's humor.

"Listen, if we opened a restaurant, would you be interested in being the chef? You would have full say over everything," Damian proposes.

Sady smiles and sips some water, clearly overwhelmed by the proposal. "Do you open a strip club for everyone who gives you a good blowjob?" he replies.

Lilly chokes on a sip of wine before spitting it onto her empty plate and laughing.

"Sweet Jesus…" Faith's whisper makes us all burst out laughing after the moment of absolute silence.

"I'm not kidding. We've been trying to diversify our investments for some time, and why not a restaurant?"

What I thought was just a joke is an actual proposal. I study Sady's face, who is suspicious, to say the least. "Because it takes millions of dollars in investment capital?" he tries to explain.

"Which we have," Thomas intervenes.

"Are you serious? You just met me two hours ago."

"Haven and Nicholas have known you for years. We trust them," Simon adds.

Sady looks at me. I shrug and nod, confirming that they're really crazy for thinking about doing this, but I'm not surprised by it.

"Full control over everything? Menu and staff included?"

"We don't know anything about running a restaurant," Damian admits. "Give me your phone number. I'll give you a couple of days to think about it. When I call you, I want an answer."

Sady's eyes widen but he says nothing. He types his number into Damian's cell phone and then turns his incredulous gaze on me again. I smile at him and shrug again. What can I say? I'd be amazed too. It took me months to understand the dynamics of this group. Knowing their stories, I understand why they keep picking up strays and giving them homes. Sady has dinner with the homeless in Los Angeles because he has no one waiting for him in his immaculate apartment. Like a dog sniffing out hopeless cases, Damian found him and offered him a leg up.

CHAPTER 25

Simon

The last two concerts before the break that separates the American leg of the tour from the rest of the world, starting with Europe, flew by without us even noticing. My mind and energy were focused on Haven and the person who wants to hurt her. It's strange how suddenly all my worries about what the press would say about us seem ridiculous compared to what she's going through.

Two weeks have passed since the investigator's visit, and although she's always smiling and trying to behave normally, I realize she looks over her shoulder when she thinks no one notices. Those few times when we go out, she prefers restaurants that have tables against the wall, where she can observe the whole room in front of her.

At first, we were undecided whether to return to Los Angeles after the tour because we're almost sure the person who follows her is based here. But we came to the conclusion that he has a way to travel because when he stole Haven's underwear, we were in entirely different cities, in states thousands of miles away.

New York or Los Angeles, it wouldn't have made any difference to her safety. Here, however, we're closer to the documentary's production company. Since Nicholas and Haven are busy editing the first episodes, we thought we'd rent a huge house that will accommodate us all. Instead of moving people working on the project to New York, having a room with all the equipment they need to work on the documentary, here is more practical.

I'm preparing a sandwich while watching Michael play with Liberty and Levi in the pool. Faith sits on the edge and has the nervous look of a mother watching her children swimming near an erupting volcano. She doesn't say anything because she knows Michael is the most reliable person on the face of the earth when it comes to her children, but every now and then, I see her wanting to grab Liberty and drag her out of the water when Michael drops her for a few seconds. The truth is that at almost four months old, that little girl could swim in the ocean if it weren't too cold.

"What the hell's wrong with you? Why that face?" I ask Nicholas as soon as he sets foot in the living room and crosses it to reach me.

His stride is furious, his face a mask of disappointment with veins throbbing on his forehead. He's almost scary with his few days' beard growth and eyes red-rimmed from too many hours in front of a monitor. He wraps his hands around my waist and rests his forehead on my shoulder when he reaches me.

"I'll kill him. I swear I will kill him if he goes on like this."

I don't need him to name the guy to know he's talking about Shane, the film editor the production company hired to finish this project. When he entered the house on the first day, he turned up his nose and began giving orders with the attitude of a know-it-all because, according to him, Nicholas doesn't deserve the role he had.

Nicholas had told us, almost word for word, about Shane's insulting speech the first time the two started working in front of the same computer. "Let's make one thing clear right away, kid. You don't have any experience in a production company. It's not like shooting independent films; do what I tell you and shut up. I don't care if you have the right connections or give great blowjobs, I'm not going to ruin my reputation with your mediocre work…"

In all honesty, he seems like one of those stuck-up snobs who discredit independent films because he feels threatened by movies that don't follow Hollywood's rules. The same movies that often reach audiences traditional production companies don't.

"Have you already thought about where we can hide the body, or do you want me to figure that out? I don't have much to do this afternoon. I'll look for the best place to bury him if you want." I make him smile.

"What if the police come looking for him and find some loose dirt in the backyard?" he teases me.

"We'll plant a rare protected species of flowers over it, so they won't be able to dig up the corpse."

This time his laugh lights up his whole face, and I'll never get tired of looking at him when he's happy. It reminds me of the child full of dreams who entered the foster family years ago and showed me his toothless smile, sticking out his hand to shake mine. I lean over to kiss him and put my hands in the dark curls that are now too long. Nicholas forgets not only to cut his hair but also to eat and drink if he's concentrating on a project he's passionate about.

His tongue slides over mine and his hands slip under my shirt, touching the skin of my back. I'll never get used to the electricity that runs through my muscles straight to my heart whenever his fingers are on me. I slide a hand down to his ass and pull him to me, feeling his erection inside the sweatpants.

"Are you happy to see me?" I whisper in his ear and then nibble his lobe and elicit a small choked groan.

"I'm always happy to see you, but we have to stop if you don't want to traumatize two kids." He nods his head to the pool where Michael finally got Liberty out of the water, saving Faith's sanity.

"Or we can always move away…" I motion to the pantry door a few steps from us.

We don't have to think about it even for a second. We slip between the shelves of canned soup, flour and tomato sauce, and close the door. When I kneel before him and pull down his pants and boxers in a single move, his erection welcomes me as if he'd been waiting for me. Nicholas leans his back against one of the shelves and slips his hands into my hair while my tongue savors its entire length, from the base to the tip, and then I open my lips until I wrap it and push it into my throat.

"I don't think I can resist," he whispers as he desperately tries not to push his hips toward me.

I move my hands to his ass and push for him. I don't want him to hold back. I want to give him the pleasure he seeks so desperately. A choked moan comes out of his chest when we hear someone walk through the kitchen and go out to the pool on the other side of the door. There's no time to prolong his agony without risking being seen, so I grab his erection with one hand and squeeze, increasing the rhythm and making it sink into my mouth until I feel him stiffen and pour his pleasure into my throat. I never thought having oral sex with a man could please me this much, especially being the giver instead of the receiver.

When I get up and pull his pants back up, Nicholas draws me to him for a kiss that leaves me breathless. I found out he likes to feel his taste in my mouth.

"When do we take care of this?" he whispers, resting his hand on my erection that's obvious through my jeans.

"Not now. There's someone in the kitchen," I tell him before opening the pantry door and coming face to face with Evan and Michael looking at us. Our manager is surprised. My friend has a knowing grin.

"I told you they were fucking in the pantry." He laughs before heading back to the pool.

Apparently, we weren't as discreet as we thought, but Evan doesn't seem bothered. "Is Haven in the studio?" he asks, and we quickly realize he has news for her. Whether good or bad, we can't tell.

"Yes," Nicholas tells me. "Do you want me to go and call her?"

"First help me figure out the best way to give her the news. We think we've found the name and address of the man who's been following her. I know she's so strong and tough, but I think she's scared. I need your help to tell her."

"No." My voice is so firm that the other two look at me, surprised. "I know how she is. She'll want to solve this situation with a confrontation. I want to see the guy first."

"You want to go and talk to the guy? Are you crazy?"

Nicholas's voice is as agitated as his expression. He turns to Evan: "Can the police do anything? Can we go to them?"

Our manager shakes his head. "There's no evidence. They don't go knocking on someone's door without having something tangible. And you won't either. We have no idea if he's dangerous or not," he scolds me.

"I'm not going to sit here and wait for something to happen to her. Give me that address, Evan. I don't want to argue with you. I'm not going to do anything stupid. I just want to see his face and tell him to stay away." I reach out my hand toward him, not knowing if he wrote the address on a piece of paper or in an email. I don't care.

Evan inhales and shakes his head before moving away from the kitchen counter.

"Where are you going?" Nicholas is as perplexed as I am.

"I'll drive." The resignation in our manager's voice would make me smile if not for the nervousness squeezing my stomach.

***

Eleven minutes. The time it takes us to get from Los Feliz, the neighborhood where we rented the house, to Burbank, where the man lives, is eleven minutes. I don't even have time to think about what the hell I'm going to say because we're already in front of his house. A complex of eight apartments on two floors joined by an exterior corridor with brown railings and bars on the windows.

Eleven minutes is the time it takes this fool to reach our home. Time enough for a shower, a coffee, or to cook the pasta Haven loves so much. Eleven minutes to give this man a chance to ruin her life. The irony is that this city is so congested it takes hours to cross it and reach the beach, but we rented a house eleven minutes from this man.

The anger smoldering inside me is so huge I don't realize that Nicholas is saying my name. "Have you changed your mind? Can we go home and let the private investigator find enough evidence to give to the police?"

He looks at me as I shift my gaze from the number eight painted in white on the dark door to his face. "No. I was just thinking about what I'll say."

Nicholas looks at me sadly, perhaps thinking I'd change my mind on the way. He's worried about me, about my criminal record that could get me into trouble if the guy sues us for threatening him. I've thought about the consequences myself, but we can't wait until he hurts Haven for the police to intervene.

Evan shakes his head but says nothing. He follows a step behind me when I take the flight of stairs that leads us upstairs. I knock on the door vigorously, and no one answers for a few minutes, but from the apartment next door, I see the curtains moving by a breath.

The complex overlooks the back of a windowless warehouse. We're separated only by a strip of asphalt where cars are parked. It's a closed road, and there's no coming and going of pedestrians. I imagine anyone would be curious to know why three men, one in sweatpants, one in jeans, and one in a suit and tie, are knocking on the neighbor's door on a Thursday afternoon. These apartments have paper-thin walls. We can hear someone snoring in the unit next door.

I knock another time, but no one comes to open it. I put my ear to the door, and I can't hear a sound inside. I try to peek through the window, but heavy curtains block any view of the inside.

"Let's go. He's not here. Maybe he's at work." Evan tries to get my attention, placing his hand on my arm.

"Or maybe he's snooping around our house spying on Haven," I snap.

I take my wallet from my back pocket and open the compartment where I keep two small metal tools to pick the locks.

"What the hell are you doing?" Evan whisper-shouts at me when I try the handle to see if, by any chance, the door is open.

When I stick the first piece of metal into the lock and lower myself slightly to see where to put the second, Evan grabs me by the arm. "Simon, let's go. I didn't bring you here to break into someone's house," he hisses with gritted teeth.

"He broke into our bus," I counter.

Nicholas chuckles. "You keep tools to pick locks inside your wallet?"

I raise my shoulder and smile at him. "Old habit, I guess."

He shakes his head and sighs. "Evan's right. You can't go in there. You could get arrested. Don't do something stupid, Simon…" he begs, but it's too late. I push the door open without a sound.

"Oops," I say, pretending to stumble and putting one foot over the threshold.

Glancing inside, I see something I didn't expect. There's

a kitchen and living area, a standard room with dark wood furniture in square, clean lines. But the creepiest part is that everything is so tidy it looks almost sterile. You don't see a single speck of dust on any surface. The towel hanging from the oven handle is perfectly centered, the four kitchen chairs are all tucked under the table at identical intervals. The rectangular coffee table in front of the sofa is positioned precisely halfway between the couch and the cabinet with the TV.

"All this tidiness is making me nervous." Nicholas's whisper behind me makes me spin.

Both he and Evan entered the room and left the door open. They look around with the same bewildered expression as mine. I don't know why, but I didn't expect a clean freak to be stealing panties from girls. I imagined a house full of monitors and tech stuff to spy on women inside dressing rooms at shopping malls. Maybe this is exactly how he's managed to get away with it.

I walk toward a small hallway.

"Simon, let's go…" Evan hisses quietly. "Don't push your luck."

I don't listen to him. I open the first door to a small dark bathroom; from what little I can glimpse, it has the same maniacal order as the living room.

The door on the other side leads to the bedroom. Neat, like the others, with a single bed, a closet, and a dresser. The only difference here is that there are sheets of paper resting on the dresser. I approach and see they're arranged perfectly like the rest of the apartment, but when I look more closely, I realize they're photos. Photos of Haven, to be exact, taken in the most mundane moments: having coffee, chatting with the roadies, doing laundry. All images that invade her private life during moments when she's most vulnerable, unconsciously exposed to danger. Every single shot reveals that he could hurt her if he wanted to. The power he has over her.

"I found something…" I call the others inside the room and in seconds they're next to me.

"That's the pass Haven lost," whispers Nicholas horrified as he points to the object dangling from a nail on the wall next to the dresser.

She didn't lose it. It was snatched from her. The man was so close he'd touched it, grabbed that pass, and perhaps cut the strap it hung from with a blade. He was so close he could've stabbed her, and we couldn't have done anything. The sour taste that rises in my throat is hard to swallow. I clench my teeth and inhale. If he were here, there's no doubt in my mind I'd beat him to death.

"Don't touch anything. Let's leave and call the police," Evan commands, and this time I listen. Perhaps this evidence will be enough to incriminate him.

When I leave the room, followed by Evan and Nicholas, I find myself face to face with a couple of officers with their guns pointed at us. We're all so surprised that the two police-men say nothing. I slowly raise my hands to my head and get on my knees. Nicholas and Evan next to me do the same. The two frown and linger on my face. The wide-open door lets in enough light to make us recognizable.

"Do you know who I am?" I ask them.

"Of course, we know who you are. Your face is on all the damn TV channels lately. But don't think your fame will help you. Don't move," replies the larger one with shaved hair.

"We don't want to stop you from doing your job. Handcuff us, do what you want, but please listen to me."

Handcuffing us is a quick business for the two of them. The biggest one renders us helpless with our hands behind our backs, while the other points the weapon at us. We don't resist, and they don't get carried away. When he grabs me by the elbow and helps me stand, I turn to him and look him straight in the eye.

"If you saw me on TV, then you must know who Haven, our girlfriend, is, right?" I ask him and he nods. He's studying me like he's trying to figure out if I'm under the influence. I don't think he expected to find me when a nosy neighbor called the police.

"We entered this apartment because the man who lives here broke into our tour bus and stole her underwear. Panties he found in her laundry basket." When you mention stealing panties to a cop, you get his attention. It's a sick act that no one would ever dismiss without checking it out first. "If you go in that room, on the dresser are photos of her taken while he followed her, and a backstage pass stolen from her months ago. I bet if you look in the drawers, you'll find panties."

The guy studies me for a few seconds but then motions for his colleague to go check. When the slightly shorter and stockier cop comes out, he looks like someone who's just learned his day got much more complicated.

"He's telling the truth. There are photos of a girl, a concert pass. I don't know if the panties are in the drawer, but I can't look without a warrant."

"Call someone to come and check," he orders him, and the man goes out on the landing to talk on his radio with the police station.

"Thank you."

"Don't think this changes anything. I'm taking you to the police station anyway. This is private property, and I doubt you have the keys or permission to enter."

"No problem. We just need this person not to hurt Haven."

He drags us out of the apartment and into the back seat of their car.

"I can't believe this," Evan whispers.

"Don't tell me you've never been in trouble." I chuckle as I lean over Nicholas, who looks both amused and worried. I bet he'll make me pay for this.

"No, Simon. I never ended up in prison for breaking and entering. And to think I drove you here! You're going to give me a heart attack." He leans against the seat, resigned.

"Come on. If we weren't here to keep you young, you'd be an old couch potato," I joke.

"I'm thirty years old, Simon. I am young…and very stressed."

We all burst out laughing at this absurd situation we ended up in. The more we try to stop, the more our laughter becomes uncontrollable, to the point of tears, and Evan getting the hiccups. When the two policemen get into the car and take us away, they glance in the rear-view mirror and shake their heads, causing another wave of laughter to fall over us.

In the police station, sitting in a room without windows and cold fluorescent lights, they ask questions that we answer honestly. They don't try to separate us because, as cooperative citizens, we confess without resisting. We clearly tell them what happened, in detail, emphasizing how sick the guy is. We asked them to verify the complaints made by Haven's mother years ago to convince them of the seriousness of our claims.

When they leave us alone, Evan rests his forehead on the big gray table in front of us. "Simon, you know you can never ask for another favor for as long as you live, right?" He studies me carefully when he raises his head. "From now on, if I tell you to do an interview naked at the top of the Empire State Building, you'll do it without complaining. Without the slightest hesitation."

I smile and look down at my hands. I realize I got carried away, but I'd do it over again if given the chance. I've never been afraid to get my hands dirty to save the people I love.

Nicholas chuckles next to me.

"Don't laugh. That goes for you too." Evan gives him a stern look.

"I didn't do anything!" My boyfriend tries to defend himself.

The door opens again, and the same policeman who brought us here and interrogated us sits across from us with a bunch of papers in his hand. "You're the luckiest bastards I know."

We look at him in surprise, waiting for him to explain.

"Less than thirty minutes after we took you away, they caught the guy in the apartment, and now he's here confessing about his obsession with Haven." He looks up at us and folds his arms, studying us for a long moment. "He doesn't even want to file a complaint against you. You get to leave with a pat on the back."

"So there won't be any charges against us?" The hope in Evan's voice is so obvious it makes me smile.

"No, you'll have to sign some papers, but that's it. You'll walk out of here as free citizens."

I breathe a sigh of relief at not having to end up in court again.

"I've never made two arrests in one day and obtained both confessions without even asking for them. You guys suck as criminals," he jokes.

"Is that man admitting that he wants to hurt Haven?" Nicholas's voice trembles, sounding either fearful or angry.

The policeman looks at him, shakes his head, and rubs his hand over his face. "I shouldn't tell you anything, but he's crazy." He frowns. "His obsession with your friend has lasted for at least fifteen years. We found not only the panties you were talking about but other things in his house too. Including a teddy bear."

"He broke into her house when she was just a teenager. He must have taken it then."

The man shakes his head and inhales deeply, raising his face to the ceiling. When he lowers it, his expression is less stern. "This time, it worked out for you, but don't do that again. He could've been armed and killed you. I know you had the best intentions, but don't play detectives. You were very lucky to get out of this without something worse happening."

The message reaches us loud and clear. Another bullshit stunt like that, and we'd end up in prison—or worse, six feet under.

A knock on the door makes us all turn to another agent who smiles greeting us. "The gentlemen who have come to pick them up are here," he announces a little too cheerfully.

"We're coming. Give me a minute to get these signed." The policeman waves the folder in his hand.

"Oh, no. They specifically asked to come in here." He chuckles and steps aside as Damian, Michael, and Thomas fill the small doorway that divides us. Cell phones in hand, they start clicking.

"We couldn't miss an opportunity to get pictures of our manager behind bars," Damian announces with a grin. Nicholas and I can't hold back a chuckle.

"Murder is still illegal, right?" Evan turns to the policeman, who's chuckling as much as we are.

"Only if you get caught." He winks as he gets up to let us out.

Haven is with them. A few steps away, she's watching a man talking to two detectives in a large room full of desks and policemen. Hands handcuffed behind his back, he grins crazily with wide eyes. He looks ordinary enough: ash-colored hair combed to the side, glasses, pale skin, shirt tucked into a pair of khakis. Quite a contrast to the junkies drooling on the desks and guys with tattooed faces. Your classic "average person" who disappears in a crowd, anonymous, harmless, someone you wouldn't keep the door open for because you don't even realize he's behind you.

"That's him, isn't it?" Haven looks at the policeman accompanying us outside.

"You don't have to meet him. Come on, we'll leave this

way." He points to another corridor.

"No, I want to talk to him."

The policeman freezes on the spot and frowns. His gaze shifts between Nicholas and me just behind her, but we don't know what to tell him.

"Please. This person has been stalking me for more than ten years. I just want to know why."

The man inhales deeply, undecided about what to do, then nods and beckons her to follow him.

"You know you probably won't get an answer, right?" I whisper in her ear as we approach.

Haven looks at me, smiles, and nods. She's calm, and that helps me not to be nervous too.

When the man looks up, his eyes light up. "Haven! We were just talking about you. I was telling them how you are my muse, how you sing just for me."

The detectives interrogating him assess this odd scene, perhaps undecided whether to intervene or not.

"Why me? Why did you choose me?" Her voice is firm. I didn't imagine she could be so collected in a moment like this.

"What do you mean why? You're perfect! You come from outer space. We'll get rid of all those piercings and tattoos when we get home, but you'll be perfect again." His voice is so calm and serene as he says this nonsense that it makes me shiver. Nicholas is as tense as a wild animal ready to attack.

"You took pictures of my partners and me and gave them to the press. Why?"

The man suddenly becomes gloomy and aggressive. He tries to get up from his chair, and we take a step back while the detective in front of him stretches out his hand to make him remain seated.

"Because they're the filthy animals that took you away. They've hidden you all these years to keep you away from me. They're filthy pigs and everyone needed to know. Everyone needed to know what they looked like, so they could defend themselves."

His voice is a hiss of hatred and in this moment I finally realize the risk I put Nicholas and Evan in, entering that house.

"Haven, let's go…" I drag her and Nicholas down the hall to where the others are waiting for us. The angry shouts of the man follow behind us.

"Everything okay?" asks Damian as we approach.

Haven smiles and nods. "Actually, yes. I've spent weeks wondering what the hell I had done wrong to get that person's attention. I thought I was too flirty, provocative, enticing… I thought back to my entire career, dissecting it for an explanation, an attitude of mine that could have been misinterpreted, that had triggered his obsession. I just realized there's nothing. He's crazy. Whatever I did, whatever decision I made, the result would not change because the problem was not me. The problem is in his head: he can't tell the difference between reality and fantasy."

Her words bring a relieved smile to everyone's faces, aware that finally, this chapter is really over.

Nicholas

Seven years earlier

I open my eyes to the phone ringing on the bedside table. I already know who it is without even looking, and my heart sinks into my stomach. One ring, just one, like every other birthday, and I wonder why. I don't know if he wants me to know that he thinks of me or if he tries to call me, but then he reconsiders and hangs up.

Every year as my birthday approaches, my tension grows. Every year I wonder why I keep that phone on at all. Mixed feelings stir inside my chest. While I'd like to answer and tell him I miss him, I also wish I could just cut off forever this last line of communication I've kept with the past and convince him that I'm over him. As soon as the idea of losing him forever makes its way into my chest, however, my heart hammers so violently it almost escapes my throat. Maybe my heart wants to run to him and let him hold it hostage for another year.

I grab the old phone held together by duct tape and open it. A missed call by a number I don't have in my contacts but know by heart. I sit down and stare at that call. Like every year, the struggle not to call back wears me out until I'm nauseous. Like every year, I put the phone in the drawer, exhaling a big sigh as I close it again.

I get up and get dressed quickly, grab my wallet with the bit of money I have left, and decide to treat myself to breakfast with a cappuccino and a muffin in a café, instead of the usual disgusting slop my roommates and I drink every morning.

I slip my wallet into an inner pocket I've sewn into my pants and go out into the only place I can afford to live: Compton. One of the most dangerous neighborhoods in Los Angeles, where you have a chance in twenty-nine of ending up a victim of a violent crime. When people think of Los Angeles, they imagine the Hollywood mansions, Rodeo Drive, the beaches in Santa Monica, or, further north, Malibu. The truth is that the cost of living here is so high you end up living in a place where your chances of being killed in a shootout are higher than getting a part in a movie.

I walk fast and head down to one of the cafes not far from our apartment. A hole-in-the-wall with bars on the windows and the door glass smashed by a bullet in the center. The only one in the area that stays open round the clock, but where I don't dare to set foot after dark.

Walking in the alley behind the place, I notice pink hair almost hidden by a garbage bag that looks heavy. I run toward the person about to be crushed by the bag's weight and help them throw it into the bin, much higher than them.

When we finally manage to put it into the smelly dumpster, I turn to the tiny figure and find two hazel eyes scrutinizing me with curiosity. Heavy makeup, piercings on her face, and hair that looks like it just came out of a blender can't hide the beauty of this girl.

"Actress or screenwriter?" I ask her the stupidest question in the world. When I'm nervous, I can't put one word after another to compose a full sentence.

She looks at me like I'm crazy and, perhaps, even with a bit of terror in her eyes.

"Sorry…stupid joke. They say every bartender or waiter in Los Angeles has a script in their drawer, either to sell it or act in." I rub a hand on the back of my neck, but I see her smiling and relaxing.

"Neither. You? Actor or screenwriter?" Her voice has a mocking tone that makes me smile.

"Director."

She bursts out laughing. "You chose the biggest shark tank. Congratulations, that takes courage."

I don't know why, but the way she says it seems like a sincere compliment, and I blush. When she goes around me to get out of the alley, I feel the need to stop her, to talk to her again.

"Would you like to have a coffee with me, so you can tell me how you ended up in Los Angeles without being an actress?"

She turns and studies me for a few seconds, clearly uncertain whether to consider me an awkward kid or a possible serial killer. "Okay, but not here. I just finished my shift, and I don't want to set foot in here again until tonight." She smiles and gestures for me to follow her.

We take a bus to Venice Beach, then stop at a Starbucks before sitting on the beach, looking at the ocean, and talking about films so old that some are still in black and white.

We spend hours talking about movies, soundtracks, passion for old films, and critically evaluating the new ones. The ease with which she discusses topics like photography or editing ignites a fire inside me. I've never met anyone with such a vast knowledge of what's going on behind the camera. Usually, I'm dealing with actresses who worry that the light or camera angle is showing their cellulite. This woman is a breath of fresh air that makes me forget Simon, my birthday, my fears, and my worries.

"Have you tried to send your resume to some production companies? Maybe starting as a production assistant and then working your way to the top."

I look down at the sand, remembering the opportunities I've missed because I don't have the capacity to stab people in the back the way so many in this business do. My cheeks burn with shame. "I'm afraid this isn't a good industry for those of us who don't know how to kill to survive. I don't think I have the balls for this job," I confess aloud what I never dared to admit even to myself.

Her brown eyes study me for a few long seconds, then she looks back at the ocean in front of us. "You threw yourself in the garbage to help a complete stranger. You have a good soul. You'll see that, sooner or later, you'll get to the top without sacrificing your moral integrity. People with such big hearts can only do great things in life."

Her words warm me like a blanket in winter. A soothing balm that heals my wounds. I had no idea how much I needed to hear this until I heard it from her determined voice. There's no trace of mockery in it.

I don't dare to answer, but I gaze at the waves crashing on the sand until I notice her get up and remove the sand from her pants.

"See you around," she says, as if she were confident in the possibility of meeting twice in a massive city like Los Angeles.

"Can I at least know your name?"

"Haven."

I nod with a smile. "Nice to meet you, Haven. I'm Nicholas."

"See you around, Nicholas." She tilts her head and smiles at me before turning around and walking with her head held high as if she owned the world. I see her disappear into the crowd without turning back even once.

CHAPTER *26*
Nicholas

As the images scroll across the production company's office screen, my leg bounces under the chair. Next to me is Shane, the film editor, and next to him, five bigwigs from the production company that will air the documentary.

We are watching the first finished episode. It will be the fiftieth time we've seen it, with different people from the team, tweaking it a bit with every viewing. This time, however, it's for the big bosses. Aaron Steel himself is standing behind us, with his black hair and ice-gray eyes looking at the screen with a blank face, his arms folded across his chest in his thousand-dollar suit. The broad shoulders, narrow waist, long legs, and regal bearing all reinforce an image that terrifies everyone who works here. He has the reputation as an axman, but to tell the truth, since he began helping his father more actively, the production company has churned out quality films that have deservedly won several awards. If he decides this documentary isn't good, however, all our efforts will be in vain.

When the credits roll over the screen, I don't dare turn around and see his expression. No one breathes, but when I hear the door open then close immediately, I turn around to see what's going on. Aaron is gone. I turn dumbfounded toward the other people in the room and their smiles confuse me even more.

"It's done! Bring me the finished block of the first eleven episodes, and then we'll discuss the timing of the second half of the season," says Reginald Rickman, the producer who's handling the project.

I look at him, disoriented. "He just walked out of the room without a word. How can you say it's done?"

The people next to me chuckle like I'm the new kid who doesn't know how the world works. And indeed, I am. I feel like a goldfish in a shark tank.

"Trust me, if he didn't like it, you'd have left this room in tears," Reginald explains with the patience of a father teaching his son a basic life lesson.

The poison that comes out of Shane's mouth next is lethal. "Christ! To think there are people with years of experience and they gave the job to you. You really are great at blowjobs, aren't you?"

If I didn't need him for the rest of the documentary, I'd punch him in the face. The others look at him with a half-embarrassed laugh as we get up to leave the room. I don't even respond and give fuel to his insinuation, perhaps because I know that on some level, he's right. If it hadn't been for Simon, I would never have had this job. On the other hand, I know I've done a great job and deserve this recognition.

"Nicholas, can I talk to you?" Reginald stops me, and Shane glances furiously at me but eventually leaves with the others and closes the door behind him. Shane is an asshole, but Reginald is still the boss, and even he doesn't dare challenge his decisions.

"Don't let him bother you. He's been a backstabber for

most of his career, and despite being good at his job, has an attitude that pisses off everyone so he never gets very far. It eats at him when someone new comes along and does a good job."

He points at the chair in front of him, across from the desk.

"Do you think I did a good job?" I focus on the final part of his speech. I don't want him to know that Shane plays on my insecurities and makes me doubt myself. The few times I've met him, Reginald has struck me as an honest, straight-forward guy, but he's managed to become one of the biggest sharks in the tank, and you don't get to that level without eating some small fish along the way.

He smiles and nods, leaning against the back of the arm-chair to scrutinize me carefully.

"You did a great job. Before agreeing to take you on board, I carefully studied the projects you worked on. As much as the Jailbirds wanted to have someone they know around, I would never have given you the job if I had any doubts about your abilities. This is my production. I don't leave it at the mercy of a rookie because a rock star throws a tantrum." His tone is calm but firm, making it clear who's in charge, pulling the strings of the whole production.

"Whew, so I'm not in this office to be scolded." When he bursts out laughing, I feel like a naïve child who has to learn to play with the grown-ups if he wants to be part of the group.

"No, you're here because I have a job to offer you."

His words shake my insides like a stirred-up can of soda. I feel the blood drain from my face and then return like an explosion that makes my ears ring. I'm in the offices of the largest production company in the country, from one of the oldest and most established stations in America. To be told there's a job offer for me means this is the moment when I have to take the leap of faith that divides me from obscurity to being a name to contend with in this business.

"I'm listening."

"A friend is looking for a director for an independent film with a decent budget. It will land at all the major film festivals. It's a documentary about activists fighting to prevent the construction of oil pipelines on Native American sacred lands. I liked how you handled this documentary and wanted to give him your name."

I recognize this as one of those moments that can change the course of my life. When I came here this morning, I was hoping with all my heart to see my documentary get to the streaming platform—nothing else. And I'll leave this place with the chance to see my name on a poster at the Sundance Film Festival or the Toronto International Film Festival. A dream I've harbored since I was a child but never thought could be achievable.

I'm so overwhelmed I can't even swallow. When I find my voice, the words come out thick. "Is there room for another person besides me in this project?"

Reginald studies me with curiosity for a few seconds, maybe wondering why I'm not jumping for joy in this chair, but in all honesty, it's such big news I'm paralyzed. "Haven?"

I nod. I asked for her to be part of the package once. It's not out of the question to imagine I'd ask for her again.

"He didn't specifically mention two open positions, but I don't think there will be any problem discussing this. Think about it, and when you've decided, call him directly at this number. In the meantime, I'll give him your name." He extends his hand with a business card. I don't even dare to read the name as I put the card in my pocket.

"Thank you," I say, getting up from my chair.

"Nicholas, if I may give you some advice: never give in to the temptation to compromise your integrity to do some dubious project for money or fame. There's a need for people like you in this business. Someone who works from his heart and not his wallet. We need someone with your values to keep the Hollywood dream alive…the real one, not the one contaminated by greed."

His words elicit a wave of emotions that almost makes my legs give out from under me. It's not every day you hear something like this from Reginald himself. I'll never be the most sought-after director for films with billion-dollar budgets, but maybe I'll be able to make a name for myself as someone who makes films that reach your heart.

I nod and leave the room in a whirlwind of so many emotions that I only realize I'm in the parking lot when I see Max waiting for me, leaning against the SUV with darkened windows.

"Are you alright? You're a little pale," he says, opening the door.

"I think I just got an offer to direct a huge movie. A real film, the kind that comes out in theaters."

"And you're this pale because *you think* you got the job? I'd better get you home before you realize you really have the job, or I'll have to stop and give you CPR." He laughs as he closes the door, and I sink into the car seat, exhausted but with a smile I can't contain.

***

"What are you doing out here alone? The others are all inside to celebrate the series. You know you're sort of the guest of honor, right?" Haven's quiet voice distracts me from my thoughts. I look at her as she snuggles between my legs on the poolside deck chair.

Inside the house, the guys called catering to celebrate the first eleven episodes of the documentary. We saw the pilot together. They were moved, complimented me, and made me feel important, but above all, like part of their family. It's the first time in my life someone's so happy for my successes; besides Haven, no one ever expected great things from me. But they have this way of making you feel part of a solid group that supports you and pushes you to give your best.

"I'm coming. I'm just a little dazed, that's all."

Haven stares at me for a few seconds, sensing something is worrying me.

"Today, they offered me the director seat of an independent documentary film that they'll be presenting at several international festivals," I say when her insistent gaze makes me squirm.

Her eyes get huge, and I recognize the excitement that creeps into them. It's the look I've seen every time she's been proud of me. "That's wonderful! Why didn't you tell me before?"

I shrug and look down, handing her the business card I've

been turning around in my hands since this afternoon.

"Alan Leery? Alan Leery's producing the documentary? He's an Academy-Award winning producer. This film must have a serious budget, not like the ones we're used to." She looks at me in disbelief, passing her gaze from the card to my face and then back to the card again.

"I haven't accepted yet."

She stares at me, her mouth wide open, as if I had just confessed to a murder. Her expression is so incredulous it would be comical if I weren't more nervous than I've ever been in my life.

"Why not? It's the opportunity of a lifetime. You've been waiting for this for ten years."

"I want to ask if it's possible to bring you too. Complete package or there's no discussion. What do you say?" Hope is palpable in my voice.

Haven smiles at me but shakes her head. Her sweet gaze does nothing to calm the panic rising in my stomach. "Not this time, Nicholas. This is your chance to shine like the Hollywood star you are, not mine."

"I won't do it without you. I don't want to leave you behind." The words come out in a whisper, barely getting past the lump that tightens my throat.

"But it's not what I want, Nicholas."

Her words freeze my chest. "You loved working with me."

She smiles at me and puts her hand on my cheek. "I've loved working with you. I've learned so much, I've loved every single moment, but it's not my dream. The other day, Simon asked me what I wanted to do with my life. What I would do even for free because nothing else would make me happy.

My dream is to act. I love it, I love to transform myself and become someone else for a few hours, but I hate Hollywood, its rules, its compromises. What happened to me scarred me so bad it scares me even to think of going back to some of those people. But maybe Broadway is the change I need. Of course, there's competition there too, but it doesn't scare me. The snakes that hide under the Los Angeles sun terrify me. I'll go back to New York with Simon and try out for some small productions."

Haven, my Haven. Her words frighten and cheer me at the same time. I'm glad she's decided to spread her wings and fly again. She stayed in her cocoon for so long I was afraid she would never get out of it.

"What if I can't do it without you?"

She smiles at me and kisses my lips lightly. "Nicholas, you're the one who taught me everything about this work. I've always been a diligent assistant, but the truth is you have always guided me. You know how to do this job better than anyone else. It's time for you to start walking without this pink-haired crutch by your side."

"Are you sure?"

"I'm sure, Nicholas."

"How are we going to see each other if we're all three busy with our work?"

She shrugs and smiles at me. "We'll just fit it into our lives. Even if you lived in Los Angeles, you'd still be traveling a lot for your projects. What difference does it make whether you're flying to Los Angeles or New York?"

She's right. The life we've chosen is not a routine one. One city or another makes no difference, and I'm glad Haven has found her way.

"Should I call him?"

She hands me the card and urges me to do so.

"Now? It's ten in the evening."

"If you wait until eleven, it'll be worse, right?"

A chuckle escapes my lips before grabbing the phone and dialing the number. My heart hammers so hard in my chest that after the second ring I'm tempted to put it down, but I'm caught by surprise when a voice on the other end answers.

"Hello?"

"Alan? This is Nicholas." Words die in my throat from the nervousness, and the silence on the other side isn't helping. "I think Reginald Rickman told you about me," I add uncertainly, while Haven looks at me with a singular curiosity.

"Yes, I know who you are. Sorry, I was just watching one of your shorts, and I got distracted."

"Seriously?" I blurt out before I can stop myself. Alan Leery watching one of my shorts might actually give me a heart attack.

"Of course. Do you really think I'd give the job to someone whose work I haven't seen? When Reginald gave me your name, he sent me links to your films. Why have I never heard of you around Hollywood? You're good, kid."

My heart explodes in my chest, and I have to make a superhuman effort to stay focused on the conversation. "I don't hang out much at Hollywood parties." I smile, grateful for his sincere laugh.

"I guess you're calling me because you're interested in the project, right?"

"Yes, but I also wanted to know if it's a problem if I finish shooting the documentary I'm working on first. The first half is already finished, but the second part is still in progress. I wouldn't want to leave the job in someone else's hands."

I hear some movements on the other side, and I'm terrified I've pushed my luck for a moment. If Alan wants you for a movie, you give up everything and make that movie.

"No, no problem. Reginald gave me an overview of your timeline. That bastard doesn't give up easily." He laughs as he rustles what sounds like sheets of paper. "I have time for a meeting tomorrow at ten. If that works for you, I'll send you the address of my office."

"That's fine. I'll be on time."

Another laugh fills the phone. "You'll soon learn that punctuality in Hollywood travels at least a couple of hours late."

"I'll be on time being late, then."

He laughs again and, after a quick greeting, ends the conversation.

Haven stares at me anxiously.

"I have to go to his office tomorrow morning at ten…or noon…I'm not sure. I'll be ready by nine."

She throws her arms around my neck. "I'm so proud of you."

I tighten my grip around her waist. "There's no guarantee yet. Let me at least go to tomorrow's meeting."

"Stop underestimating yourself. Tomorrow you'll go to the meeting, Alan will adore you, and you'll become the most famous director ever."

I laugh as she grabs my hand and pulls me up. She drags me inside the house and gets into a chair before announcing,

"Nicholas has a meeting tomorrow with Alan Leery for a job as a director."

They all look at me stunned and then burst into applause, shouts, and compliments. Simon approaches me and holds me in an embrace so tight he almost suffocates me before kissing me passionately, ripping the earth from under my feet. The frenzy overwhelms me, the hugs, the pats on the back, make me light-headed.

Getting the job was one kind of thrill, but sharing it with these people, their sincere smiles, the joy in their eyes is what makes this moment unforgettable, precious, something to tuck away in the corner of my heart and pull out when times get tough.

Nothing's set in stone yet, but even if it goes badly tomorrow, I'm sure these people will still be here, ready to support me and pick me up after every fall.

I used to be terrified at the idea of not having Haven with me, but I realize now that I have not only her but every single person in this room beside me, toasting in my honor and sharing my joy. Every shred of doubt or sense of inadequacy slips from my veins until it disappears completely from my heart for the first time in my life.

CHAPTER 27
Haven

I breathe in the ocean air, close my eyes, and enjoy the sun that warms my face. I put my hands in the cold November sand, no less pleasant, and I savor its consistency. All these months on the road with the Jailbirds' tour, living a hectic life, made me forget how relaxing it was to come here to Venice Beach and spend a few hours lulled by the sound of the waves. And now I can also enjoy my newfound freedom.

I never really understood how much those violations of my privacy undermined my self-confidence until that man was arrested. Subconsciously I was looking for an explanation, a wrong attitude on my part that might have encouraged them. Understanding there's no fault on my part makes me free to walk the streets without looking over my shoulder, and it gives me back the self-confidence I'd lost.

"Now I understand why you live in Los Angeles." Simon's voice on my right reminds me of reality.

I look at Nicholas on my left, leaning on one elbow, basking in the sun with a smile from ear to ear. "Maybe you should use your house in the Hollywood Hills a little more, it's empty for most of the year. Have you ever stayed there for more than a weekend?" he asks curiously.

When we found out that Simon has owned a house in Los

Feliz for years and rarely uses it, we stared at him, shocked, for at least five minutes until we realized it was just an investment for him. Coming here alone, with the Jailbirds on the other coast, makes no sense for him. He'd rather hide away in his home in Connecticut when he needs to disconnect from the hectic life of Manhattan, which is still forty minutes away from his family.

"No. But I could start now. When we're on a break from the tour and don't have to be in the studio, maybe we can come and enjoy some sun. You can go to work, and when you get home from the set, we'll be sprawled in the sun drinking a cocktail by the pool," he jokes, leaning on his elbows and throwing us that playful look I see on his face more and more these days.

"Okay, but when the two of you are busy in New York, I'll look for something there," Nicholas proposes. "I'm not going to stay in an empty house while you're enjoying nights in front of the fireplace."

I smile at their plans for the future because, as complicated as it may seem, I have no doubt that we love each other so much we'll find a way to spend time together.

"Haven…"

A voice I haven't heard in years tightens my stomach. I turn around to look, my back to the ocean. Simon and Nicholas move closer when they recognize my mother's tense face. Years have passed, but her beauty has not faded even by a breath. Wrapped in a pair of white pants and a jacket of the same color, her long dark hair is striking, looking more severe than her face reveals.

"Mother…"

A small, tense smile appears on her face. She never liked me to call her that because she always preferred to pass for my sister or friend, never as a woman who has an adult daughter.

"Can we talk?"

"After more than eight years?" I snap more out of the turmoil of emotions that trigger me at seeing her again than for the real annoyance of it. I've imagined this conversation for so many years that I'm scared it's really happening now.

My mother's face darkens slightly, but it's not with the usual annoyance when I did something she didn't like. There's a vein of pain in her expression I've never seen.

Simon and Nicholas remain motionless and silent beside me. I believe they have no idea how to behave either. I stand up and see them hesitate.

"I'm not going very far. If I need help, I'll give you a nod," I tell them, motioning toward the ocean.

They seem to hesitate for a second, but then they both nod. My mother watches them, and a smile, this time almost loving, appears on her face. We walk in silence to the shore. Neither dares to look at the other. As a young girl, I had little to tell her. Now no word seems suitable after all the years of silence.

She speaks first. "I brought you documents that could help you with the stalker. They contain what the private detective I hired at the time had managed to find. I think they can be useful to you when you're in court." She hands me a red folder full of papers.

I take it and study it. It's as heavy as a boulder, and I don't dare open it. I don't want to know what I risked years ago by leaving.

"Thank you, I'll give it to the lawyer, though it would have helped to know this a long time ago when I had no idea what awaited me when I left the house…or went into my room." My words are as sharp as my gaze. My icy tone mirrors what's in my chest.

I rest my gaze on her, and she lowers her head with a sadness I've never seen. There is no more arrogance, and I'm not used to it. I wonder what happened to her.

"I thought I was protecting you. I thought hiring those bodyguards was enough to keep you safe. I slept for months on the couch in the hallway, ready to protect you," she confesses, looking up and showing me all the sincerity of her words.

I didn't know. When I'd asked her why she'd moved it to right outside my room, she said the light was better to bring out the color of the pillows. I remember thinking how stupid my mother was. I feel guilty for thinking it now, but I didn't know the real reason for her decision, and the mere memory makes my anger resurface.

"He could have killed me," I hiss at her. "I could have died at eighteen."

"I know. I never considered that you'd run away from home," she whispers, and all this calmness, admitting that she made a mistake, doesn't help appease the anger that boils inside me. On the contrary, it makes it resurface in waves that I don't know how to contain.

"What did you think would happen? You pushed me into David's bed and then asked me to apologize publicly. You humiliated me! You made me feel as dirty as he did. How could I stay in that house when I had no one on my side?"

At my raised voice I finally see a bit of that vitality she

carried with her when I lived with her. "I was trying to protect you. I was trying to help you choose what I thought was best for you," she replies with a little more fervor than before. "I tried to do what a friend would do: mitigate the damage when the mess is so big that you can't hide it."

"I didn't need a friend! I needed a mother who would protect me and keep me away from David, who wouldn't buy me skimpy clothes, who wouldn't practically push me into his bed. You realize that what he did was not only a crime but it completely shaped my life, right?" I spit out all the anger I feel inside.

I see her clenching her lips and lowering her gaze. Guilt disrupts her calm face. "When I had you, I was just a kid myself. I didn't know how to be a mother. I tried to pass on to you what I'd learned, but without the pressure I had on me. I tried to give you freedom, to direct you in what I thought was the right way. I pushed you into David's arms because that's what my mother always did with me. For me, there were never any other alternatives, and when you came into the world, I tried to raise you as best I could without anyone's help. I knew I was wrong when you left, but it was too late. The damage I had done was so irreparable I didn't know how to make up for it."

These are not excuses, just the raw truth, and I hadn't predicted it would hurt so badly.

"If you hadn't burned all the bridges with your mother, you would have had someone to give you a hand," I spit at her angrily.

My mother always spoke to me very detachedly about my grandmother, but she never gave me the impression that she was a bitch. Strict and demanding for sure, but not a bad person. The bitter smile on her lips almost makes me feel tenderness for her. It's an expression so defeated it almost turns into resignation.

"When I confided to my mother that I was pregnant, she told me that she would disown me if I kept the bastard. No one should know about the pregnancy, and nothing should ruin that perfect body I had for years. And so she did. *She* burned every bridge with you and with me."

I look down, and a sense of helplessness and empathy toward the woman who gave me life tightens my chest. "Why didn't you ever tell me? Why would you tell me she exists, but not tell me the truth?" It's not an accusation, but curiosity about a decision that must have been hard for a nineteen-year-old girl.

"Because I didn't want you to know that your grandmother would have preferred you dead. I wanted to spare you that pain, but I did worse by hiding it from you."

I don't know what to answer. I've always had this vision of my mother as a fickle and impatient woman who couldn't even be bothered to call her own mother, but I'm realizing that much of what I saw was actually a mask she wore. Maybe to protect herself or me or simply maintain appearances, the supreme rule of Hollywood.

"Thanks again for the documents. They will certainly be useful in court. The accusations are solid, and he has confessed, but adding his obsession with a minor can help," I add after a long silence.

"I'm glad they got him. When it first happened, there were never enough clues to give this person a face." She seems genuinely relieved that the situation has been resolved.

I feel like smiling for the first time since seeing her. The anger has slipped away, leaving an almost comforting sense of emptiness. After years of angry thoughts about your mother, it's a strange feeling when it finally deflates and lets you breathe.

"If it weren't for those two idiots and their manager who got arrested, they would never have found the evidence to put him away." I point out Simon and Nicholas, who are intent on observing us. Their bodies close, fingers intertwined.

I look at my mother and find her smiling. She seems almost loving, an expression I never saw on her face when I lived with her. Her appearance is always perfect, her youth intact, thanks to years of cosmetic surgery, but there's a veil over her gaze that makes her appear more mature.

"I'm glad you've found someone who loves you and protects you." She doesn't look at me as she says it, but she studies the two guys watching us, trying to discern how it's going.

"You have nothing to say about the fact that there's two?" I'm curious, not trying to provoke a reaction.

Her gaze rests on me again, and that loving smile doesn't disappear. The mere sight of it makes my heart waver in my chest. How many times during my adolescence did I wish for this kind of mother and never got it?

"Haven, you've always had so much love to give that it doesn't surprise me that you need to divide it between two people."

Her words hit me in the chest, and I find myself out of words. I look down at the sand and breathe deeply.

"You know that if you ever want to come by, come to dinner with your guys, my door will always be open for you, right?" The hint of hope in her voice makes me look up at her.

I nod. "Maybe we'll try coffee somewhere first, okay?" I'm not ready to reconnect with her yet, but I can give her a coffee date before deciding whether to cut her off from my life forever.

She nods and smiles at me. I turn around and walk toward Simon and Nicholas, who are waiting for me.

"Haven..."

I turn to her.

"If you decide to support the other victims and continue in court against David, call me. I'll come to testify."

I'm seriously thinking of joining the other sixteen women and girls who have decided to come forward and sue David Freewood for sexual assault. It will be challenging to go to court to tell my story in front of everyone, but at least this time, it will be my decision, not because some paparazzo has put me on the front page. It's a step I have to take to close that chapter of my past and make sure he doesn't hurt anyone else.

"Thank you," I say from my heart. Her support means a lot to me in this situation.

She looks down and shakes her head. "Don't thank me. It's the least I can do to apologize for what I've done."

Her words hit me straight in the heart, and I struggle to find the words, so I nod and smile at her before turning around and going back to the guys.

"Is everything alright?" Nicholas blurts out as soon as I sit down with them.

"Yes, she apologized and offered to help me with both the stalker and David, should I ever decide to go to court."

Simon and Nicholas hold me, and I'm grateful for their

affection and presence. "Shall we go home?"

I nod as we approach the car that takes us to the luxurious house in the hills, but the truth is I'm already at home wrapped in their arms.

***

As soon as we enter through the door of the house we've been holed up in for a month now, chatter from the living area attracts our attention.

"Simon, grab your checkbook because we're buying this house!" Damian thunders as soon as we enter the living room, and we find them all there, including Levi and Liberty, sitting on the sofas with so many papers scattered across the floor it almost scares me. The three of us look at each other, bewildered, trying to figure out what the hell is going on.

"Besides the fact that nobody pays with checks anymore, can you explain why we're buying this house? Yeah, we like it, and it's comfortable, but don't you think it's a little much just for the holidays? We can always rent it," Simon objects.

"And that's where you're wrong," Lilly explains. "This house is perfect. Besides having a studio for Nicholas to work on his films, we thought we could move the gym to the garage and convert that huge space into a recording studio. We could come here to produce our albums without necessarily being tied to New York."

Our confusion must still be obvious because Michael gets up and makes us sit on the only section of the sofa that's free.

I curl up in Nicholas's arms.

Thomas picks up where Lilly left off. "We know Haven wants to break into Broadway and spend a lot of time in New York, but who says we can't come here to record when she's free? So, you can stay closer to Nicholas, who will spend much of his time here. We can record anywhere, as long as we have the right equipment, but Nicholas can't really move his production work. Why not buy this house and make everyone happy?"

Their faces are all turned toward us, full of expectation. I look at Nicholas and see him with teary eyes and a look of embarrassment on his face. "Would you really buy a huge mansion just to accommodate my work?" His voice breaks with emotion.

Michael leans over and frowns. "You're our friend's partner. You're part of the family. Why wouldn't we?"

Nicholas rubs a hand over his teary eyes while Simon wraps his arms around his neck and draws him into a hug before lightly kissing his head. "What do you say? Are we doing this?" he whispers in his ear.

Nicholas doesn't have the strength to respond. He simply nods and squeezes me into a grip that almost melts me. I watch as they all rejoice at our answer and immediately grab their cell phones to call, I assume, their accountants. There's no hesitation in their gestures, no doubt. I have no idea what it's like to grow up in juvie, to help each other survive, but what these people have learned down to their bones is how to be there for each other in the most generous ways possible.

I take out my cell phone and film this moment. It may not end up in the documentary, but I want to remember forever the exact moment when Simon, Nicholas, and I became a family, the kind you'd fight for. The generosity of their gesture is so ridiculously undeserved and unexpected there's no way to describe it in words, so all I can do is capture the looks of happiness that fill this room.

CHAPTER 28

Simon

"Are you sure you want to go out? We can stay in the room and rest if you want." Haven's voice comes through the door of the hotel bathroom where I've been locked up for forty minutes. The shower water flows over me, washing away the chills and stomach spasms I've had since that damn plane started vibrating like it was blasting us into orbit. Even the rock-solid walls I'm leaning against now aren't even enough to calm my fears.

"Simon, are you okay?" Nicholas's hand reaches me in the shower.

I turn to him and Haven, both with worried expressions. I didn't even hear them come in.

"Yes. I'm fine. I just have to recover a bit. Too much stress for my body."

It's rare that I experience such a severe panic attack that none of the people around me can calm me down. I shut off the shower water and Nicholas passes me a towel and helps me get out. Their arms envelop my body and wipe my shriveled skin.

I get out of the bathroom, sit at the foot of the bed, and breathe. Next to me, on either side like guardian angels, the two of them look at me like I'm a wounded animal.

"I'm fine, I swear. I'm just physically worn out, but I'll recover. Going out, eating something, will help me get my strength back." I smile to reassure them.

"When you said you were terrified of flying, I had no idea it was this bad," Haven whispers, still in disbelief. I think she and Nicholas were beside themselves. I saw the tense faces of Damian and the others, but they're used to traveling by plane with me. This time I put on a show.

"It was the turbulence. When it's that violent, it's hard to contain my panic attacks." I'm a little ashamed. Traveling by plane should be something an adult should be able to do without so much drama, but for me, it's an irrational fear I can't overcome. Fortunately, we can afford to take a private jet and not terrify the passengers of an entire commercial flight.

Nicholas inhales and shakes his head. "I'm glad to know there's something that actually rattles you."

I look at him perplexed, and Haven does the same.

"Don't think I'm crazy. Ever since we were children, I've always thought of Simon as my hero, never afraid of anything. I'm happy to discover he's a human being with fears and vulnerabilities like the rest of us." He caresses my cheek.

"I was your hero? Wow, you really set the bar low." I chuckle, mystified that he thought that about me. At the time, I was terrified that I wouldn't be able to protect him.

"Idiot. I know you went out of your way to keep me hidden from our neighbor. I pretended to not notice, but I listened to your conversations. I listened carefully. I knew he had his eye on me, but you sacrificed yourself, even ending up in juvie, to keep him from touching me. You're more than a hero to me. In spite of everything, you allowed me to live a normal life," he confesses serenely, while I'm speechless with emotion.

I didn't think he was aware of all that. I thought I'd always been discreet and kept him in the dark. I wanted him to have a normal life, like all the other kids. I look down at him, on the hands resting on my leg.

"You've taken off your leather bracelets," Haven whispers and smiles as much as I do. I've never seen him once without the leather cuffs that cover the scars, now faded with time and almost invisible.

"I came to terms with my past and decided it was time to let it go and look toward the future," he admits, looking down.

I reach out an arm and hold him to me in a grip so firm he laughs and tries to push me away, at least until Haven joins in to help me.

"Okay, if we want to go out with the band, you have to let me go because if you keep hugging me like that, I'll fuck you both." He chuckles, pushing us until we let go and free him from our grip.

Haven gets out of bed first. "Let me get up. I promised Michael we'd join them for dinner, and I don't want to hear his insinuations about why we didn't show up."

Nicholas and I reluctantly follow her and put on some clothes. Although I'd like to stay here all evening moaning and panting, I need to put something in my stomach and get my strength back after the long flight.

We walk into the hotel lobby, and find everyone there, ready to go out, bundled in their heavy jackets. London in February is particularly cold. Only Liberty, who's playing in Damian's arms, is without her coat as it makes her sweat too much.

"Finally, you've arrived! We thought you were engaged in…um, sexual intercourse." Michael catches himself as Faith looks at him and immediately puts him back in line. I smile hearing Michael avoid using swear words; it's like watching a penguin try to manage stairs without falling face-down.

"It's not like we do it every five minutes. We can control our instincts," Haven jokes.

"Really?" counters Damian as he hands the child over to her parents. "Lilly and I were like rabbits in the early days." He winks at his partner.

"Only the early days?" She raises an eyebrow.

"Can we go out to dinner instead of dwelling on who gets it longer? Literally." Thomas gets up from the couch where he's sitting next to Iris. The dark circles of exhaustion from the trip here are evident. We're lucky the first concert of the European tour is in two days and we have the opportunity to rest.

Evan announces, "Outside on the sidewalk, several fans and some paparazzi are waiting. If you want, I'll call security and make them leave before getting in the van that takes us to the restaurant. There's no underground garage or back door easily accessible with that big of a vehicle." He's always ready with a solution to our problems.

"Do we really have to take a van?" Nicholas proposes with a hint of embarrassment.

"I know you're famous and attract attention, but we're in London, we have the opportunity to enjoy it on a clear day, and the restaurant is less than fifteen minutes away. Can't we walk?"

I look at the faces of my friends and try to determine what they think. After all, it's a high-tourist area where everyone walks around. It's more challenging to get a van there without running over anyone than to walk. We're choosing between fifteen minutes of hiking and forty minutes of sitting in traffic as pedestrians cross the road.

"You know what? That's a great idea. I'd like to enjoy a city where we have a concert for once with my family. Levi visits most places from behind a darkened window. It would be nice to enjoy a place like it should be, wouldn't it?" Michael ends the sentence by ruffling the boy's hair, and he lights up with a smile at his father's proposal.

"I want to! My friends think we live like criminals inside a bus because I never post pictures of the outside."

"Do you think it's feasible?" I ask Evan hopefully. I would like to please Nicholas for once, who's turned his life upside down because of my work.

"Sure, why not?" He shrugs and beckons us toward the door.

"Michael, can I keep Liberty? That way you, Levi, and Faith can enjoy the walk." I see them exchanging a curious look at my offer, and after bundling her under layers of heavy clothing so she can hardly move, they put the baby carrier on me. All I can see are her big blue eyes inside the bundle.

I hold her to me and look at her as she raises her head and looks at me curiously. I've never carried her like this before, only on a few rare occasions when Michael put her in my arms, and I study her reaction. She seems unaffected by my presence. She's so used to being carried around by anyone in our group, my arms don't feel strange to her.

"Can you see where we're going or have your parents covered your eyes too?" I ask her as we walk out the door, Nicholas and Haven holding me in a hug, intrigued by my enthusiasm toward a baby I've hardly dared to touch. Liberty replies with a smile, a high-pitched scream, and two bumps of her legs that I barely feel—the only part of her body she can move considering the amount of clothing she's wearing.

As soon as we're hit by the cold London air, a series of excited screams rise from the sidewalk next to us. A small group of about ten girls shivering in the cold take out cell phones in the hopes of taking some pictures together. Near them, the paparazzi go wild.

We approach the teenagers. Damian and Michael start signing autographs and taking pictures, Thomas and I joining them.

"How long have you been out here?" I ask one of the girls with blue hair and a face red with cold. I grab the pen and sign a corner of her "Back to Jail" tour poster.

"Since this afternoon when you arrived," she replies timidly as she rubs her hands.

"You're freezing. Aren't you worried about getting sick?"

"I just have cold hands, nothing unbearable." She tries to downplay it, but I see her thin legs covered only with black leggings, trembling from the cold.

Next to me, I watch Nicholas from the corner of my eye, filming this encounter with his cell phone. The chatter around us is constant as we take the time to talk to our fans. I lean over to take a picture with the girl and hear my name called by the paparazzi trying to get my attention.

"Simon, apparently, you're the one with the dirtiest sexual taste of all!" The joke of one of the photographers makes me turn toward him, not without first noticing the girl next to me rolling her eyes.

"How old are you?" Her voice, which was shy before, becomes more confident as she calls out to him. I turn to see her raise an annoyed eyebrow. "We've been talking about poly-amory since the sixties, and it was accepted back in the nine-ties. You're thirty years late, which is obvious from your jeans that are two sizes too big." She puts him in his place among the amused chuckles of his colleagues.

I don't even bother to respond to the man, but instead pause to observe this girl. She can't be twenty years old and she has no problem defending me and my relationship. If I had any doubts that our fans would take it badly, she's living proof that all my worries were in vain. I smile at her and thank her with a slight nod, then I get Evan's attention, who's been watching us like a hawk from a more secluded position.

"The day after tomorrow, you'll be at the concert?" I ask her as our manager approaches.

She nods self-consciously, as if my presence makes her nervous. This is new to me.

"Are you coming with someone?"

"With a friend of mine." And she gestures to a girl not far away who comes closer.

"Is it possible to get them a backstage pass? To let her watch the show from the side of the stage." I never ask Evan for things like this, and the smile on his face is as big as the stunned expression of the two girls.

"Of course, give me your details, and I'll leave the passes at the VIP entrance. If you don't know where that is, ask one of the staff, I'll make sure everyone knows your names and gets you to your destination." He pulls out his phone and starts organizing with his usual efficiency.

"Thank you. I don't know what to say…thank you very

much." Words get stuck in her throat and her eyes become shiny with tears.

"Hot cappuccino coming through!" I turn to see Haven making her way loaded with two huge trays of Caffè Nero that she begins to distribute among those present.

"You got coffee for everyone?" I ask shocked.

"We couldn't let your fans freeze to death."

A scream of appreciation from Liberty makes me smile.

I did not believe you could fall more in love with a person, but Haven, with her small gestures of generosity, surprises me every day. I move my gaze from her to my friends walking toward the restaurant after saying goodbye to everyone, and I realize that this moment could not be more perfect. After years of torment, I feel the pieces of my life falling into place, filling those spaces I could not fill.

Nicholas's hand slips into mine, intertwining our fingers; Haven, on the other side, clings to my elbow and rests her head on my shoulder. I squint for a moment and inhale, finally feeling free and complete, wrapped in a sense of peace I've never felt until now. Thousands of miles from New York, with all the people I love around me, I finally feel at home.

CHAPTER 29
Nicholas

The light that filters through the windows wakes me up. A pair of solid arms squeeze me from behind, Simon's warm chest resting on my back while Haven is snuggled up at my chest. They both breathe while I enjoy the moment of absolute peace before tonight's concert. It's the one that kicks off the tour outside the United States, in London, and it feels like I have entered a parallel reality.

I never had enough money to travel outside the United States. To tell the truth, I never even had enough to get out of New Jersey or Los Angeles, and since Simon returned to be part of my life, I have traveled more miles than in my entire existence.

I extricate myself from the embrace that keeps me anchored to this bed, trying not to wake them up. As soon as I get out from under the covers, Haven complains a little until Simon stretches out an arm and draws her to himself. I smile when our girlfriend emits a small satisfied grunt as she sticks her head into the hollow of his neck. Sleeping in three has its advantages because when one of us gets up, the other two never have to face a bed that cools down.

I step out of the suite bedroom and stretch as I approach the massive window of the living area overlooking the Thames.

I stop to observe its lazy flow, the dark gray color that matches today's plumb sky. From a distance, you can see the London Eye, on the other side the Tower Bridge, The Shard. Every corner of this city is a mixture of ancient and modern that makes you feel like an enchanted child.

Simon took us on a tour yesterday, guiding us through a city that has hosted their concerts dozens of times. He says whenever they visit, they try to stay a few more days to enjoy the vibrant atmosphere of theaters, shows, live music. I've always been fascinated by New York and what it has to offer, but the truth is London can very well compete with the Big Apple. It's like the older and wiser sister, who doesn't give a damn about how she dresses but knows the best places to have fun. London is a jumble of wonderful styles and people to savor.

Haven's arms wrap around my torso, and her slender body leans against my back.

"What are you thinking?" she asks, peeking her head out from behind me to look out the window.

"That I'm lucky."

"Lucky?"

"To have the two of you, to be able to travel the world, to do a job I like. There's nothing I'd change about my life now."

Simon's arms wrap around my neck, and he kisses me lightly on the cheek.

"I can only agree. Right now, I don't miss anything."

"Would you like to record an interview for the documentary?"

I watch him study me and nod before kissing my lips. It wasn't scheduled. There are no questions prepared by Iris. Maybe it will never end up in the documentary, but I think this moment perfectly shows the Simon I've always loved, and I want the world to see the best person I have ever known.

"I'm going to change. Where do you want to film?"

"On the couch with the view of London behind you would be perfect," suggests Haven, and I can only agree.

I watch them as they prepare, smile, almost synchronized in their movements. It was easier to let Simon into our daily lives than other people. It's as if we've found that missing gear that made our relationship perfect.

On a piece of paper, I write down some questions that came to mind just before I fell asleep wrapped in their warmth, when my happiness skyrocketed and turned into something beautiful I needed to express.

I pass the questions to Haven as she sits on the couch, scrolls them quickly, then looks up at me, her lit with a love that in this waning light seems luminous. Simon takes a seat next to her and looks at us with curiosity.

I stand behind the camera, with the computer in front of me.

"What's that little thing that always makes you smile?" Haven starts.

Simon seems caught by surprise, perhaps because he was expecting questions about his job rather than something so personal. He rubs a couple of fingers on his lips and raises his face to the ceiling, his eyebrows furrowed. When his mouth curves into a smile, I know he has the answer.

"There is a moment, before going on stage, when we're all together to prepare and focus before the show. The tension is palpable, but I feel so damn lucky when I look at my friends and realize it's always the four of us doing what we love. That feeling of contentment no one can take away makes me smile every single time since we started. It's a moment, a fraction of a second, that then turns into adrenaline, ready to go on stage. If I couldn't find that reason to smile anymore, I'd know it's time to stop."

Haven nods and takes a few seconds to absorb his response, to fully understand what Simon feels.

"What's your first thought when you wake up?"

He crosses his arms over his chest and tilts his head to the side.

"If you had asked me a year ago, I would have replied: 'I have to water the plants.'" He laughs, and we join him. "But more recently it's been: 'It's nice to start another day.' It's the first thing I think when I'm still sleepy and tight in the embrace of the people I love. I think about how lucky I am to share my life with them and can't wait to get up. For the first time in my life, I have a reason to be excited to face the day ahead."

I feel my heart accelerate in my chest and slam into my ribcage.

"What's the most precious thing you have?"

"My friends." He doesn't think about it for a second before answering. "The most precious thing I have is not an object but a feeling, a bond. I'm not just talking about my bandmates, but about that little intimate circle that includes companions and children...my partners, together with theirs." He looks at us both, and I understand how important this moment is for him. "I could end up on the streets, and it wouldn't bother me, but if even one of them passed away, I think I'd die."

And I'm sure of that. The bond between the four of them is something rare. The circumstances that led them to know and protect each other were so extreme that the bond they formed was impossible to destroy. They're united in something more than a family. That's why their approval of our relationship was necessary to Simon. If even one of them had not been happy, I believe Simon would have given up altogether, closing himself off inside his shell.

"What is your greatest fear?"

He looks down and watches his hands play with the edge of his shirt before raising his eyes on me. He looks at me when he speaks his words. "To see the people I love suffer." He looks back at Haven. "I'm afraid I'll see them suffer, and I can't do anything to help them. I experienced that fear in my skin once, and I will never forget the sense of helplessness that paralyzed me."

"Do you want to tell us about it?" Haven's voice is just a whisper, as if she's afraid saying it out loud could awaken the sleeping demons in Simon's chest.

"The day the police came into the house to arrest me, I wasn't alone in my room. I shared it with the person who had been by my side constantly during those years. We were kids, and we were strong for each other. He had become the most important person in my life, and even today, sometimes, I dream about his desperate look when the cops handcuffed me and took me away. There was a terror so deep in his eyes that it froze the blood in my veins and stopped my heart. His cries as they took me away have remained branded on my soul, and nothing can erase them. At that moment, a deep fear crept into me of seeing someone I love suffer again. The person who is now part of me, the person I am. I don't exist without that terror that sometimes still awakens me."

I feel the lump in my throat getting as big as a boulder, and I thank heaven that it is Haven asking the questions. Right now, I wouldn't be able to choke out a single word.

"If you could meet yourself as a kid, what advice would you give him?"

Simon smiles, almost melancholic.

"To be honest, always. First with himself, but also with others. Hiding for fear of what people think of you doesn't solve your problems, it amplifies them. Sometimes reality is hard to deal with, but it's always better than a lie that eats away at you like a disease you can't cure and ultimately kills you. I was afraid to tell everyone that I love two people, that my family is not 'traditional.' I feared the pressure we'd get from the outside would implode our relationship, never realizing it was me who was sabotaging it from within. People's opinions can't hurt you or make you change your mind if what you feel inside is really what you want, what is right for you. The words of strangers can only destroy something you yourself have doubts about."

I'm proud of the path Simon has taken. I'm honored to be present when he decided to take control of his existence and his feelings to the point of becoming someone who smiles at life rather than distrusting it.

"Simon, are you happy?" Haven's voice trembles, charged with the emotion all three of us are feeling.

"Yes." No indecision, no explanation. Just the awareness that his response reflects what he feels in his soul.

I turn off the camera, close the laptop and approach them, sitting on the couch and savoring the happiness that flows under our skin when we're together. Haven's lips rest on Simon's as he holds her in a hug. My tongue savors her skin, and my fingers sink into her pink hair. I hear her sighing, moaning, enjoying Simon's hands slipping under her shirt until he reaches her breasts.

I draw her to me until her back rests on my chest, and I enjoy the desire painted on Simon's face until, one button at a time, I open Haven's shirt and expose her perfect body to my partner's eyes.

Simon stretches his hands toward her jeans after taking off his shirt. He unbuttons her pants so slowly that I feel her quivering under my lips, kissing her neck, my teeth savor the delicacy of her skin. He pulls off her pants, panties. I slide her shirt on the floor, then her bra. I play with her nipples and make her shudder while we watch Simon pull off his pants and boxers, standing naked in front of us. Without shyness or hesitation, only that unconditional love that pours over us while watching us, he slips between our partner's legs and savors her most intimate parts, licking, sucking with such hunger that Haven soon explodes in an orgasm that makes her tremble. I hold her in my arms and press my erection against her back, unable to look away from our companion, who feasts wildly on her.

Simon looks up at me. His tongue tastes Haven's body as he climbs up to reach me, until he presses his lips on mine and takes possession of my mouth, of my moans when Haven pushes her ass against my erection almost making me explode inside my pants. Simon's fingers slip through my hair in a grip that won't let me go. His tongue explores my mouth, leaving me with the heady taste of Haven, her sweetness, and her excitement I've tasted firsthand many times. When he detaches himself from me and lets me breathe, his eyes lock on mine and set fire to every part of my body.

I push him with one hand until he lays on the couch, Haven, still panting, straddling his hips. Simon's eyes never leave mine when I get up from the sofa and slowly undress for the two of them; they look at me with desire in their eyes and shortness of breath. The vision of Haven moving sinuously on Simon's hips, teasing his erection until he groans, makes my erection twitch. Simon's hands are clasped on her hips to guide her until he sinks into her with a long groan of pleasure. A slow gesture that makes her close her eyes and throw her head back.

I take the opportunity to take a seat behind her, kiss her neck until I slip my hands under her arms, and enjoy her soft breasts under my fingers, turgid nipples that I tease with my fingertips. I follow her movement and, as she moves on Simon's erection, seeking that pleasure that will make her explode, with one hand, I descend between her buttocks, exploring the openness she's never granted to anyone but me.

I feel her holding her breath when I open the lubricating gel we left here on the floor last night and lower myself again to look for her butt. My fingers gently creep in. I kiss her neck and feel her relaxing in my arms. Simon, below her, slows down the pace of the thrusts, letting her get used to the intrusion of my fingers, caresses her on the thighs, on the belly, until he climbs to her breasts and sensitive nipples. Haven's arms rise until they reach my head, my hair where she sticks her fingers, her head resting on my shoulder. Her breath becomes shorter and shorter, almost reaching pleasure, stopping just before achieving it.

Simon's hands reach out and grab her arms, pulling her toward him, holding her in a hug, kissing her, and swallowing her moans as I push my erection against her opening, slowly sinking into her. I stop, wait for her to get used to it, to relax, allowing me to go deeper. It is a slow agony to hold back, not give in to my instinct, and sink into her with all the lust I feel growing inside. But when I arrive at that long-awaited destination, the groan that shakes me inside makes my legs tremble so much I almost give in and collapse on them.

It's the most intimate connection we have. Feeling Simon move through the thin wall that separates me from him, being enveloped by the warmth of Haven that welcomes us both, giving us her total trust, is an experience that almost makes me come faster than a kid. But when I begin to move in her, following the rhythm dictated by Simon, every cell of my body becomes part of that pleasure that all three of us seek.

Sweaty skin moves, rubs, and seeks contact faster and faster. Our breathing is labored. Our hands explore, caress, clutch flesh that has become one. The thrusts become intense, the lunges longer and longer, the synchronized rhythm seems like a dance that only the three of us know how to do. We are three bodies united in one soul, three hearts beating in unison, three pleasures that explode one after the other until we tremble, quivering with that intoxication only the three of us together can feel.

I collapse on Haven's back, erasing the distance that kept our bodies separate. My arms wrap her and Simon in one squeeze as we try to catch our breath. If happiness is the only thought that fills my head in the morning when I wake up, the sense of belonging is the feeling that invades my chest right now. We belong to each other in a tangle of limbs, breath, and souls that no one will ever be able to untangle again.

EPILOGUE
Haven

"Are you ready to go?" Simon's voice is full of excitement.

We've been to several red carpets since we've been together, but this one feels special. *A Legend in the Making* about the life of the Jailbirds received several Emmy nominations, including Best Documentary. If he wins, Nicholas will have to go on stage to receive the award. I have never been so proud of him and the success he has achieved with this work. That's why I share Simon's excitement and nervousness when the limousine pulls forward to let us out in front of the wave of photographers barricaded behind a row of velvet cords.

"Nervous but ready," whispers Nicholas squeezing our hands.

"It's showtime," laughs Simon. When they open the door from the outside, the photographers' flashes begin to shoot, blinding us.

The first to get out is Simon, who extends his hand to me, helping me get out of the car in the long dress I'm wrapped in. Last, the one nominated to win one of the most coveted prizes in film with his first real meaningful work. Nicholas's face is a mixture of embarrassment, emotion, and happiness. I think he's overwhelmed by all the attention. I turn to Simon and think I've never seen so much pride in a person's eyes.

We walk through the tight space that separates us from the endless line of journalists ready to interview him. In front of us, other guests pass from one microphone to another to answer questions, smile, and say how excited they are to be here tonight. And it's true. The emotion that squeezes your stomach at such a high-profile, important event is intoxicating.

We all stand still in front of the board of the sponsors of the evening, motionless in our best pose, under the constant roar of the photographers who immortalize our every move. They call all three of our names, but the real star of the evening is only one, and when I glance at Simon, I see him nodding and reaching out to me. We move a few feet away to let the spotlight focus on Nicholas.

Nicholas turns in our direction, frightened, but immediately gets a grip on himself when he sees we're not so far away. This is his night, and Simon doesn't want to obscure it with his weighty presence. We delight in seeing him so embarrassed in front of the cameras, especially having to handle them himself as the center of attention.

"Do you think he's breathing?" Michael chuckles behind us with Thomas and Damian just behind watching him.

"No. I think he stopped when he got into the limousine," laughs Simon and us with him.

"Do you want me to go and see if they have oxygen backstage?" teases Damian.

When he finally manages to move a few steps in our direction, his gaze is almost wild, and the smile seems plastered to his face.

"When does this torture end?" he pleads, barely moving his lips for fear the photographers will notice his impatience.

"You're just at the beginning," I tell him, turning him toward the journalists and giving him the nudge he needs to take a few steps toward the entrance.

Me, Simon, and the rest of the Jailbirds, including Evan, stay a couple of feet behind him, accompanying him at each stage until we reach the theater hosting the event. We manage to get to our seats only a few minutes before the opening ceremony because it's an endless succession of hands to shake, people to greet, pats on the shoulder, and small talk. We're exhausted when we finally manage to sit our asses down in our chairs.

The ceremony is a slow parade of awards, jokes, and performances that only prolong our agony. As we move forward, it's not just Nicholas who gets quiet. Damian, Michael, and Thomas, sitting in the row behind us, have stopped making comments and jokes. Sitting between me and Simon, Nicholas squeezes both of our hands, the tension palpable in every breath.

When our tense faces appear on the giant screen behind the hosts, we know that the time has come for Nicholas.

"I'm dying. I'm going to die," he whispers as the documentary images and those of the other candidates scroll across the screen.

Simon and I squeeze his hands, ready to support him no matter what happens, but neither of us dares to say a word. We're both afraid our hearts will spill out of our mouths, given how fast they're beating. My hands are sweaty, sticky, but I don't think Nicholas notices since his hands are just as cold and wet.

The host turns to the audience at the end of the footage and takes forever opening that damn envelope. I hold my breath when that little triangle of paper rises out of the cardboard inside. He reads it, smiles, doesn't utter a single word, and I feel like I'm dying. I pray with all my heart that Nicholas will be the one to take the stage tonight, to take the prize he deserves for all the work, the passion he puts into what he does.

"The winner for Best Documentary is...*A Legend in the Making!*"

The screams that explode around me are deafening. Behind us, Thomas, Michael, and Damian pounce on Nicholas, burying him. He almost seems not to believe it, not to understand what's happening, but when the realization hits him, his eyes well up with tears and a smile stretches across his entire face. He turns to me, kisses me on the lips, then turns to Simon and kisses him on the lips too.

My hands and legs tremble with so much happy energy I can't get up from my chair. In front of us, Aaron Steel rises from his seat, perfect in his tuxedo, turns to Nicholas, extends a hand, and then pulls him in and pats him on the back. I've never seen him give so much affection in public. He has the reputation as the iceman, but right now his smile seems genuine. Perhaps because this is the first award he's won since managing to take more control over the production company, snatching it from the protective clutches of his father.

"See? When you ask for my help, good things happen!" he says to Evan, winking.

I get up to let Nicholas out and walk with Aaron to the stage. I sit next to Simon and enjoy his emotional embrace. We throw a glance toward Evan, who, despite the smile, seems tense.

Aaron rattles off his speech thanking the big shots that work with him with no emotion, only consummate experience and years spent perfecting the ice sculpture enveloping him. When he finally defers to Nicholas, holding his prize so tightly I am afraid it's stuck to his palm, his eyes and his voice are a mixture of emotion and fear.

"I don't have a list as long as Aaron's to thank. I've just arrived in Hollywood, and this is my first job. I haven't been able to make many enemies yet." The audience laughs and notices a slight smile that curves Aaron's lips. "But I know for a fact that there are two people who should be here with me on this stage tonight because, without them, I would be nobody. Without their strength, support, and unconditional love, I would not be here to hold this prize, terrified it would fall and break into seven or eight pieces…"

Another little laugh from the audience, and Nicholas's gaze looks for us where we are sitting. "Haven, Simon, this award is for you."

His words vibrate with all the emotion in his chest, and when I turn to Simon, tears of joy streaming down my cheeks, I find his eyes wet also with emotion and pride staring at the stage where Nicholas stands in all his glory.

The roar of applause and whistles of encouragement last an eternity, and when we sit down and compose ourselves, I feel my chest spread open with relief. I didn't realize how worried I was about his disappointment until I saw him take the stage and felt overwhelmed by joy.

"So Aaron is the big fish you know in the production company? How the hell did you hook someone so high up?" Damian asks Evanwhat all of us are curious about.

"He's my brother," Evan admits in an angry mutter.

"What?" Simon's eyes and mouth open as wide as all of ours.

"You're the son of Aaron Steel, Sr.? We thought you were from Texas!" says Damian.

Evan shrugs but stares at his brother and Nicholas, returning to their places. "We have a house there too," he comments vaguely, obviously not wanting to talk about it.

No one pushes for more out of respect for Evan, who decided to keep this detail hidden for so many years. But the news is so shocking we look at each other a little disoriented until Damian thunders in laughter, attracting the attention of the people sitting around us, and we chuckle with him.

"What did I miss?" Nicholas sits next to me.

"Nothing, just that we've been looking dumb for ten years," smiles Simon, who leans over my seat and kisses him on the lips.

Nicholas is confused by the answer, but we'll explain it to him tonight, when we're at home, in pajamas, in our bed tailored for three. We'll tell him not once but ten, a hundred times, even more when our children ask us what we felt when he said our names on that stage.

Because while the credits will eventually roll on this ceremony, the spotlight is turning to the opening credits of the long and exciting adventure that awaits us.

***

As an indie author, I sincerely appreciate you reading and helping spread the word!

If you loved Showtime, please consider leaving a quick review. Reviews help readers like you find books they'll love.

***

Sign up for Erika Vanzin's newsletter to get free short stories, exclusive deals, and more:
https://www.erikavanzin.com/newsletter.html

BOOKS BY ERIKA VANZIN

ROADIES SERIES

Backstage

Paparazzi

Faith

Showtime

THE HUNTING CLUB

The producer: Aaron

About the author

Erika Vanzin is the Italian Amazon bestselling author of the rock star romance Roadies Series. After traveling around the world with her husband, she settled down in Seattle, enjoying the marvelous Pacific Northwest. She brought from Italy a couple of suitcases, fifteen boxes full of books, and her most successful novels translated into English.

While she is not writing, she enjoys reading books, watching the Kraken hockey games, and working on DIY projects.

Keep in touch with Erika via the web:

Website: https://www.erikavanzin.com/

BookBub: https://www.bookbub.com/authors/erika-vanzin

Goodreads: https://www.goodreads.com/author/
show/14437720.Erika_Vanzin

Facebook: https://www.facebook.com/erikavanzinauthor

Instagram: https://www.instagram.com/clumsyeki/

TikTok: https://www.tiktok.com/@erikavanzin

Twitter: https://twitter.com/ErikaVanzin

Newsletter: https://www.erikavanzin.com/newsletter.html

Acknowledgements

Showtime is a book dedicated to those who have felt different, unable to conform to what society imposes. I dedicate this book to all of you because without your colors, the world would be much grayer. It would be much poorer without your battles.

Keep coloring outside the lines because we need brave people who question the rules.